I0582630

THE REDEEMING AFFAIR DEEPENS

THE REDEEMING AFFAIR DEEPENS

A novel by C.B. Lane

FIRST EDITION

ISBNs:
Paperback: 978-1-80227-798-2
eBook: 978-1-80227-799-9

Published by PublishingPush.com

Acknowledgements

Many thanks goes out to the Publishing Push team, but especially, Sophie, Stacy and the incredible designer of both my front covers, you are all awesome.

To my husband, for being my rock, my support, and my sharp eye over the story.

To all my supporters out there who read, experienced and loved my first book.

Lastly, of course, to those who waited so patiently and so eagerly for this, you know who you are, this is for you.

Contents

Acknowledgements v

Chapter One 1

Chapter Two 25

Chapter Three 48

Chapter Four 61

Chapter Five 88

Chapter Six 109

Chapter Seven 137

Chapter Eight 156

Chapter Nine 180

Chapter Ten 194

Chapter Eleven 212

Chapter Twelve.. 233

Chapter Thirteen 249

Chapter Fourteen 274

Chapter Fifteen.. 293

Chapter Sixteen 316

Chapter Seventeen 345

Chapter Eighteen... 367

Chapter Nineteen 388

Chapter Twenty.. 400

Chapter Twenty-One 425

Chapter Twenty-Two 446

Chapter Twenty-Three... 471

Chapter One

Light filters into the bedroom and warms my stubbly cheek. A forelock of my hair tickles my eyelids, I brush it aside, rub my eyes and hoist myself out of bed. I pad across the carpeted floor and draw the curtains. The late spring sun glimmers through the vast high-rise buildings. I slide the window open; the morning traffic roars from the streets below, pedestrians, merely small specks, rush around. Freshly bloomed trees and brewed coffee invade my senses. Manhattan is, as ever, alive with activity. A whisp from the wind blows through my long, unruly hair. A clatter from the kitchen gets my attention. I pull my pajama bottoms on before heading out to locate the source of the noise. My fiancée, Rachael Clarke has her back to me in the kitchen. I lean against the door arch and tap my lips with my index finger as I admire her slim hourglass figure, perfect ass, slender legs, and long mahogany hair

1

that drapes down her back in thick, luscious waves. I walk in slowly and hook my arms round her waist. She gasps and turns in my arms so that we're nose to nose. I marvel at her warm hazel eyes catching the sunlight as I run my hand across her slender jawline. Tendrils of hair with hews of red and purple frame her beautiful face, and her rosy cheeks lift as she smiles her special smile that she reserves for me.

"Good morning," she says.

I rub my nose down the length of hers and plant a kiss on her full lips.

"Good morning," I whisper.

She strokes my arm once before turning back to the espresso machine, her hips brushing my waist. My breath catches.

"Coffee?" she asks.

"Please."

I place my knife and fork down on my plate after consuming the best eggs Benedict in New York, lovingly prepared by Rachael. I rest back in my chair, hands clasped together on my stomach. She takes a sip from her coffee, hiding a smirk.

"What?" I ask, arching a brow.

"I can't believe we're getting married tomorrow."

I sit up and lean across the table.

"It sure came quick, huh?"

She taps her mug, her white gold engagement ring clinking against the china.

"Yeah."

She sighs and flicks her long mahogany mane behind her. The diamonds on her ring project miniature rainbows on the walls and ceiling.

"You're not regretting this, are you?" I ask, dreading her answer.

Her eyes dart to mine and widen slightly, then she smiles again, stands, and walks round the table. She perches on my lap, I wrap my arms round her slim frame as her fingers rake through my hair, making it flop briefly into my eyes. *Damn hair.* I brush it aside and stare up at her. She leans down and plants a kiss at the corner of my mouth, her rosy scent invading my nostrils.

"Of course not. I've never been so excited. Why do you think so little of yourself?" she asks.

I shrug absentmindedly.

"It's just after everything I'd done with the O'Malleys. I just thought-"

She places her fingers over my lips.

"You're nothing like Tobias. Never think that… Anyway, he's gone, remember?"

My mind briefly flies back to that night five months ago. We were confronted at the Red Hook Grain Terminal. I was tied to a chair; the horror of seeing Rachael in his slimy clutches, her police uniform torn in several places; her blood curdling scream after he took her upstairs, a gun to her head, Tobias' evil, smug grin and finally, me attacking him and plunging into the dirty water below. He hasn't been seen or heard of since. His body still hasn't been found. *He could still be-.*

"Hey," she whispers, as she strokes my chin, bringing me back to the now.

I look back up at her.

"Don't go there," she continues.

I grin at her, then her mouth seeks mine once more.

With one final stroke across my cheek with my razor, I rinse the blade under the faucet and wipe the last of the shaving foam from my face and stare at my reflection. My brown floppy hair, still damp from a shower, sticks to my forehead, and curtains my blue eyes, no longer rimmed with dark circles. I brush the hair from my eyes and glance down at my hands. My nails are manicured and well cut, no longer chapped and broken around the edges. A towel is wrapped round my waist and my biceps glisten with beads of water. I smile at myself. There was once a time when I loathed this person, for all the wrong choices he made and all the bad people he hung out with; but in the last six months, this man made the best decisions of his life and he's about to get married to the woman that he loves and who saved him in so many ways.

"You're a lucky son of a bitch," I mutter, placing the razor down on the vanity unit.

Rachael pops her head round the door just as I slip on my underwear.

"You got a text from Trent. He's on his way," she says.

I sigh as she steps closer and wraps her arms round my broad shoulders.

"Must I go?"

She purses her lips then runs her hand down my jaw.

"It's tradition not to see the bride before the big day, remember?" she says.

Screw the traditions. I grimace and she chortles.

"Don't worry, it's only for the night, then you're stuck with me," she continues.

I chuckle. *She always knows how to lighten the mood.*

"There're far worse people I could be stuck with. I think I won the wife lottery."

She sports an all-tooth grin as I press her against me for the millionth time, taking a moment to appreciate her sweet scent and glossy hair that brushes my face.

Rachael follows me out of the apartment complex; while our doorman, Tom carries my luggage out onto the busy sidewalk. Trent, my best friend since high school, stands against a cab; his black hair, spiked up at the front, glimmers from the sunlight and his legs are crossed at the ankle as he taps the roof of the cab with his index finger. He waves and regards us with his gleaming light blue eyes. Tom walks to the cab and slips the luggage into the trunk, then steps back onto the sidewalk and tips his cap at me.

"Thanks, Tom," I say.

"No problem, Mark. Best wishes to the both of you," Tom replies, smiling.

He turns to Trent.

"Sir," he greets.

Trent nods, then Tom heads back inside.

"Morning, bud. Ready for tomorrow?" Trent asks, his eyes moving from me, then to Rachael.

"As ready as can be."

He smirks, stands up straight and walks towards me. He drapes an arm round my shoulder in a firm one-armed hug.

"You'll be fine."

He turns to Rachael.

"Hey, sis-in-law."

He scoops her up into his arms and swings her round, causing a nearby elderly couple to skirt out of the way. They grumble incoherently and scowl at us. I raise my hand by way of apology, and they carry on walking. I clear my throat, causing Trent to release Rachael and peek over at me, a lopsided grin plastered on his face.

"Once you're quite finished pawing my fiancée and nearly injuring half of New York, I think we'd better go," I quip.

"Sorry, man. I've always wanted a sister, and it's just good to see you both again," he beams through perfect white teeth.

"You only saw me last week."

Rachael tuts and jabs me with her elbow. He chuckles and pats me hard on the back.

"I can never stay away from you for too long. Let's go. See ya', Rachael," he says with a quick wave before climbing into the cab.

I turn back to her. She picks at her fingernails and looks down at the ground. I hook my index finger under her chin and lift gently until our eyes lock, blue to hazel.

"Until tomorrow... wife."

She smiles and hugs me hard.

"Until tomorrow, husband," she muffles into my shoulder.

Her warm breath radiates through my shirt. I pull away and plant a delicate kiss on her right cheek, then slide in beside Trent and close the door. He gives the driver his address and the cab merges onto Amsterdam Avenue. I look out the back window and wave at her until we turn into West 62nd and she's out of sight.

We pull up outside Trent's apartment on West 47th Street. I step out of the cab and stare up at the white brick building with black fire escapes bolted to the walls. Trent walks past me and unlocks the main door. I follow him inside and we take the stairs. He pushes his front door open and strolls inside, I trail after him and observe the familiar surroundings; a sparsely decorated apartment with dark wood floors and white walls, a couple of beige couches, one of which is folded out into a bed and lined with blue sheets. *Déjà vu.* A shelving unit stands in the corner near the window, piled high with CDs and DVDs; an HD TV is mounted on a plain brick wall on the opposite side of the room; a dining table with a couple of blue chairs stands near the small integrated kitchen. This is the place I once called home. Trent shrugs out of his denim jacket and hangs it on a hook near the front door. I remove my shoes and carry my luggage over to the bed-couch. He rummages noisily in the fridge nearby.

"Beer?" he calls, holding up a couple of bottles of Bud Light.

"Please."

He kicks the fridge closed and comes to join me as I perch myself on the foot of the bed. He flops down beside me and holds his bottle aloft.

"To married life," he announces.

"Here's to that."

We clink bottles and we both take a sip.

"I thought we'd meet up with a couple of the boys later, *if* you're up for it... Call it your bachelor party," he says.

I look at him and arch a brow.

"Trent, we already had my bachelor party. Remember the camping trip?"

Mitch pulled up at the Rip Van Winkle campgrounds, ready for our weekend of camping.

Trent jumped out of the Ford F-Series and began to unload.

"We'll pitch up here. Next to the river," he said, pointing at the ground.

Mr. Clarke, Rachael's father, and chief of police, climbed out of the truck and came to stand beside me.

"Great choice," he concurred.

"Mark, help out," Trent called as he started to unravel the tent.

"I've never done this before."

He laughed.

"Don't worry, there's nothing to it."

I shrugged and started to pitch my first tent.

An hour later, the tent still lay in a flat, crumpled mess on the ground.

"Just thread the pole through," Trent shouted.

"It doesn't go there. Read the damn instructions," I shouted back.

He threw the tent on the floor and stomped off towards the river.

"Where you goin'?" Rex called.

"For a break."

I sat on the ground with Mitch, Rex and Mr. Clarke who all stared at me. I glanced down at my feet and kicked the soil out from underneath. At that moment, I'd have preferred to have been back in Manhattan, in my apartment with my beautiful fiancée. Trent returned and placed his hand on my shoulder.

"Sorry, Mark," he said.

I stood up and patted him on the back.

"Me too. Let's get this done," I said, picking up one of the poles.

Finally, after another thirty minutes, some more bickering, and Mr. Clarke's expertise, the tent was finally erected.

"Everybody in!" Mr. Clarke announced.

Trent grabbed his sleeping bag and shot inside.

"Dibs on this corner!" he said, dropping his bag into the back-left corner.

"Fine," everyone said in unison.

Night fell over the forest, we all sat round a blazing fire which spat and hissed as ember floated into the sky. We roasted marshmallows over the fire, the heat warmed my hand; we sang songs... badly and told each other ghost stories. Midnight came and went, and the guys were in the tent, asleep. However, I was restless and sat outside in the dirt, draped in an old pair of gray sweats, my chest bare. The cool wind whipped through the trees, blew my long hair into my eyes and bit into my bare flesh, causing my nipples to pucker. I wrapped my arms round myself and rubbed my chest to seek warmth. The nearby river sloshed over the rocks, trout jumped out of the water and landed back in with a splash, frogs croaked in the darkness and owls hooted above. The tent unzipped behind me, I turned, and Mr. Clarke emerged wearing blue striped pajamas and holding my leather jacket in his hands.

"You might need this. Don't want you getting sick before the big day," he said.

He draped it over my shoulders, I pulled it round myself, blocking out the chilly air.

"Thanks," I said.

"Can't sleep?"

"No."

He sat beside me and rested his arms on his bent-up knees.

"What's on your mind?" he asked.

"I'm just nervous... you know, about the wedding."

He nodded and removed his glasses.

"It's perfectly normal," he said.

"It is?"

"Of course. I was the same as you before I married Sara. I sat in this very same spot with my brothers, fearing that she was too good for me. But you know... you just make it work."

"How?"

He chuckled to himself.

"Rachael loves you, Mark, and I know that you love her. Just look after her, be open and honest with her, keep loving her. You'll be fine."

"Thank you, sir."

He smiled and tapped my knee lightly.

"Colin," he corrected, then stood up and swept himself off.

"Try to get some sleep," he continued, then ducked back inside.

I stared up at the starry night sky and inhaled deeply. *It's normal to be nervous. Just keep loving Rachael and you'll be fine; that'll be the easiest request in existence.*

"Yeah, that was fun. Skinny dipping in the river?" Trent says.

"We did *not* skinny dip. Thrashed you at horseshoe toss though."

He laughs and takes another sip; the condensation runs down the bottle and drips onto the floor.

"Anyway, we can't go out tonight. We need to pick up our tuxedos," I continue.

"Yeah, I thought of that." He checks his watch. "We'll pick them up in about an hour, drop them off here, then we're heading back out, whether you like it or not."

I snort.

"So… you're kidnapping me?"

He rubs his chin and smirks.

"Yeah, guess I am."

I exhale.

"Okay, fine, but just one drink," I say, extending my index finger.

"One drink, promise," he says, holding both his hands up.

I wake facedown, my pillow and face covered in my own drool. *'One drink' he said. 'We won't be out long' he said. Damn it, Trent.* I sit up, wipe the moisture from my mouth with the back of my hand, and grimace at my soaked pillow. *Gross.* I climb out of bed and pinch my forehead while slowly heading for the bathroom. I splash my face with cold water and hunt inside the vanity unit for some pain relief. I find some aspirin and quickly throw two tablets into my mouth. I check myself in the mirror. Despite my foolishness last night, I don't look too bad. Trent reverberates the apartment with his snoring. *He'll have complaints from the neighbors with that racket.* I snigger and check my phone. *May 6th, 2017. Why does that sound familiar?* I sit on the lone white bathroom stool and think. Nothing jumps out at me. I shrug and leave the bathroom, ready to climb back into bed, but on my way, I notice two large bags hung up next to the front door. I approach slowly and unzip one. A smart black tuxedo, complete with an ivory vest and a black bow tie. *My tux. Shit! I'm getting married today at 1 p.m.* I check my watch hastily; 10:30 a.m. *Oh god.* I rush to Trent's bedroom and barge in without knocking. He sits up quickly but then groans and flops back down.

"Trent, get up," I say, pulling at his covers.

"Leave me alone," he moans, swatting at me through the covers.

"Trent, c'mon. I'm getting married."

He sits bolt upright again and stares at me, his eyes widen and his forehead creases.

"Damn," he says quietly, before leaping out of bed, nearly toppling me over.

"What are you doing standing here? Get in that shower," he demands, shooing me towards the bathroom.

I'm freshly showered and doing up the last few buttons of my white linen shirt before tucking it into my pressed tuxedo pants. My hair is combed back, it's a little uncomfortable, but I want to look my best for Rachael today. Trent sits on the couch to my right, tying up his shoes. There's a loud knock on the door and he goes to answer it as I drape my bow tie round my neck. Alison, Trent's mom, walks into the living room. Her blonde hair has grown a fraction since I last saw her, its wavy and hangs just past her shoulders. She's wearing a short-sleeved lilac dress with matching heels, hat, and purse. She pauses when she sees me and observes me with her light blue eyes. I blink at her and look down at my attire, suddenly anxious that I don't look presentable.

"Mark, you look fantastic," she whispers.

I beam at her and step into her open arms. When we pull away, she glances at my undone bow tie.

"Here, let me help you," she says.

I lift my chin and let her tie it. *When was the last time someone did this for me? I feel like a child again.* When she's done, I collect my jacket from the couch and slip it on. I hold my buttonhole in my hand, a pale pink plush rose, and attempt to place it, but it sags limply. She smiles, removes it, then re-pins it effortlessly to my breast.

"There. Now you're perfect," she declares, placing her hands on my shoulders.

She turns to Trent and sweeps an invisible piece of lint off his shoulder.

"And Trenton, you look great too," she gushes, kissing him on the cheek.

He rolls his eyes and steps back; his cheeks flush a little.

"Mom," he whines.

I snigger. *They didn't seem to notice.* I root in my luggage for a clean pair of socks. Finding a black pair, I unfurl them. A small leather box falls out onto the bed. *Odd.* I pick it up and open the lid. Inside is a small card with a message written in Rachael's tidy italic handwriting.

To my husband to be.
What can I say that I haven't already? These last few months have been a roller-coaster ride of ups and downs, but there's no better person that I'd rather go through it with. Words can't express how much I love you and how excited I am

to call you my husband. You have shown me so much love,
adoration, devotion, and loyalty in such a short period of time.
I can't wait to spend the rest of my days with you. See you this
afternoon with much love and excitement.
Rachael (future Mrs. Flint) xxx.

The backs of my eyes prick with unushered tears. *God, I love her.* I place the card back into the box and stare down at her wedding present to me. A pair of silver cufflinks with an 'M' and an 'R' entwined with each other. Alison peeks over my shoulder.

"They're beautiful," she says.

I glance at her.

"They are."

I carefully take each one out of the box and clip the cufflinks through my sleeves, wearing them with pride. Trent peeks at his watch and gasps.

"We need to go. It's 12:15."

Alison shrieks, making me jump as she fishes her car keys quickly from her purse.

"C'mon boys. Let's go," she says, holding the front door open.

Alison parks her car just outside of the east entrance of Central Park. I climb out of the front passenger seat, careful not to crease my suit. I cross to the other side of the street and am swiftly joined by Trent and Alison, who walk either side of me.

"Where did you say Rex and Mitch were meeting us?" I ask Trent.

He peeks at me out the corner of his eye.

"At the entrance is what they said."

"Have you got the rings?"

His eyes shoot up to mine and he pats himself down hastily. *Oh no.* I stop in my tracks and both me and Alison stare at him.

"Trent?"

He grins widely and produces the box from his pants pocket.

"Ha, got you."

"Ah, you bitch," I groan.

He slaps me on the back and laughs loudly. She sighs heavily and swats at him with her purse. He ducks out the way and continues to laugh as I scowl at him.

"Not cool," I say.

He squeezes my shoulder and gives me a small shake.

"It was pretty funny though."

I roll my eyes, ignoring his jibes and continue walking.

"Let's go. We don't want to be late."

Rex and Mitch are sitting on a bench next to a bronze statue of Samuel Morse. Their suits match my own apart from their bow ties which are burgundy. Rex's blonde hair is combed back, and Mitch's curly copper hair shines in the overhead sun. Rex taps Mitch on the knee and points in our direction. They hold hands then stand and make their way over.

"Hello, everyone," Rex enthuses.

"Mark, you look dashing," he continues.

"Thank you," I say.

"You remember Mitch?" Rex says, pointing towards him.

"I do," I say, turning to Mitch who outstretches his hand.

"Congratulations," he says.

I shake his proffered hand as I regard him, his brown eyes shine as he beams at me.

"Enough of the small talk, we should get going," Trent interjects.

I check my watch. Christ, he's right, we're going to be late if we don't hurry.

"This way," I call, pointing to a path on our right.

Trent scoffs and fishes out his phone.

"I'll bring up directions."

I stare at him.

"Don't you trust my judgement?" I joke.

He laughs and nudges Rex in the ribs.

"The last time he tried to get to the Loeb Boathouse, he entered through the west entrance… Seriously, the west, way over there," he gestures with his finger.

I look away and rub my nose.

"I was new here. Besides, me and Rachael have walked this route half a dozen times while we were planning the wedding, I'm sure we'll be fine."

He waves his phone in the air, his brow furrowing.

"Hey," I click at him.

"You know something that doesn't need signal?" I tap my head. "Follow me."

I turn on my heel and head down the winding path, tailed closely by the rest of my wedding party.

We walk through the gate and towards the front entrance of the Loeb Boathouse. Gold and white balloons are tethered to the iron fence and a sign reads: '*Welcome to Mark & Rachael's wedding*'. We head inside where a young man dressed in a white shirt with a black apron smiles at us.

"You must be the groom," he says.

I nod and his smile broadens, then he gestures with his hand.

"This way."

We follow him into the ceremony room; it's decorated with rows of white chairs on both sides, a white runner down the middle of the aisle is scattered with pale pink rose petals, glass lanterns with flickering candles inside are placed beside the aisle seats, an arch is beautifully decorated with flowers and hanging ivy woven together. A string quartet plays 'Canon in D Major' softly in the background. Some guests are already seated including Sara, Rachael's mom who's dressed in a maroon frock with a red rose pinned in her brown hair. She's chatting animatedly with two men who I've never met before. Rachael's paternal and maternal grandparents coo and wave as I walk towards the front. My side is practically empty aside from Mr. Levitt, my boss at the Neapolitan Hotel; he's middle-aged, with white hair and spectacles. He's dressed in a black suit with a ridiculously colorful tie. He's accompanied by his wife and son, who's in a wheelchair. Rex and Mitch take their seats on my side as does Alison. Trent joins me up front. I take a deep breath and glance at the clock above the door; 1:10 p.m. Rachael's late. *Where is she? I hope she hasn't changed her mind.* I shake my head and clasp my hands together in front of me. Trent grips my shoulder and leans down to whisper in my ear.

"You alright?"

I look at him and smile weakly, but the truth is, I'm terrified. Sweat beads on my forehead which I wipe away with the back of my hand and my gut is in knots, making me a little queasy. Sara leaves her seat and walks over to me.

She strokes my arm delicately, observes me with brown eyes and produces a grin that stretches across her narrow face.

"Hello, Mark."

I nod at her then embrace her quickly.

"How are you feeling?" she asks.

"Nervous."

She nods and pats my arm again.

"Deep breaths. You'll be just fine."

The two men she was talking to earlier approach us. One looks to be in his early sixties, he's tall and lean, his dark brown hair is combed back, and he has hazel eyes. The other looks younger and is much shorter, but like Sara, he has brown hair and hazel eyes. I shake each of their hands in turn then glance at Sara.

"Oh, Mark. My apologies. These are my brothers, Danny and Stephan."

She points to Danny, the older one, then Stephan, the younger brother. I greet them both.

"It's nice to meet you," Danny says.

"You take care of our Rachael. She's one in a million," Stephan says.

"I'll do that," I say.

Sara cuts in between them.

"We should take our seats. She'll be arriving any minute."

Danny and Stephan turn and resume their seats next to Evelyn and Royce, their parents. Reverend Rowlands enters the room, wearing a dark suit and carrying a black book with some papers sticking out of it. He's in his late sixties, with white hair, green eyes, and a kind smile. He approaches Sara and greets her warmly before doing the same to Trent and myself. He steps under the arch and flicks through his book. Sara leans in again.

"He agreed to do this as a favor for me. I'm at his Sunday mass most weekends," she explains.

"Rachael told me."

She smiles, pats my arm again and takes her seat.

I stare at the overhead clock for the billionth time; 1:25 p.m. *What if something's happened to her?*

"Hey," Trent taps me on the shoulder.

He fishes a handkerchief out of his pocket and hands it to me.

"You might need this. You're sweating."

"Really? I hadn't noticed."

I take it from him and dab my drenched forehead.

"Relax. She'll come through for ya," he says.

I exhale again, trying to rid the sickly butterflies. The string quartet stops suddenly, and the room falls silent.

A waitress pads into the room and whispers into the lead violinist's ear. Trent nudges me.

"Here we go," he whispers.

I straighten my jacket and clasp my hands in front of me again.

"If everyone could please stand for the entrance of the bride," Reverend Rowlands announces.

Everyone gets to their feet as the quartet launch into 'Strangers In The Night', Rachael's favorite. Louise, Rachael's younger sister walks into the room smiling widely, blue eyes shining, and mahogany hair swept over one shoulder. She's wearing a long burgundy gown and gripping a small bouquet of pale pink and white roses with burgundy peonies all woven together. Behind her is Steph, Rachael's best friend and colleague on the force; she has an African American complexion, her dark brown eyes regard me warmly and her black hair is braided and like Louise, it hangs over her shoulder. She has a matching frock and bouquet. Lastly, Sasha, Steph's fiancée, who I've only met a couple of times these past few months; she's thin and tall with pale skin, red hair, and light blue eyes, she walks closely behind Steph, a huge grin on her face. Then finally, there she is. *Rachael.*

Chapter Two

My mouth dries as I lay eyes on my beautiful bride. She's in a tight fitted lace gown that clings to every perfect curve that she has; a floor length veil trails behind her, hanging from her perfect mahogany hair which is tied into a messy bun with glinting floral diamond studs; a pearl necklace drapes around her slender neckline, and drop earrings gleam from her earlobes, my wedding present to her. She clasps a large bouquet with diamantes sparkling from the center of the roses and peonies. Her perfect smile lights up the room and a few tendrils escape her bun, framing her beautiful face as she slowly makes her way towards me. Colin walks beside her, his hand resting over hers as she grips his arm; he's smiling widely, dressed in his finest police uniform, the rim of his golden cap shimmers, and his blue eyes well up with tears behind his specs. The knot leaves my gut and tightens in my throat as I hold back my own emotion. They come to a stop beside me, Rachael hands her bouquet to Louise who stands beside the other bridesmaids. Colin smiles down at Rachael then kisses her on both cheeks.

"I love you," he whispers in her ear.

He turns to me and places her warm hand in mine. My eyes lock with Colin's.

"Thank you," I say.

He clears his throat quietly, then takes a seat beside his wife at the front. I turn my steady gaze back to my bride as a large smile covers my face.

"Hi," I whisper.

"Hi," she replies, her fingers tightening round mine.

"You're gorgeous."

"So are you. You scrub up well."

My nerves slowly melt away as the music from the string quartet ceases. It's just Rachael and me. Reverend Rowlands takes a step forward and clears his throat loudly, commanding everyone's attention.

"You may be seated," he announces.

"Dearly beloved, we are gathered here today on this fine afternoon to witness the joining in matrimony of Mark Jonathan Flint and Rachael Jean Clarke."

The reverend smiles down at us both and I give her fingers a squeeze. He asks the congregation if anyone knows of any impediment to our marriage. *I was dreading this bit.* The tight feeling in my throat returns, but I quickly swallow it down. The room stays silent. Rachael exhales and peeks at me.

"Phew," she mouths.

I stifle a chuckle as some muffled titters and sighs emit from our guests. Reverend Rowlands then asks us each in turn to declare that there's no legal reason why we can't be joined in marriage. We both declare clearly and loudly that there isn't.

"And now I invite you both to offer your vows to each other."

He looks at me first, smiling.

"Mark?"

I take a deep breath and gaze at my Rachael smiling at me. I take a piece of paper from my inside breast pocket and read out loud, my words ringing out over the throng.

"I, Mark Jonathan Flint do take thee, Rachael Jean Clarke to be my lawfully wedded wife. I solemnly vow to safeguard and protect you. To laugh with you and cry with you. I promise to always be your rock and your savior in times of need. I promise to keep you safe by my side, to trust and honor you. Forsaking all others, through the good times and the bad. I will love you deep with all my heart till death do us part."

Tears shine in her eyes and her cheeks flush an enchanting rosy pink.

"Rachael?" the reverend prompts.

She takes a calming breath.

"I, Rachael Jean Clarke do take thee, Mark Jonathan Flint to be my lawfully wedded husband. I give you my promise to be your faithful partner, in sickness and in health. I promise to stand by your side in good times and in bad. I will share your sorrow and your joy. I will love you unconditionally, upholding your goals and dreams, and bring you solace in times of need. I will cherish you and keep you safe by my side until death do us part."

I wipe the corner of my eye, trying to hold back the wave of emotion that crashes over me.

"You two will now exchange rings as a symbol of your abiding love. A ring is a constant circle. Unbroken and everlasting. A symbol of pure unity. So, too, will be your commitment to each other and to this marriage, from this day forth, till death do you part. Could we have the rings please?"

Trent jumps up and hands the open ring box over. Rowlands removes Rachael's ring and hands it to me.

"Mark, place the ring on Rachael's finger."

I position it at the tip of her left ring finger.

"Repeat after me," Reverend Rowlands says. "Rachael, I give you this ring as a sign of our enduring faith in each other, our unity, and our everlasting love."

I repeat the words, loud and clear, and slip the ring fully onto her finger. Rowlands hands Rachael my ring.

"Rachael, place the ring on Mark's finger and repeat after me... Mark, I give you this ring as a sign of our enduring faith in each other, our unity, and our everlasting love."

She sounds out the words sweetly for the rest of the congregation to hear, then she pushes the ring fully onto my finger.

Rowlands clasps both of our hands in his.

"Love is the reason we are seated here today. Marriage is founded on love. These two have pledged their love for each other in the sight of God. We honor them and wish them strength, courage, and trust to grow together, to learn from each other and remain true to each other no matter on the path that life shall lead them. Mark and Rachael, you two have agreed to be married and to live together in matrimony. You have declared your love to everyone here today and promised to uphold that love with your vows. With the power vested in me by the state of New York, I now declare you husband and wife."

He releases our hands and I beam at Rachael. My heart soars.

"Mark, you may kiss your beautiful bride."

"Finally, we are one," I whisper.

She smiles warmly as I lean in, place both hands on either side of her face and kiss her deeply. The room erupts with a rousing applause. I grasp her soft fingers gently and turn to face everyone. Steph, Louise, and Sasha beam warmly at us both as they clap enthusiastically. Trent squeezes my shoulder and leans in close to my ear.

"Congratulations, bud."

I smile and nod at him briefly, then lead my beautiful Rachael in her full-length lace gown back down the aisle where a couple of waiters hold trays with flutes full of champagne. I take two, then hand one to Rachael.

"Mrs. Flint," I smile.

"Thank you, Mr. Flint."

"Are you ready to party?"

She beams her mega-watt smile at me.

"Bring it on."

Taking a sip of Laurent-Perrier Cuvee Rose, Colin wraps up his speech.

"Welcome to the family, Mark. To the bride and groom, Mark and Rachael," he announces clearly, holding his flute aloft.

"Mark and Rachael," the room choruses.

Rachael's cheeks redden as she smiles and quickly takes a sip of her champagne, I don't think she likes having this much attention on her, I don't either. I take a calming breath as I'm due to make my speech shortly, but I take a moment to look around at our opulent surroundings. Me and Rachael sit alone at the top of the room facing the rest of our guests. The sun shimmers off the lake behind us as it slowly begins to fade. The tables are draped in fresh crisp white linen and mini cherry blossom trees as the centerpieces, surrounded by tealights and mirrors. There's a loud buzz in the air as guests chatter and laugh among themselves. A waiter approaches our table and hands me the microphone. I peek at Rachael who reassures me with a warming smile and a tap on the hand.

"Knock 'em dead," she whispers.

I smile, kiss her on the cheek and stand. I clink my knife against my glass. The room falls silent, and all eyes are on me.

"Good evening, everyone. On behalf of my wife and I, we want to thank everyone for coming here today to share this special day with us. You know, a year ago, I never thought any of this was possible. I lived a life that I'm not proud of, but that's behind me now. The first time I met Rachael wasn't your typical love story… she slammed my head against the hood of her car."

I pause as the guests erupt into laughter. I chuckle with them.

"It hurt like hell, but I couldn't be more grateful than I am today. Thank you to the Clarkes for accepting me into your family today."

Sara and Colin wave at me and I wave back.

"Thank you to Trent, for putting up with me all this time. You're my best friend. Thank you for being my best man today. I remember how uncomfortable you were when I asked, I know you hate the attention, so thank you again. To Alison, thank you for being my support all this time. We were only reunited a few months ago, but it's been the best to see you again. A special thank you to the bridesmaids, Louise, Steph and Sasha. Don't they all look gorgeous today?"

Everyone cheers and claps as Louise covers her face and appears to be turning red.

"And of course…"

I glance down at my beautiful wife who grins at me.

"Thank you to Rachael for agreeing to be mine today. She has taught me a lot in the short space of time that we've known each other. You taught me to love, you showed me that beauty really does exist. I love you with all my heart."

I bend down quickly and kiss her on the cheek, followed by cooing from our guests.

"Lastly, I'll sign off by saying, there are a few people who I wish were here today, but they are here in spirit. My parents for example… They died when I was very young, and my grandma who-."

Tears well up in my eyes, and a large lump forms in my throat. I'm out of words as I'm transported back to a dark, dank apartment, and the young six-year-old boy who screamed for his parents and wept on the couch. *No. Not now.* A lone tear strays down my cheek, but I dash it away quickly. A warm, tender touch brushes my arm and Rachael stands. She takes the mic from me and continues.

"We end here with a special thank you to all my family who have taken in Mark as one of our own. Alison, a huge thank you to you and Trent. You're like a mom to him and it's heartwarming to see you two together. Trent, he doesn't express it enough, but you're like a brother to him. Thank you everyone for being here today."

We both resume our seats as a rousing applause fills the room. She hands the microphone back to the waiter, clutches my hand and leans in close.

"You okay?" she whispers.

I nod and kiss her on the lips.

"Thank you," I whisper back.

She cocks her head to the side.

"For what?"

"Saving me."

She grins and leans her head against my shoulder as Trent makes his way towards us to make his speech. He's had a couple of glasses of champagne. I hope he doesn't embarrass anyone. I take a large swig from my glass and brace myself.

"Good evening. I've drawn the short straw- I mean, I'm honored to make this speech today, but please forgive me, public speaking is not my thing."

This gets a laugh from everyone.

"Let me start off with saying, doesn't Rachael look stunning today?"

Everyone cheers and applauds loudly. Her cheeks turn a fetching rosy pink. I cover her hand with mine and grin at her which she returns.

"I have a few embarrassing tales to share… sorry, Mark. Like his first encounter with Rachael, when I first met him, he was battered and bruised. He was never any good at protecting himself. Thank God I came along."

I press my fingers against my temple and exhale as the guests laugh some more.

"But in all seriousness, I love this guy, he's been my best friend and brother for a long time and if I were gay, I wouldn't hesitate."

More laughter and a few whistles emit. Trent titters, then glances down at Rachael and smirks crookedly.

"Rest assured, I'm not. So, he's all yours. Enjoy him."

She chuckles and bows her head.

"We were separated in our youth after my mom took a job here in New York and Mark was left in Chicago. I spent many evenings wondering if I'd ever see my friend again, but not too long ago, he came crashing back into my life... or I crashed into his. In either case, you can take it literally..."

Rachael and I chuckle as do the guests.

"Imagine my surprise when I discovered that Mark Flint, the man who was useless with women had got himself a crush. And my god, what a crush she was. He would not stop chasing her, he would not stop trying to win her round. Looks like he succeeded! Today, my best friend tied the knot. I just wanna say..." He raises his flute. "Congratulations, to both of you. Mr. and Mrs. Flint everybody," he declares.

"Mr. and Mrs. Flint," everyone choruses.

Rachael taps me on the shoulder, and I lean over.

"Trent's pants," she whispers into my ear.

I furrow my brow and look over at him. His zipper is down. I rise from my seat and hold my hand up, making my way over to him.

"If I could interrupt for a minute," I say.

He squints his eyes at me as I lean down to his waist and zip him up. Everyone, except for Trent bursts into fits of laughter. Alison smacks her hand against the table, unable to contain herself. Louise covers her mouth, stifling her laughter as she reverberates her shoulders. Trent turns beet red and purses his lips. He places one hand on his hip and flicks the mic with the other while the laughter dies down.

"…And that… is what best friends are for…" he says.

The crowd laughs again as do Rachael and I.

"Now, let's all get shit-faced and forget that ever happened. Enjoy the party," he quips further.

"C'mere, buddy," I say, stretching my arm out.

He walks towards me, and I hug him tightly with both arms.

"Thanks, Trent."

"Thank *you*."

He chuckles and pats my back as we're greeted by a round of applause from our congregation, then I release him.

"Get back to your wife before I strangle you," he says.

I wink and sit myself back down next to Rachael.

"Shall we cut the cake?" I whisper.

"Sure."

The DJ is ready to pump some tunes as Rachael and I make our way to the dancefloor. I take her hand and tug her into my arms as she envelopes me with hers. The guests close in around us, forming a circle. The sweet, soulful voice of Diana Ross' 'When You Tell Me That You Love Me' fills the room. We slowly sway together in time with the music. Out the corner of my eye, I notice Colin hand Sara his handkerchief and she dabs her eyes with it. I quickly tear my gaze away and am all eyes on Rachael. Everyone fades from my vision as I bury my face into her shoulder and plant a delicate kiss there. *I don't want this moment to end. I would gladly stay like this for eternity, just Rachael and me alone in our bubble.* I croon softly into her ear as we continue to sway slowly. She melts against my arms.

"You're a terrible singer, but I love you."

I laugh and press my forehead to hers as others begin joining us on the dancefloor.

Trent and Rex are demolishing the dancefloor to 'Gangnam Style' with their jackets thrown to the side and their bow ties hanging loosely round their necks. They hop around like drunken crazed baboons. I sit down at the bar to rest my feet and glance over at Rachael. She's at the other end of the dancefloor, her veil long ago discarded and draped over a nearby chair as she laughs with Louise and Steph. I sip my champagne and watch her, utterly mesmerized that she chose me. A hand rests on my shoulder. I glance round as Alison perches onto a chair beside me.

"I'm so proud of you," she says.

I smirk at her, then look back towards Rachael.

"Your grandma would be too. She's smiling down on this place. She's here, I know she is."

"I really missed her today, Alison. I wish my family were here."

I hang my head. She places her hand on mine.

"We are. Now, you've made it bigger," she says.

I turn my attention back to Rachael. She's now swaying softly on the dancefloor, wrapped in her father's arms.

"Why are you so good to me, Alison?" I ask.

She smiles as her eyes rim with tears.

"You're my boy."

I blink at her as her smile broadens, then she taps me on the hand once more and gets to her feet.

"I should go and make sure Trent doesn't get into any more trouble," she laughs, pointing with her chin.

Trent is now jumping in circles around Rachael, he looks utterly ridiculous, his hair flings out of place and his bow tie lies in a crumpled mess on the floor. Rachael and Colin both swipe at him until Louise grabs his arm and sits him down.

"Oh my god," I chuckle as I press the bridge of my nose against my knuckles before looking up at Alison again.

She smirks, then heads towards Sara. I down my drink as Alison's words rattle around in my head; *"You're my boy"*. We've been separated for a long time, but she's been like a mom to me ever since I reunited with her. It's been years since I felt such parental love and devotion. I get to my feet quickly and go after her.

"Alison?" I call.

She glances over her shoulder and turns round so that she's facing me fully.

"This is going to sound ridiculous," I say.

She crosses her arms under her bosom and cocks her head to the side.

"Try me."

I exhale deeply.

"Can I call you 'mom'?" I say in a rush.

Alison's mouth pops open, then she pulls me into her arms and hugs me hard, making all the air escape my lungs.

"Oh, Mark. I would be honored," she weeps into my shoulder.

I pat her gently on the back and close my eyes. Soaking up the warm feeling that spreads through my veins.

I offer my pleasantries to our guests as I make my way to the dancefloor to reunite with my wife who is currently ending a dance to Beyonce's 'Run the World' with Steph, Louise, Sasha, and Sara. The music transitions into Frank Sinatra's 'I've Got You Under My Skin'. I stand behind her, taking a moment to inhale her heavenly scent that ignites my soul.

"My beautiful bride, may I have this dance?" I say smoothly, close to her ear.

She peeks over her shoulder, a huge smirk spreads across her face like wildfire.

"It would be my pleasure."

I take her delicate, perfectly manicured hand in mine, then pull her flush against my body and sway to the tune that croons around us.

We walk towards the exit of Central Park, down the lantern lit path, followed by our wedding party who chatter excitedly. Louise holds the end of Rachael's dress to avoid the mud. Rachael's arm is tucked into the crook of mine, my jacket covers her shoulders to shield her from the chilly breeze. Our transport is waiting, a retro 1950's yellow taxi, complete with a chauffeur dressed in old fashioned clothing, ready to take us to the Hilton Hotel near JFK. The guests gather around us as Rachael smiles, turns her back to them and throws her bouquet. The female guests shriek and all charge for it like field players in a baseball game. It lands in Trent's arms; all eyes turn on him. He grimaces and tosses it at Rex, who holds it aloft and cheers. We pose for a few more photos as the guests snap away with their phones, then I hitch up Rachael's dress and help her inside before sliding in beside her. The chauffeur closes the door and drives away as everyone cheers, whistles, and showers the car in rice. She waves out the back window, then leans her head against my shoulder and sighs quietly.

"What a day," she breathes.

I lean down and kiss the top of her head.

"The best. My hair was kinda irritating like this though" I say.

She sits up and observes my slicked back hair. She smiles and ruffles it with her fingers, so it flops back into my eyes.

"I prefer it like this anyway."

I blow it out of my eyes then comb it aside.

"Me too," I smile.

She sighs again and rests her head back on my shoulder as we stop at a red light.

I carry a weary Rachael over the threshold and into our suite.

"I've always wanted to do that," I say.

"Hmm…" she groans, looking up at me and smirking.

I set her onto her feet gently.

"There's no one else that I'd rather do that with," I say.

"Me neither."

I marvel at our surroundings; white walls, grey patterned carpet and an HD TV mounted on the wall. Our luggage rests next to the couch, dropped off earlier by Sara. Rachael slumps onto the bed and exhales deeply.

"Would you be a dear?" she asks, raising her white heel-clad foot from under her gown.

I smile and bend down to unstrap the heel from her right foot, followed by her left, then prop both feet on my lap and massage them firmly. She groans softly and lolls her head back against the pillows.

"You're my hero," she says.

"You too, honey."

I stop massaging, clamber over her, and kiss her once again. She rakes her fingers through my over-long hair. She places a finger on the corner of my mouth and rubs firmly.

"What's that?" I ask.

"You've got more makeup on your face than me."

"Really?"

I get up and walk into the bathroom as she follows. I look in the mirror. She's right. My cheeks and mouth are covered in lipstick marks. I chortle.

"I should get this stuff off my face," she says, walking out of the bathroom to root through her luggage.

"No. Let me do it."

She turns to me.

"Really?"

"Yeah. How hard can it be?"

She sniggers as she pulls out the makeup remover and cotton pads, then hands them to me. I take her hand and lead her back into the bathroom where I sit her down on the lone chair in the corner. I gently wipe the makeup from her face. After fifteen minutes, it's gone.

"Ah, there you are," I coo softly.

"You don't like makeup?"

"Sure. I just prefer the real you."

She smiles up at me and starts removing pins from her updo. I stand back and lean against the wall, appreciating the masterpiece in front of me. Gradually, waves of mahogany hair cascade, resting across her shoulders and down to the tops of her breasts. When the task is complete, she shakes her hair and rakes her fingers through it to level it out. My breath hitches in my throat and her eyes slowly drift over to meet mine.

"My god. The Venus de Milo would need a lot of work done to match your beauty," I say.

She tilts her head to one side, as her cheeks blush an enchanting pink. I lean down in front of her, place my hand on her check and gently guide her gaze back to mine.

"I mean it," I clarify.

Her lips twitch, then she strokes my arm deftly, stands and leaves the bathroom. I watch after her before looking in the mirror, exhaling my held breath. I make to exit the bathroom but freeze in the doorway. She stands at the foot of the bed, slowly unbuttoning the back of her dress. She glances over her shoulder at me and smirks. My mouth goes dry. I lean against the doorjamb and cross my legs, enjoying the floor show. She unfastens the final button with her slender fingers and the elegant lace trails down her body and pools around her feet. I widen my eyes and lick my lips. My god, she's wearing white thigh-high stockings attached to a garter belt, matching lacy panties and a tight corset that accentuates every luscious curve that she has. She steps out of the pool of lace, bends over to collect it from the floor and drapes it over the armchair in the corner of the room. I stride over towards her, my intentions clear, but she grabs the collar of my shirt, halting me.

"Uh-uh. Not so fast."

She shoves me onto the bed, making me gasp. Her pupils dilate and her breathing shallows as she crawls over my lap and straddles me just above the waist. She slowly peels my jacket from my shoulders and tosses it to the side. I don't dare break my gaze from her heated hazel depths. She grins slowly exposing her straight white teeth, then she leans down and nips at my earlobe, making me gasp again. Her sweetly fragrant hair tickles my face as she continues her assault. My fingers dig into the sheets underneath me as every nerve ending and hair follicle on my body stands to attention. She stops her sensual assault as doors slam and guests talk and laugh loudly in the corridor. She frowns for a moment, then leans down and grips my bottom lip between her teeth. She unfastens my bow tie and gets to work on my shirt buttons while planting kisses on my chin and neck, grazing her teeth along them on the way down. I slowly raise my hands and place them onto the warm, soft swell of her breasts. She bats my hand away and flattens me against the mattress, pressing her hand firmly against my half-bare chest, her fingers raking through the smattering of chest hair. I shut my eyes and groan.

"Not yet," she admonishes in a sultry manner.

She finishes the task of unbuttoning, removing, and discarding my shirt while gripping my toned upper arms firmly, then she presses her lips against mine. I wrap my arms around her back and fondle the clasps of her corset. *She's not denying me this time.* We both come up for air as I draw vital breath into my lungs. She smiles down at me, her hair curtaining her face.

"Your turn," she says as she dismounts me.

I jump off the bed, rip my shoes and socks off, and struggle out of my pants while she regards me, hiding a smirk behind her fingers while tapping her philtrum. *Okay. Let's try this again.* I march over and pull her from the bed. She attempts to brush me off, laughing as she does, but I grab her wrists, put her arms behind her back and hold them in place with one hand. I place my mouth to hers and deepen the kiss. Our teeth clash painfully, but I don't care. I slowly walk her backwards until she's pressed up against the wall. I draw away, remove her panties in one swift move, then hitch her stocking-clad leg round my hip. She twitches her arm and I release the pair of them, she unbuttons my underpants to release me, then I move forward slowly until our hips join. She groans softly in my ear then takes a fistful of my hair and tugs hard, making me yell. I pick up the pace as she matches my rhythm. We're all tangled limbs, erratic breaths and mingled tongues as we collapse onto the bed and continue slowly, reveling in each other until my body can stand the wait no more.

I lie on my back and stare up at the ceiling, a hot and sweaty mess. Rachael lies with her back to me, breathing deeply. She's removed her corset so I can admire the dip in the small of her back and her fine shapely waist. I reach over and slowly rub some life back into her shoulders. She hums her approval before turning swiftly so that we're nose to nose.

"That was very nice," she whispers.

"Start our married life on a high, right?" I smirk.

Her eyes twinkle and she rubs her nose down the length of mine. I peek at the bedside clock and note that it's nearly two in the morning. *Crap! We're due at the airport in five hours.* I cover us both with the duvet and switch off the bedside lamp.

"It's late, we should get some sleep."

She cuddles in close, entwines her legs with mine and kisses my bare chest.

"Good night, wife," I whisper into the darkness.

I feel her lips lift against my skin.

"Good night, husband."

I entwine my fingers through hers then close my eyes and slowly drift into a happy and sated sleep.

Chapter Three

———∽———

The sun beams through our hotel windows and a light breeze blows through the curtains. The roar of the lapping ocean is carried on the breeze. I glance out at the white sand and the clear blue sky. It's so crisp, so perfect. I bend down and proceed to unpack our luggage. Rachael has changed out of her turquoise summer dress and is now sporting a rather revealing navy-blue bikini. She lies stretched out on a sun lounger on our balcony, soaking up the Punta Cana rays. I smirk and quickly pull on my swimming shorts, then join her outside. I stand over her and admire her slim figure, long delicate legs, amazing hips, toned belly, and perfectly formed breasts. I run my hand delicately down her side, she jumps awake and lifts her aviator specs, smiling brightly.

"Mark," she croons.

I bend down and peck her softly on the lips.

"You'll burn."

She frowns then leans down and picks up a small white tube. She tosses it at me, and I catch it. *Much to my amazement.* I examine the tube of sunscreen and blink at her. She grins and rolls onto her stomach.

"Could you put some on my back?" she asks.

"As you wish."

I throw my leg over the lounger and straddle her just above her ass. She giggles and I massage a handful of lotion firmly onto her back. She sighs then rests her face to the side, giving me an opportunity to appreciate her.

"Let's go back to bed, I'm too hot out here," she says.

I furrow my brow and slide off. She rolls over then stands.

"It's only 5 o'clock, I'm not tired."

She grins.

"I wasn't planning on sleeping… were you?"

My mouth falls open. *Oh.* She grabs my hand and I follow in her enticing wake. She pulls a string on her bikini, and it unravels slowly. I lick my lips instinctively and can do nothing but stare.

"Now what?" she shrugs.

I lunge for her, our lips locking. She groans into my mouth and returns my assault with her own heated ador. I walk us back slowly until we both collapse onto the bed, the springs protesting. We never break our precious contact, until I make her mine all over again.

We split a goat's cheese flatbread and a bottle of red wine in the on-site restaurant. She stares off into the distance while she chews slowly. I clear my throat. She shakes her head and stares at me.

"Penny for your thought?" I ask.

"Looking forward to horse riding tomorrow?"

I take another piece of flatbread and contort my mouth.

"I don't know the first thing about it."

She chuckles and covers my hand with hers.

"There's nothing to it, I'll help you… Unless you'd prefer to cancel?"

I consider this for a moment or maybe suggest that she can go alone. *Don't be stupid, you're on honeymoon. She can't go alone.*

"No, of course not. It should be fun."

The blazing sun beats down on top of us making my hair stick uncomfortably to my face. *I've never hated my floppy hair more than I do now.* I'm mounted on top of a slow brown horse, who refuses to do as I tell it. It stops again but this time, I can't get it going and I'm losing the tour group.

"C'mon. Let's go," I shout, spurring it hard, but it doesn't budge.

I kick frantically. It lowers its head with me still holding the reins. I'm thrown forward and land face down in the sand. Rachael laughs as she comes to a stop beside me.

"Are you okay?" she splutters.

I lift my head and shake the powdery sand from my hair.

"I hate sand," I grumble.

She dismounts her horse and grabs my arm, pulling me to my feet.

"The Caribbean was a bad choice if you don't like sand," she laughs.

"Well, I hate being sprawled out on it, at least."

I laugh and brush myself down.

"Wait till I tell Trent," she says, still doubling over with laughter.

"He'd never let me live it down. Look, I hope you don't mind, but I'm going to head back to the hotel and grab a shower."

"Do you want me to come with?"

"It's okay. You enjoy your ride."

I brush a loose tendril of hair from her eyes and hook it behind her ear. My thumb lightly grazes her soft warm cheek.

"I'll see you later," I continue.

The tour guide returns along with the other guests.

"Are you alright, sir?" he asks in a thick Hispanic accent.

"Yeah, just fine. I'm heading back."

"You don't want to finish?" he asks.

I wave my hand up in a dismissive gesture.

"Nah, I'm good."

He frowns, but then smiles.

"Okay. Everyone else, let's get going," he calls to the group.

Rachael quickly clambers back onto her horse and smiles down at me.

"Be careful," I say.

She runs her hand through my sticky hair.

"Always," she says, then she follows in line with everyone else.

A flash of light and a low rumble wakes me. I sit up in bed, the thin sheet pools above my waist. *What's the time?* I glance over at the clock; 5:45 a.m. I look down at my side, but Rachael is absent. I scan the room and find her outside, standing on the balcony draped in her silk white gown. I climb out of bed, pull on my underpants and go to join her. I wrap my hand round her waist and kiss her on the cheek. She looks over, then another flash of light illuminates the side of her face briefly. We both stare out at the beach; the waves crash aggressively against the shoreline and the palm trees are blown ferociously.

"There goes our swim," she says.

"Well, we've got the hot tub."

I gesture with my head to the corner of our suite where the large jacuzzi bath sits. She smirks and titters.

"Foam and champagne it is, then."

"Now?"

She looks over at the clock on the nightstand.

"It's a little early. We should try and rest through this storm."

We go back inside, and I close the patio doors in a vain attempt to shut out the roar of the storm. We climb back into bed and lie down. She nuzzles and kisses my chest gently until her breathing evens out. She's asleep. I kiss the top of her head and close my eyes.

Me and Rachael stand hand in hand at the Loeb Boathouse as Reverend Rowlands pronounces us husband and wife. I kiss my beautiful bride as our guests cheer with glee behind us. She smiles warmly at me but her smile fades as she glances back at Rowlands. I follow her glare and there he stands. Tobias. He scowls deeply through his piercing green eyes, his black slicked hair is slightly out of place, his yellow decaying teeth are visible as his scowl slowly turns to arrogance. He's in his charcoal pinstripe suit, a red carnation is pinned to his left breast, and he holds his revolver in his left hand. The guests scream and begin to flee.

"Until death do you part," Tobias sneers.

He raises the gun, points it at Rachael and pulls the trigger. A white flash and she's gone. Tobias' laughter echoes around the room.

I sit bolt upright in bed and wipe my face. I'm drenched in sweat. *What was that about?* I stare down at my side, but she isn't there. Terror claws at my throat, threatening to overwhelm me. I leap out of bed and search the suite.

'Rachael?" I call desperately.

The bathroom door flies open, and she stands in the doorway, her eyes wide, her hair brushed over one shoulder and her mouth forming a perfect 'o'.

"Oh, thank God you're okay," I say.

"Of course I am. Why wouldn't I be?"

"Well, it's just…"

I trail off not wanting to relive my nightmare. *Why is Tobias back to haunt me? Why now?* She switches off the bathroom light and steps closer.

"Mark, what is it?"

"It doesn't matter."

I wrap her into my arms and inhale her scent, which goes a long way to calming me. She wraps her arms round my back and squeezes me close.

"Talk to me," she whispers into my shoulder.

I pull away and run my hands through my hair.

"I can't."

I flop onto the bed and stare up at the ceiling. The storm rages on outside, the rain now patters the balcony, reflecting my bleak mood. The bed dips as she climbs beside me and drapes an arm round my naked chest.

"Please. Tell me what's bothering you. Was it a dream?" she presses.

I know I can't shake this. I have to give her something.

"Do you know where Tobias is?"

She sits up, her mouth falling open.

"Why?"

I prop myself up on my elbows.

"I dreamt he was at our wedding… with a gun. What if this is telling me something? What if he's back? If anything happened to you because of me-" I speak in such a rush, my voice raises several notches so that it doesn't sound right to my ears.

"Nothing is going to happen to me," she says quietly.

"Is he back?"

She sighs and looks down at her fingernails. *That can't be good.*

"I'm not sure. We never recovered his body. So, I just don't know. I'm sorry."

I survived the fall from the Grain Terminal, so he must've too.

"He's still out there, isn't he?" I whisper.

She opens her mouth but then closes it again and shakes her head.

"We're safe. Nothing is going to happen. If, in the slight chance that he's still out there, the police will be ready. Trust me."

"You're sure?"

She smiles and presses her forehead to mine.

"I promise. It was just a dream. It's going to be okay."

I smile and kiss her delicately.

"Thank you," I whisper.

"For what?"

"For being mine."

She pulls away and leans back on her arms.

"Shall we get back to our honeymoon? I think the jacuzzi is calling for us."

I laugh as she gets up from the bed, saunters over to the tub and turns the faucet on.

"Care to join me?" she smirks over her shoulder.

Our honeymoon is nearly at its end. There's been no more talk about Tobias since my nightmare a few days ago. We both lie stretched out on the hot sand under pale blue parasols. Rachael lies on her front, her legs crossed and flicking back and forth in the air behind her as she reads 'Pride and Prejudice'. One arm is tucked under my head as I stare up at the cloudless, blue sky. A gentle breeze blows through the nearby trees, the waves crash against the shore, couples walk across the beach and a few children play noisily in the sea. I stand up and brush myself down, she peeks at me over her glasses.

"I'm going for a swim to cool off. You coming?" I ask.

She closes her book.

"I'll watch."

I strut through the blazing hot sand and stride into the refreshing sea. The waves lap at me as I wade in until I'm neck deep. I raise my hand and wave at Rachael who's now sitting up, chewing on the end of her glasses. I breaststroke back towards the shore as she gets to her feet and heads into the sea herself. She swims towards me and wraps her arms round my neck.

"Changed your mind, I see?" I smirk.

"I couldn't resist."

She kisses me and runs her hands through my wet hair.

"Must we go home?" she sighs.

"New York beckons."

She nods and briefly, her mouth turns down. It doesn't last, she peeks at me out the corner of her eye and sweeps her arm through the water, splashing me.

"Hey," I protest and splash her back until we're in a full-on water fight.

A lifeguard blows his whistle and shouts at us in Spanish. Some people on the shore laugh at us, others shake their heads and frown.

"Oops," she mouths.

"We should get out," I say.

We swim back and lie under our parasols. She wipes her face and hands with a towel then tosses it at me, so it drapes haphazardly over my head. I laugh and pull it away.

"That's my shower for the day," I quip.

"No, it's not," she says, laughing.

We walk hand in hand across the white sand just as the sun starts to sink into the far horizon. The waves lap the shore, and the breeze cools my damp heated skin. I stare in awe at my Rachael as she combs her hair away from her face and fastens it effortlessly with a hair tie. She turns and stares at me through her specs and smiles.

"Let's sit for a while," she says.

"Sure."

She releases my hand and sits down. I sit beside her on the warm sand, she lays her head across my lap, and I entwine her ponytail round my wrist.

"I've had a wonderful time. Thank you," I say.

She leans up and pecks me on the lips.

"Thank *you*."

I look out across the ocean, utterly content as the last of the remaining sun disappears over the horizon and dusk soon becomes night.

We sit in the airport lounge and wait for our American Airlines flight home to New York. It's just past eleven at night and I'm exhausted. I read the Stephen King novel Trent leant to me to kill the boredom. Rachael reads a local newspaper. I glance over occasionally but I have no interest in news. She folds the newspaper up and places it down beside her. She sighs and rubs her eyes. I close my book and place it in my rucksack.

"You okay?" I ask.

"I'm nervous about returning to work, it's unlike me."

I furrow my brow and try to scramble for a response.

"You'll be fine, you've settled into your promotion well I think."

"It's a lot more responsibility. It was sprung upon me so quickly."

I take her hand.

"Honey, if this is too much for you..."

She raises her hand in her usual way of silencing me.

"I'll find a way to cope."

"You'll be great. You never cease to amaze me."

She blushes slightly then glances up at the flight board and places her hand on my lap. Our flight number is called.

"We're going home," she says, getting to her feet.

"We're going home."

Chapter Four

W e touch down in New York just after 3 a.m. The plane taxis across the runway as Rachael squeezes my hand. It goes numb and my knuckles start to pale. I wince and hiss through my teeth. She stares over at me and releases.

"That's quite a grip you've got," I joke, shaking life back into my dead hand.

"Sorry, that will be thanks to the police academy," she laughs but then stops and rubs her stomach.

"You alright?"

"I hate take-off and landing the most when I fly."

"Discomfort?"

"My ears pop and I get queasy."

"We're down now, nothing to worry about."

She sits back in her seat and glances out the window. The plane comes to a stop outside the terminal and with a slight jolt, the tunnel connects to the side of the aircraft. The flight attendant makes an announcement welcoming everyone on board to New York and informs us that it's 55 degrees Fahrenheit. Rachael stands from her seat and collects my rucksack from the overhead compartment. I stand to help but people push and shove past me.

"Maybe we'll wait until it clears out a bit," she says.

I nod and sit back down. Within minutes, it's quieter. She stands back up and proceeds to the exit. We both thank the pilot and stewardess as we leave and make our way into the terminal. Colin, Sara, and Louise stand with a sign that reads 'welcome home'. Rachael runs into the open arms of her mom. I join them and shake Colin's proffered hand.

"Welcome back, son," he grins.

A warm feeling spreads through my chest and constricts my throat. I haven't been part of a proper family for a long time. I smile at him, then hug Sara and Louise as Rachael greets her dad. We continue to the carousel to collect our luggage. Colin grabs the bag, puts his arm around Rachael, then we leave the airport and head towards Colin's BMW.

Colin pulls into the underground garage of our apartment.

"Just over there, Dad," Rachael instructs, pointing to a vacant spot.

He parks up next to Rachael's white Mercedes and switches off the engine.

"Do you want to come in?" she asks.

"If you don't mind," Sara says, turning in the front seat to face us.

"Of course not."

I open my door and climb out, then take Rachael's hand and she too climbs out followed swiftly by the rest of the family. I link my arm through hers and we head towards the elevators.

We alight on the fifteenth floor. I grab our luggage and walk down the corridor. *Home sweet home.*

"Have you got the keys?" Rachael asks me.

Everyone stares at me. I shrug my rucksack off and lay it on the floor.

"I think they're in here."

I check all the pockets and compartments of the bag but can't find them. I stare at her, my eyes widening.

"They're not in here."

"What?" she furrows her brow and pats her pockets quickly.

She tuts and pulls the keys from her jeans.

"Sorry," she chuckles.

I mockingly pretend to wipe sweat from my brow. She unlocks the door, and it swings open.

"After you," I gesture.

She steps inside and I follow. We take our jackets and shoes off then she slumps onto the couch.

"It's good to be home," she says.

I sit beside her and place my hand around her shoulders.

"Dear, you look exhausted. Shall I get you a drink?" Sara asks.

Rachael shakes her head.

"I'll get them," she says.

"No, you stay where you are," Sara says, flapping her hand at us.

"Thanks, Mom."

Sara walks into the kitchen. Louise sits beside me, and Colin slumps into the nearby armchair.

"Did you guys enjoy your honeymoon?" Louise enthuses.

"It was lovely, wasn't it, Mark?" Rachael grins.

"Best time of my life."

"What did you get up to?" Colin asks.

"Not much, we spent most of our time soaking up the sun on the beach... Oh, and Mark landed face first in the sand after falling off his horse," she says, nudging me in the ribs.

All their heads turn in my direction as the backs of my ears heat.

"Not my most glamorous moment."

Sara returns with a couple of glasses of iced water. Rachael and I take them, and I tip the cool glass back as the welcoming glacial liquid washes down my throat and refreshes me.

"We'll leave you be now. You two should get some sleep. Come on, Colin, Louise," Sara says.

"Aw," Louise whines.

"I'll see you soon," Rachael says.

They all make their way to the front door. Me and Rachael follow, she hugs her dad.

"Thanks for picking us up," Rachael says.

"Of course."

Colin opens the front door, gives us a final wave, then they're gone.

"I'm going to bed," she says.

"I'll join you."

We discard our half-drunk glasses of water and walk into the bedroom. We get undressed quickly and slip onto the soft, cloud-like mattress.

"Thank you for a wonderful honeymoon," she whispers.

"Thank *you*."

She kisses me gently on the lips, then pulls the duvet tighter around herself.

"So, when do you go back to work?" I ask.

She breathes gently. No response. I lean up on my elbow. "Rachael?"

I peek over at her, but she's fast asleep. I pull the duvet over her a little more and stroke her cheek with my index finger, then lie down and drift into a deep sleep.

The shadow of the Red Hook Grain Terminal looms over me. I walk to the water's edge and stare out across the East River. The stench of the water invades my nostrils. I crinkle my nose and turn to walk away. The sound of water splashing stops me in my tracks, I look to my right and Tobias emerges from the river, dripping wet and scorning. I gape at him. Before I can say anything, he draws his gun from his jacket and fires past my ear. A high-pitched scream of a woman rings out behind me. I turn and Rachael grasps her chest, her fingers redden with blood. I catch her as she falls while Tobias cackles behind me.

I gasp awake and am soaked in sweat... again. I look to Rachael's side of the bed. She's still sleeping peacefully. *What's happening to me?* I place my head in my hands and rake my fingers through my over-long hair. I slowly slide out of bed, grab my robe from the back of the door, slip it on, tiptoe out of the room and make my way to the lounge. I stare out the window at the street below, the early morning light is starting to peek through the skyscrapers. I breathe in deeply and rest my forehead against the cool glass. *What's wrong with me? Why am I thinking about him again?*

"Mark?" Rachael says softly.

I turn to face her. She stands in the middle of the room in her silk gown. I sit on the couch and rub my face. She sits beside me, and her warm eyes stare deep into my soul.

"What's wrong?" she asks.

"I dreamt of… *him* again. Why is this happening?"

She arches her brow then she rubs her hand down my back.

"I thought we spoke about this. You're safe. You have nothing to worry about."

"But, what about you?" I ask.

Her mouth forms a hard line as she folds her arms and sits back.

"I'll be fine. If we ever go after him again, I won't be alone. I'll have a large team with me. Please, just try to relax a little."

I sigh and lower my head.

"I'm trying."

"I know you are. We'll find him, trust me."

I take her hand in mine and pull her to me.

"I know you will, but for now, I'd like to go back to the grain terminal."

She sits up and stares at me, her eyebrows shoot up.

"You sure that's a good idea?"

"It was the last place I saw him. I just want some closure."

She frowns but then picks up her cell from the coffee table.

"It's a crime scene at the moment, but I'll try to pull some strings."

She gets up from the couch and begins dialing.

"I'm sorry if this has burst our just married bubble," I call as she walks back towards the bedroom.

She looks over her shoulder.

"I just want you happy, Mark. If this is what's going to help, then I'm happy too."

She half smiles, then shuts the door behind her.

It's nearly seven in the evening as we sit on the couch watching The Notebook and eating Chinese takeout. Rachael places her empty box on the table and sips her red wine.

"Oh, I forgot to mention, I spoke to Dad. He's willing to let you on the crime scene but only if you promise not to touch anything," she says, wagging her finger at me.

I pause the film and stare at her.

"Thank you. I promise."

"We go in the morning. Steph will be meeting us there."

I smile, but my earlier nightmare gnaws at me, I push it to one side, refusing to think any more about him and continue with my meal. She resumes the film and rests her feet on my lap.

Rachael wakes me, already in her Sergeant uniform.

"Time to go," she says.

I sit up in bed and rub exhaustion out of my eyes. I glance at the alarm clock; 6:15 a.m.

"It's so early," I groan, laying back down and covering my head with the duvet.

She laughs and pulls the duvet off the bed.

"Get up, lazy bones. This was your idea."

"Hey," I protest and pull her down onto the bed.

She laughs and slaps my bare chest as I press her to me.

"You should wear this at home more often; it's very sexy," I croon, fingering her uniform.

"Mark!" she laughs, feigning disgust.

She slaps me playfully again, then gets up off the bed before I have a chance to grab her again.

"Get up," she orders.

"Okay. I'm up."

I get out of bed, stretch, and proceed to get dressed.

Rachael swirls her car keys round her fingers, then presses the fob. The car flashes to life and I climb into the passenger seat. She glides delicately into the driver's seat and starts the engine. It purrs to life as she reverses slowly out of her space and maneuvers out onto the busy streets of Manhattan. Frank Sinatra croons softly in the background as she hums along to it.

"What got you into the old music?" I ask.

"It's classy and it has heart. Do you like it?"

I listen to Frank sing a little more and picture her in her long lace gown walking down the aisle towards me, accompanied by 'Strangers In The Night'.

"He's wonderful."

"Glad you like it."

She presses down on the gas, and I'm thrown back into my seat as we drive through the opening of the Hugh L. Carey Tunnel.

We're drawing ever closer to the grain terminal, and I'm nauseous. My nightmare from yesterday refuses to leave my thoughts and I'm starting to regret my decision of asking to come here. Rachael parks up and switches off the car.

"You ready?" she asks.

"Yeah."

She places her hand on my lap.

"You have nothing to be afraid of," she says.

I nod and climb out of the car. I walk round to her side and take her hand while staring up at the roof. Tobias and I once stood there, fighting. It's where we last saw each other and where he pulled me into the dirty river below. I shiver, despite the heat.

"You don't have to do this," she says.

"It's fine."

We stride towards the back of the building, the gravel crunching underfoot. The site is roped off with multiple police vans and cars parked up.

"Rachael!" a familiar voice calls out.

Steph runs towards us and hugs Rachael.

"I missed you so much. How was your honeymoon?" she gushes.

"It was wonderful. Thank you, Steph."

Steph steps away and looks at me.

"Mark, hello."

"Hi, Steph."

She gives me a quick one-armed hug before releasing me and leading the way to the crime scene.

"I'm sure Rachael already mentioned to you that you must not touch anything," Steph instructs.

"You have my word."

She pulls the tape up to let us through and I stand in the gloomy shadow of the grain terminal, mold overspreads the concrete walls like a mourning veil. Piles of rubble and twisted metal are scattered around us. The water laps nearby, officers call out to each other, and a tugboat horn sounds in the distance.

"Do you mind if I look around?" I whisper to Rachael. She furrows her brow, then nods.

"Just…"

"I know. Don't touch."

I walk to the water's edge and look out, but a harsh flashback of my nightmare hits me, the gunshot and Rachael's scream rings in my ears. I head back towards the building, press my back up against the wall and slide down until I'm sitting on the dusty floor. I place my head in my hands but quickly snap out of it; I can't let her see me this way. I stand back up and brush myself off. I'm about to return to her, but something catches my eye on the shore near the water. I squint my eyes to get a better look and step forward slowly. There's something behind this large boulder, I push it to one side and see a black pinstripe jacket with a fresh carnation pinned to the breast. It takes me a moment to register, but then realization hits. I gasp and rush back towards Rachael. She stares at me as I barrel for her.

"Mark, you look like you've seen a ghost," she says.

"You're not far off. Come with me."

I grab her hand and pull her with me. She follows round the side of the building and to the site where I found the jacket. I point in its direction.

"Look," I say.

She stares at the jacket.

"So?" she asks, shrugging.

"*So?* That's Tobias' jacket. He's been here, recently."

"Mark, a discarded jacket doesn't mean anything."

I blink at her, and my mouth falls open.

"That carnation is fresh. Who else could have put it there?"

She rests her index finger against her lips.

"I dunno. Maybe one of his old followers?"

I try to calm myself down a little and think about this.

"Maybe."

"Thank you for bringing this to our attention. We'll take it for evidence. Davis!" she calls.

A young male officer hurries over.

"Yes, Sergeant."

She points at the jacket on the floor.

"My husband found this. Bag it, tag it, and send it to forensics."

Davis nods, then pulls some gloves out of his belt and slips them on. He bends down, collects the jacket, and proceeds to place it in a clear bag with 'Evidence' labelled on the front.

"Are you officially on-duty?" I ask.

She stares at me.

"Not till tomorrow, why?"

"You wanna go for a stroll in the park? Get something to eat?"

She beams and links her arm through mine.

"I'd love to."

We walk side by side through Central Park while we each enjoy a salted pretzel. The sun beams through the tree branches, leaving spots of light across the sidewalk; the leaves on the trees are in full bloom, filling the park with different shades of green and hews of pink from the nearby cherry trees. Several dog walkers and joggers are out enjoying the morning air. I try to blow my hair out of my face, but it sticks to my forehead. *I've never liked the heat.*

"I'm hot. Can we sit?" I ask.

"Sure.

We cross over Bow Bridge, and I reminisce my proposal just a few short months ago. We sit on the same bench where me and Rachael met properly a short time before that. Jeez, how far we've come since then. We both continue with our pretzels and watch the row boats on the lake, full of couples and families. She laughs suddenly and I turn to face her.

"What's funny?" I ask.

"It's amazing, isn't it?"

"What?"

"Us. We met on this same bench only seven months ago. We proved everyone wrong, now we're married."

She twists her engagement and wedding rings round her finger.

"I'm lucky. I never thought I would be in love again after…" she stops and clasps her hands together on her lap.

"Never mind," she sighs.

She's remembering her scumbag ex-fiancé. That will never do. I take her hands in mine.

"What happened? Between you and… *him?*"

I try not to sound bitter, but it's hard when I think of how someone could hurt Rachael so much. She blinks at me twice, then shakes her head. I hold my hands up.

"If you're uncomfortable, you don't need to tell me."

"No. It's okay."

She sits up straight and squares her shoulders, but her eyes rim with tears, and I feel awful for bringing it up.

"He was a traffic cop… we met at work," she starts slowly.

I overheard an argument months ago between Rachael and her father, regarding me. I recall him being brought up then.

"Yeah. I heard."

She peeks at me out the corner of her eye.

"You heard? When?"

"When your dad raided the Neapolitan. After I left the room, I heard you and him argue about… Craig, is it?"

"Yeah. Why didn't you mention that earlier?"

"It just didn't seem relevant. I didn't want to reopen old wounds. Do you still want to talk about it now?"

She nods and takes a deep breath.

"Things were good to start with, but they always are I suppose. Shortly after we got engaged, he started to act… strange. He took a vacation from the 'stresses of work' and went travelling in Asia. I stayed behind to continue with my duties."

She pauses and wipes her eye.

"He returned a month later and his interest in me had completely diminished. He started avoiding me at home. I did some digging and found a photo in his wallet… of a woman. Naturally, I was furious and confronted him. He denied it at first but then admitted that he had met and slept with another woman he met in a bar… I dumped him on the spot."

I'm suddenly boiling with rage. *How dare he?*

"Bastard," I seethe through gritted teeth.

I put my arm round her, desperate to touch her and pull her to me. She rests her head on my shoulder as we continue to watch the row boats drift by.

"Thank you for telling me. If I ever meet him, I'd like to punch him," I say more to myself, but she giggles and sits up.

"I don't think you'll get that chance. He was let go from the force shortly after we broke up. Apparently, he harassed someone else at work. I haven't seen him since."

"Is he still in the city?"

"Who knows? Anyway, I don't care. What do you wanna do now?"

"Shall we head back?"

She smiles, then takes my hand.

We finish our tofu salad with a glass of iced lemonade. I push my empty plate away and rest back in my chair.

"So, back to work tomorrow?" I ask.

She peeks over.

"Unfortunately."

I sniff, then get up and clear away the plates. She follows me into the kitchen and watches over my shoulder as I load the dishwasher.

"Would you like me to do that?" she asks.

"I'll manage, thank you."

She slaps me playfully on the behind and waltzes out of the kitchen. I stare at her long legs and the gentle sway of her hips as she leaves. I hurriedly finish what I'm doing and head into the lounge to join her.

"I have an early start in the morning. I think I'll go to bed," she says.

I yawn and check my watch. *8:15 p.m. Man, the day flew by.*

"Me too."

We walk into the bedroom together as she pulls her flowery summer dress over her head, then climbs into bed in just her underwear. I unbutton my jeans as she props herself up on her elbows and watches me. I crawl in beside her and she lays across my chest. I deftly stroke her hair and inhale her sweet scent, committing it to memory.

"I'll miss these days," she whispers.

I look down at her.

"Me too, but I'll always be here."

She leans up to kiss me quickly, but her kiss changes from sweet to intense. She combs her fingers through my hair and deepens the kiss. I push her down against the soft mattress and slowly we become lost in each other once more.

The early morning sun shines through the gap in the curtains. I roll onto my back and reach across the bed, but Rachael is gone. I'm suddenly wide awake and sit up. She stands at the foot of the bed with her back to me. She's already in her uniform as she looks in the mirror and ties her hair effortlessly into a neat bun. She finishes up and places her police cap on. I smirk.

"Looking good, Mrs. Flint."

She whirls round and smiles at me.

"Good morning. I didn't hear you get up."

My eyes travel greedily up and down her body before coming to a stop at her name tag under her badge, 'Sergeant Clarke'. I frown, as does Rachael. She looks down at her name tag momentarily then sits on the edge of the bed beside me.

"I was going to tell you about that. I'm still known as Rachael Clarke at work."

My frown returns and I can't shake the cold stab of disappointment that strikes my gut.

"You're not ashamed of me, are you?" I ask.

She gasps, her hand flies to her mouth.

"Mark, how can you say that?"

I twist the duvet in my hands. She strokes my face softly which encourages me to look back at her.

"I'm Flint everywhere else," she says.

"Okay."

Her eyes search mine for any clue of hurt. I plaster the most dazzling smile I can manage to try and reassure her.

"Okay," I repeat.

She grins, then gets to her feet.

"I'd better go. I'm running late as it is."

She leans down and kisses me.

"Have a good day at work," she says.

"You too."

She stands up straight and leaves the bedroom. I listen for a moment and hear the front door open, then close, she's gone. I flop back down onto my pillow. She's still Clarke at work. I don't know whether to be hurt by this or not. Is she ashamed that she's married to an ex-felon? Is it because I was once an O'Malley boy? I sit up suddenly and mentally slap myself. *Stop this. It's her choice.* I shake my head and check the alarm clock on the nightstand, 6:45 a.m. I jump out of bed. I need to be at work in fifteen minutes. I hurriedly throw on my over washed jeans and an old white shirt then race out of the bedroom, grab my jacket along the way and fly out the front door.

I walk as fast I can while dodging and weaving around the other commuters. I don't know why I thought it was a good idea to grab my leather jacket; even though it's nearing seven a.m. it's warm out here. I shrug off my jacket and wipe the bead of sweat running down my face with the back of my hand. I'm close to the Neapolitan Hotel now, I sure hope it has air conditioning. I push through the double doors and am welcomed by the cooling breeze of the air conditioner. I could stand in its cold blast all day, but I've got work to do. I head for the elevators but spot Trent and Rex sitting at their desks in a whispered conversation. They both glance in my direction, I smile and offer a quick wave. Trent jumps up from his desk and barrels towards me. He swamps me in his usual over-enthusiastic bear hug, I rasp and pat him on the back.

"I've missed you so much, bud. How was your honeymoon? How's Rachael? Are you enjoying married life?" He barrages me with his usual gusto.

I hold my hands up and he falls silent, his eyes crinkling at the corners.

"One question at a time, man. Yes, my honeymoon was wonderful. Rachael's fine. Married life is going well so far."

He grins widely.

"How've you been?" I ask.

He blows out.

"Busy. The high season has started early. Reservations are flooding in."

"That'll give me plenty to do."

He nods then looks over at Rex who's still at his desk.

"I'd better get back to work," he says.

"Me too."

He pats me on the shoulder then returns to his desk. I press the call button to summon the elevator, one arrives in moments, so I step inside. I comb my damp long hair out of my eyes as my mind drifts back to Rachael, I hope she's okay. The elevator jolts to a halt and the doors slide open. I step off and proceed to make my way to the staff room. Debbie, my supervisor, steps out of one of the bedrooms, a vacuum in her hand. I head towards her as she turns to face me.

"Mark, welcome back," she smiles.

"Thank you. Where do I start?"

She puts the vacuum down and places one manicured hand on her hip.

"I believe Mr. Levitt wants to talk to you before you begin."

"Oh. Where is he?"

She gestures with her head down the corridor.

"Staff room, I think."

"Thanks."

I proceed down the hall, swipe my access card and enter the staff room. Mr. Levitt's inside, leaning against the small counter beside the kettle and nursing a cup of coffee.

"Good morning, sir," I greet.

He peers up and smiles.

"Mark, welcome back, son. Did you have a good honeymoon?"

"It was lovely, thank you. Debbie mentioned that you wished to see me?"

He puts his mug in the sink.

"Would you join me in my office for a moment? I have something I need to talk to you about."

I swallow.

"Sure."

He gestures towards the door with his hand, then leaves the staff room. I follow him down the hall and into his office. He strides behind his desk, removes his gray jacket, places it on the back of his chair and sits down. I sit in the chair opposite him and place my jacket on my lap. Mr. Levitt's specs shine as he smiles at me.

"It's a hot one," he observes, looking out the window.

I nod and swallow the lump forming in my throat.

"Relax, Mark, you're not in trouble," he chuckles.

I breathe out my held breath and sag into my seat.

"I needed to talk to you about something important," he continues.

I sit up straight and square my shoulders.

"As you are probably aware, we get extremely busy this time of year. My front of house team is doing an amazing job already, but Hannah, you remember Hannah?"

I remember Trent introducing me to her the first time I came here.

"Yes, sir."

"She's been moved to a different department. Now, we're a little short staffed on reception. How would you feel about being front of house?"

I gape at him for a moment. *A promotion!*

"With Trent and Rex?" I ask.

He smiles.

"Exactly. Call it a promotion."

I can barely contain my amazement.

"Thank you, sir, but what about the rooms? They need cleaning."

His smile broadens.

"Don't worry. We have plenty of staff to deal with that."

I can't believe what I'm hearing. I sit frozen to the spot, gaping at him.

"Well, Mark, what do you say?"

"I-I well, I'd love to. Thank you, sir."

He stands up and offers his hand. I jump from my seat and take it. He eyes my scruffy clothes.

"You'll need to look presentable when the guests arrive. Do you have a suit?" he asks.

I look down at my dirty jeans and shirt.

"Yes, sir, I do."

"Well then, I'll see you Monday morning. Nine a.m. Sharp."

I grab my jacket from my seat and make my exit from his office. I open the door then pause.

"Thank you again."

He looks up from his computer screen, nods once, then waves me out. I stroll towards the elevators and ride back down to the lobby. I glance over at Trent, but he's flooded with queuing guests. We catch each other's eye briefly. I do a phone gesture at him; he nods quickly then returns his attention to the couple at his desk. I head through the double doors and emerge back out onto the sidewalk. I clap my hands together. *Wait until I tell Rachael.* I begin to make my way home, but crowds of people shout ahead of me. I look towards the source of the noise and see a man running with a few cops in hot pursuit. Pedestrians are shoved aside; some get knocked to the ground. I press my back up against the wall as the man flies past me.

"Stop!" a cop shouts.

A female officer races past me. I double take before I notice. Rachael. I follow quickly, keen to see what happens.

Members of the public attempt to stop the fleeing man, but they get pushed aside. She's still hot on the man's heels. He runs straight into traffic causing a taxi to screech to a halt. He beeps at him and shouts out the window. The man continues to flee to the opposite side, then jumps a fence effortlessly. I stop and watch as best I can. Rachael jumps the fence after him then draws what looks like a taser.

"Freeze!" she orders, but the man foolishly ignores her.

Seconds later, the fleeing man seizes up and falls to the ground with a thud. My eyebrows shoot up and I whistle through my teeth. *Thank God, she didn't use that on me.* She grabs hold of the man, stands him up and places a pair of cuffs round his wrists. I cross the sidewalk and continue to watch from a distance as a squad car pulls up and she loads him into the back while reading him his rights. She slams the door shut and the car speeds away. She removes her cap and wipes her forehead before looking in my direction. Our eyes lock as she walks over slowly.

"Mark, hey."

She throws her arms round me in a dramatic display of affection causing several pedestrians to look, while others hold their phones up. She pulls away quickly and clears her throat.

"That was impressive," I say.

"It's the job. Why aren't you at work?"

I beam and she glares at me.

"What?" she asks.

"I've been promoted. I start Monday."

She squeals and hugs me again.

"We'll celebrate tonight," she gushes.

Her radio crackles to life.

"Any available units? We have a 10-53 on East 37th on Madison. Please respond."

She presses a button.

"This is Sergeant Clarke. I'll be right there."

She looks back at me, her brow furrowed.

"I have to go," she says, then she turns and heads in the opposite direction.

"Rachael," I call.

She turns and stares at me.

"Keep kicking ass. I love you."

She laughs, then blows me a kiss.

"Always. I love you," she calls back, then she turns and continues to stride away. I watch after her until she rounds a bend and is gone from my sight.

Chapter Five

———

I dry the beads of water that run down my skin, then I roughly towel dry my hair and pad to the closet. I slip on a pair of clean underwear and reach for my navy-blue collared shirt. It slips off the hanger and drops to the floor. *Damn.* I bend down to pick it up and eye the cardboard box at the back of the closet. *Grandma's box.* I quickly slip the shirt over my head, then lean back down to lift the box gently and place it on the foot of the bed. I open it up. Inside is Grandpa's old brown leather biker jacket. I can smell the history from this old thing, it's torn and tattered, but it was once loved. I look back inside the box to find several photos, piled neatly in the corner. I pick them up and examine each one in turn; a small passport sized photo of Grandma, she smiles warmly in her beige wool knit sweater that she always wore; underneath is the letter that she wrote, I unfold it and read it twice. I wipe the corner of my eye and stare back at her photo.

"Thank you," I whisper.

I turn my attention to the other photos; Mom and Dad's wedding, they beam at the camera, I've never seen them so happy before; then the three of us, Mom, Dad, and me, I can't be any more than three months old in this photo, piercing blue eyes and a shock of dark hair. *Wow. Scruffy, even back then.* Mom smiles warmly as Dad rests his hand delicately on his new son. *What changed them? How did our family fall apart?* I endeavor to find out what happened to them. I still have so many unanswered questions. Maybe Rachael will help me? I shake my head. She has enough to worry about already. I'll find out on my own, one way or another.

It's approaching seven p.m. and Rachael still isn't back. I contemplate calling her, but decide not to, she might be pursuing another unfortunate schmo, and I don't want to distract her. Maybe I'll cook dinner. I'm awful in the kitchen, but I'll give it a go. I roll up my sleeves and wash my hands in the kitchen sink then look in the cupboard for some inspiration. An omelet maybe? I find her cookbook and start by cracking some eggs and whisking. I add in some spinach and tomatoes, then pour the mixture into a hot frying pan.

It sizzles and spits ferociously, prompting me to raise my arm to shield myself from its scalding wrath. The front door clicks open.

"Hello," Rachael calls.

I exit the kitchen.

"Good day?" I ask.

"Busy."

She unbuttons her uniform and removes her cap.

"I'm going to get changed," she says, walking to the bedroom.

I sit on the couch and turn on the TV as she sticks her head out of the bedroom.

"Is that burning I smell?"

I jump off the couch and run into the kitchen. *Crap, not again.* I switch off the stove, I've burnt dinner… again. She enters the kitchen and looks over my shoulder, she tries to keep a straight face but sniggers.

"Sorry," I say, frowning at the blackened omelet.

She places her arm round me.

"You tried."

I throw the ruined omelet into the trash and quickly rinse the pan.

"I've never been good at cooking," I chuckle.

She frowns slightly, then collects the ingredients from the fridge.

"I can teach you, if you like," she says.

"I thought Louise was the chef extraordinaire."

She laughs as she rolls up her sleeves.

"I dabble. Besides, I've been feeding you fine. Haven't poisoned you yet."

I twist my mouth and titter.

"Best keep it that way."

She smirks.

"Yeah, lets. Anyway, make the mixture as you did before."

I grab a clean bowl from the cupboard and begin to make the mixture. She directs me with my whisking tactic.

"It's all in the wrist," she says.

I pour the mixture into the hot frying pan and make my way out the kitchen.

"No," she calls.

I turn and purse my lips.

"Never leave the food unattended. It needs to be flipped soon."

I walk back into the kitchen and stare at the sizzling eggy mixture. She thrusts a spatula at me. I blink at her.

"Fold it in half, like this."

She takes the spatula and demonstrates. I lean over her shoulder.

"You can do the next one," she says as she dishes up the first omelet.

She remakes the mixture, and we wait a few minutes for it to cook. Again, she hands me the spatula.

"Your time to shine."

I swallow, then gingerly place the spatula underneath and fold it in half. It rips slightly but it's mostly intact.

"I did it," I beam like an overexcited child.

She laughs and applauds; I bow at her praise.

"The test is in the taste. Let's eat," she says.

I pick up both plates and place them on the table.

Rachael places her knife and fork down on her empty plate.

"Mm. That was really good," she says.

I grin as I finish mine.

"Thank you for the cooking lesson."

"It was fun."

She gets up and begins cleaning up.

"I can do that," I say.

"You cooked, I'll clean."

She takes my empty plate and places it into the dishwasher.

"Wine?" I ask.

"Please."

We sit on the couch together; Rachael's feet are propped on my lap as I massage her soles softly. She reads her book while I surf through the TV channels. She closes her book and places it on the arm rest.

"Oh yeah. I thought you'd like to know. We've had the results back from the forensics team on the jacket you found."

I stop massaging and glance up.

"And?"

"They weren't Tobias' prints or of anyone known to the police."

"So, what does that mean?"

She sighs.

"Inconclusive. Sorry."

"But whoever left that flower must know him or be him. Maybe he was wearing someone else's prints, he used to do it all the time."

She sits up and rests her chin against her knuckles.

"Maybe. We can't be certain though. But for now, just try to relax. Whoever it is, we'll find them."

"I know you will. You always do."

She smirks and her cheeks turn a fetching pink.

"I do."

She checks the time on her cell.

"Is that the time?" she says.

She stands from the couch and stretches.

"It's late. I'm going to bed. Good night, Mark."

"Night."

She heads into the bedroom and closes the door. After a few minutes, I'm beginning to feel lonely without her. I turn off the movie and go into the bedroom. She's already tucked up in bed, fast asleep. I get undressed and as gently as I can, so as not to wake her, I climb into bed and lie down. She rolls onto her side so that she's facing me and drapes her arm across my chest. I admire her beauty for a moment before my eyes become too heavy and I can stay awake no more.

Rachael left for work early this morning and I don't start my new job until Monday, I'm on my own. I get changed out of my navy bathrobe and into a pair of dark blue denim jeans and a checkered shirt. I walk into the lounge and sit on the couch but can't help feeling restless. *Crap, I was meant to call Trent last night.* I grab my cell from the bedroom and dial his number. It rings a few times and I'm about to hang up, but he answers just in time.

"Yeah, hello," he says quickly.

"Hey, Trent, it's me."

"Hey, bud. Sorry, I just got out the shower. You okay?"

"I'm fine. Sorry I didn't call last night. Are you at work today?"

"Not till tomorrow. Why?"

"You wanna grab a drink, have a catch up?"

"Sure. I'll be over to pick you up shortly."

"Great. Wait- What? Pick me up? I didn't know you could drive."

Trent laughs loudly.

"I passed my test recently. Don't you remember? I'll be over soon."

I hang up. Trent drives? That's a scary thought. I remember playing a round of golf with him and his mom for his fifteenth birthday. His mom let him drive the golf cart. He drove like a mad man before plowing us into a sand trap. I titter to myself. *It took hours to get the cart out and Trent was no help.* I sit on the couch and wonder what he'll turn up with, I'm excited to spend some time with him, but I'm dreading the ride.

My cell vibrates against the coffee table. I answer it. Trent's voice comes through the receiver before I have a chance to speak.

"I'm outside," he says.

"I'll be right down."

I hang up and head for the front door, picking up my leather jacket along the way, but then recall the heat from yesterday, so I place it back on the hanger and leave. I ride down in the elevator then stride through the lobby, past Tom and out the door. I look around for Trent's car but can't see him. A vehicle beeps. I look around again and spot a man wearing full leathers and a helmet with a satchel draped around one shoulder and down his back. He's straddling a black and red motorbike. He flips up his visor on his bike helmet and waves at me. I roll my eyes and approach, eyeing the bike. Trent pulls his helmet off and ruffles his hair.

"Whaddya think?"

I continue to stare.

"I'm not getting on that thing, I'll walk."

He frowns, then pats the bike.

"This is my BMW F800GT, and you will treat her with respect," he grumbles.

I hold my hands up.

"Sorry."

He shuffles forward slightly.

"C'mon, climb on."

I blink at him, then continue to stare at the bike.

"I've never been on a motorbike before, Trent. I don't know if I can."

"I'm not asking you to drive it, am I? Just climb on."

"I haven't got a helmet."

He kicks the support stand of the bike and climbs off, removing his bag. He opens it and pulls out another black helmet before thrusting it to me.

"Here."

I take it from him.

"You'll need something leather too," he says.

I arch a brow.

"I don't have any-."

Grandpa's old jacket.

"Be right back."

I rush inside and hurry back up to my apartment. I unlock the door quickly and dash to the bedroom where I grab the cardboard box from the closet and fish inside for the brown leather jacket. I pull it out and dash back downstairs where I regroup with Trent. He smiles when he sees me.

"Nice jacket. Let's go."

He throws his leg over the saddle and starts the engine. The bike roars to life and my anxiety returns swiftly.

"Don't be nervous," he says, patting the saddle.

I take a deep breath and sit behind him. He slips his helmet on and I do the same. He looks back at me.

"Now, hold on."

"To what?"

He puts his feet up on the pedals.

"Either wrap your arms around me or hold on to the metal bar behind you. Your choice."

I grab hold of the bar with both hands and grip it tightly. The bike pulls away gently and merges into traffic.

Trent weaves at speed in and out of the busy traffic, dodging past a yellow cab which starts to come into our lane. The cab beeps at us and curses out of his window. I grip the metal bar behind me so tightly that my fingers start to go numb.

"I don't like this," I shout over the wind.

"Almost there," he shouts back.

I close my eyes tightly, not wanting to see anymore. Mercifully, the bike's engine stops, I open one eye and look around. He gets off the bike as I gingerly climb off, but my legs are like Jell-O. I trip slightly, but he catches me and pushes me back up. I take the helmet off and hand it back to him.

"Was that fun?" he chuckles.

I furrow my brow with a what-do-you-think expression. He laughs harder.

"I'll take that as a 'no'. It's fun when you get used to it."

"I don't know if I'll ever get on that thing again."

He heads towards the bar entrance. It has an old English vibe about it; glass paneled doors and dark wood. The name is painted in gold into the dark wood above us, 'The Stag's Head'. A large silhouette of a stag is pasted on the main door. I've never been in here, but I've heard good reviews from Rachael's dad.

"Me and Rex come here a lot," Trent says.

I look at him as he smiles, then he shakes his head and opens the door. We walk in together and sit at the first table we find.

"I'll get the first round. Whaddya fancy?" he asks.

"Whatever you're having."

He nods and retreats to the bar. I admire my surroundings; it has a log cabin feel. The bar is dark oak, some walls are wood paneled, and others are brick. There's a fireplace in the corner, but because it's spring, it isn't lit. Trent returns with the drinks, he sets them down on the table, then pulls a chair out and sits beside me.

"I've got orange juice because I'm driving, but I thought you could do with some booze," he says.

"Thanks."

He sips his orange juice and I take a welcome sip from my glass. It tastes like lager, but I'm not sure.

"Stella Artois. Like it?" he asks.

"It's a little bitter, but it's nice."

I take another quick sip and turn to face Trent, eager to tell him the good news about my promotion.

"Starting Monday, I'm front of house with you and Rex," I say.

He looks at me over his glass while taking another sip from his juice.

"I heard. Good job."

He slaps me on the back.

"I'll be in charge of your training," he continues.

I splutter into my drink and cough. He hits me on the back again. I wipe my mouth with the back of my hand.

"Is that a problem?" he asks, cocking his head to the side.

"No. Prefer to work alongside you rather than... *her*."

Trent's eyes roll to the side and his mouth twists.

"Debbie's not that bad."

"No, I mean..."

"Oh right. Melissa. Was it true she was working for Tobias?"

I grimace.

"Yep."

"Jesus. What happened to her?"

"Not sure. Rachael never went into too much detail, something about Witness Protection or something."

"Witness Protection?"

"Tobias was blackmailing her."

His mouth drops open.

"Anymore word on where the bastard is?"

"No. Hopefully he's... gone."

Trent sucks in his lips and runs his finger across the edge of the table.

"Anyway, onto happier things," I say, desperate to change the subject.

We've been laughing and bantering for the last couple of hours. Tobias is once again pushed into the back of my mind. I'm starting to feel lightheaded from the two lagers that I've consumed. I'm now onto the orange juice with Trent. If he expects me to ride on his motorcycle again, I can't be drunk. He looks towards the bar area and stares at something, I follow his gaze but don't see anything unusual. There's a man with his back to us wearing skinny jeans and a denim shirt. He has combed back blonde hair and chats happily with the bartender.

"Excuse me," Trent says.

He gets up from the table and approaches the man, he places his hand on his shoulder, the man turns. Rex.

"Trent, what a lovely surprise!" he gushes.

Trent points over at me and I offer a small wave at them both. Rex's grin grows wider. He collects his drink from the bar and walks with Trent to our table. He sits beside Trent and stares at me.

"It's so good to see you again, Mark. How's that lovely wife of yours?" Rex enthuses.

"She's good, thank you. How's- um."

I look down at my hands and desperately try to remember his partner's name. He was at the wedding... and my bachelor party. I should know who he is by now. I look back at Rex. He smirks.

"Mitch."

"Right. Mitch. Sorry. How is he?"

"He's good."

"Is he still working at the hospital?" Trent pipes up.

"He is. In fact, I have something I need to tell you guys," Rex bounces in his chair.

We both lean over the table and look at him. He produces a face splitting grin.

"We're getting married!"

Trent high-fives him.

"Well, you did catch the bridal bouquet," Trent says.

We all laugh and Rex shunts Trent's shoulder.

"After you thrusted it at me!" Rex says.

"Well, anyway. Congrats! This calls for a celebration."

Trent heads for the bar again and leans against it as he talks to the bartender. Me and Rex exchange a look before he quickly returns, carrying a bottle of champagne and three flutes. He pops the cork and pours us each a glass.

"To Rex and Mitch," he says, holding his flute aloft.

I chorus with him as Rex flushes.

"Congratulations," I say, taking a sip of champagne.

The three of us stagger out of the bar laughing loudly.

"Looks like you'll have to push your bike home tonight," I laugh, shoving Trent slightly.

"Nah way. I'll leave it here for a while. Maybe Mitch will take it home for me?" he directs his gaze at Rex.

"I can ask," he shrugs, pulling his cell from his pocket.

I check my watch; 5:30 p.m. Rachael should be home soon.

"Thanks for the company, boys. Think I'd better get home," I say.

I stagger away.

"Mark?" Trent calls.

I look over my shoulder and arch a brow.

"Wouldn't it be easier to get a cab?" he asks.

I shake my head and lean against the wall. I'm a little queasy.

"Nah. I need the air. Gotta sober up a little before I get home."

He frowns but regains his composure.

"See you Monday," he calls.

I wave my hand up.

I walk through Central Park, tripping on my own feet from time to time. It's mild with a cooling breeze blowing softly, rippling the leaves on the trees. My vision starts to blur, and I become short on breath, so I stop at a bench and sit down. After a few deep breaths and a rest, my vision returns, and I feel less nauseous. I get back to my feet, but a man sitting nearby catches my eye. He appears to be in his late twenties, wearing a dark suit and a pair of dark rimmed glasses, which he keeps adjusting. He's staring in my direction, not moving an inch, just staring. I squint my eyes, trying to recognize him, but I don't. I look over my shoulder to see if he's staring at something else, but no one's behind me. I choose to ignore him. *Time to head back.* I turn and stride in the opposite direction, trying to rid the man from my mind.

I walk a few blocks, the fuzz and dizziness slowly leaving my head. I head past Columbus Circle, but I have a creeping sensation that I'm being watched. *Oh. Not this again.* I glance over my shoulder, but nothing seems unusual. I walk a little faster, but I can't shake the feeling. A black car drives slowly alongside me. I can't see the driver due to the heavily tinted windows. I start running but the car follows closely. I dodge left into a nearby alley and the black car screeches to a halt. Pulling my phone from my pants, I hastily dial Rachael's number, but it goes straight through to answer phone. I leave a frantic message.

"Rachael, I think I'm being followed. I'm in an alleyway just past Columbus Circle. Please help."

I look over my shoulder but continue running. A light blue van pulls out suddenly, knocking me over. I bang my head against the cold, hard concrete making my head spin.

A flurry of activity occurs; doors open, and people shout incoherently. I scramble to my feet and make my leave, but a man dressed all in black, his face covered by a balaclava grabs the collar of my shirt.

"You're going nowhere," he says.

I swing round and punch him hard across his jaw, he staggers backwards and falls to the ground. I look down at him, then try to make a run for it, but two other men also dressed in black clamber out the back of the van and point automatic rifles at me. I gape at the guns and stand frozen to the spot. My palms go cold and clammy, and my heart palpitates against my ribs. They walk slowly towards me.

"Hands up," one orders.

I comply. The other pats me down swiftly, digs my phone from my pocket and throws it into the nearby trash can.

"Get in," he orders, pointing to the van.

I look at the blue van. My heart thumps harder in my chest and a bead of sweat starts to form. One of the men hits me round the head with his rifle, making me stumble forward and clutch the brick wall. A shock of pain lances down my spine.

"Get the fuck in!" he shouts.

I raise my hands again and slowly walk towards the van. A white car pulls up and a woman scrambles out. Rachael

runs towards the van that I'm being loaded into. Her eyes
bulge, her mouth slacks and her hair flies around her.

"Mark!" she screams.

They throw a bag over my head, blacking her out as they
toss me into the van. The door slides shut with a bang, the
tires shriek, and the van speeds away throwing me forward.
A lone gunshot rings out and my heart flies into my throat.
Shit. Rachael! The bag is suddenly torn from my head and
the masked man looms over me. The other two sit up front.

"What do you want with me?" I say, backing myself into
the corner.

"You talk too much. Put him to sleep," the driver says.

The man pulls out what looks like a taser and approaches
me.

"That's not necessa-."

A searing, burning pain shoots through my neck. I feel
weak. I try to fight away the darkness, but the pain comes
again, and my surroundings go dark.

I wake with a start, and flinch as pain races through my
skull and down my spine, seeping into every sinew, muscle,
and bone in my body. I spin my head round frantically. The
room is vast, but dark, lit only by a few narrow windows.
The walls are moldy with a strong stench of death. Aisle after
aisle of dilapidated seats, and dusty perished books litter

the debris covered floor. I try to stand up but can't move. I look down and notice that I'm tied to one of the seats. I pull hard, groaning. I need to get to Rachael. *I need to know that she's unharmed.* The restraints hold firm and after all my struggling, I'm exhausted. A masked man walks into the room and stares in my direction. He cocks his head to one side. I frown and struggle once more while he downs the last of his drink from a glass bottle and throws it at me. It smashes at my feet, jolting me. He walks towards the dilapidated door where he just entered and leans against the doorframe.

"He's awake. Fetch the boss," he shouts.

More men shout in the distance, but I can't make out what they're saying. The masked man takes one more look at me, lights a cigarette, then exits. I try one last attempt to struggle free, but they don't budge. I sit back again, my heart races and the pain in my body intensifies. Loud footsteps echo outside of the room. I sit up and look towards the door. A tall, broad figure, shrouded in the shadows enters, followed by two men wearing balaclavas, both armed. I eye the automatic rifles and swallow hard. The figure stares towards me, then looks back at his companions.

"Leave us," he orders.

I know that voice, but it can't be. I stare at the shadowed figure, my anxiety growing.

"Why am I here?" I ask.

The man cackles.

"You're here for an opportunity."

An opportunity?

"Who are you?"

"You don't know me? I never forgot about you... Mark Flint."

He walks into the light, revealing greasy, black slicked hair. The dusty stale light illuminates his wicked green eyes albeit his left one is paler than before. A long scar runs down the left side his face, starting at his brow and ending at his chin. He smirks, displaying his yellowing decayed teeth. My worst fears are confirmed. *It's him. Tobias is back.*

Chapter Six

My mouth falls open.

"Tobias?" I whisper.

His grin broadens.

"But I thought you were…"

"*Dead?* A part of me is. The part of me who underestimated you," he growls.

I gape at his scar. That must've been where I slashed him after we fell from the grain terminal. His eyes squint and he raises his hand to his scar.

"It's the new me," he smirks.

He walks closer, looking me up and down. As he nears, I flinch.

"Correct me if I'm wrong, but I'm not the only one with a scar," he crows.

I swallow, a cold shiver runs down my spine. He opens his jacket and pulls out a switchblade. I stare at it. *He's going to kill me.* He leans down and rips through the denim near my right thigh. I flinch again and can do nothing but watch as he examines the large scar on my leg.

"It's not as bad as mine. You got off lucky, Mark. People can't see yours. You hide it away, keep it under cover, be ashamed of it even."

"Lucky?! You nearly killed me and Rachael!" I bellow.

Tobias smiles, his bitter breath of cheap booze and cigars invades my nostrils, making me want to gag. He walks round the back of my chair and pulls on the cuffs that bind my wrists. They bite into my flesh, and I close my eyes, trying to absorb it, not wanting to give him the satisfaction of knowing that he's hurt me, but then he cocks his gun. I scrunch my eyes tighter and my mouth dries. Rachael's face is all I can see. Smiling. Laughing. Lying beside me. *I love you, Rachael.* A gunshot echoes off the walls and rings round the dilapidated room. I go limp, parting my hands from each other. *Wait a minute.* I reopen my eyes and raise my hands up in front of me; the cuffs are still on my wrists, but the chain is broken. He shot it off. I jump out of my seat and swing round to face him; he's now pointing the gun at me.

"Don't try anything clever," he spits.

Lines form above his brow into a deep creased scowl, then he smiles and holsters his gun. I rub the pain from my wrists around the cuffs.

"I can only apologize for the means of getting you here," he says.

"Where am I?"

"That doesn't matter."

I strain my ears for a clue.

"Well, by what I can tell, we're by the water. I can hear it lashing outside," I start.

He sniggers.

"Very good. Anymore detective skills?"

I look outside the shattered windows to find thick, overgrown trees and vines that seep into the building.

"We're probably on an island somewhere as I can't hear any trace of the city. There's a lot of vines and trees outside, and they appear to have settled into the building nicely. Nature has taken over. You should consider cutting them back," I continue.

He nods and scoffs.

"Very good, but enough of that. I brought you here to talk to you."

"What is it that you want with me, Tobias?"

I fold my arms and take a step back.

"I have a proposition for you, like I said earlier."

He walks towards me, but I back away further.

"Last time we spoke, when I had your beautiful Rachael at gunpoint, you said that if I let her live, you would rejoin my crew. I didn't believe you at the time, but I'm offering it now. Rachael is alive... is she not?"

I purse my lips as he stares down at my arms, his forehead creasing. He lunges over and grabs my left hand.

"I take it from this ring on your finger that you're no longer a single man," he says, raising my left hand up to my eye level.

I snatch it away and stare at my platinum wedding band.

"Try to convince me that it wasn't *her* who put that on your finger."

I stare at him for a moment, but then tear my gaze away and look down. He laughs.

"You betrayed your principles, Mark. Never get friendly... or sleep with an authoritative figure."

I stare back at him, my fists clenched.

"They're not my principles, they're yours," I seethe.

He nods slowly.

"Sure. So, do we have a deal?"

I can do nothing but laugh.

"You've got to joking."

His eyes bulge and his lips thin.

"Do I look like I'm joking? A deal is a deal. If you agree, everyone in your life, Rachael, her family, your little friends at that hotel, me and the boys will leave them be."

I blink, then shake my head. He steps forward again, but I walk back.

"I wouldn't be crazy enough to make that mistake again, Tobias."

"Is that a 'no', Mark?" he says, raising an eyebrow.

"I won't rejoin you. I have a life. I will not sacrifice it for a life of lies with you," I growl.

He laughs.

"You're already living a life of lies. You really think that police officer wife really cares about you? You're lying to yourself."

I clench my fists tighter and grit my teeth. He looks down.

"Truth hurts, don't it, old friend?"

"I don't believe you."

He paces the room in front of me.

"All I ever wanted to do was help you, Mark. I gave you a life while everyone else abandoned you. I'm the only friend you have."

"No," I say, shaking my head.

He sighs.

"You are truly lost, Mark. It breaks my heart to see you this way. I did offer, but you've left me no choice. Rusty!"

A large balding stocky man, covered in tattoos enters the room and stares at Tobias.

"Yeah, boss."

"I think Mark needs a little time out."

"Sure, boss."

Rusty cackles as he pulls something from his jacket and comes at me with it. I try to throw a punch at Rusty, but he dodges me fast and kicks me to the dusty ground. I scramble to my feet and raise my fists, but my arms get pinned to my sides from behind by another man. I try to swing round, but he holds firm.

"We'll talk a little more when you've come to your senses," Tobias says, then he clicks his fingers.

Rusty lunges at me again and the same searing pain from earlier shoots through me and I'm plunged into the darkness once more.

My head throbs aggressively as I slowly open my eyes, making me screw them shut again. It's pitch black, waves crash in the distance, hallow winds whip past the building and rustle the leaves. I slowly lift my head and straighten my body, my back protesting. I groan but notice a tight sensation around my face and a foul taste of the fabric jammed in my mouth. *Rachael, I hope you're okay and you can find me.* I test my hands. *Yup. Tied up. Again.* It was handcuffs before, now the coarse sensation of rope rubs against my wrists. I can't hold out for a rescue this time. Tobias is not a man of patience. I'll have to do this on my own. I struggle fruitlessly until footsteps click outside the room. I pause and wait as the footsteps quieten. I pull at my restraints again, but the rope slowly and viciously bites at my skin. My wrists feel like they're on fire, but all I can think about is the last time I saw Rachael's face; terrified, hysterical, the gunshot. *Will I see her again? No. Don't think like that, Flint.* My mind shifts to her heavenly smile during our wedding photo shoot, her head thrown back in ecstasy on our honeymoon, her rosy scent, and her warm hazel eyes. I'm getting out of here. I gently rotate my wrists and the binding slowly lowers down my hands. It gets tighter and more painful as it moves towards the knuckles. *Keep going. Don't stop. She wouldn't want you to.* I hold in a breath, relax my hands and I rotate them a few more revolutions. The heat builds up in my hands, but I don't stop. The binding slips past my knuckles and my hands are free. I bring my hands up to the back of my head to find the knot to the gag in my mouth. *It's just like untying a shoelace, only its dark and you can't see.* A loose thread tickles my fingers, I get hold of it and pull. It unravels in my hand, I drop it onto the floor, stand from the chair and make for the door. I open it cautiously and look up and down the dark, dilapidated corridor. Nothing. Staying low, I chance heading left and towards the cool breeze that I feel blowing in. That must be the way out. I head past several doors, the debris and glass crunches under every footstep I take. Voices laugh and chat loudly in the room ahead. I pause, rest my hand against the damp, dirty tiled wall, and peek round the corner. Several of Tobias' men are armed and camped around a burning barrel, one is polishing his weapon with a lint cloth while the others jerk around nosily.

"Should we check on Flint?" one asks.

"Nah. He'll get what's coming to him when the boss returns," another says.

"From what I heard, he didn't sound so easy to bring in, like he's toughened up."

"It's just luck. Don't let that concern you."

"I'm just sayin'-"

"Hey! I said the boss'll deal with him. Now, shut up."

I take a deep calming breath and tread past, staying as low and quiet as possible. All I can see are tall trees in the darkness. No sign of New York. I tread gently, leaves and twigs crunch beneath me. I spin my head round, observing every direction, but the guards are ignorant. The trees are blown above me as I continue slinking through the tall stems of grass and pass the ivy-covered trees. Resistance pulls at my right leg, rustling the grass. I turn round; the rip in my jeans is snagged by one of the tree branches. I lean down slowly and start prizing the branch from my leg. It pricks my fingers, but I keep pulling at it. I yank the branch off my jeans, but it produces a loud tear as I tumble over into the soil.

"Hey. What's that? Go check it out," a voice calls behind me.

Gotta move.

"*Me?*" another voice speaks.

"Yeah. You. Or do you wanna explain to the boss why you couldn't be bothered to do your share?" the other man says.

I move quickly but silently until the voices fade from earshot. The waves get louder and less trees surround me until I find myself on the shore. There's nothing but water in front of me and the twinkling lights of the city beyond. *Oh no.* I rake my fingers through my hair.

"He's escaped! Find him!" a voice booms from behind.

Shit. I look around frantically and notice a broken-down dock next to an old plant with a large chimney protruding from the roof. *Now what?* A loud whir looms in the distance. I look ahead as a large spotlight draws closer to me. A blue and white helicopter with the NYPD crest hovers over the island. The spotlight blinds me, but it's the most relieving feeling. I wave my arms above my head, but a gunshot rings past my ears.

"There he is!" a guard shouts, pointing.

"Lower your weapons!" a distorted voice from the helicopter demands.

One of the guards shoots at the helicopter, but a red dot illuminates on his chest.

"Lower your weapons and get down on the ground with your hands on your heads! Final warning!" the officer commands.

"Fuck," the guard says.

They drop their rifles with a loud thud, lie face down on the ground and place their hands above their heads. Two armored officers rappel down, then proceed to cuff them. An NYPD boat docks nearby, and the goons are taken aboard. Another middle-aged male officer walks towards me.

"Mr. Flint?" he says.

"Yeah?"

"You alright?"

"Could be better."

"Let's get you aboard."

He attaches me to his harness, then we ascend into the helicopter.

The helicopter touches down. The door slides open, and Officer Davis helps me out.

"You alright?" he says.

"Sort of. Is Rachael okay? Where is she?"

"She's fine. I'll take you home. She's waiting for you."

He walks me to his cruiser where I'm placed inside and driven back into the city.

I push the front door open. Rachael paces the living room, her hand pressed to her face with her cell to her ear.

"No. He's still not home yet, Mom. He's been gone for seven hours. The helicopter took off, but I haven't heard from them since."

I lean against the wall and watch her, relieved that she's alive; frantic, but alive. She draws her hand away from her face and looks in my direction. She freezes, then quickly turns back to the cell.

"He's here."

She hangs up and runs into my arms, nearly knocking me over. I wince as my blistered wrists chafe and my head and back throbs, but I hold her tighter, embracing her familiar scent. She weeps uncontrollably into my shoulder, her tears soaking my already stained shirt. I gently push her away and wipe a stray tear with my thumb.

"Don't cry. I'm here."

Her face crumples once more and she buries her head into my chest.

"Oh god, Mark. I thought… I-."

"Hey, it's okay. I know."

She releases me and wipes her eyes with both hands. I walk further into the living room and slump onto the couch, resting every muscle. She's beside me in moments, she examines my face and my wrists which are both blistered. She looks me up and down, her hands running all over my body.

"Who did this to you?" she asks.

I'm flashed back to being restrained in that dirty run-down hospital, Tobias' evil sneer, the large scar that covered his face, and the smell of death and rot. I shiver and wrap my arms round my body.

"Mark, who did this?" she asks again.

I look at her.

"Tobias."

She sits back, her eyes widen.

"You saw him?"

I nod and lay back, staring up at the ceiling.

"Did he do this?"

She points down at the rope burn marks on my wrists, her mouth turns down and her eyes are ablaze.

"No, that was me… escaping. He tied me to a chair, and I got myself free. Hurt like a bitch though," I say to lighten the mood.

She gapes at me and lays her head on my chest.

"You escaped all on your own?"

"No."

She leans her head up, her eyebrows furrowed.

"My mind was occupied by thoughts of you. You gave me the strength to get free. The NYPD arrived. I never would have gotten out alive if it wasn't for you."

She smiles up at me as her eyes begin to glaze over. I run my knuckles gently down her smooth cheek and plant a tender kiss on her lips.

"I missed you," I say.

"I missed you too. Trent was real torn up when I told him you'd been taken."

"Damn, I should call him."

I reach into my pocket, but then remember the assholes throwing my phone into the trash when I was taken.

"I don't have my phone. They threw it away."

She sits up straight and smirks her secret smile. She fishes into her pocket and hands me my phone.

"I recovered this at the scene. Don't worry, it's been sterilized."

I turn it over in my hands, the screen and casing are covered by a large crack. *I doubt this will work like it used to.* I stare back at her.

"Did they hurt you? I heard a gunshot when I was driven away. I was afraid that-."

She shakes her head and smirks again.

"That was my gun. Shot a man that was driving the black car. Took him in for questioning. He never mentioned Tobias, refused to in fact. I knew he was an O'Malley though; he had a red carnation tattooed on his left wrist, like the rest of his schmucks… No offence."

"None taken."

"We demanded a location, got him to sing eventually with Dad's help and we launched the helicopter immediately."

I brush her hair away from her face and kiss her again.

"My Rachael. You really do think of everything, don't you?"

"For you, anything."

She locks her forehead to mine and stares into my eyes.

"I'm so glad you're safe."

She presses her body flush against mine, making my breath catch in my throat, then she leans down slowly and kisses me deeply. I lie on my back on the couch with her on top of me as she continues her sweet embrace. The kiss changes from loving to something more fervent. Her pupils dilate and her breath becomes shallow as she looks down at me.

"Maybe we should go to bed?" I say.

She grins and shakes her head slowly, curtaining us both with her hair.

"There's nothing wrong with staying here."

She sinks her teeth into my lower lip and tugs slightly making me groan. I squeeze my eyes shut then she kisses me again and our lovemaking begins, slowly and at her pace.

We lie together, sated and panting on the couch. Rachael still rests on top of me, her head lolled against my shoulder as her breathing slows. She peeks at me and smiles.

"Thanks for that," I grin down at her.

"Feel better?"

I nod and wrap my arms round her bare back, clutching her to me and enjoying her warmth that washes over me in waves, cleansing the dark memories from the depths of my soul.

"What do you want to do now?" she asks.

"I'm real tired. Let's go to bed."

She sighs and climbs off me then stands beside the couch as I sit up. Her eyes stray down my body and stop at my blistered wrists. She sniffs and rubs her eye with her index finger. I look at the deep red marks and smile up at her.

"They're not as painful as they look."

She cocks her head to the side, her mouth twisting.

"I'll grab the first aid kit, deal with those, then we'll get some rest," she says, turning on her heel and heading into the kitchen.

She returns with a small green bag and places it on the coffee table. She kneels on the carpet in between my legs. Taking both my hands in hers, she turns them over and hisses through her teeth.

"Really. This isn't necessary," I say.

"Just… sit still."

She roots in the box, then pulls out several packets and a pair of small scissors. She rips one of the packets open using her teeth and holds a small wipe.

"This is an antiseptic. It may sting a little," she says.

"Do you have to?"

She frowns and nods once.

"Mark, I must. We don't want infection getting in."

I exhale and lay both hands on my lap. She scooches a little closer and starts dabbing at the wound. I squeeze my eyes shut and suck in a breath. *Man, that smarts.* The sensation stops, making me open one eye. She stares at me.

"You okay?"

"Yeah," I breathe quickly.

She continues and I close my eyes again, blotting out the pain.

"Finished," she says.

I open my eyes and look down at my wrists, they've been cleaned, and a dressing now covers the hideous marks. They'll bruise no doubt.

"Thank you."

She smiles and pulls me to my feet.

"Shall we go to bed now?"

I nod and she leads the way. We slip into bed together and she snuggles into my arms.

"I was so scared you weren't coming back," she whispers into the darkness.

A lump forms in my throat as the fear threatens to choke me. I quickly swallow it down and pull her close.

"I'll always return to you," I say.

She bends down, her hair tickling my chest and she plants a trail of feather light kisses across my sternum.

"Good night, Mark."

"Good night, Rachael."

We just arrived in New York City in a large white van. Tobias jumped out from the passenger side, opened the back and we all filed out.

"Welcome to our new home, boys," he said.

I looked out across the Hudson.

"Okay, boys. Start unloading all these boxes. Place them in the warehouse over there," he ordered.

It was mid-August and the blistering summer sun beat down on us as Adam and I lugged a heavy box into the warehouse.

"Screw this life. I'm moving on in a month or two. You should come with me," Adam said.

We put the box in the corner and went outside for another. I removed my white shirt and wiped my face with it.

"What are you planning to do?" I asked.

He shrugged and patted me on the back.

"I'll flee the city and Tobias. Go into hiding for a while, then settle down, get myself a wife and kids," he said.

"That sounds nice."

He nodded and wiped his forehead with his arm.

"Better than this life."

"Get back to work," Rusty shouted.

We rolled our eyes as he turned his back and grabbed another box.

"Be ready soon," Adam said, winking at me.

I shake my head, snapping out of my daydream and turn to the espresso machine. I open the cabinet and retrieve another mug to make Rachael one. I place the mug underneath and press the start button.

"Morning, sugar," Rachael croons, startling me.

I swing round and smile at her. I cup her face in my hands and kiss her hard.

"Good morning."

She peeks over my shoulder at the steaming coffee machine.

"Is that for me?" she asks.

I look back at the now filled cup.

"Yup," I say, picking it up and handing it to her.

She takes a sip.

"Mmm. That's good. Thanks, Mark."

She strides out of the kitchen as I collect my mug from the marble counter and follow her. She sits on the couch, and I sit beside her. I drape my free arm over the back of the couch and gently stroke her bare shoulder with my thumb. She takes another sip then sets it down on the table in front of us.

"Are you working?"

"Not today. Dad put me on leave after you were taken. Said I was too close to the case. I'm back at the start of next week."

I'm thrilled. I get the whole weekend, just Rachael and me.

"What would you like to do today?" she asks.

I think hard, then an idea hits me. Something I've been dying to do.

"How about a boat ride?"

She blinks and rests her nimble fingers under her chin.

"Staten Island Ferry?"

I laugh.

"Not that kind of boat. A rowboat, in Central Park."

"You old smoothie. I'd love to."

I put on my black jeans, checkered shirt, and black chucks. Rachael's in a simple but elegant white blouse, a pair of pale skinny jeans, and white chucks. I'm tying up my last shoe just as Rachael's cell vibrates. She checks the number and frowns.

"Be right back," she says and darts into the bedroom.

I stare after her and my heart sinks slightly. *I hope that's not work calling her back in.* I lean against the wall and fold my arms. My cell vibrates in my pocket, I dig it out and answer it without checking the number.

"Trent, I was planning to call," I say.

"My. You're slipperier than I gave you credit for. That was an interesting stunt you pulled. Gotta say, I'm impressed," Tobias' voice sneers.

My heart sinks as my breathing shallows.

"Oh, Jesus Christ, Tobias. Give it up. When are you going to give a guy a break?" I hiss.

He laughs.

"When *I* get bored. And as you know, I don't bore easily. Especially where you're concerned."

"The police aren't going to stop. We'll find you."

He sniggers.

"Keep telling yourself that, sweetheart. I'll see you soon. Oh, and Mark… you need to get out while you can. You're starting to sound like a law-dog."

The line goes dead. I pocket my phone just as Rachael reemerges, smiling. It fades when she sees me as the knot tightens in my stomach.

"What's wrong?" she asks.

"Nothing."

She steps forward and runs her hand down my cheek.

"You're pale and as cold as ice. What is it?"

I sigh and run my fingers through my hair.

"Tobias called."

She steps back, her eyes bulging.

"When?"

"Just now."

"What did he want?"

"Nothing important. Just acting big and mighty as normal."

She sighs and shakes her head.

"We'll stop him… soon. I've had enough of this bastard," she growls.

"Yeah, me too. Anyway, I don't want him to spoil our day. Who phoned you?"

"Nothing to worry about. It was only Mom."

Thank God. She collects my rucksack from the floor and slings it over her shoulder.

"Let's go," she says, heading for the door.

We stroll hand in hand through Central Park and towards the Loeb Boathouse. Memories of our wedding flash through my mind. *What a day that was, everything I ever dreamed of and more.* Now, my beautiful wife walks by my side loving me like no one else. We walk past street artists who sketch different landscapes, and various street musicians play an assortment of instruments. We head past Bethesda Fountain as the cool spray of the water hits my skin. We arrive at Loeb Boathouse. I stop and look for the boat rental area. She pulls at my hand, leading the way.

"This way," she instructs, pulling me towards the water's edge.

She lets go of my hand and speaks to a middle-aged man with dark hair, looking after the boats. She palms him some money and waves me over. I approach slowly.

"I was going to pay," I whisper.

She raises her hand dismissively as the man directs us to one of the boats which is moored on the jetty. She climbs in and sits on the wooden seat. I climb in after her and sit next to the oars. The man pushes the boat from the jetty, down a slope and into the water. I grab the oars and with all my upper body strength, the boat glides smoothly along the lake. There's a lot of boats filled with young families as the children scream and squeal, and couples laugh and joke together. I continue to row smoothly as she leans back and soaks in the sun. She flops her hand down into the water and splashes gently. We start to go under Bow Bridge. She looks up at the bridge and smiles sweetly at me.

"What?" I ask.

"This bridge has a lot of memories," she breathes, playing with her engagement ring.

I smile and look up at the bridge, remembering the day I proposed to her. She places her hand back in the water and splashes me. I'm dripping wet and soaked through. She bursts into fits of laughter. I shake my arms in a futile attempt to dry off.

"What was that?" I chuckle.

She shrugs.

"You looked like you needed cooling off," she splutters.

I let go of the oars and grip the sides of the boat tightly, then I start swaying from side to side, rocking the boat. She widens her eyes and grips onto the side.

"Stop that!" she shouts.

I rock harder as people in the other boats look on and frown, but I don't care.

"Feeling seasick?" I laugh.

"Mark!" she cackles.

I rock a little more, harder this time. Not knowing my own strength, the boat capsizes, throwing me and Rachael into the cold water. Ducks fly away. I resurface and look around for her, she's already swimming towards me. We both grip onto the capsized boat and attempt to right it again. She tuts.

"Good job," she coughs.

I grin an all-tooth smile as we manage to right the boat. I push her back in, then climb up myself. She shakes herself off and wrings her hair.

"That brought back some memories," she giggles.

I smile; the Uniphere at Flushing Meadows, the day I confessed my love for her.

"That's my shower for the day," I quote.

She beams as I grab the oars and start rowing back to the jetty.

"We should head home," I say.

She nods. Slowly, we approach the jetty with the boat owner staring at us and shaking his head. He steps forward and pulls our boat out of the water and moors it. Me and Rachael step out quickly and leave the Loeb Boathouse. Our clothes drip all over the sidewalk and people stare at us, their brows furrowed and avoiding us.

"That was fun," she says, taking my hand.

"Definitely."

"I don't think you'll be welcome back there," she narrows her eyes at me.

"It was worth it."

We head for the exit and make our way back home.

Tom opens the front door for us and eyes our now damp clothes. Rachael smiles at him as we walk in.

"Morning, Tom," she greets.

"Rachael, Mark. Been for a swim?" he asks, stifling a laugh.

"Something like that," I chuckle.

We stride towards the elevators and ride up swiftly to our floor. A loud ping sounds, and we step out, our wet shoes dampening the carpet. She frowns at the footprints left in our wake.

"I'll have to apologize to Mr. Jenkins for that," she says.

I unlock the door, but before stepping inside, we take our shoes and socks off and hang them on the radiator. She heads into the bedroom and returns promptly with some dry clothes. I step into the lounge, but she shoos me away.

"Get your wet things off my carpet!"

I jump off the carpet.

"Into the bathroom," she points.

I turn on my heel and head towards the bathroom. She closes the door and begins to remove her wet clothes. I pull my checkered shirt over my head, but it sticks to my skin. I pull hard and finally get it off. Next, I take my pants off so I'm standing only in my underpants. Rachael stares at me.

"What?" I ask.

She eyes the scar on my leg that Tobias left when he stabbed me. She pushes me back towards the lone stool. I sit down as she kneels on the floor and strokes my scar. She frowns up at me, then looks away. I cup her chin with my thumb and gently turn her face so that she's looking back at me.

"It doesn't bother me. Okay?"

"It never should have happened. When we were standing on that roof and I watched you fall, I thought…"

She looks away again. I slide off the stool and kneel on the tiled floor with her.

"It was a horrible night, I know, and we both know that he's back, but you said it yourself, the NYPD are ready."

I stare deep into her hazel eyes. Finally, she cracks a small smile and wraps her arms around me. I hug her back, like my life depends on it. I don't know how long we've been kneeling on the floor in each other's arms, but my knees start to ache. I stand up and pull her to her feet. She combs my hair out of my face and kisses me gently.

"You need a haircut," she says.

I look at myself in the mirror, it's so long, it flops over my forehead and nearly obscures my vision. I flick it out of my eyes and smile at her reflection in the mirror.

"I'll give Rex a call," I say.

"I can do it."

"What? Call Rex?"

She laughs.

"No. I can cut your hair for you."

I blink at her.

"Have you done it before?"

"I used to cut Dad's hair."

"Okay."

She smiles and sits me down on the stool again.

"I'll be back in a minute. Don't move," she says.

I raise my arms and smirk.

"Where else am I gonna go?"

She smirks back and walks out of the bathroom. I hope she knows what she's doing. She comes back in seconds carrying a comb and a pair of scissors.

"We need to wash your hair first," she says.

I stand up, slip off my underpants and step into the shower to wash my hair. She stands on the other side of the cubicle, staring at me. I smirk at her.

"You can join me," I invite.

"If I do that, you're never gonna get a haircut."

I pout but continue to soap and rinse my hair. After I'm done, I step out and she hands me a towel to wrap round my waist. I quickly do so and sit back down on the stool. She deftly towel dries my hair then examines me closely.

"What length would *sir* like?" she asks.

"I'd like it out of my face."

"I like it floppy."

"Okay. I'd like it away from my eyes."

"Ah, an excellent choice," she says, then she takes a lock of hair in between her fingers and snips.

Chapter Seven

S he steps back and admires her handiwork.

"I think I did pretty good. What do you think?"

I admire myself in the mirror; it's still floppy, but it's out of my eyes.

"Much better."

I take her in my arms and kiss her.

"Thank you."

She brushes loose hair clippings from her clothes.

"You're welcome. Want some lunch?" she asks.

"I'd love some."

I glance down at all the hair trimmings on the floor.

"You do lunch. I'll clean up here," I say.

"Agreed."

We had a quick, easy lunch and now, we relax on the couch together. Rachael's delicate legs rest up on the couch, her head rests against my shoulder while she reads a magazine. I flick through the channels on the TV, but nothing sparks an interest. I sigh deeply, switch it off then stand up. She sits up while closing her magazine, throws it onto the coffee table, then stares up at me and crosses her arms.

"I'm going out for a run," I say.

"Okay."

I stroll into the bedroom and get changed into a black tank top, gray sweatpants, and blue sneakers. I grab a water bottle from the fridge, then walk back into the lounge. She looks me up and down. I lean over her and plant a tender kiss on her lips.

"Back soon," I whisper, then stand up straight and head to the front door.

"Mark?" she calls.

I turn round.

"Yeah?"

"Please be careful."

I kiss her forehead.

"I will."

"Let me know if anything happens."

I pull my battered cell from my pocket.

"Sure will."

"Does that thing still work?"

"Just about."

I put it back.

"Okay. See you soon."

I peck her on the lips once more, head out the door and stride down the corridor, pumped for my upcoming run. *I need to burn this excess energy.*

I exit the elevator and walk briskly down the corridor. I push the front door open and slam the door shut, harder than intended, making me cringe. *Oops.* Rachael peeks round the corner from the lounge and smirks at me.

"Are you sure that's closed?" she asks.

I crack a half smile. She steps closer and cocks her head to one side.

"You're all sweaty. Take those things off. Give them to me, I'll put them in the laundry," she says, beckoning with her hand.

I slip my tank top over my head and hand it to her, then pull off my sweatpants. She continues to stare.

"Anything else?" I chuckle.

"Socks, please."

I take off my sneakers, then remove my socks and hand them to her.

"You know, I can do my own laundry."

She turns and enters the kitchen.

"Nah, it's fine. You can do it next time."

I pad into the lounge and flop onto the couch, clad only in my underwear, and prop my feet up on the coffee table.

"Get off!" she calls.

She storms over and bats my legs, forcing me to retract them and place them on the floor.

"How was your run?" she asks.

"Like jogging down memory lane."

"Where'd you go?"

"Over Bow Bridge, round Bethesda Fountain, past Loeb Boathouse and back home."

She grins slowly, then combs her long mahogany hair out of her face.

"You okay?" I ask.

"Sure."

I cock my head.

"What's up?"

She clears her throat.

"The guys that… Nah, never mind."

"No. What?"

She sighs.

"The guys that… kidnapped you; they've been charged with kidnap, attempted murder and as accessories to Tobias' organization. They're due to be sentenced by Justice Miller next week. We're hoping for lengthily sentences for each of them."

"Well, that's good. How many are there? Three?"

"No. The officers swarmed the old hospital shortly after you were extracted from the island. They found three more inside trying to escape. So that makes six."

"And Tobias?"

"He couldn't be found."

I groan and lie back against the soft cushions. She rests her hand on my knee.

"I know this is frustrating, but he will be caught. I promise you."

I take her hand in mine and raise it to my lips. I kiss her knuckles and brush her fingers through my stubble.

"I know."

"But for now, I would like you to be accompanied to work by Trent on Monday."

I arch a brow and open my mouth to respond but she rushes on.

"Just for a few weeks... please, Mark. This is important to me. I need to know that you're safe."

I sigh and collect my phone from the table.

"Okay. For you," I say and dial Trent's number.

Rachael helps me with my navy tie for my first day as front of house.

"I can do my own tie."

She beams up at me.

"You always say that, but when you do, it looks like a wad of crumpled Kleenex. There."

She stands back and rests her chin against her knuckles. I look in the mirror as I slip on my navy jacket.

"Not too shabby," she says.

I start adjusting my tie, but she rapidly taps my hand.

"No! Leave it."

I hold my hands up.

"Okay. Sorry."

"You look great."

I kiss her quickly on the cheek and walk into the lounge. She follows and I only just realize that she's still in her bathrobe.

"Don't you have to get ready for work?" I ask.

"My shift was changed. I don't start till later."

I glance down at my watch; 8:15 a.m.

"Trent will be here soon," I say.

She nods.

"Good. I should get dressed."

She disappears into the bedroom, and I sit on the couch. Trent was an emotional wreck when I called him to ask for a ride. He blamed himself for my kidnapping, but I told him not to be ridiculous. Rachael reemerges dressed in a pale blue flowing blouse and dark denim jeans. She sits beside me.

"Are you nervous about today?" she asks.

"A little, but I have the best teacher possible. Trent's showing me the ropes."

She laughs and rolls her eyes.

"Oh, lord."

I titter just as there's a loud knock at the door.

"Speak of the devil and he shall appear," I joke, getting to my feet.

I open the door and Trent barrels in, sweeps me into his arms and hugs me with his usual enthusiasm.

"Mark, thank God."

I pat him on the back and gently push him away.

"It's so good to see ya," he continues.

"You too, man."

He recomposes himself and offers a quick smile at Rachael.

"Thank you," he directs to her.

"For what?" she asks.

"Rescuing him."

She shrugs and places her hand on my shoulder.

"It was a team effort."

He nods then turns back to me.

"We should go."

I grab my rucksack, slip on my shoes and head towards the elevators with him.

"Don't forget your lunch," she calls.

"Already packed," I call back.

"Where's my hug?" she grumbles.

"Oh. Where are my manners?"

I rush back, swamp her in my arms and swing her round as she squeals.

"See you later," I whisper.

She kisses me and I leave with Trent.

We arrive at the Neapolitan just before 9 a.m. He parks his bike, and we head inside. Mr. Levitt is waiting in the lobby. I square my shoulders and stride towards him.

"Good morning, sir," I say.

"Morning, boys. You're just on time, I like that. You ready for your training?"

"I am."

He waves his hand towards the front desk, and hands me a piece of laminated paper which I glance at quickly.

"This is your desk, Mark. This is your login. Keep it safe," he says.

I take off my navy jacket, drape it on the back of my chair and sit down behind the desk. Mr. Levitt looks from me to Trent and back again, then he claps his hands together.

"Right. I'll leave you to it. Good luck."

He strides towards the elevators. I turn to Trent as he sits at his desk beside mine.

"Okay, Mark. Here we go."

After I've logged in, Trent begins talking me through the reservations screen. I listen closely. *God, this is complicated.* He shows me how to book in those checking in and those checking out.

"After they arrive, you need to ask for a credit card and log the details, but don't charge the card until they check out, okay?" he explains.

"Okay."

"Now, what am I missing? Uh… oh yeah, check in is at 3 p.m. and check out is at 11 a.m. I think that's all." He rubs his chin, but then shakes his head.

"Yeah. I think that's it. I'll be here if you need a hand though," he says.

I look back at my complicated computer screen and glance at the time: 10.30 a.m.

"The check-out rush will be soon," he says.

My gut knots, making me clench it. I'm not used to face to face contact.

"You'll be fine," he says.

A loud ping from the elevator gets my attention. An old couple step out with their luggage and make their way towards our desk. I pray internally that they choose Trent, but they walk straight towards me. I offer them the warmest smile I can manage.

"Morning," the man greets.

"Good morning. Are you checking out?" I ask.

"We are."

"Name please?"

"Benton."

"Okay, thank you. Did you enjoy your stay with us?" I say as I type on the keyboard.

It's nearing two o' clock and the hotel is quiet, for now. *This has been easier than I thought.* I stare blankly across the lobby, looking forward to telling Rachael about my first day. Mr. Levitt walks around the lobby with a man roughly in his late twenties, wearing a scruffy white shirt, jeans, and dark specs. *Wait, I recognize him… The guy from the park. I saw him minutes before I was abducted. Is it the same guy?* Mr. Levitt doesn't seem impressed, his arms are folded, his forehead is creased, and his lips begin to thin out.

"Trent," I whisper.

He leans in, still typing.

"Who's Mr. Levitt talking to?"

He stops typing and glances over.

"Oh. That's another potential cleaner. Jeez, he could've worn a suit for the interview or something," he tuts.

A suit? I'm shot back to that moment. He was wearing a suit that day.

"Keep an eye on him," I whisper.

He narrows his eyes.

"What? Why?"

"Something's not right about him."

He arches a brow then looks back at him just as Mr. Levitt leads the man into a waiting elevator.

Trent drops me at the sidewalk outside my apartment. I climb off and remove my helmet. He muffles something at me.

"What?" I ask.

He flips up his visor.

"Sorry. Good job today, bud."

"Oh. Thanks for the help."

He raises his leather gloved hand, gives me a thumbs up then drives away. I enter the building, offer a quick greeting to Tom, and make my way to the bank of elevators at the end of the marble and dark oak paneled corridor. I exit on the fifteenth floor just as Rachael leaves the apartment in her uniform and locks the door. She looks up, smiles, and unlocks the door again.

"Hey, honey. Off to work?" I ask.

"Yeah, I am. How was your day?"

"Long. Listen, there was a guy today, applying for the cleaning role. I swore I saw him in Central Park just before I was… yeah."

She leans against the wall.

"You think he's involved with Tobias?"

"Yes, I do. One way or another."

"What was he doing in the park, and today?"

"Nothing much. He was staring at me in the park, felt a bit strange; and today, Mr. Levitt was talking to him. He always seems to be where I am."

"What does he look like?"

"Um… late twenties, dark hair and he's always wearing dark glasses."

She contorts her mouth.

"It's not much to go on, but I'll see what we can do. Maybe I'll give Mr. Levitt a call, see if he's concerned in any way."

"Will you let me know?"

"Of course."

She smiles again, approaches me and kisses me.

"Sorry. I have to run; my shift starts soon. I was hoping for a relaxing evening together," she says.

"It's okay. Thank you for a wonderful weekend."

She kisses me once more.

"Just try not to worry," she says, before heading for the waiting elevator.

The doors slide shut, blocking her from my sight. I instinctively blow phantom hair from my eyes. *Oh yeah, Rachael cut it.* I head into the apartment. It feels empty and so lonely without her, I drop my bag on the floor and sigh heavily. *Looks like dinner for one today.* I head into the kitchen and eye the stove. I don't trust myself to cook. I look in the cabinets for something simple. *A sandwich maybe.* I take out the bread and make myself a PBJ sandwich.

I watch TV, hoping Rachael will be home soon, but I doubt it. I check my watch: 10:50 p.m. I don't think she'll be home for a while. I turn it off and slink into the bedroom where I get undressed and slip into bed. Snuggling down into the feather soft mattress and thick covers, I feel cold and alone. I roll my eyes at myself and after a lot of tossing and turning, I finally close my eyes and drift to sleep.

I'm awoken by the front door opening and closing. I look at the alarm clock; it's just past four in the morning. I listen for any more noise, but everything is silent again. The bedroom door opens and Rachael tip toes in. She gets out of her uniform, hangs it in the closet and gently climbs in beside me.

"How was work?" I ask.

She props up on her elbow and looks over at me.

"You're awake?"

"I couldn't sleep without you."

I turn over so that I'm facing her.

"Catch any bad guys?"

"A couple. You can sleep soundly tonight."

She fluffs her pillow, lays down and curls up close to me. She rests her head against my shoulder and sighs.

"Did you find any leads on the mystery man?" I ask.

"Is that what you're calling him?" she chuckles.

"Didn't take much premeditation, I know, but yeah."

"Not much. Mr. Levitt found him strange. Said he was quiet and kept fiddling with his glasses. Unsurprisingly, he won't be hiring him. Other than that, we've got nothing. No name. The name he put on his application was 'Michael Jones', but it was a dud. We'll keep looking."

"Right."

"How was your first day as front of house?"

"It was complicated, but I'll get the hang of it."

Her warm smile radiates against my bare skin.

"Of course, you will."

I kiss the top of her head as she yawns loudly.

"Good night, hon. Sleep well," she says.

"You too."

Within minutes, her soft even breaths signal that she's asleep. I drape my arm over her chest and feel full again, this time I drift easily into a deeper and more sated sleep.

The weekend arrives and my new job is becoming long and arduous, however I've had the opportunity to meet some interesting people. I've had honeymooners, businesspeople, tourists suffering with jet lag, and some downright rude people. It's been fun to work alongside Trent and Rex, sometimes they talk across me about some stupid noisy videogame, I'm not that sort of guy. It's Saturday afternoon. *I'm a whole year older tomorrow.* I push my birthday to the deep, dark depths of my mind. *I've never liked celebrating it. Not since... Don't go there.* I sit on one of the leather armchairs in the staff room, tucking into my lunch. My mind drifts to Rachael, I'm missing her so much, our shift patterns have been all over the place and we've hardly seen each other throughout the week. I shake away my depressing thoughts and continue with my falafel pitta, lovingly prepared by her. Trent walks in.

"Hey," he greets.

I nod at him and continue with my food. He collects his lunchbox from the fridge and sits beside me. He sniffs in my direction, crinkling his nose. I narrow my eyes at him and chew slowly.

"What?" I ask, my mouth still full.

"What are you eating?"

"Falafel. Want a bite?"

I wave the pitta at him. He jumps up and twists his mouth.

"Ugh. No thanks."

"More for me then."

He sits back down and opens his lunch box. He takes out half a baguette filled with what smells like salami. He takes a large bite and groans. *God. You'd think he likes that more than sex.*

"Want some?" he offers.

I shake my head.

"I'm good thanks."

"How can you eat that?"

I put the pitta down on my lap.

"This was lovingly prepared by my wife. It's delicious."

He holds his hands up in a defensive gesture.

"I'm just messing."

I finish the last few bites of my pitta, then pick up my cupcake, also made by Rachael.

"Ah. Let's have a bite," he gushes.

I hold it away from him as he reaches for it, crumbs falling from the corner of my mouth.

"This is mine," I say.

He pouts, then continues with his sandwich.

"You should try her brownies," I continue.

His face whips to mine.

"She makes brownies?"

I smile.

"Sure. I'll ask her to make some."

He nods frantically, eyes wide open like a toddler.

"So, to change the subject slightly, it's your birthday tomorrow. The big 3 and 0," he smiles.

My smile fades and I continue with my cake in peace. He nudges me and I stare at him. *I think he was expecting me to be excited or something.*

"My birthday is nothing worth celebrating, Trent," I say.

"Well, I want to celebrate. I'm sure Rachael does too."

"Sure."

Every year that my birthday draws close, I need to push the sound of my mother's voice deep into the back of my mind.

I unlock the front door and walk into the lounge. Rachael is talking on her cell. She stares at me like a deer caught in headlights. I smile and wave at her. She holds her index finger up and rushes into the bedroom. I blink at the closed door and shrug. I take off my shoes and undo my tie, then head into the kitchen to pour myself a cold drink.

"Sorry about that," she says.

I jump and turn to face her. She leans against the door arch.

"It's okay."

She saunters into the kitchen and wraps her arms round me. I put my drink down on the counter and hug her back.

"We haven't seen much of each other this week, I'm sorry," she says, looking up at me.

"We're busy with work, it's okay."

"That's no excuse. We need time for us."

I nod.

"You're right."

"Your birthday's tomorrow. Anything in particular you want?" she asks.

"I already have it. I have you, my friends, a family. It's all I've ever wanted."

She blinks up at me, her eyes rimmed with tears.

"Oh, Mark."

She presses her lips against mine, but then deepens it. Soon, we're both alight with passion. I scoop her off her feet and march to the bedroom.

"What are you doing?" she giggles.

"Making up for lost time."

We enter the bedroom and I kick the door shut behind me. I set her down on the bed and stare down at her, stunned by her beauty.

"I love you," I say.

She grins up at me.

"I love you too."

I crawl onto the bed and kiss her again. She unbuttons my shirt and pulls it open to reveal my chest. I sit up, quickly shrug off my shirt and pants, then slip into bed. She pulls her clothes off and joins me. I pull the covers over us, ignoring the heat, and let my passion for this woman fully take over.

Chapter Eight

I wake slowly, the hews of dawn shine through the gap in the curtains. I rub my eyes and check my phone; 4:50 a.m. May 28th, 2017. The day I was dreading has arrived. *Today is my birthday.* I huff and peek over at Rachael who lies on her side facing me; her long dark lashes are fanned out, her full lips are slightly parted as she breathes slowly and softly, her chest rises and falls, her hair pools round her shoulders and pillow in dark waves, her eyelids flutter on occasion. I deftly comb her hair away from her face and peck her lightly on the cheek. She groans but doesn't wake. I roll onto my back and slowly copy the gentle rhythm of her even breaths as my eyes become heavy.

It was my fifteenth birthday and Grandma set a huge chocolate cake on the table before me as I sat at the dining table doing my homework. I glanced up and stared into her bright blue eyes.

"Happy birthday, Mark," she beamed.

I looked at the cake and my mouth watered at the smell, but then I felt a cold stab of betrayal from my parents' abandonment.

"Has the mail been?" I asked, looking back down at my homework.

She took a sharp intake of breath.

"It has," she sighed.

"Anything from my parents?"

I glanced up but knew the answer. Her mouth twisted, then she sank into the chair beside me. I looked down at the oak table as tears rolled down my cheeks.

"Mark..."

She placed her hand gently on my back. I was suddenly overcome with rage. I swept my homework off the table and jumped to my feet. Grandma continued to stare at me, wide eyed. I paced the lounge, pulling at my hair. She jumped to her feet and grabbed me by the shoulders. She stared deep into my eyes as her hand brushed my face.

"Mark, I'm sorry," she said.

I took her hands in mine and kissed her on the cheek.

"Me too. What happened to them? Where are they?" I asked.

She opened her mouth but then closed it again and shook her head.

"What aren't you telling me?" I asked.

"Mark. I don't know where your parents are. I haven't had contact from them in years. I wish I could tell you more, but I just can't," she explained softly.

I nodded, trying to accept the fact that my parents didn't care and wouldn't be coming back.

"How about some cake?" she said, feigning a smile.

I collected my papers from the floor and sat back at the table as she lit each of the candles. I watched the flames flicker and dance, closed my eyes, and made a wish. *I just want to know what happened to them.* I blew hard and opened my eyes. I watched the smoke float softly into the air as I started to realize: my parents were never coming back.

My eyes snap open as I pant hard. I sit up in bed and rub my face furiously. *What was that?* I take a deep breath, trying to bring my thundering heart to heel, but it continues to hammer against my ribcage. I glance down at Rachael, she's still curled up, asleep. I get out of bed and retrieve my underpants from the floor. I slip them on, then take my robe from the door and quickly shrug it on. I open the door as quietly as I can and pad out of the bedroom, through the lounge and into the kitchen. I switch on the espresso machine and watch the steaming black liquid fill my mug. The rising sun bleeds into the night sky, sending hews of orange and red through the kitchen window.

It was my fourth birthday and Mommy was in the kitchen cooking something that made my mouth water. Daddy was out. Mommy said he was at work. I played with my train set that Grandma got me. The lights turned off. I jumped up from the floor and stared around. Mommy came out of the kitchen, carrying a chocolate cake with four lit candles that stuck out of the top. She sang 'happy birthday', her eyes shined from the candles, and her long dark hair curtained one side of her face. She placed the cake down on the coffee table and I clambered up onto the couch to watch the flames of the candles flicker and dance.

"Make a wish, big guy," Mommy said, a large smile spread across her face.

I squeezed my eyes shut and wished hard. *I hope we will always be this happy.*

I blew out the candles and smiled at Mommy. She clapped her hands and whispered in my ear.

"When Daddy returns, we have a big surprise for you."

I looked up at her and grinned.

"Can I see it now?" I asked, bouncing in my seat.

She laughed and shook her head.

"You won't have to wait long. Now, how about some cake?"
I nodded as I eyed the cake. She collected a knife from the
kitchen and cut me a generous slice.

Rachael startles me by wrapping her arms round my
shoulders and kissing me on the cheek.

"You're up early," she whispers.

I turn and frown.

"I couldn't sleep."

She steps back.

"What's wrong?" she asks.

My mind drifts back to my mother, but I shake it off.

"Nothing."

She sucks in her lips, but then smiles widely and pulls
me into her arms, hugging me hard.

"Happy birthday," she whispers, running her fingers
through my hair.

"Thank you. What are we doing today?"

She folds her arms.

"I thought you could go for a drink with Trent."

"And you?"

She shakes her head.

"Just you and Trent."

I frown.

"I was hoping to spend the day with you," I grumble.

"You will. I just thought it would be nice to see Trent for an hour or so while I make you a cake."

"You're making me a cake?"

She laughs.

"Of course."

"Chocolate?"

"What else? You can never beat a good chocolate cake."

I grin widely.

"I can't come home soon enough to try it."

She laughs and nudges me slightly. I grab my mug of coffee and stride into the lounge where I deposit it on the coffee table and sit on the couch. She joins me with a mug of her own. She sits beside me and places her mug beside mine. She sighs, causing me to glance over.

"You okay?" I ask.

"I wish I knew you more."

I cock my head to the side and take her hand in mine.

"You know me better than anyone."

"I know. I just have so many unanswered questions."

I turn my whole body so that we're nose to nose.

"Ask away," I whisper.

Her hazel eyes search mine.

"On your birthday? Are you sure?"

"Sure. How bad can it be?"

She licks her lips and rolls her eyes to the side before glancing back at me and smirking.

"How did you meet Trent?" she asks.

"We met in high school. He protected me."

"From what?"

"Life."

Her smile fades, and she rests her head against my chest.

"Has it always been hard for you?" she asks.

"I was angry with the world before I met Trent. My parents abandoned me, or so I thought at the time, and the kids at school called me 'Marky no parents.'"

"That's terrible."

I nod.

"Grandma did everything she could to make sure I had a happy normal life, but it was hard. Trent helped though; he looked out for me. He was the only friend I had, but he dropped out."

"His mom got a job here, didn't she?"

"Yeah, and… he fancied our math's teacher, asked her to the prom, she refused. That's the *real* reason why he dropped out," I joke.

She sits up and gawks at me.

"Really? He fancied the teacher?"

I nod, desperately trying to keep a straight face but I burst into fits of laughter.

"Nah. Kiddin'."

She shoves me and turns beet red.

"I can't believe I bought that."

"Sorry."

"What happened next?"

"With Trent gone, I had no one to protect me. I got into trouble… a lot. I stole from the cafeteria."

I turn away from her as I say this. *What was I thinking?*

"You stole?"

"Fifteen dollars. Petty, huh?"

"Boys will be boys."

"I paid it back, after a stern word from Grandma, God rest her soul. She said to me; 'be careful how you choose to live your life. One day, your bad deeds will catch up with you'. Looks like they did," I say.

She takes my hand.

"You're not a bad man, Mark. You're gentle and kind, and I love you."

"What made you love me?"

"When I came to arrest you that day, I saw only a frightened man. You weren't going to break into that store, unlike all the other criminals I face. You gave yourself up. I knew in my gut that you were different."

I manage a smile and raise her hand to my lips. I plant a gentle kiss on her palm. She grins and places her hand deftly on my face.

"How did you get to New York?" she asks.

"Tobias sent me on a small job in Chicago. The police were waiting. They spotted me and I ran back to the hideout with the police following. Tobias was furious, but we managed to escape. He said we had to leave Chicago. One of his lieutenants, Rusty, had highjacked a large white van a couple of days prior. We were bundled inside and driven here."

Her mouth drops open and she gapes.

"My turn to quiz you," I smirk.

"What do you want to know?"

"Tell me more about you and Steph?"

"Well, like you, she was a target to bullies. I protected her. After her father died, she was desperate to be a cop."

"She was bullied at school? She never struck me as the sort that would be messed with. You know she threatened me in jail?"

"She did?"

"She told me to stay away from you."

She laughs.

"Look how that turned out," she smiles, flashing her ring.

A thought jumps into my mind. I had no idea that Steph was gay until I met her fiancée a couple of months before we got married. I chuckle.

"What's funny?" she asks.

"Did she have the hots for you at any point?"

Her eyes widen and her mouth drops open again.

"I can't believe you said that!"

"Well, I did... so?"

"I dunno."

"You must do."

She sighs and chortles a little.

"She asked once, a long time ago. I put her in her place, said that I just wanted to be friends."

"No wonder she fancied you. I mean, look at you."

"Mark!" she quips, nudging me again.

I push her and she pushes me back, harder. I lie down on the couch and pull her down with me as she squeals and laughs.

"Your uniform is very sexy, but I like what's behind the badge," I whisper.

She laughs harder and attempts to sit up, but I hold onto her firmly and glide my hand up her thigh, pushing her silk gown aside.

"Mark, we're on the couch," she giggles.

"And? Didn't stop us before... Remember?"

She rests her weight onto her elbows and twists her mouth before her eyes come to rest on me again.

"Oh. What the hell?" she says and kisses me deeply.

I return her kiss with my own passion and as our love for each other fully takes over, dark thoughts of Tobias dissipating.

Rachael is sprawled naked across my chest as our breathing slows. I thrum my fingers down her back and she hums, her throat reverberating against me. She rolls off and gets to her feet. I roll onto my side, resting my head against my propped elbow as my eyes travel greedily up her body. She smirks down at me, then runs her fingers through my hair making me close my eyes.

"Why don't you go back to bed?" she says.

I furrow my brow and sit up.

"Why?"

She smiles then bends down and runs her nose down mine.

"Because I wanted to make you a surprise breakfast."

"Not much of a surprise now."

"Well… breakfast, then."

I stand and make my way to the bedroom with her trailing behind me. I climb back into bed and lie against the soft pillows.

"Now, stay," she says, placing her palm flat against my chest.

I laugh and pretend to pout.

"Yes, ma'am."

She giggles, then turns on her heel, and struts out of the room, her hips swaying seductively.

She reenters the bedroom, draped in her silk nightgown and holding my bathrobe over her arm. I sit up in bed, exposing my naked chest. She leans against the doorjamb and looks me up and down.

"Coming back to bed?" I ask, throwing the duvet aside.

"Maybe later. Your breakfast is ready first."

My smile melts away briefly but I decide to try and tempt her more. I throw the duvet over my head and lay back down.

"I don't wanna," I grumble.

She laughs as the duvet is pulled away from me. I hold on tighter and pull back.

"Come on," she says.

"No."

She crawls onto the bed and pulls the duvet from my head. I take my chance and lunge for her. She screams and leaps off the bed. I thump the mattress with my fist. *Dammit.* She places her hands on her hips.

"Your breakfast will get cold," she admonishes.

I throw the duvet off myself and climb out.

"I'll get you later."

Her smile broadens.

"Oh, I'm counting on it."

She throws my robe at me. I catch it, laughing.

"The neighbors will be complaining if you don't cover up."

I look down at myself and shrug.

"We can always find new neighbors."

Her mouth falls open as I quickly shrug it on. She smiles then leaves. I trail after her as she heads for the dining table. I eye the waffles with berries and the champagne cooling in a bucket of ice. I scoop her up in my arms and kiss her hard.

"You didn't need to go through so much trouble," I say.

"But I wanted to."

I let her go and sit down at the table, grab my knife and fork, and start devouring my food. *This is incredible.*

"Would you like another coffee?" she asks.

"Please," I say, my mouth still full.

She turns the espresso machine on, then joins me to start on her own. I finish off the remains of my waffles, picking up as many of the crumbs as I can.

"That was amazing."

She smiles at me through a mouthful of food, a drop of syrup dangles from her lips. I kiss her to remove it. She looks like she could melt, but before things go any further, I need a coffee. I slide off my chair and finish off with the espresso machine.

"I can do that," she calls.

I look over my shoulder as she starts to get up, but I wave my hand at her.

"You finish eating. I can manage."

She sinks down and continues with her food. I place a mug in front of her then lean against the marble counter while taking a sip of my own.

"What are we doing after breakfast?" I ask.

"As I mentioned earlier, Trent will be here shortly to take you out for a drink."

I frown, still slightly disappointed.

"Are you sure you don't want to come with us?"

"I have some things to do."

My smile fades and I look down at my coffee.

"It's only for a couple of hours. I'll see you later," she continues.

"Okay."

She gets up and makes her way towards me. She wraps her arms round my neck and kisses me gently.

"Happy birthday, Mark," she says, before turning and walking into the bedroom.

We emerge outside into the balmy air. Rachael eyes Trent's motorbike as he dismounts it. She frowns and puts her hands on her hips.

"I don't know if I trust that thing," she says, pointing at the bike.

"That's what *I* said," I smile as Trent removes his helmet.

He ruffles his hair into place, then makes a beeline for Rachael. He hugs her hard then smacks me on the shoulder.

"Happy birthday, old man," he crows.

I rub my shoulder from his over enthusiastic greeting.

"Who are you calling 'old'? *You're* thirty," I taunt.

His smile fades as his mouth falls open.

"Holy crap, you're right! We'll be going gray next."

He places his hands on top of his head. I laugh at him as she frowns at me.

"You boys will always be young at heart," she says.

He blushes slightly, then clears his throat and grips the handlebars of his bike.

"Shall we get going… old pal?" he asks, arching a brow.

I kiss Rachael, then climb onto the back of the motorbike. He hands me a helmet as I slip my jacket on, then he starts the engine.

"No drinking, Trent," she says, wagging her finger at him.

He smiles and slips his helmet back on.

"Wouldn't think of it," he shouts over the engine, then he pulls away as she waves at us.

I sit at a table in the corner at The Stag's Head and wait for Trent's return. It's noisy as most of the customers gather round the bar, watching the overhead TV, tuned into the sports channel. They shout, cheer, and boo every so often, others stumble around and look a little drunk. I stare at Trent, he's squashed in the middle of the overexcited fans, waiting to be served. I rest my chin against my knuckles, wondering what Rachael's up to. She mentioned a cake, I can't wait to try it.

"What are you thinking?" he asks, placing the drinks down.

"Nothing."

I take a sip of cranberry juice as he does the same.

"Oh. I have something for you," he says.

He leans down and fishes in his bag. He removes a parcel, then hands it to me.

"Here."

I take it, looking down at the blue paper.

"You didn't need to get me anything."

He rolls his eyes.

"Just open it."

I rip through the paper and take the lid off the box. Inside is a personalized pint glass with an inscription: *'Happy 30th Bud. Love Trent'.*

I smile at the glass and look up at him. He's biting his nails.

"It's great. Thank you."

He breathes out and slumps back.

"You like it?" he asks.

"I love it."

"Now you can knock back a few after work."

I laugh and place the glass back in its box. He holds out his hand for it.

"I'll stow it in my bag for safekeeping," he says.

I hand it back and he gently stows it away.

"Happy birthday, bud. Cheers," he says, raising his glass.

I do the same and we clink.

He glances down at his watch then jumps out of his seat, startling me.

"We need to go," he says.

I furrow my brow and stare down at my watch; 12:55 p.m.

"What's the rush?"

"Rachael gave me strict instructions. We're running late."

"For what?"

"No time to explain. Come on."

He pulls me from my seat and rushes for the door. I follow him back outside where he jumps onto his bike. We slip on our biker gear, then he disengages the kickstand and revs the engine.

We weave and dodge as we head through the Hugh L. Carey Tunnel. *This isn't the way home. Where are we going?* I lightly tap him on the shoulder.

"Why are we going this way?" I shout over the roar of traffic and wind.

"I just wanted to visit Louise real quick," he shouts back.

"Couldn't you have dropped me home first? I thought you said we were late for something."

"We won't be long."

I continue to hold onto the back of the motorbike as he speeds through and emerges out the other side. I suppose it'll be nice to see the in-laws, but I'll have to text Rachael when we get there, I don't want her to worry.

Trent pulls up on the Clarkes' driveway, then dismounts the bike and removes his gear. I follow him, removing my helmet and jacket which has made me all sweaty. He makes his way onto the porch, knocks on the front door loudly, then steps back. Louise answers, wearing a summer dress, laden with palm trees; sandals, and sunglasses resting on top of her head. She's had a haircut, no longer wavy and long, now a short and tidy pixie cut.

"Trent," she squeals, throwing herself into his arms.

I raise my eyebrows but look away and rub the side of my nose as they embrace nosily. When they are *quite* finished, Louise turns her attention to me.

"Mark, happy birthday."

She hugs me hard which I return.

"Louise, nice to see you. Nice haircut by the way."

She combs her fingers through it and beams.

"Yeah, it's the new me."

She twirls, her sundress rising slightly.

"Well, now I can tell the difference between you and Rachael."

She rolls her eyes.

"I know, right? I'm always getting that. There was this guy as the Christmas tree was going up at the Rockefeller that thought I was Rachael. Can you believe it?" she laughs.

Oh god, I thought she forgot about that.

"Yes, alright. I see Trent's sense of humor has rubbed off on you."

Her eyes sparkle as she directs her gaze back at him.

"I know, he's great. Don't you just love him?" she says dreamily, placing her hand on his shoulder.

He stares back at her and plants a kiss on her lips.

"Yep, he's one in a million," I say.

Can we go now? I'd like to see my wife.

"Come in. Mom and Dad will be thrilled to see you," she says, grabbing my hand and tugging hard.

Guess not. I follow her inside. The house is deserted, no one's in the lounge. The large stone fireplace dominates the façade of the room but is not lit; two cream couches stand opposite each other in the center; and sun rays shine through the stain glass window, emitting a kaleidoscopic hew of colors on the cream carpet.

"They're in the garden," Louise says, continuing to drag me through the house.

She leads me through the kitchen and stops by the back door, finally releasing my hand which is red and throbbing.

"They're out there, Mark. After you."

I look at Trent who drapes his arm round Louise's shoulders and glances down at her. I place my hand on the knob and swing the door open. I'm taken aback by the round of applause and cheering that suddenly hits me. I step out into the sun and blink at the throng of people gathered in the Clarkes' backyard. Everyone is here; Colin, Sara, Colin's parents Derrick and Katherine, Sara's parents Royce and

Evelyn, Rex, Mitch, Alison, Steph, Sasha, and Colin's two brothers and sister, accompanied by their spouses and children. I scan the crowd slowly until my eyes come to rest on her, my Rachael. I'm motionless as I stare at her; she's clad in the same simple, but elegant turquoise dress that she wore on our honeymoon that exposes her slender arms, cork wedge sandals that extend the length of her already long legs, and a polka dot Alice band that sweeps her hair behind her ears, exposing her delicate neckline and providing an unobscured view of her beautiful face. She beams and steps forward. I stand frozen to the spot as she reaches me. I take her hands and smile at her.

"Did you do this?" I whisper.

She nods, still displaying a perfect all-tooth grin.

"You're worth it, honey."

She turns back to face everyone.

"Here's to Mark," she calls.

Everyone shouts my name and applauds again. I turn to face Trent who still stands in the doorway with Louise.

"Did you know about this?"

He sniggers.

"Everyone did."

Rachael links her arm through mine and shows me around. I've never been in the Clarkes' backyard before. There's a barbeque being lit and a table by a row of perfectly manicured hedges, lined with an assortment of drinks. A large pool dominates the yard, the crisp, clean water ripples and twinkles in the sunlight, the sanitary scent of chlorine fills my nostrils. It looks so refreshing that I just want to head straight in, but then I remember. *I haven't got my swimming shorts. Damn.*

"I don't have anything to wear for the pool," I whisper to Rachael.

She continues to smile and lifts one shoulder.

"I thought of that. I've packed your swimwear, it's in my bag."

"Can I get changed?"

"Absolutely."

Most of us choose to get into our swimwear. Rachael looks as sultry as ever in her navy-blue bikini, the one she wore on our honeymoon, but Trent looks ridiculous in his pineapple shorts, a straw hat, and blue sunglasses. He sits on the edge of the pool, sipping a drink and dangling his legs in the water. Rachael hands me a can of ice-cold lemonade and rests her head on my bare shoulder. I stare over at Colin as he chats to his brother. I can't remember his name.

"What's your uncle called again?" I ask.

She looks up and chuckles.

"Forgotten already?"

"I only met him once, at our wedding."

She takes my hand and leads me over. Colin turns to face us as we approach.

"Dad, Mark wanted to say 'hello' to Uncle Frank."

She pushes me forward, then leaves to assist her mom with the food. I stare after her then look back at the two brothers who smile at me. They both offer me many happy returns. I grin at them both and turn my attention to Frank.

"How've you been?" I ask.

He puffs out.

"Work's hard, the wife and kids keep me on my toes but other than that, great. How are you finding married life?"

I look back at Rachael who is now sat on a sun lounger as she laughs with Louise and Steph.

"She's wonderful."

Frank looks over my shoulder then back at me.

"She was always a lovely girl. You chose well."

I nod as Alison makes her way over.

"Happy birthday again, Mark. Enjoy," Frank says, raising his glass before turning and heading over to join his wife. Alison hugs me.

"Happy birthday, my boy. Are you enjoying yourself?" she asks.

"It's wonderful, thank you for coming... Mom."

She places her hand on my cheek and hugs me again.

"I wouldn't miss it."

We talk for a while until Rachael approaches. Alison smiles at her and they begin girly talk which drags a little. I quietly pull myself away and sit at the outdoor dining area which thankfully, offers some shade from the overbearing sun that beats down. I sip my now warm lemonade and watch everyone. I haven't felt so loved and so welcomed anywhere for a while. This has got to be my best birthday ever.

Chapter Nine

—∾—

Colin joins me at the table, drinking a beer; Sara's in the kitchen with Louise preparing sides for the barbeque; Trent continues to sit at the poolside, kicking his long legs through the water. Derrick has called dibs on manning the barbeque. Rachael has finally escaped Alison and sits beside me under the parasol, my hand rests on top of hers. Colin pushes a bowl of gum drops towards her.

"Want some candy?" he asks, eyeing me and Rachael.

"No thanks, Dad. Don't you know what that stuff does to your teeth?" she says, raising her hand.

He laughs and peeks at her through one eye.

"Coming from the girl who said she wanted to live in a candy house when she was ten."

"Dad!" Rachael flushes.

I snigger. She whips her face at me.

"Candy house?" I smirk.

She clears her throat and gets up from the table.

"Thanks, Dad."

She walks towards the pool and raises her hands above her head revealing a perfect cleavage. I widen my eyes and look around at the other guests. *Is Trent watching this?* I look towards the pool's edge, but he's gone. I continue watching her to see what she does next. She outstretches her arms in front of her and performs a perfect swan dive into the water. My eyes widen further, and my mouth dries. *My wife has a killer body.* I feel like I've gotten too big for my shorts. I peek at Colin, hoping he hasn't noticed, but he glances straight ahead. I get up from the table and head for the pool, desperate to conceal myself from the waist down. I sit on the pool's edge and slowly slip into the warmed water. She breaststrokes towards me, smirks, and whispers in my ear.

"It worked I see."

I look down at myself and clear my throat.

"What was that for? In front of your family," I hiss.

"That's for laughing at me."

I smirk and kiss her hard which she returns fully.

"Knock that off you two," Colin shouts mockingly.

She pulls away and stares at her father.

"Is there somewhere to go?" I whisper.

She blinks at me.

"Well, you know where the bathroom is," she says.

I roll my eyes.

"No. I mean for-."

I look around to make sure no one's listening.

"-some privacy…"

She gapes at me.

"Need some relief, Mr. Flint?"

"Yes."

She climbs out of the pool, water dripping off every tip of her body.

"Follow me," she whispers.

We head inside the house, walk through the kitchen and past Sara.

"Just showing Mark around," Rachael says.

"Well dry yourselves up first, you'll cause an injury with all those wet footprints," Sara admonishes.

I stare at Rachael.

"Gotta respect the house rules," she says, winking.

I roll my eyes as she departs back into the garden. *C'mon. Hurry up.* She returns swiftly with a towel to dry both our legs and feet.

"Thank you," Sara smiles as she resumes dicing potatoes.

We head up the sweeping staircase and turn left at the top. She opens a door and ushers me inside. We're standing in the same bedroom I was in when I was looking for Colin's office some time ago; the walls are littered with boyband posters, and I notice some boxing trophies.

"You used to box?" I ask.

"I was part of a club."

She strides over to me, her eyes locked onto mine. I don't dare break our contact as her smile widens and her pupils dilate. Every follicle of hair on my body stands to attention.

"You got me in here. Now what?" she asks.

"That wasn't cool, flashing me at the poolside like that."

"What? You mean like this?"

She pulls the string of her bikini. It unravels and drops to the carpeted floor, revealing her perfect physique. I look her up and down and lick my lips.

"Exactly."

She peeks towards the bed, then back at me.

"We don't have a lot of time till my family get suspicious. Might wanna make this quick."

I swallow, then remove my soaked shorts and lunge for her. She falls backwards onto the small double bed, then I mount over her. I slip my hands round the back of her head and rake my fingers through her sodden hair, beads of water run down my hands and wrists. She parts her lips and draws in a breath. Her eyelids are hooded as more droplets run down her neck. I bring her wet lips up to mine and pour my ardor and gratitude into her. She presses her cool damp hands against my stubbled cheek as she returns the kiss with her own fire. I move my hands across the back of her shoulder blades, trail my fingers down her sides and hook them around her bikini briefs. I slide them down her long legs and discard them carelessly on the floor. I hover over her, then lower myself down gently. She moans huskily as her fingernails dig *almost* painfully into my shoulder blades. She coats my face in featherlight kisses and growls deeply after each sensual movement. I pick up the pace, grunting after each thrust until the sensation overcomes me. I groan loudly as she winces and mewls beneath me, her eyes scrunch shut as she claws at the sheets beneath us.

She breathes deeply as she rests against my chest and strokes her fingers gently through the smattering of chest hair.

"Feel better?" she asks.

I glance down at her and kiss the top of her head.

"Much. Thank you."

She cuddles closer and sighs. I could lie here in our blissful bubble all day, but footsteps creak from outside the door. Her eyes widen, then she bolts from the bed and hastily attempts to tie her bikini back on.

"Get dressed," she whispers.

I jump off the bed and retrieve my shorts. I slip them on quickly as she tries to neaten her hair and straighten the bed covers. Someone knocks softly on the door and enters without waiting for a response. Colin pokes his head round the door.

"What are you two up to?" he asks.

She stares at him.

"I was… uh… showing Mark… m- my photo albums," she says, pointing towards the white bookcase in the corner.

He raises a brow, his mouth set in a hard line.

"Well, the food is ready," he says.

"Thanks, Dad. We're coming."

She leaves the room. I follow her, tailed closely by Colin. *God, he's breathing down my neck.* We head back through the kitchen and outside. Sara stands beside the barbeque serving the food onto plates.

"There you two are. What took so long?"

I glance at Rachael, but she continues to smile, unfazed by her mom.

"I was showing Mark my photo albums."

"Wonderful. Did you like the photos, Mark?" Sara beams.

Rachael peeks at me and shifts her eyes between me and Sara.

"They were wonderful," I say.

"Did you have a favorite?" Sara asks.

Crap. What can I say? Then I remember seeing a Disney photo on the nightstand when I went in there last. *That'll do.*

"I loved the Disney photos."

Sara pauses and looks at Rachael. I think I may have blown our cover. Thankfully, Sara smiles again.

"That was a wonderful holiday. Let's eat."

Sara turns away and continues with her task. I puff out and slump my shoulders.

"I don't think I've come so close to death in all my life," I say.

"Ah. Take some time to cool off," Rachael says.

She shoves me hard, using both hands. I stumble backwards and crash into the warm water. I resurface quickly, a forelock of hair sticks to my forehead. I wipe my eyes and comb my fringe away. All the guests are staring, including Trent, who doubles over with laughter. I look at Rachael who chuckles. I raise my hand to the other guests.

"Sorry," I say as I hoist myself out of the pool.

Everyone begins grabbing their plates and serving themselves. Me and Rachael hang back. I exhale and my shoulders slump.

"Better?" she whispers.

"Much. Thanks."

"Anytime."

It's just past 8 p.m. The sun begins to sink slowly into the horizon, turning the sky a beautiful deep orange. There are fairy lights that I hadn't noticed earlier draped over the hedges. They glow a magical warm white. Frank and his family play in the pool while Trent and Louise are cozied together in the corner. I sit at the dining table with Rachael, her hand rests deftly on top of mine as we watch the sunset together.

"I've enjoyed my birthday for the first time in years. Thank you," I say.

She turns to face me.

"I'm so glad."

She peeks down at her watch then gets up from her chair.

"Be right back," she says.

She squeezes past me, and I smack her playfully on her behind. She yelps and laughs then disappears inside the house. Trent sits in Rachael's seat and grins at me. I frown at his goofy expression.

"What are you looking at me like that for?" I ask.

"I know what you and Rachael were doing upstairs. You dirty dog."

I flush and turn my face away from him.

"I don't know what you mean."

He drapes his arm over my shoulder and leans in closer.

"Don't worry, I won't tell anyone."

I turn back to face him. He gives me an exaggerated wink, then returns to Louise. I shake my head and blow out. How does Trent know? Maybe he saw us go into Rachael's room? I shrug and look around for her, but she's nowhere to be seen. She must still be inside the house. Suddenly, all the lights switch off and everyone gathers around me. I stare at them all, wondering what's going on, then Rachael emerges from the house carrying an enormous chocolate cake. Everyone begins singing 'happy birthday'. She sets it down on the table in front of me and lights the giant thirty-candle sticking out of the top then she stands back and sings along with everyone else. The song comes to an end, and everyone applauds loudly.

"Make a wish, old man," Trent bellows.

Rachael and her family frown in his direction. I give him a thumbs up.

"Thanks, man," I call back, then I close my eyes and wish hard; *I wish to always be this happy.* I open my eyes and blow out the candles. Everyone claps again as Rachael walks over and hugs me hard.

"Thank you for the cake. It looks amazing," I whisper.

Her eyes shine.

"Happy birthday," she whispers in my ear, then kisses me on the forehead.

She picks up the knife that Sara brought out and hands it to me.

"You should be the first to cut the cake," she grins.

I look out at the crowd, holding the knife.

"Who wants a slice?" I announce as everyone shuffles forward.

The garden is alight again. Everyone sits in various chairs, eating slices of Rachael's cake. I tuck happily into mine, the sweet richness of the chocolate is exquisite, and I crave more. I place my cake fork down on my empty plate and lick my lips.

"That was incredible," I say to Rachael.

"I'm glad to hear it. I made it when I arrived here this morning."

"No one's gone through so much trouble on my birthday before. Thank you for an amazing day."

She leans over and kisses me. I let out a loud yawn and stretch. She cocks her head to one side.

"Are we keeping you up?"

"Not at all, but I've had a long day, I'm pretty tired."

She nods, then gets up.

"I'm going to get changed, then we'll go home," she says.

"Me too."

We thank the Clarkes for hosting a wonderful party and exchange goodbyes, then we head down the driveway. I look around for her car, but I can't see it.

"How did you get here?" I ask.

"Drove."

"Where's your car?"

She heads towards the garage door and opens it; her white Mercedes CLK is inside.

"Couldn't ruin your surprise, so I hid it."

I scratch my chin.

"Clever."

She walks round to the driver's door and slips inside. I stand on the lawn as she reverses down the drive and stops in front of me. I climb in, sink into the plush leather seat and buckle up. She pulls onto the road, offers one last wave to everyone standing in the doorway of the house, then speeds into the night, back towards Manhattan.

I'm shaken awake. I rub my eyes, sit up in my seat and look at my stunning Rachael. We're in the underground garage of our apartment.

"We're home," she says.

I climb out of the car and stand by her side. She wraps her arm round my back, and we make our way to the elevators. She presses the call button, then we stand and wait. My eyes are heavy and I'm finding it hard to stand up straight. I can feel her eyes on me, I turn to face her just as the elevator arrives. We climb on board and the doors slide shut.

"You look exhausted," she says.

"Mmhmm."

"Can you stay awake to receive your presents?"

I blink at her.

"I forgot to give them to you this morning."

"Sure."

We step out of the elevator and walk down the corridor. She unlocks the door, and we step inside. It feels so good to be home. I take off my shoes, then head into the lounge where I slump onto the couch, my head thrown back against the cushions. She disappears into the bedroom but reemerges very quickly. She sits beside me and hands me two boxes. *Two?* I stare at them both, deciding which one I should open first, but she pushes the larger of the two towards me.

"Can you open this first?" she asks.

I pick up the box and rattle it gently then tear off the paper. It's an iPhone, I've always wanted one, but they're so expensive. I finger the picture on the box, then glance at her. She clasps her hands together.

"I just thought that your current phone was a little damaged. You know, after you were… taken."

She holds up my old Nokia, displaying the cracked screen and bent casing.

"It's the same phone Tobias gave me years ago."

She drops it beside her.

"Well, I'm *definitely* glad I got you a new phone now. You have a different number too, hopefully that'll keep him at bay."

I take the iPhone out of its box and examine its sleek, silver beauty, then I turn it over and gasp. She's put a personalized cover on the back of it. It's a photo of the two of us at our wedding, during our photoshoot; she's pressed up against me, locked in our embrace with Bow Bridge in the background. I brush my fingers across the gloss finish. The backs of my eyes prick, I take a deep breath, trying desperately to keep my emotion at bay. I put the phone down on the table, then fold her in my arms.

"Thank you," I whisper into her hair.

She holds on tight to me and we embrace silently for a few minutes. She pulls away and hands me the other box.

"Another one?" I raise a brow.

She nods, but then begins picking at her nails. *A nervous twitch. Why?*

"You sure you want me to have this one?"

She places her hands on her lap and nods again. I pick up the small red box and remove the lid. Inside is a small, silver name tag. *What's this about?* I pick it up and read what it says: '*Sgt. Flint*'. I whip my face to hers. She bites at her nails as I turn to the tag again.

"I had it changed before we spoke about it. I didn't mention it earlier because… well, it was a surprise, for today. Do you like it?"

I stare at her again, place the tag back in the box and hug her again.

"I love it. This has been the best day," I say.

She hugs me tighter, then leaps from the couch.

"I think we should go to bed. Maybe with some champagne?"

She raises a perfect brow and gestures with her head. I smirk, get to my feet and look at the champagne still in its bucket from this morning.

"Let's take the whole bottle," I say.

She chuckles, then grabs the bucket and we rush into the bedroom together, my exhaustion forgotten.

Chapter Ten

Rain lashes against our bedroom window. It's finally raining after what feels like weeks of heat. I glance over to my left and smile at Rachael, still curled up, fast asleep, her hair splayed across her pillow in a mahogany haze. I bend across and rub my nose delicately against hers. She murmurs something unintelligible in her sleep, then I'm greeted by her bright hazel eyes as she wakes slowly.

"Been up long?" she asks.

"No."

She sits up, looks out the window and frowns.

"Looks like we'll need our coats," she grumbles.

"It's only a bit of rain."

"It's not so great being in it all day when you're on foot patrol."

She lies back down, hugging her pillow to her bare chest.

"I can't believe we drank the whole bottle last night. Do you feel okay?" she asks.

My head aches slightly.

"I'll live."

She stretches her hand across me and combs her fingers through my long hair, then she twirls a lock round her finger and tugs gently. I grin and brush her hair away from her face. She leans across and kisses me on the forehead, then sits up to check the alarm clock.

"Crap!" she exclaims, leaping out of bed.

I sit up, the duvet falls away, exposing my bare chest.

"What's wrong?"

"I'm late for work," she says as she hurriedly removes her uniform from the closet.

I tut at her. She stares at me in the mirror and frowns as she buttons up her shirt.

"You're a bad influence," she admonishes.

I shrug as she pulls her pants on and straps her duty belt round her waist, then she rushes round to my side of the bed, kisses me, and flies out the door before I see a shadow. The door slams shut as I climb out of bed and get ready for work myself.

I walk the busy wet streets on my way to work, I didn't anticipate just how hard it was raining. I stupidly chose not to wear a coat, so my suit is soaked through. *Mr. Levitt is not going to be happy.* I decide to run the rest of the way, I'm not far now. I quickly push through the double doors and shake myself off as best I can. Trent stares at me from across the lobby and shakes his head. I make for the elevators just as he gets up from his desk and joins me inside.

"Have you ever heard of a coat or an umbrella, dude?" he jokes.

I scowl at him.

"I didn't think it would be raining this hard."

He laughs.

"This is New York City, Mark. In the summer, it really comes down."

"Thanks for the weather forecast."

We exit the elevator and walk side by side to the staff room. I take off my charcoal jacket and drape it on the radiator, then check my pants and shirt. The pants are soaked, but the shirt isn't too bad. I look at him as he continues to regard me. He shrugs out of his own jacket and hands it to me.

"Here," he says.

I stare at him.

"But you need it."

"I'm hot anyway."

I take it and quickly slip it on. It's a little big, but it will do for now.

"Thanks for this."

He pats me on the shoulder then sits down in one of the leather armchairs.

"Don't you have to get back to work?" I ask.

"I'm on break."

I nod, then leave the staff room.

The hotel lobby is swarming with tourists and businesspeople eager to escape the rain. Me, Trent, and Rex work as fast as we can to check everyone in but some of them become impatient at my speed. A young couple with a British accent approaches my desk, the woman chews gum loudly, and the man scowls.

"We've been in line for an hour," he snaps.

No you haven't. You came in five minutes ago.

"I'm sorry, sir," I say.

The couple continue to moan that they've been on a flight for eight hours and want to go to bed. There's a point where I want to tell them to wait in line like everyone else, but that would probably get me fired. I continue to offer my apologies and check them in quickly. After handing them their room key, they snatch it from me, huff, and stomp away.

"Enjoy New York," I call.

I peek at Trent who stares in my direction.

"What was their problem?" I whisper.

He shrugs.

"You'll get used to that."

I blow out and try to forget about it. I turn back to my computer screen and wait for the next customer, hoping for better luck.

I'm getting ready to clock out, I'm looking forward to heading home and seeing Rachael, but then my cell buzzes in my now dry jacket. I fish it out and quickly check the number, it's Rachael. I smile and swipe the screen.

"Hi, honey. I'm on my way home," I say.

"I forgot to tell you this morning as I was in a rush. I'm going over to Steph's after work, we're having some girl time."

I frown but try to maintain my good mood from the last few days.

"Have a good time."

She breathes softly down the phone.

"It'd be a good chance for you to spend some time with Trent," she says just as he enters the staff room.

"What time will you be home?" I ask.

"About nine-ish."

"See you then. Love you."

"Love you too."

She hangs up, I pocket my phone and look at Trent who roots around in his locker.

"Can we hang out?" I ask.

He looks over his shoulder.

"No Rachael tonight?"

"She's having a girly night."

He grins, shuts his locker and leans against it.

"I'd love to."

"What? Girly time?"

He scoffs.

"Ha. You're a comedian. Let's do it."

Trent unlocks his front door, and we head inside. He shakes off the umbrella and stows it away in a cupboard near the door.

"Would you like a drink?" he asks.

"Please," I respond, sitting on the couch.

He roams into the kitchen, rummages in the fridge then heads back towards me with two bottles of our usual brew. I take one and we clink. He sits beside me, and we both take a sip. I look around the room and reminisce. This is where my new life started, I was reunited with Trent, and at the time, I didn't know where I stood with Rachael. *How far I've come in such a short amount of time.* He clicks his fingers in my face, jolting me.

"Where are you?" he titters.

I stare at him. He takes another sip from his bottle and narrows his eyes.

"What are you staring at me like that for?" he asks.

"We've come a long way, haven't we?"

"I haven't, but you definitely have. You're married to the woman who arrested you, that's crazy."

He nudges my elbow, making me spill beer all down my jacket.

"Oops. Sorry," he says, passing me a handkerchief.

I dab at my jacket.

"And *we* were reunited after years apart."

He smiles.

"I really missed you," he says.

"Me too."

We both take another sip, then he slaps his knees and gets to his feet.

"Enough of this mushy stuff. I want to show you that game I've been playing."

"What?"

"Uncharted. Heard of it?"

"I'm not much of a gamer."

He grabs my arm and tugs me to my feet.

"Well, you are tonight."

I roll my eyes and follow him to his room. *Might as well see what all the fuss is about.*

We've been playing for hours, and I refuse to hand the controller back to him. This is better than I thought. We both tuck into slice after slice of pizza as he continues to lunge for the controller.

"C'mon, man, my turn," he moans.

I resign and hand it back, but he rushes through each level, annoying me slightly.

"You're skipping all the collectables," I groan, but he grunts.

"I'll come back for them."

I'm shaken awake by Trent. I sit up on the couch, but flop back down, my head is killing me. His mouth is set in a hard line, then he disappears from my sight. He rummages noisily around in the kitchen cabinets and the faucet switches on. I press my fingers to my forehead and massage in small, slow circles in a vain attempt to numb my headache. He returns with a glass of water and some painkillers. I down them quickly and sip my water.

"You've had four beers dude. You dozed off," he says, his arms folded.

I will myself to sit up, but my head is pounding.

"What time is it?" I groan.

He checks his cell.

"Two in the morning."

I widen my eyes and leap from the couch. *Shit! Rachael.* I grab my phone and unlock it, the bright screen in the dim light hurts my eyes and my head protests a little more. I have four missed calls and several texts. I open each one while pacing the room:

> *Mark, when are you coming home?*
> *Are you still with Trent. R. XX.*
> *Please call me.*
> *Dammit Mark, where are you?*

I stare at him as he perches on the arm of the couch, cocking his head to one side.

"Has Rachael called you?" I ask.

He scratches his chin slowly.

"Yeah, she was worried about you. I told her you were with me."

I quickly dial her number.

"She's going to be asleep, leave her till morning," he says, but I'm desperate to talk to her, so I continue with my call.

She answers quicker than I thought.

"Hello, Mark."

She doesn't sound happy. I'm in trouble. I try to right this as best I can.

"Rachael, I'm so sorry."

She breathes down the phone, so I hurry on.

"I had too much to drink and…"

"I know. Trent told me everything."

I swallow hard.

"I really am sorry. I lost track of time."

She's quiet again, so I continue.

"I'll come home now."

I start slipping my shoes on, pressing the phone to my ear with my shoulder.

"You might as well stay with Trent tonight. I'm just happy to know that you're safe. For a moment I thought that- well, you know."

"You thought Tobias got hold of me again?"

She sucks in a breath and sniffs.

"Yeah."

Oh God. I've been so selfish. The kidnapping wasn't so long ago. I put her through a lot that night.

"I'll come home in the morning, and we'll talk. I'm sorry. Believe me."

She sighs.

"I believe you."

Three words that have recently meant so much to me. She uttered them to me while I was in prison after she interviewed me.

"You have to believe me."

"I believe you."

I close my eyes as the memory washes over me.

"See you in the morning, Mark. Good night."

"Good night. Love you."

"I love you," she responds, then she's gone.

I place my phone down on the table and rub my face. *Boy, do I feel guilty.* I hate the idea of her worrying and it's my fault. Trent pats me on the back. I peek up from my hands and he's smiling at me.

"Is she okay?"

I puff out.

"Furious, but I think I softened her up. I was so selfish, Trent. Drank myself silly, then fell asleep. She's been waiting for me."

He nods, sucks in his lips and looks away for a moment before chuckling.

"I think we had a little too much fun," he quips.

"Yeah."

He stands and heads to the other couch.

"I'll make a bed up for you."

"Don't bother yourself. I'll sleep on the couch."

He stands up straight and glances over his shoulder.

"You sure?"

"Of course. It's only tonight."

He smiles, then yawns loudly and rubs his forehead.

"I'm gonna crash. Good night, Mark"

He walks into his bedroom and closes the door softly. I lay back down on the couch, scolding myself for being so irresponsible. I wish I was in bed, curled up close to Rachael, her warm body pressed up against mine. *It's only for tonight.* I'll head home in the morning and hope that she doesn't stay mad at me. I'll need to make up for this, and I will.

I unlock our front door and step inside. It's just after 6 a.m. I left Trent's early without waking him. I couldn't sleep or shake the guilt of what I did and was desperate to make this right. I head into the lounge but as expected, Rachael isn't there. I open our bedroom door and there she is, curled up in the fetal position. She looks so small. I walk round the bed and crouch down on the carpet next to her. She's asleep, her eyelids flicker intermittently. Gently, I brush my knuckles across her soft cheek. Her eyes snap open and she stares at me.

"Hi," I whisper.

She sits up slowly and folds her arms. Her heated eyes bore into me as she pats the bed beside her.

"Come in," she says, throwing the duvet aside.

I strip off hurriedly and climb in beside her. We lie down and I pull her into my arms. I've missed her warm body pressed against mine. I press my nose into her hair and inhale deeply. She smells of home. She turns in my arms so that we're nose to nose but she continues to scowl.

"You came home early," she says.

"I couldn't wait."

"So…?"

"I lost track of time."

She squints her eyes.

"What were you two doing?"

"Just playing games, ate pizza…"

She raises her eyebrows.

"Anything else?"

"…drank too many beers."

"Mmhmm."

She turns her back to me. I lean my head over her shoulder.

"Did you have a good time with Steph?"

"It was lovely, but we're not talking about that right now."

She props herself up.

"You frightened me last night, Mark. I came home and the apartment was in darkness. I called your cell to see whether you were coming back or staying out: no answer. I left it for a while and tried again: still no answer. I really did fear the worst. You didn't return any of my calls or texts and I contemplated calling the NYPD for help, but I called Trent. He told me everything. I was relieved that you were safe but furious that you didn't let me know."

Her cheeks are flushed as she finishes her tirade. I sit back, my eyes rounded and my mouth dry.

"I'm sorry," I say again.

She sighs and her shoulders slump.

"I know you are, but sometimes that's just not enough."

She gets out of bed, dressed in a gray tank top and shorts. She slips on her robe and exits the bedroom. I sit, paralyzed for a moment. She's angrier than I feared. I didn't mean to worry her. I was just having too much fun. I leap out of bed, grab my robe, and go in search of her. She's in the kitchen, her hands rest against the marble counter, and her head bows as steam rises from the espresso machine. I approach slowly and wrap my arms round her waist. She stiffens and turns slowly.

"Do you forgive me?" I ask.

She runs her hand down my arm. I absorb this contact between us.

"I don't want to be the sort of wife that nags her husband to come home. Of course you can hang with Trent. We all need time with our friends but, it was just… I really thought Tobias had you again."

I stroke my hand down her face.

"I thought I lost you that night, Mark. I still dream about the day you were taken. I know we're both shaken but I need to know that you're safe."

I kiss her gently, then pull her into my arms. My gut knots painfully as my guilt hits DEFCON 1.

"I was selfish last night. I lost track of time due to some silly video game and I drank way too much booze. I don't blame you for a second if you want to stay mad at me."

She presses her forehead to mine.

"I forgive you. Just please, let me know next time. If you want to stay out, that's cool, but I need to know. Please, Mark. Just till things cool down with the Tobias case."

"Okay."

She smiles then kisses me again, her arms wrap round my neck as we embrace for what feels like minutes. When we come up for air, she checks the clock on the wall.

"Do you have work today?" she asks.

I shake my head.

"Nope. Do you?"

She smiles.

"No. Looks like it's just you and me today."

"Those are the best days. Let's go and get breakfast."

I walk through the front door, having finished another busy week at work. *Something smells good.* My nostrils are swamped by a bold and tangy aroma. I remove my shoes, jacket, and tie, then unbutton the top two buttons of my shirt and follow the scent, discarding my jacket and tie on the couch. I stop in the kitchen doorway to find Rachael stirring something on the stove. I sneak up behind her and snake my arm around her waist. She jolts, then she whips her head to meet my gaze.

"Hi," she says.

"Hey. What smells so good? Besides you, of course."

She giggles and slaps me on the shoulder.

"Stop it. Just doing some ratatouille. It'll be about fifteen minutes."

"Great. What've you been doing today?"

"Mm, nothing exciting. Y'know; chores, groceries. Could you set the table for me please?"

I collect a pair of placemats and cutlery from the drawer, walk into the lounge and place them on the dining table.

"How was work?" she calls.

"Busy, as expected. Need a hand?"

"Nah, I'm alright."

I sit on the couch and turn on the TV. A loud knock rings out from the front door. I lean over on the couch.

"Ah, damn. Mark, could you get that?"

"Sure. You expecting anyone?"

"No. Maybe it's one of the neighbors."

"Yeah, maybe to complain about all the noise we've been making. *Uh?*"

She laughs.

"Get the door..."

I smirk as I walk down the hall and open it. A tall broad-shouldered man, roughly around my age with light brown eyes, and short, dark buzz cut hair stands on our threshold. He's wearing baggy jeans, which are ripped at the knees and a Yankees shirt. I look him up and down and cross my arms.

"Hello. Can I help you?" I ask.

He clasps his hands in front of him, rubbing his thumbs together.

"Sorry, I didn't mean to disturb you. Is Rachael here?" the stranger asks.

How does he know Rachael? Who is this guy? A colleague, maybe?

"Uh... Sure. Who you are?"

He steps forward a pace, making me step back.

"I'm um... an old friend."

"Uh huh. Hold on."

I lean back inside.

"Rachael," I call.

"Yeah?"

"Could I borrow you for a minute?"

I hear a small clatter, then her soft footsteps as she pads out of the kitchen and down the hall.

"What's up?" she asks.

"There's... an 'old friend' here to see you."

I arch a brow as does she.

"Who?" she asks.

I shrug my arms.

"Dunno. Some guy."

Her mouth sets in a hard line then she walks past me and freezes in the doorway. She blinks a few times as a wide grin spreads across the man's face.

"Hey, babe," the man says.

Babe? I grab her arm and open the door wider so we both stand in the doorway.

"Who is this guy?" I hiss.

Her mouth falls open, then she licks her lips and looks from me to the stranger.

"Uh... Craig, this is my husband, Mark... Mark, this is Craig... my, um..."

She purses her lips and shifts her eyes.

"Ex-fiancé?" I whisper.

She nods once then looks down at her hands and picks at her fingernails. *So, this is Craig? The cheating scumbag ex?*

Chapter Eleven

I scowl at the slimeball that stands on *my* threshold as he ogles *my* wife. His eyes are out on stalks. *My bad vibe detector is close to detonation.*

"You look… wow. Amazing. I've really missed you." Craig says.

He moves towards her, a large sickening smirk spreads across his face as he outstretches his arms. Rachael raises both her hands and steps away. The slimeball's smile turns to a deep frown and his arms flop down like a deflated balloon. *Yeah. Hands off, asshole.*

"You've got a lot of nerve coming here," she says, venom dripping from every word.

"I just wanted to see how you were," he says.

A firm 'v' forms in between her brows.

"Odd time to check now, *isn't it*? But, hey, since you're here, yes, I'm fine."

He holds his hands up.

"Why are you being like this? This isn't how I remember you at all."

She stutters and throws her arms around.

"BECAUSE ITS OVER. YOU HAD YOUR CHANCE AND YOU BLEW IT!"

I'm putting an end to this.

"You need to leave now," I say.

"Hey, button it, mop top. I wasn't talking to you," he says, drawing his finger close to my nose.

I'm about to erupt. I'm not taking this. I grab his wrist with my left hand and draw back my right into a fist, but she grabs my shoulder.

"Mark. Easy. Easy," she says. *It works.*

"Yeah, Mark. Be a good boy," he sneers.

I struggle, but she keeps hold.

"Shut up, Craig," she hisses.

"I'm only joshin'. Doesn't your new beau know how to take a joke?"

"Please. Go," she says quietly.

He looks at me, then at her, before stepping back with his hands held up.

"Okay. I can see you two are happy together. But, Mark–"

"*Mr. Flint,*" I growl through gritted teeth.

"Whatever. If you get bored of her, and I know I did, I know a few girls."

My blood boils violently through my veins. *Right, no more.* I grab his collar. She doesn't intervene this time. I throw a fast right hook, making contact with his jaw. He stumbles backwards then collapses onto the floor. He groans and clutches the left side of his reddening face.

"The lady. Told you. To go," I spit.

I shake the soreness out of my hand as I stand over the crumpled heap on the floor.

"He hit me! Arrest him!" he whines.

Shut it…

"He defended my honor if that counts."

He looks frantically back and forth between the two of us again with a stupid horrified look on his face, his pupils dilate and his jaw slacks, revealing blooded gums and teeth.

"You've changed. You're deluded," he directs to her.

"Yeah. You're right. I have changed. I'm not falling for your bullshit anymore. You're lucky I don't cuff *you* for stalking. Now get out, before I call security."

He struggles to his feet, blood streaming down his chin. He wipes it off with the back of his hand.

"You made a big mistake, buddy," he growls, eyeing me.

I watch him as he staggers down the hall and into an elevator. The doors close silently. *Finally. He's gone.*

"C'mon," I say, clutching her waist.

I steer her inside and shut the door.

"You didn't stop me that time," I say.

"He deserved it. He had plenty of warnings."

"Felt good. Are you okay?"

"Yeah. Just a shock seeing him again, after all the pain he caused me."

"Well, I thought I'd give him as good as he gave. You're not going to bring me in for assault?"

"No. Even if he reports it, I'll vouch for you."

"Thanks. Anyway, haven't we got ratatouille to eat?"

She looks over to the kitchen and back at me.

"Yep. Get comfy. I'll serve up."

I finish up the last of the ratatouille and sit back with a glass of white wine.

"That was great," I say.

She offers a weak smile and sips her wine. *Something's wrong.*

"Are you okay?" I ask.

"Why did he have to come back here? I made it clear to him the last time we saw each other that I didn't want him in my life anymore."

"He's a fool. Now he suddenly becomes desperate to win you back after two years apart?"

"Yeah. He was always late off the mark."

"Well, his loss is my gain. But hey, I got my opportunity to sock him. It was worth it."

She chuckles before she downs her wine.

"I bet it was. I was half tempted to do it myself."

"Well, he better not bother you further, for his sake. Now, maybe its best if we forget about that jerk?"

"Yeah, I think we should."

She gets up from her seat, walks over to me and perches on my lap. She strokes her fingers through my sideburns then kisses me.

"Thank you," she says.

"For what?"

"Protecting my honor."

I smile and run my hands down her hips.

"What are husbands for?"

She kisses me again and I return it as I move my hands up to her warm cheeks.

Me and Trent clock out after another long and tedious Monday. I collect my leather jacket from my locker just as he hands me my black biker helmet.

"I'll take you home," he says.

I slip on my leather jacket then we head down to the lobby where we pass Hannah along the way. She turns as we pass and offers us a quick wave.

"Have a good night, boys," she calls.

"You too," he says, smiling.

We push through the double doors and emerge out into the balmy heat. We dodge and weave through the heaving streets and round the corner that leads to the underground garage of the hotel. It's much cooler down here, and quieter, albeit the buzzing and flickering of the overhead lights and a few cars driving past. We arrive at his bike; he strokes the bodywork, then throws his leg over the saddle and grips the handlebars. I chuckle and place my hands on my hips.

"What?" he asks, slipping his helmet on.

"If I didn't know you better, I'd say you love that thing more than Louise."

He fastens the clasp round his chin, his blue eyes just visible through the visor.

"It's close," he laughs, his voice muffled.

He pats the seat behind him, I climb on and grip the bar behind me.

"You ready?" he calls.

"As I'll ever be."

He pulls up outside my apartment. I climb off and remove my helmet.

"Thanks for the ride, Trent. I was thinking, would you like to come up with me? Say 'hi' to Rachael? Maybe play some poker?"

He cocks his head to the side, then removes his own helmet.

"You know, I've never been able to beat her," he jokes.

I shrug.

"There's still time."

He smiles, then nods.

"Thanks, Mark. I'd love to."

"Great. Park down there, next to Rachael's car."

I point towards the entrance of the underground garage as he slips his helmet back on and drives into the garage.

I unlock the front door and we both step inside.

"Mark?" Rachael calls.

"Hi. Look who I've brought home."

She's sitting on the couch, legs crossed with her head buried into her Jane Austen book. She looks up at us, abandons the book and walks over quickly.

"Trent. Great to see you."

She hugs him, which he returns.

"Hey, where's mine?" I moan.

She giggles and hugs me too, then examines Trent's leathers as she pulls away.

"You know, I'm very anxious about you guys riding around on that thing," she says.

"Yeah, me too."

He frowns at me, and I hold my hand up.

"Don't worry. I'll keep him safe," he says, patting me hard on the back.

"I'm sure you will. Well, make yourself comfortable."

He walks into the lounge and sits on the couch, removing his leather biker boots and leather jacket. I head for the bedroom to put my old leather jacket back into the cardboard box. When I return, Trent is still seated on the couch, holding a can of lemonade. Rachael sits beside him, also with lemonade. I head into the kitchen and help myself to one before joining them both. She glances at me and kisses me deftly.

"Did you have a good day at work?" I ask.

"It was hot with all my gear on, but otherwise, same old. What about you two?"

She looks from me to Trent.

"Same old," we respond in unison.

She nods, then takes a sip of soda.

"Do you fancy a game of poker?" I ask Rachael.

Her eyes dart to mine and she grins widely.

"Still undefeated," she crows, crossing her arms.

"Yeah yeah. Our luck is due to change."

She sets her drink down, then stands and heads to the chest of drawers beside the TV. She opens a drawer and pulls out a deck of cards.

"Can it be strip poker this time?" he jokes, nudging me.

I roll my eyes and shove him.

"Not on your life," she laughs.

"I win again," Rachael crows.

Trent and I throw our cards onto the floor.

"Damn. How did you get so good?" he whines.

"Me and Dad used to play all the time. He's the one person I can't beat," she says.

He raises an eyebrow.

"Really? I need to ask him for some pointers," he says.

He looks down at his watch, then gets up from the floor.

"I'd better be going," he says as he collects his leathers and pulls them on.

He heads for the door, opens it, and turns to face us.

"It was nice spending time with you again."

"You too," she smiles.

He glances at me.

"See you tomorrow," he says.

"See ya."

He closes the front door behind him. I head back into the lounge and start clearing the cards from the floor. She sits on the couch and sighs.

"You alright?" I ask, glancing up at her.

She grins and nods. I place the deck of cards on the coffee table and stretch.

"I've got work early in the morning. Think I'll go to bed," I say.

She yawns and checks her watch.

"Me too."

Another week draws to a close and I look forward to the weekend. Both me and Rachael have been busy with work, but I'm looking forward to seeing her again this evening. Trent logs out of his computer as do I.

"Wanna go out for a drink?" he asks.

I stare at him. That does sound appealing, but at the same time, I want to see Rachael.

"Thanks, but I should be getting home," I say.

His smile fades. *Maybe just a quick one, Rachael will understand. She encourages me to spend time with Trent.*

"You know what? I'd love to," I say.

"Great. I'll invite Rex, he misses you," he smiles.

We head up to the staff room where I retrieve my cell and call Rachael. It rings for a few seconds, then her sweet voice comes through the phone.

"Mark."

"Hey. Just to let you know that I'm with Trent tonight."

"Thanks for letting me know. Don't drink too much this time."

I flush, remembering the last time I was with him. *I won't be repeating that.*

"I promise."

She's silent for a moment.

"Have a good time."

"Thank you."

We both hang on the line.

"You can go now, Mark."

"You first."

She giggles.

"Mark, hang up."

"I don't wanna."

"Do as you're told for once."

"It's not my style."

She laughs loudly.

"Goodnight, hon. Love you."

"Love you too."

Silence again.

"*Bye...*" she says in a sing-song voice and hangs up.

God. I love that woman. I pocket my phone and smile to myself before turning back to Trent. He grimaces at me, his nose crinkling.

"What?" I ask.

"Gross, man."

I scowl.

"You'll get used to it."

His forehead creases.

"*It's not my style,*" he says mockingly.

"Really? Because you and Louise seem to be doing just fine. I saw you on my birthday, canoodling in the corner all night," I say, shunting his shoulder.

"Coming from the guy who snuck upstairs and spent a few private moments with his wife."

I go beet red. *He's not going to let that go anytime soon.* I clear my throat and check my watch.

"Let's head to the bar," I say, opening the door.

The Stag's Head is loud and packed as always. Everyone is out enjoying their Friday evenings. Me, Trent, and Rex sit in a booth away from all the commotion.

"So, I would like you and Mark to be my best men at the wedding," Rex enthuses.

Trent beams and squeezes Rex's shoulder.

"Wow. I've been best man twice in a year. I'd be honored."

Rex smiles at him, then they both turn to me. I've never been to a wedding apart from my own. I don't know how to be a best man.

"Thanks, Rex, but I don't think I'd be very good at it."

They both groan, then Rex reaches across the table.

"Please."

It can't be that bad... Trent managed.

"Sure, thanks Rex. I'm sure Mr. Miyagi can show me some tricks," I say, peeking at Trent.

He flinches back, his brow furrowed, but he smirks.

"It's settled then," Rex says.

He leaps from his seat and hugs me hard. I pat him on the back until he finally releases me.

"Thank you," he beams.

"Anytime."

He takes his seat again and sips his orange juice, then he glances down at his watch.

"I wonder where Mitch has got to?" he says, looking around.

I find myself mirroring him, but then Rex is up again and rushing towards Mitch. Me and Trent watch as they hug. Trent rolls his eyes and continues with his drink. I laugh at him.

"What?" he says.

"How does Louise put up with you?"

He shrugs.

"It must be my good looks."

I place my fingers to my temple.

"Uh huh."

Rex and Mitch join us. Trent shimmies across to make some room.

"Sorry I'm late. Emergency at the hospital, and the traffic was *awful*," Mitch says before letting out an exaggerated breath.

"An emergency?" Rex gasps.

"Yeah. There was a drunken altercation. Two guys battered each other good."

"Will they be alright?"

"They'll live. Once I patched them up, the police took them in."

Trent huffs and rolls his eyes.

"People like that. They had it coming," he says.

I take another swig as Mitch turns to me.

"Oh, Mark. Hi again."

"Mitch. Congratulations on your engagement."

He smiles.

"Thank you."

"How's the planning coming along?" Trent asks.

"It's fun, isn't it, Rex?" Mitch says.

He nods.

"How's Rachael?" Mitch asks, staring back at me.

"She's busy, but she's well, thank you."

He smiles, then he and Rex turn their attention to Trent as they begin discussing suit fitting dates for the wedding. I continue with my drink as my mind drifts to Rachael. I hope she's keeping herself busy, but I do miss her. I check my watch; my eyes widen; it's nearing one a.m. *Shit! I didn't think I'd be out this late! Not again…*

"I'd better go," I say as I lurch from the table.

"What's the matter, bud?" Trent says, standing.

"I need to get home."

He checks the time, and his eyes bulge a little.

"Yeah. Totally lost track of time. I'd better be going too."

I shake Mitch and Rex's hands in turn, then Trent walks outside with me. It's cold and I wrap my jacket tightly around myself.

"You going to be okay?" he asks.

"Sure. Why not?"

He furrows his brow, his forehead creasing.

"Maybe you should get a cab home."

I'm about to insist that I'll be fine, but then I remember the last time I left the bar. *Right. Tobias…*

"Good idea." I concede.

He raises his hand. A cab screeches to a halt in front of us. I climb inside and give the driver my address. Trent leans against the open door.

"It was nice hanging witcha," he says.

"You too."

I smile and shut the door. *Rachael will be worried sick. Again…*

The apartment is dark and deserted. Maybe Rachael's in bed. I take my shoes off and pad to the bedroom. The bed's empty. *Where is she?* I'm shot back to my old, dank apartment when I was six. My parents' bed was empty that night, the apartment was cold and dark. The sound of my desperate cries ring in my head. I press my hands against my face and rub, then rake my fingers through my hair until I grasp the back of my neck. *Get outta there.* I flop my arms down to my sides and breathe, then switch the bedroom light on and sit on the edge of the bed. I pull my phone out of my pocket to call her. It goes straight through to answer phone. A lump forms in my throat. *What if Tobias got to her?* I swiftly call Steph, answer phone again. Maybe they're together? I tap out a quick text to her.

Honey. I'm so sorry I was home so late. I lost track of time. Please let me know you're safe. I'm so worried. Love you.
Xxxx.

I get undressed and climb into bed. I'm sure she'll be home soon. I lie awake and wait for the sound of the front door, but it doesn't come. I continue to wait, occasionally glancing at the alarm clock, but the apartment remains silent. I check the alarm once more; its nearing four in the morning. I sigh, then turn over in bed and drift to sleep; cold, alone, and afraid of what has become of Rachael.

I wake abruptly; 8 a.m. *Dammit. Late for work.* I hope to find Rachael curled up beside me, but her side of the bed remains vacant. I climb out of bed. My eyes are sore and heavy as I hurriedly get dressed and rush out of the empty apartment. I run most of the way, my mind swimming with thoughts of her, she hasn't responded to my call or my text. I need to know that she's okay. I'll phone the 17th precinct when I get to the hotel. I'm sure she's fine. I rush round the bend, dodging through the busy morning streets. The hotel is now in sight. I stop, there's two police cars parked outside, their red lights flashing. I approach slowly and peek through the glass doors of the hotel, the lobby is empty, albeit a few guests. I head inside to find Trent already seated at his desk, typing. He looks up and waves. I raise my hand in a half wave, but I'm so low. I'm scared for Rachael. I check my watch; 8:30 a.m. I don't have time to call now, I'm late enough as it is. I head to my desk and sit down.

"Hey, you alright?" he whispers.

I nod and quickly proceed to log in. Mr. Levitt steps out of an elevator and stands in front of my desk. He frowns down at me, his arms folded, his mouth set in a hard line and his brow furrowed.

"Sorry I'm late," I say.

I stare at Trent who looks from me to Mr. Levitt.

"It's my fault, sir. I kept Mark up late last night," Trent interjects.

Mr. Levitt rips his gaze from me and turns to look at him.

"Continue with your duties, Mr. Wilkinson."

He turns his stare back to me.

"Join me in my office, please."

I swallow hard, shakily get to my feet, and follow him into the waiting elevator. I ring my hands together and rake my fingers through my hair.

"Is something wrong, sir?" I ask.

He peeks across at me, then looks straight ahead at the shiny closed doors until the elevator jolts to a halt with a loud ping and the doors slide open. Mr. Levitt steps out and strides down the corridor, I trail after him, not daring to breathe another word. We enter his office. Rachael and Steph, dressed in their uniforms, are sitting inside. They both stand as we enter and look from me to Mr. Levitt.

My heart hammers in my chest and I slump my shoulders. *Thank goodness. She's okay.* I approach her, desperate to hold her and tell her how sorry I am, but she raises her hands and shakes her head subtly. I stop, frozen to the spot. *What's all this about?* I look around the room and gasp when I see the safe at the back of the room, open and empty, surrounded by police tape. My mouth falls open, I stare back at Mr. Levitt, who continues to frown deeply at me. I turn my gaze to Steph; she shakes her head and looks down at the carpeted floor. I look towards Rachael; her eyes are glazed. She sucks in her lips, sniffs, and stares down. *What's going on? Why am I here?*

"What's happened?" I whisper.

Steph steps forward, her thumbs hooked into her belt.

"I think it's very obvious what has happened, Mr. Flint."

I blink at her. Why is she referring to me like that? I look again at Rachael, but she keeps her eyes downcast.

"Mark Flint, you're under arrest for robbery," Steph continues.

I whip my gaze back at her, my eyes widening. My mouth is immediately dry, and I step back.

"What!?" I bellow.

"You have the right to remain silent," she says, unbuckling the cuffs from her belt.

I step away, my hands raised.

"I didn't do this."

She grabs me by the wrists. I twist and writhe frantically.

"Please. I didn't do it!" I shout.

"Mr. Flint. Don't resist," Steph demands.

"Wait!" Rachael shouts.

Everyone in the room stops and stares at her.

"Rachael-," Steph snaps.

She raises her hand and steps forward.

"He's my responsibility," she says, unstrapping her own cuffs.

She walks slowly towards me and slaps the cuffs on me without making eye contact.

"Rachael," I whisper, but she shakes her head.

"Rachael, please."

"You have the right to remain silent," she says quietly.

She shrugs out of her police jacket and drapes it over my cuffed hands. She grips my right upper arm then steers me out of Mr. Levitt's office and down the corridor. She keeps hold of me as Steph walks behind us.

"I didn't do this," I whisper again.

Rachael peeks at me, a lone tear runs down her cheek. She takes a deep breath, then stares straight ahead. We exit the elevator in the lobby and stride past Trent. He jumps up from his seat and dashes over. Steph stops and raises her hands, stopping him in his tracks.

"Mark, what's going on?" he shouts.

"Sir, stay where you are," Steph says.

I look back at him, his mouth is held open, his eyes bulge and he's panting. I'm taken outside into the heat and loaded into the back of Rachael's police car. She climbs into the driver's seat as Steph enters the passenger seat. I lean forward.

"I didn't do this," I attempt once more.

Rachael continues to face forward, but Steph turns in her seat.

"There'll be time for all that when we get there," Steph says.

I sit back. My stomach is doing somersaults and I think I'm going to be sick. I want to curl up into a tight ball and die. I haven't felt this low in months. I've been arrested for robbery... again. Only difference from last time, she's my wife now.

Chapter Twelve

We arrive at the Metropolitan Correctional Centre, a miserable, beige building with a black wired fence outside. Rachael remains silent and refuses to look at me. She parks up and climbs out, swiftly followed by Steph. Rachael walks round to the back passenger door and opens it. I climb out, but my knees are shaking. Rachael grabs my arm and begins leading me towards the entrance. I stop, dig my heels into the ground and stiffen my legs. Rachael tugs at my arm and stares at me, her eyes are still glazed, and her bottom lip trembles a little.

"Mark, come on. Don't make this harder than it already is," she whispers.

"But I didn't do anything! You know me!" I shout.

Rachael sucks in her lips and sniffs just as Steph approaches and grabs my other arm, yanking me hard.

"Come on," Steph barks.

I lower my head and allow them to steer me into the all too familiar surroundings.

I've once again been put through the grueling ordeal of being fingerprinted, photographed, and logged into the system. After I've changed into a hideous orange jumpsuit, a familiar guard starts walking down the hall towards us; He's middle-aged, balding, tall, and broad with a round fat face. Both his arms are plastered with tattoos, his muscular physique bulges through his tight blue uniform. The keys rattle against his hip. It's the head guard: 'Mr. Burly'. I groan and flop my head forward; his sarcasm is the last thing I need right now. He stands in front of me.

"Well, well. In trouble again," he sneers.

Rachael scowls at him.

"That's enough," she demands.

Mr. Burly's smile is wiped from his face which cheers me up a little, but then he takes my arm and proceeds to lead me to my cold, smelly jail cell. He opens the door and releases me. I walk inside then he slams the door shut and stomps down the corridor, his heavy footsteps radiating off the cold concrete walls. Rachael stands on the opposite side of the bars and stares in at me, her mouth turned down as all color drains from her face. I walk over and grip the bars.

"You know I didn't do this," I whisper.

Her eyes rim with tears once more then her hand covers mine. The first loving touch she's given me today. She slowly leans forward and rests her head against the solid metal. I lean in until our noses are almost touching. She blinks, her eyes start to go red, and a lone tear strays down her cheek. She tears her gaze from mine and stares at my platinum wedding band.

"Rachael, look at me."

She keeps her eyes downcast, and I can bear it no more. I move as close to her as the cold cell bars will let me.

"Please look at me."

Slowly, her hazel eyes meet mine.

"You know me. I promise you. I. Didn't. Do this. If you need proof, go and see Trent. He'll vouch for me."

She shakes her head once and a small sob escapes her mouth. She lets go of my hand, places her nose against mine and our lips touch deftly. She sobs once more as she breaks away.

"I'm so sorry, Mark," she whispers, then she rushes down the cold corridor and out of sight.

I watch after her as best I can until the loud metal door slams shut. She's gone. I rest my forehead against the cold metal. I can almost feel my heart rip in two, as a cold stab strikes me through the chest. I step away from the bars and slowly walk over to the heavily eroded concrete wall. I press my palms against my face and rake my fingers through my hair, then pound the wall with my fist. I lower my head and scrunch my eyes shut, hoping that when I open them again, I'll wake up from this nightmare.

Minutes turn to hours, hours turn to days, and still I've heard nothing about what's going on. I'm woken by a loud bang on the bars. I roll over on my hard mattress, Mr. Burly sneers at me. I roll my eyes and stand up.

"You have a visitor," he says, then walks away.

I walk to the bars and look down the corridor; it's Trent, looking in every direction. He stands outside my cell.

"Hey, bud," he whispers.

I reach through the bars; he looks at my hand then takes it and squeezes gently.

"I thought you could do with a friend," he continues.

"Has Rachael been to see you?" I ask.

"She has."

"What did you tell her?"

"The truth. That's all you need, right?" he half smiles.

"Then why am I still in here?"

"She said she had to check the CCTV in the bar where we were that night."

I groan and bang my head against the bars. He steps back.

"If I had just text her…"

"There's nothing you could've done to prevent this."

I stare at the wall, clenching my fists.

"I hate to see you like this," he says.

I look back at him.

"You've got to help me, Trent, please."

He steps closer and leans against the bars.

"I promise you, Mark. You will be free. Justice will prevail."

"How much longer am I going to be in here?"

"You need to ask Rachael that question, but I'll do anything I can to help."

Loud footsteps and a rattling of keys echoes off the concrete walls. We both glance up the corridor, Mr. Burly's coming back.

"Time's up," he orders.

Trent looks back at me one last time.

"You will be free," he insists, then he's led away, leaving me alone once more.

Mr. Burly returns moments later and opens my cell door with a loud creak.

"Time for your exercise," he says in a strangely friendly voice. Rachael must have scared him.

"Must I?"

He steps forward and produces a pair of cuffs.

"I'll take that as a 'yes'," I say.

He snaps them round my wrists and leads me out. We follow the small procession of other prisoners that are also being collected and we're all marched to the large cage.

I sit as far away from the other prisoners as I can, some of them occasionally stare at me, unsettling me further. I look around the perimeter of the cage, there are guards keeping watch, but that does nothing to soothe my dark troubled soul. *Why didn't Rachael let me explain? Why did she bring me back here? I thought she was on my side.* Tobias' words that he spoke not so long ago come flooding back. *'You're already living a life of lies. You really think that police officer wife really cares about you? You're lying to yourself.'* I don't believe it; she didn't do this to hurt me. I'm snapped out of my thoughts by two tattooed men walking towards me; one is tall and slim with long, greasy blonde hair, and a scar on his right hand; the other is short and rat-faced with a receding hairline and several missing teeth. I stand from the bench and attempt to walk away but they corner me and sneer down their noses.

"I think I recognize this one," one sneers to the other.

"Mark Flint, right?"

"Yeah, who are you?"

One cackles. I look down at their tattoos, both have red carnations on their left wrists. *Tobias' boys.*

"*Zzzap!*" he mocks, lunging his hand close to my neck.

I step back and place my hand to my neck.

"You kidnapped me for Tobias."

He smiles grotesquely and spreads his arms out, his stale breath making me need to wretch.

"You're a smart one," blonde greaseball says.

"Well, that makes one of us."

"*Ooh...* Fiery little bastard ain't ya'? You're nothing like how the boss spoke about you."

"Sorry to disappoint."

"Yet here you are, again."

I clench my fists.

"And why are *you* still here? You think Tobias *really* cares about you? I was with him for a long time, and he betrayed me. He'll throw the two of you under the bus as well and forget about it twice as fast."

Their eyes bulge. Greaseball throws a punch at me, I jump back and counter him with a strike of my own, pounding him in the gut. He doubles over and gasps, clenching his stomach. The other wraps his arms round me, pinning my arms to my sides. I charge backwards, slamming him into the fence, then kick back. He releases me, grunts, and coils up on the floor, his hands gripping his crotch.

Greaseball kicks my legs out from under me and I fall hard on my back. He grabs the collar of my jumpsuit, pulling me up slightly, then punches me across the face and stomps on my stomach, making me rasp for air. The cage door opens, and the guards tackle the greaseball off me. He wriggles and grunts against their hold while two other guards pull the rat-faced thug away who continues to mewl. They're both led out of the cage. The pain finally registers, it lances through my head and torso. Another guard appears in my periphery; Mr. Burly. I struggle up to my feet as he grips my arm. I wince.

"You need first aid," he says, leading me out of the cage and taking me back to my cell.

He lowers me onto my bed and stares down at me.

"Stay where you are."

"Where else will I go?"

His lips thin as he stands up straight and heads for the door.

"I'm going to get the first aid kit," he says, locking the door behind him.

I shakily get to my feet and, while gripping my stomach, stumble towards the cracked mirror that rests over the grimy sink. I'm a mess, I have a black eye, and my nose and mouth drip with blood. I wipe my nose with the back of my hand and sit back down. Mr. Burly arrives with a first aid kit. He kneels in front of me and takes out a couple of antiseptic wipes. He proceeds to dab at me gently making me wince some more.

"Do you see why I hate exercise time, now?" I growl.

He looks up but continues with his task.

"All prisoners are required to have exercise time," he explains, still dabbing at my bloody face.

"Even if this happens?" I say, pointing to my face.

"You threw the first punch."

"No, he tried to punch me first. I dodged and defended myself."

He sighs then closes the first aid box and stands up.

"Get some rest," he says then shuts my cell door and walks away.

I lie on my cold hard mattress with a small piece of fabric to cover me. I lie awake for hours, listening to the cockroaches scurrying around and drips of water from the leaking corroding pipes overhead. My mind drifts back to Rachael. The love of my life. My wife. *The woman that's arrested you twice now.* Why couldn't she have looked further into the looted safe before assuming it was me? She knows me better than that. Maybe she's looking into it now. Is she thinking about me? I roll onto my side as my exhaustion takes over.

I sit bolt upright, light streams into my cell through the small filthy window above me. My back and neck stiffen as I slowly get up. I rub my neck and sit on the edge of my bed. I glance towards my cell door and jump. Rachael stares at me through the bars, dressed in white jeans and a pale blue camisole. I rub my eyes. *Am I dreaming?* I stare back slowly, she still stands before me, but she's so pale, the rosy glow of her cheeks is no longer there. Her hazel eyes are red rimmed, and her nose is slightly pink. She has dark circles under her eyes and her hair is barely held in place by a hair tie. I get to my feet. She smiles slightly, but then gasps.

"What happened to your face?" she rasps.

"I was beaten up. What does it look like?"

She flinches.

"I just thought you'd like to know how the investigation is going."

I lean in closer.

"What have you got?"

"I went to the bar; I checked the CCTV. You were seen there at the time of the robbery. I've interviewed Trent, Rex and Mitch. All their stories matched, and they heavily vouched for you. I spoke to the cab firm, one of the drivers recalls picking you up. All this evidence has been handed over to the judge. You'll be out of here by dinnertime."

My mouth falls open and I grip the bars.

"You mean it?"

She nods and strokes my fingers.

"Be ready. I'll be back later," she says, then she turns on her heel and leaves.

I stare down the empty corridor, feeling happier than I have been these last couple of days. I'm out of here… today. All the same, I can't help feeling betrayed by her. This jail time was unnecessary, and I can't understand why she didn't let me explain right away. I sit on my bed and try to think of a reason, but I have nothing. I'll endeavor to ask her when she comes to collect me.

Hours have passed since she came to see me, and I'm still stuck in here. I walk over to the window and look out at the city. The sun starts to fade into the horizon as footsteps click down the corridor. I turn round to face the door, Rachael and Mr. Burly appear. He unlocks the door, and it creaks open. She's wearing a red, long sleeved checkered shirt, light denim jeans and white chucks. Her hair is tied loosely and is swept over her left shoulder. Her cheeks have regained color and her eyes are less red rimmed, now clear, and bright. Mr. Burly's thumbs are hooked into his belt loops as he glances towards her. She smiles, steps forward and holds out her hand to me.

"Mark, you're free," she says.

I stare, frozen to the spot.

"C'mon," she says.

I place my hand slowly into hers. She grins and squeezes my fingers slightly, then we exit the cell, past Mr. Burly and past the other prisoners who wolf whistle at Rachael.

"Hey! Flint! I'll be seeing you real soon, and so will the boss!" the blonde greaseball shouts.

"That's a nice piece of ass you got there, Flint! When the boss is through with ya', maybe he'll have a little fun with her. Hell, he might let us take turns," another shouts.

I whip my head to them, scowling. Mr. Burly slams his baton against the bars, producing a loud ring.

"Shut up in there! The lot of ya'!" he demands.

She tugs at my arm, and we continue walking down the long concrete corridor, through the heavy metal door and past the front desk where we stop. She points to a small room on the right.

"Get changed in there. I'll wait here."

She releases my hand and steps back as I head inside, desperate to rid myself of this awful orange jumpsuit. I reemerge a few minutes later, dressed in my work suit that I was arrested in. We exit the M.C.C. and step out into the cool New York air. I stop and inhale deeply, ridding my lungs of the foul stench of mold and stale standing water. A light breeze blows through my hair, I close my eyes and absorb all the senses. It's still a little warm from the past couple of days but I don't care, I'm free. I walk alongside her, desperate to get home and sleep in my own bed with my beautiful wife, but my gut twists and I'm hit with a wave of nausea, my sense of betrayal comes into full force. *How could she do this to me?*

"Taking me to another police car?" I hiss.

"No police car," she says as we round the building.

She presses her key fob and her white Mercedes flashes to life. She climbs into the driver's side as I sink into the heated leather seat on the passenger side. She starts the engine and pulls out into traffic.

We sit in silence throughout most of the journey, the radio is on, cutting through the quiet but I'm not listening to it. I can't control the hurt that I continue to be haunted by. Rachael pulls into the underground garage of our apartment and pulls into her designated space. She cuts the engine and faces me. I look away from her and quickly climb out of the car. She follows and rushes round to my side.

"You okay? You're very quiet," she says, taking my hand.

I look at her delicate fingers wrapped round mine. I draw my hand away. She stares at me.

"Mark, I'm sorry," she whispers.

I sigh loudly and walk towards the elevators.

"Please talk to me," she says.

I turn to face her.

"Why didn't you let me explain when you arrested me?" I ask.

She blinks and gapes.

"We have to follow the information we're given at the time. Your DNA was found on the scene."

I furrow my brows.

"My DNA?"

"Your hair and fingerprints."

"That's impossible."

"It's what was found."

How did someone get my hair and prints? I rest my hand on my head and twist my mouth. *Tobias.* He's the only man that has reason to hurt me. Him, or his men, they must've taken some when I was abducted. I'm suddenly hit with rage; I turn to look at her as she continues to stare at me.

"You knew I was taken by Tobias. Couldn't you have figured out that maybe he took my DNA?" I shout.

She gasps and tries to approach me, but I step out of her reach.

"You were caught on CCTV at the safe," she says, her voice rising.

"Well, it obviously wasn't me, I was at the bar. I told you I was spending time with Trent," I bellow, my whole body shaking.

"I worked hard to get you out of there, Mark," she whispers.

"Well, why did I have to be in there at all!?"

I glare at her, panting heavily.

"Do you even care about me?" I ask.

She steps back, a large 'v' forms between her brows and her mouth drops.

"I didn't sleep the whole time you were in there. I stayed at work, even when my superiors ordered me to go home. I wanted you out of there. I knew you were innocent. We just needed the evidence to prove it. Doesn't that show you how much I care about you? How much I love you!?" she shouts.

I throw my hand up in the air, groan and stomp off towards the ramp that leads to the street. Frantic footsteps echo behind me.

"Where are you going?" she calls.

I keep walking, hang my head, and jam my hands into my pockets. She grabs my shoulders and stares into my eyes.

"Where are you going?" she repeats.

I brush her hands off and look down at my feet again.

"I need some air," I say, then turn and walk away from her.

I fight every urge to look back as I walk farther from our apartment. I stop and look over my shoulder, she's not following. I can't face her when she's angry. *That's because you made her angry, you idiot.* I sigh, then continue down the street with no real destination. *Where am I going? Why am I here? What am I good for?* I'm free again, and I'm more bitter than the last time I was freed. *What do I do?* An idea pops. *Trent. I need a friend to talk to.*

Chapter Thirteen

———

I buzz Trent's intercom and wait. The clouds loom dark and heavy above, reflecting my bleak mood. The wind is colder now, and whips round me. I pull my jacket tighter around myself and buzz again, longer this time. He still doesn't answer, I huff and begin to walk away but his voice comes through the intercom.

"Yeah, who's this?"

"Trent. It's me."

He's silent, then the front door buzzes open. I push through quickly and fly up the stairs. By the time I get to the top, he's waiting for me. I rush over and hug him hard. He pats me gently, then pushes me away.

"What's up?" he says softly.

"I don't know."

He frowns and gestures me towards the couch. I walk inside and sit down. He retreats into the kitchen and returns with a couple of bottles of Bud Light. He hands one to me and I take a large swig. He sits beside me.

"What happened to your eye?" he asks.

"I had a fight in jail."

He gasps.

"Does Rachael know about this?"

I nod and take another sip.

"Where is Rachael?" he asks.

I shrug.

"At home, I guess."

He furrows his brow and leans in closer.

"Why aren't you there with her?"

"I had a fight with her as well."

He sits back in his seat.

"What? You mean you-"

I scowl at him.

"No! Why would you think-"

He raises his hands.

"Okay, okay. Sorry."

I puff and flop back against the cushions, then I scrunch my eyes shut and place my hand over them.

"What did you fight about?"

I release my hand and stare at him with a 'what-do-you-think' expression.

"She arrested me, Trent."

He nods.

"Y'know, she came to me after you were arrested. She was beside herself," he says.

"And how do you think I felt?"

He grunts and rests his hand behind his head.

"Look, I know it can't have been easy for you, Mark, but Rachael had no choice, she explained everything," he says.

I glance back down at my bottle; the wet condensation runs down my thumb.

"Do you still love her?" he asks.

I peek at him.

"I think so."

His mouth falls open.

"You *think* so?"

I put the bottle on the table and play with my hands.

"Mark, how can you say that?"

"She arrested me. How do I know she won't do it again?"

"She loves you. She didn't want to do it. Couldn't you tell?"

The vivid images form: she marched me down the corridor of the Neapolitan as a tear rolled down her cheek, the tender embrace she gave me after I was locked up, the sweet delicate kiss. It hits me hard in the face. She was torn up. It was clear to see.

"I want to believe it," I say.

"So, why don't you?"

"I dunno. Maybe a criminal marrying a cop was a bad idea. Maybe Tobias was right, she doesn't care, I'm lying to myself."

He scowls and slaps me across the face. I scurry to the opposite side of the couch.

"What the hell!?" I say, raising my hand to my heated cheek.

"Look, I know you're mad at her, you have every right to be, but don't throw your marriage away for this psycho who's out to destroy you. You're letting him win," he says.

I stare at him, my cheek still throbbing.

"Fine, but was the slap necessary?"

He shrugs.

"It was the only way to make you see sense."

Still hurt though.

"What do I do, Trent?"

"That's up to you, but I'll ask again. Do you still love her?"

I roll my eyes to the side and think about all the fun times we've had together; our first date at Storico; her slipping on the ice rink and pulling me down with her; teaching me to cook; arranging the surprise for my birthday; falling into the Unisphere, and our first kiss. I smile and look back at him.

"Yeah, I do. I love her so much. More than anyone will ever know. She's my world."

He smiles and pats my knee.

"That's what I thought. You wouldn't have chased her as hard as you did if you didn't care. Now, go home and tell her."

I stand, abandoning my half full bottle and march to the door, but then stop.

"I don't know if I can."

He flops back.

"Ah, Jesus Christ. Why not?"

"I was so horrid to her."

He stands and places his hands on my shoulders.

"Tell her you're sorry, tell her what you just told me, then… give her time, that's all you can do."

I nod, then open the door swiftly. I glance back at him once more.

"Thank you," I say.

He smiles, then waves me out.

"Go home to your wife."

I rush out the building and stumble onto the street. I raise my hand to hail a cab. It stops and I climb in.

"Where to?" the driver says, turning in his seat.

I hurriedly give him my address; he nods and pulls away. I sit back and wait to see Rachael again. It's time to right my wrongs.

The cab nears my apartment, but we're stuck in gridlock traffic. I tap my seat and check my watch frequently. I huff and sit back, trying to distract myself with how I intend to apologize to her. The traffic creeps forward every few minutes. *I'm not waiting a second longer.* I open the cab door and jump out. The driver turns in his seat, his eyebrows raised as I quickly palm him fifteen dollars.

"Keep the change."

I sprint home as fast as I can. My feet pound the sidewalk as my lungs tighten to the point of bursting, but I ignore the pain seeping into my legs and chest as I pick up the pace, weaving the crowds and dodging traffic. I'm sweating profusely, my shirt sticks uncomfortably to my skin. I wipe my forehead but keep going. I'm growing more desperate by the second and fearing that my earlier outburst may have driven her away. I'm a couple of blocks from home now and my shirt is soaked through, but finally, after the most agonizing run I've ever been on, I make it to our apartment block. Tom rushes forward and opens the door for me.

"Thanks, Tom," I wheeze, resting my hands on my knees as I rasp for breath.

"Evening. Been for a run?" he greets.

"You could say that."

He frowns slightly and eyes my suit.

"Odd gear for exercise if you don't mind me saying."

I offer a half smile, take off my jacket and lean against the dark paneled wall.

"I don't want to probe but is everything okay?" he continues.

I stare at him.

"Of course."

He squints an eye. I shake my head and scoff.

"Nope. I messed up."

He steps a little closer.

"I'm a good listener if you want to talk."

"I've been in a lot of trouble, Tom. Me and Rachael fell out, I said some things that I wish I didn't."

He nods and places his hand on my shoulder.

"You know, Mark. I've been married for nearly fifteen years. Marianne drives me mad on her best days, but I love her to bits."

"Fifteen years? I hope me and Rachael can make that."

He laughs.

"I believe you will. Marriage isn't without its challenges, but it certainly has its rewards."

"How do you make it work?"

He removes his hat and wipes his forehead.

"Know when you've made a mistake. Say you're sorry, show each other that you love each other. Simple really."

"Thanks, Tom."

He nods and I rush over to the waiting elevator. It rides up painfully slowly; tenth floor, twelfth floor. *Come on.* I stab at number fifteen repeatedly in a vain attempt to speed it up, but it finally arrives on our floor with a loud ping. I rush down the corridor and stop outside our door. My gut knots tightly. I hope she'll forgive me. I comb my fingers through my hair, then hover my hand over the doorknob, take a breath and step inside as quietly as I can manage. I place my jacket on the hook, close the door and take off my shoes. She emerges in the doorway, dressed in her nightgown. She leans against the door arch. Her eyes are narrowed and hooded, and her lips form a thin line.

"Where've you been?" she grumbles, folding her arms.

I walk up to her, desperate to hold her, but she backs away. I drop my hand, deflated but not defeated.

"How about a glass of wine?" I offer.

She stares for a moment, then finally, the corner of her mouth lifts.

"I could do with some wine."

I head into the kitchen and take out a bottle of white from the fridge, pour us both a generous amount, then rejoin her in the lounge. I sit beside her, hand her a glass and she instantly takes a swig.

"What I said was wrong. I shouldn't have lashed out at you like that. It wasn't your fault; you were only doing your job. I'm sorry," I start.

She sits back against the cushions.

"You know, it was the hardest thing I've ever had to do since becoming a cop. I arrested my own husband. How do you think that made me feel?"

"You were just doing your job."

"I never wanted my job to include that."

"I understand that, and I don't blame you."

She taps her index finger against her plump bottom lip.

"Obviously you do. You were mad at me."

"I was… and it was wrong, but I had some sense slapped into me by Trent."

"I was going to ask you what was wrong with your face."

I rub my cheek. *Is it that bad?*

"We spoke. He put everything into perspective. It was unacceptable how I acted. I'm sorry. I'm crazy about you, Rachael. I don't want to lose you."

She puts her wine down on the table, then leans into me and kisses me on the lips. I return it with my own passion, desperately missing her touch. She breaks away and stares deep into my soul.

"You're not going to lose me. I love you. You're stuck with me… till death do us part, remember?" she whispers.

"Till death do us part."

I link my fingers through hers, then lean in and kiss her again. She pulls away and gets to her feet.

"I've had a stressful day, I'm going to bed," she says.

"I'll stay up for a while."

She frowns then heads towards the bedroom.

"Good night, Mark," she says.

"Night."

The bedroom door closes. I flop my head back and stare up at the smoke alarm on the ceiling, it blinks intermittently. I groan and place my hands over my eyes while thoughts nag and swirl in my mind. *Tobias won't stop. He's trying to ruin me... in every way.* I slowly remove my hands from my face and sigh. *I must stop him. I don't know how, but I'll find a way.*

The morning traffic report wakes me. I quickly slam it off, hoping that it doesn't disturb Rachael. I roll over to face her and I'm greeted by her bright hazel eyes.

"Morning. Sleep well?" she asks.

"Not bad. You?"

She nods and props herself up on her elbow.

"Good thanks."

She sits up in bed and glances at the alarm on the nightstand; 8:48 a.m. She throws the duvet aside and climbs out, she grabs her uniform from the closet and proceeds to get dressed. I watch for a moment then also climb out of bed, retrieve my crumpled suit from the floor and start to get ready for work but then a thought hits me. *Do I still have a job?* I was arrested for robbing the place.

"Do I still work at the Neapolitan?" I ask.

She swings round, her cap in her hands.

"Have you spoken to Mr. Levitt?" she asks.

"I haven't had time."

She arches a brow then walks out of the bedroom, leaving me alone. I don't know if I could ever go back there, even though I didn't rob the place, I'm ashamed and embarrassed. Mr. Levitt's angry expression as I was cuffed comes back to mind. I shake my head and follow after her. She's sitting cross legged, half-dressed on the couch, speaking on her cell.

"This afternoon? That's fine. See you later."

She pockets her phone and looks at me. I cock my head to one side.

"I just spoke to Mr. Levitt. He was reluctant to let you back into the hotel but has agreed on a meeting."

"Oh, when?"

"This afternoon."

I suck in my lips and lower my head. Her soft footsteps approach me then she places her hand gently on my face.

"What's wrong?" she asks.

"I appreciate your help, but I can't go back in there."

"Why?"

I walk towards the window and stare out to the street below which is already full of life.

"I shamed myself."

She places her hand on my shoulder, but I don't face her.

"You have nothing to be ashamed of, you're innocent."

I peek over my shoulder.

"I'm sorry I did this to you," she continues.

I turn and place my hand against her cheek.

"I don't blame you."

She steps away and exhales gently.

"I'd better get ready for work," she says, then walks back into the bedroom.

Rachael left for work an hour ago without much of a goodbye. I sit in the silent apartment and think. She clearly feels bad for the arrest, she was only doing her job, but I still struggle to understand why she wouldn't talk to me on the way to the prison. I kept insisting to her that I didn't do it, but she wouldn't listen. I shake my head of these thoughts, it's not her fault, it's Tobias'. That murdering psychopath isn't going to stop until he ruins my life or I'm dead, whichever comes first. I stand from the couch and walk around the lounge, my hands on my head. My thoughts continue to taunt and nag. I try to call Trent, but he doesn't answer, he must be at work. I rush into the bedroom and quickly get changed out of my nightwear and into my jogging gear, I need to go out for a run to burn off my excess energy. I leave the apartment as fast as I can and rush to the elevators. I punch the call button and wait. A loud ping announces its arrival, I bolt inside and press for the underground garage, I'm not much in the mood for conversation this morning, so I choose to avoid Tom. I arrive at the underground garage and proceed to walk up the ramp that leads to the street. I make a sharp left and head in the direction of Central Park. I stroll through the packed streets, dodging the pedestrians pushing and bumping their way past each other, but as I near Central Park, the crowds thin out. I stand by the wall of the East entrance and begin my warmup exercises, then after one more deep breath, I head into the park and begin my run.

The sun beats down on my head. I'm rejuvenated, but at the same time, this heat is unbearable. I ignore the discomfort as I sprint past Ramble Rustic Bridges, over Bow Bridge and past Bethesda Fountain. My thoughts continue to nag. Tobias is relentless. I run harder, trying desperately to run from my demons, my feet slap the concrete, but the dark storm clouds continue to loom in my mind. I stop to catch my breath and sit on a nearby bench. I take a sip of cool water then splash my face with it. *What is it this man wants with me? Why me? Was it because I wanted out? Anyone who leaves Tobias' crew eventually winds up dead. Maybe he's pissed that I'm still breathing.* I place my head in my hands and pull at my hair. What if it isn't me he wants? What if he's really after Rachael? After all, he hates the police, and she's been after him for some time. I'm taken back to the day Colin was shot; Sara's words come back to haunt me; *'Rachael could be next.'* He failed once before, but he won't give up. She must be next. I try to think of a way to stop her from getting hurt, but my cell vibrates in my pocket, halting my thoughts. I take it out of my pocket and check the number: Rachael.

"How's work going?" I ask.

She puffs out.

"Manic. It's all systems go here. Listen, I forgot to tell you. Can you be at the hotel by one?"

I check my watch; two hours to go.

"No problem."

"Good, see you later," she says, then she's gone.

She continues to sound distant; I don't know what I can do to get us back on track. I'm missing her happy, care-free side, but at the same time, I feel miserable too. The stress of the situation is getting us both down and if we're not careful, it could tear us apart.

I arrive back home, hot, sweaty, and out of breath. I slip out of my sticky grey tank top and sweatpants then head into the shower. I turn on the faucet, cold water splashes down onto my shoulders, I hang my head and watch beads of water drip down my fringe. I place one hand on the tiled wall and stand still, not bothering to wash myself. I feel so low. In an hour, I have to face Mr. Levitt again. What am I going to say to him? I raise my face to the streaming water. I want to cleanse myself and hope it makes me feel better. I turn the temperature up and wash myself, trying not to dwell on my meeting. I need to focus my energy on what I can do to get me and Rachael back on track. Tom's words come back to me. *'Marriage isn't without its challenges. Know when you've made a mistake. Say you're sorry, show each other that you love each other. Simple really'*. I crack my first smile of the day and switch off the shower. Grabbing a towel from the rail, I wrap it round myself. I won't lose her over this misunderstanding. We'll talk tonight and work this out. My happy, care-free Rachael will return. I head into the bedroom with a new goal and proceed to get dressed into my suit, ready for my meeting with Mr. Levitt. I can do this.

I stand outside the hotel and check my watch; 12:55 p.m. I take a deep breath and as confidently as I can, stride through the double doors and into the polished marble lobby. Trent sits at his desk, he looks up and raises his hand, offering me a small wave. I return it quickly, then head for the elevators and ride up to Mr. Levitt's office. As I walk down the hall towards the staff access door, I remember that I don't have a pass. I arrive at the door, it's ajar. I head inside, then stand outside Mr. Levitt's office. Rachael and Mr. Levitt are talking, but I can't make out what they're saying. I take another deep breath, my gut knotting tightly as I knock. The voices cease.

"Come in," Mr. Levitt booms.

I open the door and step inside. Rachael sits by the desk, still in her uniform. Mr. Levitt is sat at his desk, wearing a dark suit. They both stare at me when I enter, Mr. Levitt removes his specs and places them onto the table in front of him.

"Take a seat, Mark," he says.

I sit beside Rachael, who glances briefly in my direction before squaring her shoulders and turning her attention to Mr. Levitt. I attempt to do the same, I sit up straight and give my full attention to him as he glares at me from across the table.

"Now, Sergeant. What can I help you with?" he starts, glancing at her.

She clears her throat.

"I would like you to consider giving Mark his job back."

He raises his eyebrows.

"I can't do that."

I clasp my hands together and stare down at my shoes. This is worse than I thought it'd be.

"Can I ask why?"

"I trusted Mark once. He ruined that trust."

"How?"

He clears his throat and sits back in his seat.

"He's a criminal."

She blinks at him once.

"But you knew that when you hired him. Mark was only let out of prison when you took him on."

"I did, but I never thought that he'd steal from me."

"Sir, please, I didn't do it," I say.

She raises her hand at me, then glances back at him.

"Mark was found innocent. He was framed," she says.

"Framed? By whom?" he asks.

She takes her police cap off and rubs her forehead.

"I can't go into too much detail as it's an ongoing police investigation. All I can do is assure you that he was not the culprit or involved in any way. At the time of the robbery, he was in a bar with friends."

He blinks a few times before diverting his gaze at me.

"Mark, anything you wish to add?" he asks.

"Rachael covered everything, sir. I was in a bar with Trent and Rex. I didn't commit the crime."

He places his specs back on and rubs his head.

"Thank you, Mark. I would like to speak to Rachael alone for a minute if I may?"

I look at her, she smiles and nods. I get to my feet and make for the door in double quick time. I open it, but then stop.

"Thank you for your time," I direct to Mr. Levitt.

He stares at me for a moment, then smiles.

"Good seeing you again," he says then proceeds to wave me out.

I leave the room and lean against the wall. I sink to the floor and rest my palm on my forehead.

"So, how'd it go?" Trent says.

I look up slowly. He smiles down at me. I get to my feet and brush myself off.

"I dunno."

He stares at the closed door.

"Is Rachael still in there?"

I nod. He pats me on the back.

"You'll be okay. She'll get you back here," he says.

"Do you believe that I didn't do it?"

He laughs.

"Well, unless you can be in two places at once. I know for a fact you didn't."

I smile at him, then the door opens, and she steps out.

"Thanks for your time," she calls, then exits.

She looks at me and Trent.

"You'll know soon," she says.

He smiles at us.

"Speak to you later," he says.

He walks down the corridor towards the staff room.

"Let's go," she says, taking my hand and heading for the elevator.

"What did he really say?" I ask.

She presses the call button then peeks at me through her dark lashes.

"I'll talk to you about it when I get home."

"What are you doing now?"

She looks down at her uniform.

"I'm still on duty, I'll be home by seven."

We step into the elevator and ride down to the lobby.

"Why can't you tell me now?"

"It's a long story. It'll be better if we do it at home with a glass of wine."

"But you told Mr. Levitt."

"Just trust me on this. I promise, we'll talk tonight. I'll tell you everything."

We arrive in the lobby. I take her hand and stride across the marble floor and out the double doors into the balmy heat.

"I'll see you later," she says.

"'Kay."

I turn and head towards a street crossing.

"Mark," she calls.

I look back at her. She walks up to me and kisses me on the cheek.

"Get home safe," she whispers.

She turns on her heel and walks in the opposite direction. I stare after her until she disappears into the crowd, then I turn and make my way home.

I head into our apartment and shut the door behind me. I stand in the hallway and feel utterly numb. The eerie silence unsettles me further. I walk slowly into the bedroom and stare at my reflection in the mirror. I barely recognize the miserable, blue eyed, scruffy haired man staring back at me. I turn away, suddenly awash with anger. I take my jacket and tie off and carelessly throw them into the closet, then I remove my shoes and throw them across the room with a loud clatter. I sit on the edge of the bed, my mind thankfully quiet for now. I lie down and drape an arm over my eyes, wanting this nightmare of a day to come to an end.

The front door slams shut, startling me awake. *How long was I out?* I prop myself up on my elbows and check the alarm; 7:45 p.m.

"Mark?" Rachael calls.

I slide off the bed and get to my feet.

"Mark," she calls again.

I head out of the bedroom and lean against the door frame. She sags when she spots me.

"There you are. Are you okay?"

I flop onto the couch.

"Yeah."

She sits down beside me and stares.

"No," I say.

"Yeah, I had a feeling. You've been off all day."

"I don't know what's happening to me, Rachael. I don't recognize myself anymore."

Her mouth drops open, then she snuggles up close.

"Ah, c'mon, it can't be as bleak as that."

"It is, Rachael. I don't know who I am."

She sits up and strokes my face with her thumb.

"I'll tell you who you are; you're Mark Flint and I love you."

"Do you?"

Her mouth drops open again and she flinches.

"Course I do. I thought we resolved this last night."

"Then what aren't you telling me?"

She swallows, then clears her throat.

"During your brief prison stint, another robbery took place… at the bank, next door to the 17th precinct. They got away after a short shootout with us. Thankfully, no one was hurt. However, when we analyzed the crime scene, we found traces of your hair and prints, just like at the hotel."

I squint my eyes and sit up straight. *This doesn't make any sense.*

"More of my DNA?"

Her mouth turns down and she nods once.

"Yeah. Doesn't make any sense. You were in prison."

"Yes. I remember…"

"None of us could understand. Why would they do that?"

I think hard. This isn't Tobias' M.O. So why? Then an idea pops.

"He's doing it to humiliate the police. And me. He's sending a message, the police can't protect me, he runs this city, or he's deluded enough to believe anyway."

"That's crazy."

"He digs crazy."

She titters.

"He sure does."

"So, does Mr. Levitt know?"

"He does. We've been tracing three armored trucks around the city, each loaded with stacks of cash. We believe one belongs to Tobias."

"Why?"

"One was reported stolen shortly before the hotel heist. I'm sorry, I should have told you."

"Then why didn't you?"

She rubs her philtrum.

"I didn't want you to worry."

"It could have saved both of us a lot of hurt, Rachael. You know I'm always happy to help you if I can."

"I know that and I'm sorry. No more secrets from now on."

I sit back.

"So, anything else I should know?" I ask.

"I mentioned that we're tracing the trucks. One of the drivers was arrested and questioned. It was confirmed by the security company that he's one of theirs, it's clean."

"One down, two to go."

"Yep. Everyone at the precinct is monitoring the other two. Checking traffic cams, tracking their movements, y'know. With any luck, we'll pin Tobias with this one."

"Good. Good."

"Anyway. I bought you something else for your birthday."

I blink at her.

"What? Another one? Honey, I love the two presents you got me already."

"I know, but after everything that's happened recently, I think this is the best time to use it."

"Use what?"

She gets up from the couch.

"Wait here," she says and disappears into the bedroom.

I watch after her but dare not move. I listen carefully; a squeak of a drawer opening, followed by rustling. She returns, carrying a piece of paper. She hands it to me. I look at the folded paper, then back at her.

"What's this?"

"Open it."

I unfold it and read what it says, it's a hotel reservation for somewhere that I've never heard of.

"Bear Mountain?" I ask.

She grins and takes the paper from me.

"It's upstate from here. I thought it would be nice to get away, just you and me."

"What has this got to do with Mr. Levitt?" I ask.

"I told him about the trip. He said that you need a break to get away from the stress, return to New York with a fresh mind, then he'll consider taking you back."

I smile. Does this mean that she's got my job back?

"When do we do this?" I ask, pointing at the paper.

"This weekend. We leave on Friday. Return on Sunday."

"How do we get there, fly?"

She laughs.

"It's only upstate. I'll drive."

"I'd love to. Thank you."

She leans down and kisses me.

Chapter Fourteen

~~

"Wake up," Rachael whispers, nipping at my earlobe.

"Mmm," I grumble, and pull the sheets around myself.

"Get. Up."

I crack one eye open and peek at the alarm: 3 a.m. I scrunch my eye shut and pull the duvet tighter.

"C'mon, Mark. We need to pack."

"It's not Friday yet."

"Um. Yeah, it is."

"Um. No, it's not."

"Check your phone."

I flop my arm out of bed and feel around the nightstand for my phone. I pick it up and unlock the screen. The bright light dazzles me as I squint and groan at the date displayed. I drop the phone on the mattress. *Oh fuck. It is.*

"Believe me now?" she asks, crossing her arms.

I flop back down and cover my face with the duvet.

"Why didn't we pack last night?" I groan.

She laughs.

"Well, I was going to, but you kinda distracted me; that's on you, buster."

I groan again and wave her away, but she pulls the duvet from the bed, leaving me exposed.

"Hey," I complain, covering my modesty.

She chuckles.

"I've seen it all before. Come on, get up, get dressed."

She smiles, then leaves the room. I get out of bed and switch on the bedside lamp. I squint in the light and rub my eyes, then grab my robe off the back of the door and head into the lounge. She's in the kitchen, kneeling on the tiled floor and rooting in the fridge.

"I can't eat now, it's too early," I say.

She peeks over the fridge door, then gets to her feet.

"As you wish."

She kicks the fridge door closed.

"Let's start packing," she continues.

She squeezes past me, her hip brushes my waist, making me suck down a breath. She opens a door in the hallway and pulls out our suitcase. Laying it down on the hard floor, she unzips it.

"I've never been to Bear Mountain before. What do we pack?" I ask.

"Well, remember your bachelor party? Hiking gear would be good."

"Oh yeah, right."

She giggles.

"It's a mountain, clue's in the name."

I snigger and the backs of my ears heat.

"Obviously."

We kneel on the floor together and sort through the clothes that we've chosen; several shirts, pants, swimwear and of course, hiking boots. She stands up, walks back into the hall, and opens another door. I watch from afar and admire her perfect back curve as she roots noisily inside.

"What are you looking for?" I call, getting to my feet.

She reemerges holding two long sticks. I look at them, then back at her.

"What are they?" I ask.

"Hiking sticks. We'll need them…trust me."

I watch as she unsnaps them so that they fold in half, and she lays them in the case on top of our clothes.

"I think we're done," she says.

I zip it up and carry it to the front door, then we head into the bedroom to get changed into something comfortable. I opt for a cream knit sweater that Alison got me for Christmas with black jeans and black chucks. Rachael's donned in tight denim jeans with a mint green camisole, matching cardigan, and white chucks.

"Ready?" she asks.

"Ready."

Rachael turns right and merges onto the 9A. She presses on the gas, and I'm thrown back into my seat. The streets are almost deserted albeit a few trucks and cars that whip past us. A hint of sunlight bleeds into the horizon, turning the sky beautiful shades of deep orange and hews of pearly pink. The Hudson River ripples and catches the colors of sunrise on our left. It's just past five in the morning and the heat already bores into me. I blow my floppy hair and remove my sweater, but it does nothing to cool me down. She glances across.

"You hot?" she asks.

"A little."

A ghost of a smile plays on her lips, she reaches across and turns on the AC. The icy chill washes over me and soothes my heated skin.

"Thanks."

She smiles across, her beautiful hazel eyes shining. I yawn and sit back in my seat. The sound system comes to life and the crooning smooth voice of Frank Sinatra fills the car. She hums along sweetly. My eyes become heavy, and I drift… Just for a minute.

"Mark."

I open my eyes and glance across. Rachael has her eyes fixed on the road ahead.

"We're nearly there," she says.

I sit up in my seat, rub my eyes and look out the window. The surroundings are unrecognizable. Pine trees whip past us, the roads are still empty and quiet. We're surrounded by lush greenery and clear blue cloudless skies.

"How much further?" I ask.

"About five minutes."

The mountains emerge in the distance and different types of trees continue to shoot by.

"It's beautiful, isn't it?" she says.

I peek over at her and smile.

"Quite stunning."

She reaches across and squeezes my knee then places her hand back on the steering wheel and looks straight ahead.

"I hope you can ride a bike," she says.

Bike ride? Wow, I haven't done that in years.

"I can't," I moaned, pointing down at my scraped knees.

Grandma smiled, bent down, and kissed me deftly on each knee.

"Nothing a Band-Aid can't fix."

She placed one on each knee then stood up, picked my bike up and patted the saddle.

"One more time," she whispered.

I climbed on gingerly and started to pedal. She ran behind me, gripping the saddle.

"That's it, Mark. You're doing it. Pedal," she called, then she released.

The bike wobbled and shook, but I held firm and pumped my legs hard. The bike levelled out and I was riding smoothly.

"You're doing it," Grandma shouted.

I pedaled in a circle round her.

"I'm doing it," I shrieked with all my seven-year-old glee.

Rachael pulls into a parking space outside our home for the next two days. I get out of the car and breathe in the aroma of fresh pine. She stands by my side as I admire the hotel; it's an early twentieth century building, built out of cobble stone with balconies at the windows and a dark tiled roof. A light pinkish path leads to the main entrance, surrounded by an array of plants and rocks. I take in the name of the place, The Bear Mt. Inn. I laugh to myself.

"What?" she says.

"I like how they named this place. Clever."

She chuckles slightly and stares at the building with me.

"I used to come here a lot."

"Really? With the family?"

She looks at me.

"Yeah. Dad's a keen fisherman. This is one of his all-time favorite places to fish."

"I didn't know that about your dad."

"There's a lot you don't yet know about Dad. He'll continue to surprise you."

I clear my throat and go back to the car to collect our luggage.

"Leave that for now. It's way too early for check in," she says, checking her watch.

"So, what now?"

"I thought we'd go for a walk, then come back here and get some breakfast."

"Sounds good."

She outstretches her hand. I link my fingers through hers, then follow her lead. *She knows this place better than me.* We arrive at the bank of a giant lake and what looks like a picnic area under several trees that provide some much needed shade. We release each other, sit on a bench, and look out over the lake. The birds sing and flit overhead, a slight breeze whistles through the leaves causing them to rustle and sway gently. The water splashes as fish emerge on the surface of the calm, still water, and waves of little bubbles form as ducks bob gently.

"I haven't been here in years. It's great to be back," she says.

"We should come back next year, bring your parents with us."

She rests her head against my shoulder.

"I'd like that."

I kiss her on the head and stroke locks of hair through my fingers as we both look out across the lake. The stress of everything that has gone on this past week melts away into nothing and is replaced with my love for this woman and the peace and tranquility of this slice of heaven.

We're seated at a small table in the corner of Hiker's Café and are handed our menus. Rachael scans what's on offer while I observe the interior. Like the exterior, the walls are made from cobbled stone, there's a large fireplace with two stag heads above it, lanterns hang from wooden beams on the ceiling, and the tables are each draped with a crisp white tablecloth. I pick up my own menu and look through the options. A young male waiter arrives, his eyes are fixed firmly on Rachael. *Seriously?* I narrow my eyes.

"Are you ready to order?" he asks, producing an all-tooth grin at her.

"Yes, I think so," she says, placing her menu flat on the table in front of her.

"Mark?" she gestures at me.

The waiter turns his attention to me.

"You go first," I say.

"I'll have the blueberry pancakes and a coffee please."

The waiter scrawls on his notepad, then looks at me again.

"Eggs Benedict please." *With a side of 'stop ogling my wife'.*

"Anything to drink?" the waiter asks.

"Coffee please."

He finishes scribbling our order then collects the menus and tucks them under his arm.

"We'll get right on it," he says.

He gawks at her once more, his eyes staying on her for too long before finally scurrying away. I scoff.

"What?" she asks.

"I think he has the hots for you."

Her eyes narrow.

"Who?"

I gesture with my head at the waiter who is now taking orders from other customers seated nearby.

"No he doesn't."

"I saw how he was looking at you."

"Well, that's too bad. I'm yours."

She flashes her wedding and engagement rings at me. Multiple angelic hews of light are reflected off them from the sun outside the window. They're a sacred talisman that proclaims her as my one and only.

"Anyway, amazing here, isn't it?" she smiles.

"It's beautiful."

I observe our surroundings once more. She leans across the table and takes my hand in hers. Her rings glimmer further, emitting small rainbows on the walls and tables around us.

"Are you happy?" she asks.

"Of course."

She sits back in her seat and picks at her fingernails.

"Why do you ask?"

She peeks up through her lashes and offers a weak smile.

"After everything that's happened, I…"

I get out of my seat, walk round to her side of the table, and kneel in front of her.

"Is this about the arrest?" I ask.

She nods slowly.

"I don't blame you… I promise."

I get back to my feet and sit down.

"What brought this on?" I ask.

She shrugs.

"I haven't been able to stop thinking about it since it happened."

I stroke her hand deftly with my thumb.

"I love you. I'm sorry for everything I said, okay?"

She smiles, then raises my hand to her lips and kisses my wedding band. Her talisman to show that I'm hers.

"Through the good times and the bad. I will love you deep with all my heart, till death do us part." I recite the end of my wedding vows, desperate to convince her.

Her pupils dilate and the corner of her mouth lifts.

"I will love you unconditionally, upholding your goals and dreams, and bring you solace in times of need. I will cherish you and keep you safe by my side until death do us part."

I melt internally, my heart filling with love, warmth, and adoration I have for this woman, followed by a swift, painful knot in the gut. I was so horrid to her, the things I said when I was released, I wish I could take it all back. None of that matters now, I just have to make up for my actions.

"Wife of mine. I love you," I whisper, outstretching my hand across the table.

She looks down at it and covers mine with hers.

"Husband of mine. Back at ya."

We laugh together over breakfast. I feel euphoric and the food is incredible. All thoughts of what's gone on back in New York City recently is now buried. Tobias looms in the back of my mind, but that's where he'll be staying. He will not spoil the happiness that me and Rachael are sharing. We finish up, and she stands to collect the check. I stand with her and grab her arm.

"I've got this," I say.

"You sure?"

"Of course."

She sits back down as I summon the waiter.

We're not due to check in till this afternoon, so we leave the lodge and step out into the warming weather. The sun has now risen fully and beams high above us. Rachael takes my hand and breathes in deeply.

"Now what?" she asks.

"Show me around?"

"Sure. There're so many things to do here."

She leads me back to the car and releases my hand. *Not what I was expecting.* I put my hand on my hip and squint. She opens the trunk, then looks over her shoulder and chortles.

"What's that look for?" she asks.

"Nothin,"

She rummages through our luggage and pulls out the hiking sticks.

"We'll need these."

"Hiking? Already?"

She strolls back towards me and thrusts one at me.

"Sure. That's what being here is all about."

She leads me towards one of the hiking trails. The park is starting to fill up now, it's almost as busy as Midtown Manhattan. As we walk deeper into the woods, I catch a glimpse of one of the hiking trail signs and blink. *Two miles?*

"I don't think I'll manage two miles," I say.

She looks at the sign.

"It's not that bad when you get started, trust me."

I bear my weight against my stick.

"Then let's go."

We've been hiking for over half an hour and I'm beginning to wheeze as we stride uphill. I stop and lean against my stick, panting. Rachael continues to stride ahead, showing no sign of slowing down for a break.

"Hey, wait up," I call, staggering after her.

She stops, digs her stick into the ground and looks back at me.

"You alright?"

"I just need a moment."

She walks back to me, removes the rucksack from her back and opens it. She pulls out a bottle of Gatorade and offers it to me. I look at the bottle and turn my nose up. *Never been a fan of the stuff.*

"Have you got any water?" I ask.

She furrows her brow, then looks in her bag again and pulls out a water bottle. I take it from her as she takes the Gatorade for herself.

"You're welcome…" she says, eying me.

"Thank you," I scoff.

She shakes her head before taking a sip as I admire the scenery. We're surrounded by beautiful woodland, and a trickling stream gushes from a small spring on my left. Other hikers stride past, talking and laughing amongst themselves.

"Where does the trail lead?" I ask.

"If you walk far enough, you can get to the top of the mountain. The view up there is breathtaking."

"I bet it's stunning at sunset."

"Much better at sunrise."

I take a slug from my water and stare at all the different trees that surround us until some movement catches my eye in the shrubbery ahead. A small gray dog walks out of the shrubs and sniffs the ground.

"Has someone lost a dog?" I ask.

She grabs my arm and leans in close.

"It's a coyote." she whispers.

I stare and blink, now recognizing the thin canine. My hairs stand to attention and prick the back of my neck.

"We should get out of here," I whisper, grabbing her hand.

She shakes her head and eyes the coyote.

"No need to be afraid. Coyotes rarely come into contact with people. He's no threat to us."

The coyote moves farther away from us and disappears back into the shrubs. I exhale and look back at her. She cracks a smile and laughs.

"What's funny?" I ask.

"You looked terrified."

"I wasn't scared."

She shoulders me.

"Sure, you weren't. Let's keep moving."

She pulls her stick back out of the dirt as I do the same and we continue to follow the keen crowds up the hiking trail.

We make it to the top at last. I'm completely out of breath but Rachael looks completely unaffected. I spot a bench and make a beeline for it, eager to rest my sore legs and feet. She stays where she is and stares out at the view. She turns and waves me over.

"Come and look at this," she calls.

I groan, get to my feet, and stand by her side. The wind blows her silky mahogany mane into her face, she combs it behind her ears and points at the view. I peek out slowly, terrified of heights, but am awe-struck when I catch sight of it. It's a clear day and there's miles of landscape spread out before us. The whole world at our feet. What looks like New York City or New Jersey is in the far distance, the Hudson River flows ahead of us, and an old iron railway bridge is on our left. I gasp at the splendor. I never knew the world could look this beautiful. She takes out her camera and snaps a few photos.

"Thank you for bringing me here," I say while staring out.

From the periphery of my vision, she lowers the camera and looks at me. She rests her head against my shoulder and stares out.

"I've always wanted to bring someone special here," she breathes.

I peek down at her.

"Did you never bring…"

Crap. Damn brain-to-mouth filter.

"…Craig?"

I purse my lips.

"Sorry."

She rests her chin against my shoulder so that she's looking at me.

"I never wanted to. I didn't know why at the time… now I do, I was waiting for you."

I beam down at her and press my lips to her forehead.

"I just wish I found you sooner," she continues.

I stroke her face with my thumb.

"Me too."

She smiles and glances down at her watch.

"We should head back, check-in's soon."

She turns to make her leave, but I grab her arm and pull out my cell.

"Wait. One for the album."

She grins and links her arm round my waist. I hold the phone aloft and snap the photo.

We take the stairs up to our room. I carry the luggage as Rachael rushes up to the third floor. She stops outside our door.

"C'mon, Mark," she calls.

"I'm coming."

I place the bag on the floor and stretch my sore back as she unlocks the door and pushes it open. I'm about to grab the case and take it inside, but she grabs it first.

"I'll take this," she smiles.

We head inside, then I close the door behind us. It's an immaculate room with cream walls and a beige carpet. The room is dominated by an impressive king-sized bed with a dark wood headboard and dark bedside cabinets to match, in the corner stands a couple of leather armchairs. She drops the luggage onto one of the chairs and flops backwards onto the bed. I titter. She props herself up on her elbows and arches a brow.

"Join me?"

I remove my shirt. She stares and licks her lower lip slowly. Without taking my eyes off her, I remove my shoes and socks. She giggles.

"I don't know what you're planning, Mark, but I like it."

She begins pulling off her own shoes and socks followed swiftly by her shirt and pants, then she sinks back down onto the bed, only in her cream panties and bra. I drink in her fantastic perfect figure.

"Now what?" she asks.

I jump onto the bed beside her. She pushes me down so that I'm flat on my back, then she straddles me just above my pelvis. I stare up at her as her bright hazel eyes glimmer down at me, and her long hair curtains her face.

"Now what?" I say.

She places her finger on my lips.

"Just stay still and shut up," she whispers huskily.

My heart picks up a few beats. *I love this side of her.* She leans down and kisses me deeply.

Chapter Fifteen

⌐∾⌐

O ur breathing slows as Rachael lays her head on
my bare chest, her warm breath heating my skin.
Her arm is draped over my waist, her forefinger
caresses my happy trail, and she glides her leg up and down
mine, stroking through my leg hair. I drape one arm round
her back, swirling locks of her hair round my fingers while
my other arm rests under my head.

"What were you thinking?" she asks suddenly.

I stare down at her, but she remains still.

"When?" I ask.

"Downstairs, in the lobby when we were checking in,
you seemed… distracted."

I roll onto my side, facing her. I've tried to keep thoughts
of Tobias at bay, but he continues to seep into my mind,
unwelcome and unbidden.

"Mark?"

"It's nothing important."

She wraps her arm round my shoulder and plants a tender kiss on my chest.

"It doesn't sound like 'nothing important'. Talk to me. What's bothering you?"

"I can't. I don't want to spoil our weekend."

"Is it Tobias? Is *he* bothering you?"

I sigh and close my eyes. I won't escape this.

"I'm scared of what he'll do next."

She cocks her head to one side and props herself up.

"What are you scared of?"

"I'm scared he'll target you. If he hurts you because of me, I couldn't live with it."

She blinks, then strokes her fingers through my sideburns.

"He isn't going to hurt me, I promise you."

"How do you know?"

"We're ready for him. Please don't worry, he won't do anything to me, I won't let him."

"You're sure?"

"I promise," she whispers.

I lean forward and kiss her softly on the cheek.

"Now. What say we get up, get dressed and enjoy the rest of our vacation?" she says.

"I'd like that very much."

We stroll hand in hand past the lake, then she chuckles and shakes her head.

"What's funny?" I ask.

"I remember when I first came here. I was only about nine at the time. Dad would get up early every morning and stand right here," she stops and points at the embankment.

"One time, Mom moaned at him; 'Can't you spend more time with your family?' just as Dad netted a huge catfish. I've never seen anything so big. He showed it off proudly to us all with the biggest grin. He thrust it at me, there's a photo of it somewhere."

I laugh.

"I never pictured him like that. I'd love to see the photo."

"I'll show you sometime. C'mon, lots more to see."

The park is packed with young families and couples. We stop at a large carousel; she stares at it and bites at her thumbnail. I watch it go round as kids and adults alike ride on various wooden animals, laughing loudly. Others stand around watching, waving, and taking photos.

"I used to love going on this," she says, her eyes lighting up.

I look back at the carousel as it begins to slow, and everyone dismounts.

"Would you like to go on?" I ask.

She whips her face to mine. Her smile could light up a room.

"Will you come with me?"

I look back at it, then back at her.

"I've never been on one before."

Her mouth falls open.

"Never?"

I shake my head.

"Nope."

She purses her lips briefly, but then grabs my hand and pulls me towards it. She immediately mounts one of the horses and pats the one next to her. I stare for a moment. *I'm a little too old for this.*

"This'll be fun," she gushes.

I open my mouth to protest but then laugh and let my childish side come to life. I step forward and clumsily climb onto the horse next to hers. She smiles then grips onto the golden bar in front of her as the carousel starts to move and the music plays. I wobble and nearly fall backwards but I reach out and grab the bar in front of me. She throws her head back with laughter, her mahogany hair flowing behind her.

"Hold on, Mark."

I grip on tighter and am overcome with a childish delight that I haven't felt in a long time.

"Isn't this fun?" she shouts over the music.

I grin and nod at her.

"I can't believe I didn't do this sooner," I call back.

She beams an all-tooth grin as we continue our ride. This is so much fun. I can't understand why I never got to experience this with Grandma. I shake my head, not wanting anymore dark thoughts today and like Rachael, I enjoy the rest of the ride as we laugh together with childish mirth.

Rachael throws her leg over the saddle and dismounts gracefully. I attempt to follow, but my foot clips the horse's neck, I stumble and fall flat on my face. She gasps, grabs my arm and helps me to my feet.

"You alright?" she asks.

I nod, rubbing my face then burst into laughter. Her mouth presses into a firm flat line but slowly, her lips twitch and we're both in hysterics.

"You don't have much luck with horses, do you?" she says.

I cock my head to the side.

"What do you…" *Oh. The honeymoon.*

"Oh yeah. Maybe I'll leave them to you."

"Good plan."

After a quick dinner at Restaurant 1915, we return to our room. Rachael kicks off her shoes and lies on the bed. She rests both hands behind her head and closes her eyes. I shrug out of my leather jacket, drape it on the back of the nearby chair and stare out the window. It's nearing eight in the evening and dusk begins to fall; hews of pink, turquoise and orange stain the sky, and a soft gail blows through the leaves on the trees. She wraps her arms round my chest and stares out over my shoulder. We watch together until the sun sinks into the horizon. I turn in her arms and kiss her.

"I've had an amazing day."

She grins.

"It's not over yet. You up for more exploring tomorrow?"

"With you, Mrs. Flint, absolutely."

She pulls her flowery sundress over her head and makes for the restroom.

"I'm going to take a shower," she says.

My mouth dries as her hips sway from side to side and her hair bounces against her shoulders and back. The door clicks behind her. I sit on the edge of the bed and try to calm, but my blood runs hot and heavy through my veins making every hair follicle on my body stand to attention. I rub my face and switch on the TV to calm my frantic heart. The gush of running water resonates from the bathroom. I switch off the TV, jump off the bed and creep towards the door. I open it as quietly as I can and peek inside. She has her face raised to the stream of water; her eyes closed. The warm moist air makes my shirt cling to my skin, the mirror has already started to steam up as condensation comes to rest on it. The steam gradually obscures her figure, denying me. Beads of sweat form all over my body. I strip out of my clothes in double quick time and rush forward to join her. I open the sliding door slowly and climb in. Her head is still tipped back, beads of water trickle down her face and shoulders; her hair clings to her back with the tips resting against the dip of her spine. She stretches out her arm and feels around the nearby shelf, knocking a few things off.

"Shit," she mutters, bending down.

I snatch the shampoo up from the shower tray and press it into her hand. She freezes, her eyebrows scrunch, forming a 'v', then her eyes snap open.

"Mark!" she gasps.

"Sorry. I didn't mean to startle you."

She smirks, grabs the body wash and wash cloth, then thrusts them at me.

"Seeing as you're here, would you scrub my back?"

I take the body wash and cloth from her.

"Turn around."

She turns her back to me. I squirt some soap onto the cloth, press it against her back and massage in small circles, up to her shoulders, forming a lather. She groans as the hot water cloaks us, and the sudds trickle down her body. My heart rivals the speed of a Formula One engine as I lower my hands and the cloth to her buttocks. Her knees buckle slightly as she murmurs further. *That's it. No more waiting.* I grab her and spin her round to face me. She blinks and gasps, then I thrust my lips against hers. The heated frenzied breath from her nostrils warms my philtrum as she grips the back of my head, snaking her fingers through my hair and tickling the backs of my ears. I push her up against the tiled wall and with my eyes firmly glued to hers, I close the space between us and make us one all over again. She lets out a garbled cry which I absorb with my mouth as I kiss her fiercely. She scratches her fingernails down the length of my back causing me to pick up speed. She raises her left leg and wraps it round my waist. We're an entanglement of limbs, mouths, tongues, and breaths. Sweat beads and rolls down my forehead, the heat of the water becomes overpowering. Every muscle in my body tightens and one final thrust becomes my undoing.

She grabs two soft towels from the nearby radiator and wraps one round herself before wrapping her hair in another. I step out beside her and look her up and down. *God. Even after sex, I can't get enough of her.* She smirks and throws a towel at me. It lands on my head blocking her from my sight. She chuckles as I pull it down and wrap it round my waist.

"That was a nice surprise," she says.

"Glad I could give you that."

She smiles and retreats from the bathroom. Beads of water run down my body. I dry myself off, then check myself in the mirror. Christ, my hair is getting long again and it's a mess. I comb my fingers through it in a vain attempt to make it look more presentable. A loud whir emits from the bedroom, I open the door and exit the bathroom. She's draped in her silk nightgown and is sitting cross legged at the small desk with a hairdryer and comb. I lean against the door frame and watch as she brushes her silky mahogany hair back into place. Our eyes meet in the mirror, and she grins.

"Get dressed," she admonishes.

I look down at myself then walk to the case and pull out a clean pair of underpants. I slip them on quickly then climb into bed, covering myself with the duvet and waiting impatiently for her. She turns off the dryer and flicks her hair behind her, so it falls down her back in luscious waves. She climbs into bed herself and switches off the bedside lamp. We lie down together, my head sinking into the plush pillow. She sighs into the darkness as her arm drapes over my naked torso, and her soft even breaths radiate my chest. I glance down, her lashes are fanned out against her cheek, her lips slightly parted. She's asleep. I smile and plant a delicate kiss on the top of her head. She murmurs then pulls the duvet tighter around herself. I snuggle up against her and am soon in a deep peaceful sleep of my own.

We stop off at a small café and each grab a croissant. We stroll arm in arm back to the fishing lake where we stop and sit on a bench. I eat my pastry and take a sip of coffee as I watch the fishermen.

"The reflection of the trees in the water, it's like a mirror," she says.

I stare with her. The trees and shrubs on the other side of the lake are reflected on the surface, it's so clear and calm. The image in the water gently bobs and ripples, like a soft sheet being blown in the breeze.

"It's beautiful. I can see why your folks brought you here."

She grins, then gets to her feet and outstretches her hand. I take it and stand so that we're nose to nose. Her lips are so close to mine and her warm breath washes over me. I close my eyes and inhale her sweet aroma until she pulls away and I open my eyes.

"The zoo will be opening soon. Wanna go?" she asks.

"I didn't know there was a zoo here."

"Well, there is. That way."

She flicks her head to the right, towards a nearby pathway.

"That'll be fun."

We walk round all the different enclosures. Beavers swim around behind the glass, some splash in the water while others pat down piles of logs with their thick tails. Children squeal, scream and laugh while the parents try fruitlessly to keep them quiet. Several owls stare at us from the aviary as we walk past, their bright orange eyes regarding us closely. *Unsettling in its own way.* We get to the bald eagle. Rachael stops and looks through the mesh fence.

"Such a majestic creature. Makes you proud to be American."

I look at the massive black and white bird with bright yellow feet and razor sharp talons.

"It's amazing, but you wouldn't want to be its dinner," I joke.

She giggles.

"Nah, you're right."

We follow the bustling crowd towards the bear enclosure. Two large bears lie on rocks; one appears to be sleeping; the other yawns, stretching its jaws wide and rolling its long, pink tongue out. They're huge, bigger than I expected.

"Black bear," she says, reading the information sign.

I bend over next to her and glance at the sign.

"They mostly prey on insects. Well, that's a relief," I say.

We carry on to the reptile house. It's hot and humid, compared to the cool breeze outdoors that usually takes the edge off during this time of year. We look at various breeds of turtles and lizards, but I'm fascinated by the snakes. One lies still on a rock, basking under the red heat lamp. It stares through the glass at me, occasionally flicking its tongue. I look over my shoulder, Rachael stares through the glass of a nearby enclosure.

"Hey, Rachael, check it out, it's Tobias," I call.

She spins round, her eyes widening.

"Where?" she says, glancing around.

I point at the glass. She peeks in, bursts into a fit of laughter and clutches her hand to her chest.

"You had me there," she exhales.

"Well, he's a bit of a reptile, isn't he?"

She looks at the snake again.

"At least this fella's cute… and probably less slippery."

I laugh loudly as other people stare at us, some shake their heads and furrow their brows. I raise my hand, by way of apology.

"Sorry, guys."

She links her arm through mine as we walk on.

It's early afternoon, the sun beats down and the intense heat begins to kick in. We sit in a small café, eating cheese sandwiches and drinking cool glasses of lemonade. I glance out the window at the hiking trails stretched out before us.

"You know, Mark, I was thinking, we don't really know a lot about each other."

"Mmm?" I murmur, ripping my gaze from the view.

I link my fingers together and rest them on the table. *What can I tell her that I haven't already?*

"You know me better than anyone."

She strokes her chin, then leans across the table.

"I only know snippets of your life in Chicago," she says.

I look down at my fingernails and clear my throat. A chair scrapes against the hard floor, making me glance up. She walks round and perches on my lap. I grip onto her slender waist and stare up at her.

"I'm sorry. You don't need to tell me if it makes you uncomfortable," she says.

I lick my lower lip.

"No, it's okay. What do you want to know?"

"You met Trent in high school. Any other friends?"

"No, he was the only one. I was a loner, kept to myself mainly before he came along."

"Favorite subject?"

"I didn't really like school, always got myself into trouble, but I loved playing ice hockey. I found it helped with my anger."

"Your anger?"

I nod as all the fights I got myself into flash through my mind.

"I got into a lot of fights. Grandma was called to the school more times than I care to admit."

"But Trent protected you? You told me once."

"I got into fights before Trent came into my life. I got beaten up, went to see the nurse, then stumbled into the boys' restroom. Trent was there, styling his hair."

She laughs.

"His hair's always been like that?"

I snigger.

"I could never picture him without it. Anyway, at first, I thought he was going to have a pop at me too. I stayed away as best I could, but he spoke to me in a kindly way, gave me a wad of tissue for my blooded-up nose and introduced himself. The bully came back for more, but Trent scared him away and protected me from then on. We helped each other, it was only him and his mom; his dad passed away a long time ago. After he moved, everything changed."

"You were apart for a long time, huh?"

"Thirteen years give or take. I didn't last very long at high school after he left."

"Where's Trent now, huh?" Charlie shouted as I laid on the ground next to the lockers.

I wiped blood from my nose with the back of my hand.

"No one loves ya', Markie. Who you gonna cry to, eh?"

I slowly lifted my head to Charlie's piggish face. He cackled, his beady eyes squinted, and his wide nostrils flared. He swung his foot at me and made firm contact with my chin.

"You're my little bitch ain't ya', Markie 'No-Parents'?"

He continued to chortle. Fury bubbled up inside, ready to boil over. I slowly stood up as he laughed harder. My temper couldn't manage anymore. I grabbed him by the scruff of his shirt, screamed, then lifted him off his feet and swung him hard against the lockers with a loud bang. His small eyes widened as he gripped onto my wrists. Without thought, I pounded his face with my right fist. He howled as I threw another punch, then another, and another, showing no restraint. I pulled him away from the lockers and slammed him back against it. He continued screaming, but I didn't care. I continued pummeling him as blood poured from his nose and mouth, and lacerations formed on his checks.

"MR. FLINT! LET HIM GO!" The principal yelled.

I froze, still holding Charlie and slowly turned around at the school principal. Multiple teachers and students surrounded us; some of them open-mouthed and others laughed. I dropped him to the floor. The teachers stood between me and Charlie who continued whimpering.

"My office. Now," the principal said.

I shook my head and slowly stepped back.

"Mark…" he said.

I turned on my heel and bolted down the corridor.

"Mark!" he yelled.

"Yeah! That's it! Run! Run away from your problems! Like you always do!" Charlie yelled.

I panted as I ran, tears rolled down my face as I stormed out through the doors, down the stone steps and across the field.

Night began to fall before I finally returned home. Grandma was in the lounge, pacing and talking frantically on the phone.

"No, I don't know where he is," she said.

I slammed the front door closed and hurled my school bag into the closet with a loud bang. Grandma gaped at me before turning her attention back to the phone.

"Never mind. He's here."

She hung up and barreled towards me.

"There you are, I was so worried. Where have you been?" she said.

I huffed and skirted round her, but she followed, stood in front of me and cupped my face in both hands, her warm eyes crinkled at the corners.

"Mark, where were you? What happened to your face? Has that boy been beating you up again?"

I gently prized her hands from my face and slumped onto the couch.

"They told me what happened. I know he's been giving you grief, but that's no way to act. I'll take you back there tomorrow and sort this out."

"I'm not going back," I grumbled.

"Mark, you need to go back," she said, sinking beside me.

I shot my head to hers.

"I'm not going back! I don't care what anyone says!" I shouted.

She sighed and placed her arm round my shoulders.

"I miss Trent, Grandma." I stuttered as I placed my head in my bloodied hands.

"Listen, I know things have been difficult without him. Maybe we can pay him a visit. I'll call Alison."

I raised my head up and looked at her. She smiled.

"I'd like that."

"Okay. Now, about going back to high school, maybe sleep on it?"

"No. My mind's made up."

Her smile faded.

"We'll talk more about it in the morning. In the meantime, we should pay a visit to the emergency room, get your face fixed up."

Rachael exhales.

"Wow. She sounded like a lovely woman. Took great care of you," she says.

I sniff.

"Yeah. You'd have loved her. She'd have loved you to bits too. She was really patient with me. Helped me get a part-time job after I pulled out of high school.

"What happened to that Charlie character?"

I snigger.

"Dunno'. Don't care. He's not my problem anymore. I felt like a coward though."

She furrows her brow.

"Why?"

"I ran away; didn't face my punishment. And when I was reeled into Tobias' crew, I didn't get out soon enough because I was too scared of what he'd do to me. I didn't stop Tobias from killing Adam because I was too scared."

"You are not a coward. You're the bravest man I've ever met."

"C'mon. That's not true."

"It is. You could've ran from us when we came to arrest you that day, but you faced justice for the greater good; you gave us vital information about Tobias when you could've kept it zipped; you alerted us when Tobias broke into Trent's apartment, allowing us to save him and put Tobias behind bars; and even when he broke out and held us hostage, you took a bullet for Steph when Curtis took a shot at her; you stopped Tobias from shooting me and nearly died by doing so. None of that qualifies you as a coward, not even close."

"Good to know someone has faith in me."

"We all do. You've saved so many lives. That's who you are. That's what you're capable of."

I smile and interlock my fingers with hers.

"Thank you," I say.

"Of course. Can I ask you about your grandma? Would that be alright?"

"What do you want to know?"

"What happened to her... in the end?"

Tears sting the backs of my eyes, but I sniff.

"She had problems with her heart for years. She had a cardiac arrest."

"Where were you?"

"I was with her. I called the ambulance, but it was too late… She died in my arms. She had a lot of debt leading up to her death, so the house was repossessed. I was taken to a homeless shelter, stayed for a few days but left. I was afraid and wound up on the streets. Enter Tobias."

She wraps her arms tightly around me.

"Thank you for telling me."

I sniff again but manage a smile.

"My turn."

She sits back in her seat and clasps her hands together.

"Have you always been a vegetarian?" I ask.

"No."

I stroke my chin.

"What changed?"

"After Dad caught that catfish I told you about earlier, he kept it. Mom gutted it that night and served it for dinner. I couldn't bring myself to eat it. After that, I thought about the cruelty that animals must face; it put me off."

"Fair enough," I say, straightening my jacket.

"Were you a good girl at school?"

She chuckles.

"I was what you call a 'teacher's pet', 'book worm', et cetera."

"So, you were never in trouble?"

She smirks and I arch a brow.

"Were you?"

"I got myself into trouble when I was sixteen."

"Really?"

I lean forward, resting my elbows against the table.

"I was grounded for staying out late with friends too much, so Dad wouldn't let me go to the movies with them. I was furious and stormed up to my room, then I made a rope out of my bedsheets, climbed out of the window, and went."

"Classic. Did you get in trouble?"

She blows out.

"Boy, did I. We came out of the movies and Dad was waiting, along with maybe half of the police force. I was taken home by the ear, and he screamed at me. Mom was a little softer about it, just gave me a wag of the finger and a warning."

"I can't picture that."

"That's what happened."

She shrugs and takes another sip.

"There's something I'm dying to know about that night you arrested me," I ask.

She peeks over her glass, lowers it onto the table and steeples her fingers in front of her mouth.

"Go on."

"One, did you have to hit me against the car? And two, how did you arrive so fast after Melissa called it in?"

She smirks.

"To answer your first question, yes, I did, it was quite satisfying knocking sense into you; and two, we received the call an hour before the job. We made our way there right away and watched you for a while."

"Oh yeah, Steph mentioned that before. How long were you watching?"

"I saw it all, you walking out of that alleyway, casing the building, putting your gloves on. We were ready to have you the second you gained entry, but then you sat on the floor and stared up at the sky. I felt in that moment, you were different from the other O'Malleys, you aren't dangerous like them."

She slides her hand across the table, and I take it in mine.

"Incidentally, what were you thinking… when you were sitting on the ground?" she asks.

"I lost faith in Tobias that day. I knew I wasn't cut out for the life of crime. I was going to run, but you arrested me. I've never been so thankful for that."

"Oh?"

"It led me to you. You saved me that day."

She slumps into her seat and beams.

"And you to me. I didn't realize just how lonely I was, but all of that went away when I met you. You eradicated all that for me, gave me a new purpose," she says.

I smile and stand up, walk to her side of the table, and rest my hands on either side of her chair. She looks up into my eyes.

"Then we're definitely meant to be," I say.

She reaches up and strokes my stubble deftly, then I lean down and kiss her. When we break away, I stand up straight and check my watch; 15:40. Wow, we've been talking for nearly an hour and a half.

"We should go," I say, offering my hand.

She takes it, I pull her up then we leave the café, our hands inserted into each other's back pockets.

Chapter Sixteen

———∞———

Dusk breaks over Bear Mountain. Hews of orange, pink, and aquamarine spread across the sky, like paint brushed onto a canvas from an artist's loving hand. Birds sing harmoniously in the trees overhead and the lake ripples gently; nature is alive and well. The sunset illuminates the left side of Rachael's face. We've hiked back up the mountain as the sun sinks slowly in the distance. She takes her camera off from around her neck and snaps several shots of the panorama before us. Shadows slowly shift across the old iron bridge and the Hudson River is soon shrouded in darkness as the last of the sun disappears behind the hills. She takes a deep breath, links her fingers through mine and snuggles in close. I rest my head gently on top of hers.

"I don't want to go home tomorrow. I've had the best time," she whispers.

I glance down.

"Me too. Thank you for a wonderful weekend."

She smiles, leans up and plants a gentle kiss on my cheek, then she glances at her watch and frowns.

"We should get back. It'll get cold soon."

I take her hand in mine and we follow the other hikers down the trail and back towards our lodge.

Morning breaks, I rub my eyes and sit up. Rachael is curled up beside me, her hair a shock of mahogany splayed over her pillow. Her bare chest rises and falls slowly as she sleeps soundly. I lie back as gently as I can so as not to disturb her and pull the duvet over us, covering her modesty. She groans and rolls away, but the bright sun shines in her face and she rolls back to face me, dazed hazel eyes twinkling at me.

"Good morning, beautiful," I croon.

She grins crookedly then reaches out and strokes my stubble with her nimble fingers.

"Good morning, beautiful yourself."

"Sleep well?"

"I did. You?"

"Like a log."

She sits up, the duvet pools around her waist, exposing her. My eyes travel up and down her body as the vivid memory of her riding me last night comes back. She giggles, slaps me on the arm and climbs out of bed.

"See anything you like?" she asks.

I lick my lips.

"All of you."

She looks down at herself, then proceeds to get dressed. She glances back at me as she clips on her bra, then throws my shirt at me.

"You've seen plenty," she chuckles.

I pull my black shirt from my face and get out of bed.

"I don't know about that."

I stalk round the bed towards her, making her jump away from me.

"And if I walk away?" she asks, taking a step back.

I continue stalking her.

"Then I follow."

She leaps onto the bed; the springs creak their protest as I continue to follow her path with my eyes.

"But we need to get going," she says.

I glance at the alarm.

"We have time."

I lunge for her. She shrieks and leaps away. I lie face down on the bed and try to rethink my plan. I slowly lift my head, she stares at me from the opposite side of the room, a huge grin plastered on her face.

"Don't make me come over there and get you. You're only making things worse for yourself," I say.

She leans against the wall, her legs crossed, and her arms folded.

"We'll see about that."

I rise slowly and stare. *Hmm. A worthy opponent. I like the challenge. Even Sun Tzu would have a hard time strategizing around her.* I stalk round again; she stands up straight and backs away. I bide my time and wait until I'm close enough, then I lunge. She attempts to flee but I grab her arm. She struggles and pulls against my grip. I spin her round and kiss her deeply. She presses her body up against mine. I pick her up and drop her onto the bed. She stares up at me, dressed only in her bra.

"Now what?" she grins.

"Now, we make the most of our vacation."

I crawl onto the bed with her and kiss her fiercely.

I zip up our case, having finished packing the last garment and carry it to the door.

"Is that everything?" Rachael asks, scanning the room quickly.

"I think so."

She pulls her car keys from her pocket, then links her arm through mine.

"Let's go," she says, opening the door.

We walk down the stairs towards reception. She releases my hand and makes her way towards the wood-polished desk. A middle-aged man, with a receding hair line and thick glasses, dressed in a dark suit glances up and smiles as she approaches.

"Checking out?" he asks.

"Please."

I lean against the wooden beam, crossing my legs at the ankle. I'm nervous about returning to New York. What awaits me on our return? Will Mr. Levitt give me my job back? What is Tobias planning? Have the cops traced the money that he stole? Rachael hasn't breathed a word about it on our vacation, but why should she? A feather touch brushes my arm. I jolt out of my wayward thoughts to meet her steady gaze.

"Mark, you ready?"

"Of course."

She squints her eyes and takes my hand as I collect the case from the ground.

"Where were you?"

"Never mind. Let's get home."

"Yeah. Let's."

"Did you have a good time?" Rachael asks.

"The best, thank you. I know I keep saying that but really, I've been so relaxed."

She reaches over and rests her hand on my leg before placing it back on the steering wheel. I glance out the window at all the scenery that shoots past us, and I suddenly feel a little sad to be leaving.

"We'll be back," she says.

I glance over, but she stares firmly ahead at the road in front of us.

"Maybe I'll bring you for your birthday... I bet it's stunning in the winter," I say.

She peeks over and a ghost of a smile plays on her lips.

"I've never been in the winter, so I wouldn't know."

I look out the window again, the idea appeals to me. Maybe I could bring her family along next time, I'm sure she'd love that, and maybe Trent. Thoughts of him showing off makes me cringe, but it might be fun to experience fishing with him and Colin while Rachael has some girl time. I smile at the idea. Her birthday isn't for another few months, but I fully intend to make my plan a reality.

Halfway through the journey, we've pulled over at a small truck stop for a drink and a snack. We're sat back in the car as we eat Danishes and drink coffee. Rachael blows out and peeks at the in-car clock; 12:15 p.m.

"Just another hour to go," she groans.

I finish the last of my Danish.

"Would you like me to drive?"

She looks over and blinks.

"Really?"

"Sure. It'll give you a break and reward you for teaching me to drive and helping me pass my test."

She laughs.

"You were a very trying student."

"And you were a very patient... and hot teacher."

She blushes then quickly tears her gaze from mine, roots in her purse and throws the keys at me which to my surprise, I manage to catch.

"Don't scratch the paintwork," she hisses.

I flinch and chuckle as we both climb out of the car and switch seats.

"You know, the way you talk about the car, I'd be fooled into thinking you love this thing more than you love me," I joke.

"It's close."

I laugh loudly, then buckle my seatbelt. *I hope she's joking.*

"Well, let's go," she says, sitting back in her seat.

I breathe out, my gut balls into knots then I turn the key and the engine comes to life.

"Are you sure about this?" she asks.

Now I'm nervous.

"We'll be fine."

I put the car into drive then slowly pull out, rejoining the traffic and speeding down the freeway.

We're about a block away from our apartment after being stuck in Times Square for thirty minutes due to taking a wrong turn off the 9A.

"Left, Mark. Don't miss it," Rachael instructs quickly, pointing at the garage entrance.

I turn the steering wheel sharply to the left, the tires screeching in protest.

"Steady on," she shouts, gripping onto the door.

I drive down the ramp, pull up into our designated space and cut the engine.

"Sorry," I whisper.

She glances across and shakes her head.

"Well, I was going to say that was a nice relaxing ride, but..."

She rolls her eyes.

"Honestly, you've lived here long enough."

"Sorry," I repeat as the backs of my ears burn.

She nudges me.

"I'm only messing witcha."

I clear my throat, comb the forelock of hair out of my face and climb out of the car. She scrambles out after me.

"I haven't offended you, have I?" she asks, coming to stand in front of me.

I look down into her sincere eyes and smile warmly.

"Of course not. I love your wit."

She plants a gentle kiss on my lips, takes the keys and looks back at the car.

"You didn't scratch the paint at least," she says.

"You're welcome."

I lift the luggage from the trunk, then she presses the key fob to lock the car. The turn signals blink and the sideview mirrors fold in with a satisfying hum.

I kick the front door shut and put the case down in the hallway. Rachael heads straight into the kitchen while I remove my jacket and shoes.

"You want a drink?" she calls.

"I'd love one."

I pad into the lounge as she rustles around in the cabinets. I sit on the couch just as she reemerges carrying two glasses of crisp white wine. She sits down beside me and hands me a glass.

"It's good to be home," she says.

I raise my glass.

"Good to be home."

She clinks her glass against mine, then we both take a sip.

"So, are you going to see Mr. Levitt tomorrow?" she asks.

I splutter into my glass and whip my face to hers.

"Tomorrow?"

She stares and nods.

"There's nothing to worry about. It's just a follow up."

"What time?"

"I don't know. Maybe call him?"

I blink several times and put my glass down on the table.

"I can't."

"Why?"

"Because-."

She rests her hand on top of mine.

"Mark, you have nothing to be embarrassed about. Mr. Levitt knows that now. He treats you like a son. He was more hurt than angry when you were arrested."

"You know that?"

She nods.

"He told me after you left the room. You're a valued employee, he wants you back."

I smile and kiss her on the cheek.

"Thank you," I whisper.

"Call him."

I take a large glug of wine, then pull my phone out of my pocket and dial Mr. Levitt's number. He answers on the third ring, his stern voice booms down the phone.

"Neapolitan Hotel, you've reached Mr. Levitt. How may I help you?"

I swallow and glance at Rachael who gives me a thumbs up.

"Eh, Mr. Levitt, it's Mark."

There's a brief pause.

"Mark, you're back. How was your vacation?"

"It was great, thank you. Rachael tells me that you wish to see me."

"Yes, I do. Is tomorrow good for you?"

I swallow again as she smiles.

"Sure, what time?"

"Around lunchtime if that's okay for you."

"See you tomorrow."

"Great. See you tomorrow, Mark."

He hangs up and I drop my cell on the couch.

"What happened?" she asks.

"He wants to see me tomorrow at lunchtime."

"That's good, isn't it?"

"He's going to fire me. I know it."

She rests her arm around my back and lays against my chest.

"You'll be fine, I promise."

I wrap my arms round her and hold her like my life depends on it. We sit in our embrace for what feels like hours, neither of us move or speak but then she sits up and runs her nose delicately down the length of mine.

"Pizza tonight?" she asks.

"Sounds great."

Rachael parks up on the curb round the corner from the hotel at 11:50, ten minutes until my meeting. I step out and walk round to the driver's side window. She leans out and kisses me on the cheek.

"Good luck," she says.

I smile and return her kiss quickly.

"See you later."

She nods, rolls up her window and merges back into traffic. I stand back on the sidewalk and watch until she disappears round the corner. With a deep cleansing breath, I turn on my heel and stride as confidently as I can towards the hotel. I push through the double doors. Trent sits at his desk, talking to Rex. They both glance over and fall silent. I offer a quick wave at them, Trent jumps from his seat and walks towards me.

"Hey, bud. Got your job back?" he asks.

I shrug.

"We'll see."

His smile fades then he places his hand on my shoulder and gives me a little shake.

"Good luck."

"Thanks," I smile then head for the elevators.

I knock on the mahogany door and wait to be summoned in, but everything remains silent. I knock again, louder this time, still no answer.

"Mr. Levitt… Sir?" I call.

I slowly twist the knob and push the door open. *Unlocked. Huh.* His office is empty. I step inside and sit in one of the leather chairs, waiting for his arrival but something catches my eye, a newspaper clipping hangs on the wall beside his desk. I get up and walk over to read the article.

'Twenty-one-year-old entrepreneur seriously injured in a hit and run accident.'

I squint at the photo; a young man, roughly around my size, with tied back brown hair and deep green eyes. I've seen him before. It's his son, he was at our wedding, in a wheelchair. I turn to resume my seat, but then a photo on his desk gets my attention; Mr. Levitt with his arm draped round his son's shoulders. They both stand outside a baseball stadium, wearing Yankee caps. It's dated a week before the incident.

"It's rude to snoop," Mr. Levitt says from behind.

I spin round. He's leaning in the doorway, his hands dug into his pockets.

"Mr. Levitt. S-sorry, sir... um... I thought I'd wait in your office. I didn't mean to trespass."

His eyes crinkle and the corner of his mouth lifts slightly. He walks further into the room as I rush back to my seat where I sit down and stare at my hands, my face flushed.

"Patrick. I believe you met him at your wedding," he says.

I glance up, he's sat at his desk holding the framed photo.

"Yes, sir. I remember."

"My son was doing well with his career, but then he..."

He looks away and sniffs.

"Well, he was knocked from his motorcycle by a drunk driver."

"I'm very sorry, sir."

He rests his index finger against his forehead and eyes me across the desk.

"I appreciate that. My wife quit her job in the Financial District to care for him. He's paralyzed from the waist down."

"He's a lovely guy. Great sense of humor."

He chuckles and nods once.

"Yes. He was always a mischievous one... still is."

He peeks at me, his specs shimmering from the sunlight that beams through the windows.

"Anyway, back to the matter at hand," he says.

I suck in my lips and look back down at my hands.

"We need to discuss your future here at the hotel."

I look back up at him.

"You look nervous," he says.

"Yes, sir. I am."

He frowns and rubs his forehead.

"You have nothing to be nervous about. Your wife explained everything to me... well, almost everything."

"*Almost* everything?"

He nods.

"She showed me the CCTV proving that you weren't the culprit of this robbery, but what I can't figure out is how your DNA ended up on the scene. I was hoping you would fill in the blanks."

I blink at him then sit up straight.

"I was kidnapped by my old boss about a month ago. I woke up in an unknown location, he must have taken some of my hairs."

Mr. Levitt flinches.

"Is he *that* crazy?"

I scoff.

"That's a nice way of putting it. He set me up once before, that's how I ended up in jail the first time."

He nods slowly and continues to stare.

"I was asked to rob a jewelry store. I didn't go through with it but was arrested anyway."

"Oh yes. That was because of Melissa. I didn't take her for the sort to be affiliated with his ilk."

"She was forced into it, but she saved my life. Tobias was planning to kill me."

He widens his eyes.

"My god… This Tobias sounds like a colorful character, but I'm happy to hear that you never committed a crime."

"He's out to destroy me. I understand why you no longer want me here. I'd be putting you and everyone here at risk."

He blinks then removes his specs and gets to his feet.

"That's a rather bleak thing to say about yourself. Why think that?"

My gut twists tightly.

"Mark, I have no intention of firing you."

I glance up.

"Really?"

"Of course. You're a good employee. You're so professional with your work. You run late quite a lot, that will need some working on."

"I can do that."

"The question I wanted to ask is, do *you* want to come back?"

I lick my lips.

"Yes. Absolutely."

"Then, welcome back, son."

He outstretches his hand. I stand and shake firmly.

"Thank you. Thank you so much. I won't let you down."

"I know you won't. You resume tomorrow. You may go."

I rush towards the door without a backward glance.

"Oh, and Mark?"

I peek over my shoulder.

"From now on, keep your hairs on your head, and out of my lunchbox."

He winks and I scoff.

"You have my word."

I step out of his office and close the door with a soft click behind me. I clap my hands together and rush towards the elevator. I burst out when the doors open at the lobby, a huge smile plastered on my face. I glance over at Trent and Rex and give them a thumbs up, they grin and offer one back then I rush out of the double doors and head for home, excited to have been given this second- no... third chance. I can't wait to tell Rachael.

Rachael's sat on the couch, her legs tucked underneath her, while Steph sits in the armchair beside her. They both look at me and smile when I enter.

"Mark. Hi," Rachael says, getting to her feet and pecking me on the lips.

"How'd it go?" she asks.

"I'll tell you later," I whisper.

She nods as I peek over at Steph.

"Hi, Steph."

"Mark."

"I'll leave you girls to it."

I make for the kitchen.

"Oh, Mark?" Steph says.

I stop and turn.

"About that wrongful arrest thing…"

I raise my hand.

"It's alright. You were only doing your job. Rachael and I have discussed it already. I don't need an apology."

She smiles widely and nods. I head for the kitchen again and begin to busy myself with chores.

"That was very nice of you, Steph," Rachael says.

"It was the right thing to do. I hope he forgives me."

"Sounds like he already has."

I continue loading the dishwasher, smiling to myself.

"How's everything with work?" Rachael asks.

"Oh. That's what I came to tell you, we've got a lead on that van."

I prick my ears and sneak towards the kitchen door. I press my back against the wall.

"Ssh. Steph, I don't want Mark to know," Rachael hisses.

"Why?"

"Because he'll worry. I'm back at work tomorrow. We can talk about it then."

"Sorry."

"Let's talk about something else," Rachael says more clearly.

Why wouldn't she want to talk about it now? She knows that I'm aware of the security vans that they're pursuing. Is there development on the case? Tobias, perhaps? My head swims with all the possible scenarios. Desperate to rid the thoughts, I switch the dishwasher on, but thoughts continue to swirl. How bad is this going to get? Tobias is dangerous, he must know the police are onto him. He must have a plan. *God, I hope not.*

Steph walks past the kitchen doorway and peeks her head round.

"Bye, Mark."

I turn and wave at her.

"I hope you're not leaving on my account."

"No, I'm on duty in an hour."

"Be safe," I say, turning back to the stove.

She scoffs.

"Always."

I continue to stir the rich bubbling tomato mixture but keep my ears pricked.

"Tomorrow, the hit is early," Steph hisses.

"I'll be there," Rachael whispers.

The front door closes then Rachael joins me in the kitchen and wraps her arms round my neck.

"So, there's a sting on a van tomorrow," I say.

I tap the wooden spoon against the edge of the pot, place it down on the counter and turn to face her. She gapes, her mouth held open.

"You heard us."

"I heard enough. I know you think this shouldn't burden me, but I need to know. What aren't you telling me?"

She opens and closes her mouth.

"Mark, I-," she trails off and picks at her fingernails.

I step closer and take her hands in mine.

"Please don't lie to me, Rachael. We've been open and honest with each other so far. Has there been a development?"

She stares into my eyes.

"I'm just trying to protect you."

"Protect me? I don't need protection. I want to know what's going on."

She lowers her head and huffs.

"Please?" I whisper.

"We've narrowed down which van Tobias may have stolen. My colleagues found one while we were away, piled floor to ceiling with unmarked bills. They tried to seize the van and take the driver in for questioning, but he had backup, there was a shootout. Two officers got hurt bad and the van got away. We've been tracking it though and we're after it again tomorrow."

My mouth falls open and I rub the back of my neck.

"Rachael. What if this is a trap? You could be giving Tobias exactly what he wants."

"Maybe, but we can't just cower and hide. We must go after it. A lot of innocent peoples' money is wrapped up in this. We need to get it back."

"These men are armed with automatic rifles. They'll kill on sight. You're lucky they only injured those cops. If they want to kill, they will, easily," I say firmly, pulling at my hair a little.

She steps forward and rests her hand on my shoulder.

"I know that you're scared for me, and I appreciate it, but I have no choice, this is my job. This is for you. This is for us. This is for the people of this city. Tobias is standing in their way."

"I know that. Just... be careful. I couldn't bear to lose you."

"You're not going to lose me. We're ready for this. I'll have body armor on, and I've got a big team going."

I swallow, then nod.

"Okay."

She smiles then looks over my shoulder.

"What you cooking?"

I look back at the stove and stir the mixture.

"I'm attempting veggie spaghetti Bolognese."

She leans down and smells the mixture.

"Smells good. How sweet of you."

I grin, but still feel sick to my stomach. My appetite has vanished.

"How was the meeting?" she asks.

"It was good. I got my job back. I return tomorrow."

She squeals and hugs me hard.

"Congratulations. I'm so proud of you."

She kisses me then bends down and roots in the fridge.

"This calls for a celebration. How does Bollinger sound to you?" she says, holding up a bottle.

"Boll-y-... what?"

She laughs.

"Bollinger. Mom got it for your birthday, don't you remember?"

I take the bottle from her and read the label, expecting it to be wine. *Ah... its champagne.*

"Sounds nice."

She grins then pops the cork and pours us both a glass. I take a sip, it's delicious, fruity, fresh, and crisp.

"Congratulations," she says.

We clink glasses and take another sip of the champagne, but my thoughts continue to grind. Rachael is chasing down Tobias and my worst fears are realized; there's nothing I can do to protect her this time.

A feather touch glides through my unruly hair. I slowly prize my eyes open. Rachael is perched on the side of the bed, already dressed in her uniform, smiling down at me. I rub my eyes and yawn loudly.

"Sorry, I didn't mean to wake you," she says.

"That's okay," I say, sitting up.

"I'm off."

I hold onto her hand and brush it through my stubble.

"You be safe. You hear me?"

She moves my hand to her lips and plants a gentle kiss onto my knuckles.

"I'll be fine."

She stands from the bed and walks towards the door.

"I'll be home in time for dinner, you'll see," she smiles as she twists the doorknob.

"Rachael," I call.

She looks back.

"I love you."

She grins then quickly rushes over and kisses me hard, her tendrils tickle my face and I absorb her sweet aroma.

"I love you too," she whispers against my lips.

She leaves the bedroom, leaving me laying alone in bed, then the front door slams shut. She's gone. I crawl out of bed, my mind is congested with my biggest fears from the deep, dark place that I wish didn't exist. Hopefully work will keep me on my toes. I retrieve my suit from the closet and begin to get dressed as the eerie silence creeps into my subconscious. Why is this happening? Oh god, I hope she's going to be alright. I mentally slap myself. *Get a grip, man.* I spray myself with deodorant. I'll need it today and not because of the sweltering heat. I quickly check myself in the mirror. *Christ, I'm pale.* Hopefully some color will return on my walk to work. I grab my bag, slip on my shoes and with one last long exhale, I exit the apartment.

It's an overcast day, but the heat still bears down onto the city. Pedestrians are out in full flow, some carry umbrellas under the crook of their arms in anticipation of rain. I glance up at the sky as the clouds grow ever darker. I keep my head down and round the bend towards the hotel. I push through the doors and make a beeline for my desk. I can't be bothered with the staff room today, so I tuck my bag under my legs. Trent comes out of the elevator holding a thermos and bobbing to music which blares through his headphones. He sits beside me at his desk and taps at his phone screen. The music ceases, he removes his headphones and smirks at me.

"Welcome back," he says.

I high five him.

"Good to be back. I'll need the distraction today."

His mouth contorts and he leans in a little closer.

"What's going on?"

I open my mouth just as a few guests depart the elevators and head towards us.

"I'll tell you later," I hiss, then sit up straight and plaster the biggest smile I can manage just as two elderly ladies approach me.

"Good morning, ladies. Checking out?"

I sign out of my computer and stand, ready for my lunch break.

"I think I'll go out for lunch today. You coming?" I direct to Trent.

He smiles and leaps from his seat.

"Sure."

I grab my bag, slip it over one shoulder and head through the lobby, my smart shoes squeaking against the marble.

"Where were you thinking?" he asks when he catches up.

"Let's see where we end up."

We step outside, greeted by the now pouring rain. I take off my jacket and place it over my head in a futile attempt to keep dry.

"Somewhere close, I think," he says, shielding himself with a newspaper.

"Summer's fun here," I snigger.

We head left, but multiple sirens wail through the chatter on the streets and the lashing of the rain as it pounds our surroundings.

"What's going on?" he hisses in my ear.

I look back towards him just as a large blue armored van shoots past with several police cars on its tail.

"Driver. Stop your vehicle and come out with your hands on your head," a loud voice orders from a speaker on one of the cars. *Rachael.*

She's the lead car in pursuit of the van. I watch as the cruisers attempt to surround it. It veers sharply to the right, smashing into one and sending it into a tailspin. People around us scream and scatter in different directions. I follow the chase as Trent grabs my arm.

"Where are you going!?" he shouts.

"That's Rachael."

"There's nothing you can do, Mark. We need to go."

"No, Trent. I can't."

He places both hands on my shoulders.

"Listen, I'm sure she'll be…"

Another loud bang pierces my ears, followed by glass shattering and distorted sirens. My heart jumps into my throat.

"Oh god," I whisper, and run towards the noise, dropping my jacket.

"Mark!" Trent bellows, his loud footsteps splashing behind me.

I race round the bend, everything goes numb, all that can be heard is my deep uneven breaths as my feet pound the drenched sidewalk. I stop as a large crowd blocks my path. They whisper to each other, point, and some hold their phones aloft. I push through until I'm at the front. A cruiser is upside down on the sidewalk, its front bumper buckled in, dents and crevices cover the body work, and the driver door is torn clean off and lies beside the car. All the windows are shattered, and shards of glass litter the sidewalk. The wheels still turn, and smoke hisses from the hood. Trent stands by my side and stares at the car.

"Oh. Holy. Shit," he whispers.

Several officers climb out of their cars, then cordon off the area while others stop the oncoming traffic and try to disperse the crowd. I step forward a few more paces, but a male officer holds out his hand.

"Keep back, sir," he says.

I glance over his shoulder. Steph is crouched on the ground beside the wreckage. She grabs someone and begins pulling them free. *Please don't be Rachael.* She places the officer onto the wet ground and covers the officer's torso with her jacket. I try to get a better look and flinch. Everything goes into slow motion. Lights flash from the other police cars, muffled shouting and wailing sirens draw ever nearer. Steph's arms are round my shoulders as she leads me through the cordon and towards the figure on the ground. Steph talks to me, but I can't make out a word she's saying. I collapse and crawl on my hands and knees through the broken glass. The moisture from the rain seeps through my clothes. A female cop is covered in blood, her uniform ripped in several places, her mahogany hair out of place. My face screws up as I gently ease her onto my lap. It's my Rachael. I cradle her to my chest; tears stream uncontrollably down my face. The anger and grief clash together as I let out a loud inaudible wail.

"Rachael!"

Chapter Seventeen

———∾———

My world caves in on itself and I can't acknowledge what's going on around me. *This must be a nightmare. It has to be.* I continue to cling to my beautiful, unresponsive wife desperately, while the crowd around us begins to disperse, safe for Trent whose mouth is open, and his eyes are glazed.

"Oh, Mark," Steph sobs.

I stroke Rachael's bloodied wet face and kiss her forehead.

"Rachael?" I whisper but she remains still and quiet.

Tears continue to roll down my face unrestrained and my whole body shakes.

"Rachael, please," I sob, resting my forehead against her chest.

Steph stands and rests her hand on my back.

"I'm so sorry," she whispers but I don't look at her.

I stare down at Rachael, limp in my arms.

"Please don't leave me," I cry.

"The ambulance is coming," Steph whispers.

I cradle my beautiful wife in my arms and scream further. Cackles of laughter erupt from the distance. I slowly turn to face a dump truck on the other side of the street; its front is crushed in, and smoke emits from the radiator; surrounded by police cars and S.W.A.T. The driver is held at gunpoint and dragged forcibly from the truck. He falls onto the hard concrete, laughing. I'm overcome with such rage that I've never experienced before. I gently lie Rachael on the ground and slowly get to my feet. I dash the tears away that continue to roll down my face as more sirens blare closer. The driver is pulled to his feet by a pair of officers, and he turns his hideous smile to me.

"Hey, Marky! How's the wife?" he caws.

The red mist descends, and I clench my fists tightly.

"The boss says you'll be joining her *real* soon!"

Fucking bastard. I'll fucking rip him in half. I charge towards him, but my arms are grabbed from behind. *Let go of me!*

"Mark, easy, easy… calm down." Steph says.

"HE KILLED HER! I WANNA FUCKING KILL HIM!" I bellow.

Trent stands in front of me, his hands pressed against my chest.

"Hey, Mark, buddy. Rachael's still alive. They checked for a pulse."

I stop trying to shake free.

"She is?" I whimper.

"Yeah, of course she is. You wanna be with her? There's room in the ambulance."

"He ain't gonna stop until you're gone, Marky! Until you're *both* gone!" the driver shouts.

Another shot of adrenaline-fueled rage streaks through my veins as I struggle against Steph and Trent's hold.

"Hey, chill, chill," Trent says.

"Get him outta here!" Steph orders.

Several officers struggle with the bastard before tossing him into the back of a police van. I look over at where Rachael was. Two paramedics strap her onto a gurney, she's now wearing a neck brace. They load her into the back of the ambulance, and I bolt over.

"I want to come," I say desperately.

One of the paramedics looks back at me as the other starts their tests.

"Are you family?" he asks.

I flash my ring at him as my patience hangs by a thread.

"I'm her husband."

He sucks in his lips and gestures with his head.

"Come on then."

I jump on board as they slam the doors shut and speed away.

I grip her bloodied police cap in my hands as we speed through the city, the sirens wailing. This can't be real. I pray internally that I'll wake up. I sit beside the gurney that holds my beaten up, unconscious wife. I bury my head in my hands, my heart leaps into my mouth, as I continue to pray. I've never been religious, but in this moment, I will do anything to guarantee that she'll return to me. *Please be okay. Wake up. Come back to me.*

"All vitals appear good," the paramedic says, his dark eyes shine, and he smiles down at me.

"Then why is she still unconscious? How long will she be like this?"

He sinks down onto the seat beside me.

"It's hard to say. The doctors will be able to run further tests when we arrive and hopefully, they'll tell you more."

She remains still and quiet, a white sheet covers most of her body, albeit her hand that rests delicately on her chest.

"Can I touch her?" I ask.

"Of course."

I lean forward and gently rest my hand on top of hers, her hand is warm which goes a little way to soothing me, she's alive, but the relief doesn't last. What if the doctors find something worse? What if she never comes back to me? I sit back in my seat and stare up at the small light on the ceiling. I want to scream, I want to wail, I want to howl to the moon to release this pent-up pain and fury, but I can't. I must remain strong... for her. The last words she uttered to me before she left this morning flit back.

'I'll be home in time for dinner, you'll see.'

'I love you.'

'I love you too.'

At least I said that. I lean over her and plant a tender kiss on her bloodied cheek.

"I'll always love you," I whisper, as tears flow down my cheeks anew.

We finally arrive at Mount Sinai Hospital. I'm sidelined as the paramedics fly into action; they rush the gurney off the ambulance while I walk briskly alongside. They rush her through some double doors and into the ER triage, I try to follow but a nurse stops me.

"Stay back for now," she instructs.

I can do nothing but watch helplessly as they take her down the long corridor and disappear into a side room.

I stand paralyzed, staring through the glass doors and clasping her police cap in my bloodied hands. *I'm sorry.* A throaty growl of a motorcycle gets my attention. I look over my shoulder as Trent engages the kickstand, climbs off his bike, and removes his helmet. He glances towards me and barrels over.

"Where is she?" he asks.

"In there," I squeak, gesturing with my head.

"Why aren't you with her?"

"They wouldn't let me."

I place my head in my hands as a new wave of tears begin. He pulls me into his arms, and I cling to his leather jacket.

"She's going to be alright. She's tough. Let's head inside and wait," he says softly.

I pull away and wipe my eyes, suddenly conscious that we're two grown men hugging outside ER's main entrance. He wraps his arm round my shoulders and steers me inside, through the automatic doors and into the sterile surroundings of the hospital's waiting room. I sniff and my whole body trembles fiercely. I'm so cold, I wrap my arms round myself as we make our way over to the seating area.

"Does Louise know?" I ask.

"Oh yeah, and her folks. They're on their way."

He lowers me down onto a chair gently. I rest her cap on my knees and run my hands repeatedly through my wet hair as my lungs fill with the smell of disinfectant. Doctors and nurses in blue scrubs walk up and down the corridor, some carrying clipboards and others pushing patients in wheelchairs or beds.

"Right. Stay put. I'm going to try and speak to someone," Trent says.

I lower my head and weakly wave him away. He marches down the corridor and stands next to a small desk. He chats quickly to the receptionist, every so often gesturing with his hands or pointing in my direction. I tear my gaze away and stare down at the polished floor. Every breath shudders through my body, my lungs ache, probably from all that screaming and crying. I wring my hands together, trying desperately to grasp at my composure, but I can't get a hold of it. Tobias is obsessed with making my life a living hell, but he's crossed a very thick red line. That prick will pay, I'll make sure of that. I don't know how, and I don't know when, but he will pay. Trent kneels in front of me, regarding me with his clear blue eyes. I don't know how long he's been there.

"Hey. Drink this."

He lowers a small paper cup filled with black coffee into my hands. I look down at it, losing myself to the depth and darkness of it; the strong aroma overwhelms me further.

"Small sips," he says, patting me on the shoulder.

I raise it to my lips and sip gently.

Minutes tick by painfully and I've still heard nothing. Trent every so often gets up and paces in front of me, his hands clasped behind his back, but my legs are weak, rendering me incapable of movement. I hug her cap close as frantic footsteps echo down the corridor. I look up, hopeful that it may be the doctor, but its Louise followed closely by Colin and Sara. I struggle to my feet, still holding her cap. Sara jumps into my arms and weeps into my shoulder.

"Not Rachael," she muffles.

I wrap my arms tenderly round her and rock us back and forth. She pulls away and wipes her eyes.

"Have you heard anything?"

I shake my head.

"I'm sorry, no."

Colin scowls and checks his watch.

"It shouldn't take this long," he growls.

"Colin, we'll just have to wait," Sara says, stroking his arm.

I sit back down as does everyone else. Sara gasps and points at Rachael's cap.

"Can I hold it?" she asks.

I hand it to her; she continues sobbing and collapses into Colin's arms. I look to my left and offer a small reassuring smile at Louise, she returns it meekly then rests her head on Trent's shoulder as he strokes his fingers through her hair.

Minutes turn to hours but finally, a young Asian American man with dark hair, dressed in a white coat and blue scrubs walks down the corridor.

"Are you with Rachael Flint?"

"Yes," Sara says, jumping to her feet causing everyone else to stand.

"How is she?" I blurt out.

The doctor stares at me then pulls a chair up close and sits down. *That can't be good.* I sink slowly back into my seat.

"Mrs. Flint is stable. We've had to put her into a coma. She's got a bleed on the brain."

An unknown force strikes me through the heart. Sara cups her hand to her mouth as Colin rubs her shoulder.

"Is it serious?" I whisper.

The doctor frowns.

"Not sure yet. We won't know until the updated scans come back. She's currently on a ventilator."

"Can we see her?" Colin asks.

The doctor stands.

"Of course. Right this way."

We all stand quickly and trail after him towards her room.

The doctor stops outside a door and turns to face us.

"She's in there," he says quietly.

I rush towards the door, everyone else stands behind me. I swallow then slowly turn the handle and push it open. Rachael is tucked up in bed under crisp white sheets. She's wearing a blue hospital gown, her left arm is dressed in bandages, and her face is covered in cuts and bruises, visible through the mask that's over her mouth and nose; her eyes are closed, one leg rests on top of the sheets. She remains motionless as we all quietly step in. The machines beep rhythmically and the air hisses from the ventilator. Various tubes protrude from her right arm and chest. A couple of IV bags hang above her, one contains what I can only assume is water, another contains blood. *Blood transfusion?* Sara howls, making me jump then she pushes past me and runs towards the bed.

"Oh, my sweet baby," she says, stroking her hair softly.

Colin sits on the foot of the bed and rests his hand on her uncovered leg. Louise weeps loudly and falls into Trent's arms, he hugs her close and leads her from the room. I attempt to swallow the lump forming in my throat and pray this is just a bad dream, but it's not, this is really happening. Sara looks over at me and pats the bed.

"Come, sit with us," she offers.

I walk over slowly and sit on the bed beside Rachael's face. I brush my fingers against her bruised cheek, her skin is warm and rosy. Leaning down, I brush her hair from her forehead and plant a gentle kiss on it as tears start to roll down my face again. A female nurse with curly gray hair and warm brown eyes enters. Everyone looks up.

"Hi. I'm Nurse Crawford, I'm in charge of Rachael's care," she says.

"Tell me that she'll be okay," Sara cries.

The nurse purses her lips and walks over slowly.

"I'll make sure of it."

Sara wipes her nose and gets up.

"Colin, could you take me home please?"

He jumps to his feet and takes her arm.

"Please keep me informed," Sara whispers to me.

"Of course."

They exit the room as Sara continues to cry against Colin. The nurse follows them and closes the door, leaving me alone with her. I lie down on the bed beside her and snuggle up close.

"I'm sorry," I whisper, my tears refusing to subside.

"I'll get that bastard for you. I promise."

"Hey, bud."

My eyes open slowly. Trent stands next to the bed. I hadn't realized I'd fallen asleep. Nurse Crawford stands beside him.

"It's time to go," he whispers.

I look from him to the nurse, then at Rachael.

"No. I won't leave her."

The nurse steps closer.

"I need to do my checks. You can come back tomorrow morning."

"I won't leave her," I whisper, stroking her hair.

"She's safe here. I'll take care of her," Nurse Crawford says.

I look back at Trent who nods subtly.

"Okay," I resign, then lean down and kiss her on the forehead.

"I'll be back in the morning," I whisper.

I sit on Trent's couch, cloaked in blankets, feeling numb and disorientated. I shouldn't have left her, I should be with her now, trying to bring her back to us. Trent busies himself in the kitchen, but I stare at the opposite wall, feeling nothing but utter grief. He heads back to me, carrying two plates and places one beside me, I look down at it, the aroma of the stew makes my stomach turn.

"Thanks, Trent, but I'm not hungry," I say, pushing the plate away.

He frowns and places his hand on my knee.

"Just try it?"

I stare at him blankly then get to my feet and walk to the opposite side of the room, sitting away from him. He looks over at me, then starts with his own plate of food. I continue to stare at the wall as I listen to the scraping of his cutlery against his plate. The noise infuriates me.

"Please stop," I snap.

He glances up, his mouth still full of food.

"Wha?"

I wave my hand up and look down at my feet.

"Never mind."

I shouldn't take my temper out on him, but I can't help it, I'm so full of rage. Why did this have to happen? Why Rachael? I promised to protect her on our wedding day, I failed her.

"Mark, I know this has been a rotten day. We're all hurting, but she'll be fine."

I peek at him out the corner of my eye.

"How do you know that?"

"She's strong, she'll pull through and she's in the best place."

I pace the room, my hands on my face as the anger threatens to boil over again.

"You don't know that, Trent. Nobody knows what's going to happen next. Just leave me be."

He blinks, then stands up, pulls the couch into a bed, and enters his room without another word. I breathe deeply, feeling guilty as hell but having no idea how to apologize. I groan, raising my face to the ceiling then I collapse, face first onto the bed couch. My world continues to tear itself apart. I turn over onto my side and pull my cell out of my pocket. I turn it over in my hand and smile weakly at the phone case on the back, a photo of me and Rachael at our wedding, with Bow Bridge in the background. She looks so beautiful in her lace gown as she rests her hand against my chest. We both beam at the camera, my hand draped round her waist, I can still hear her infectious laugh. Tears roll down my face again, but I quickly dash them away. I unlock my cell and dial Rachael's number, it rings several times then the answering machine cuts in, her sweet voice rings through.

"Hi, this is Rachael. Sorry I can't come to the phone right now. Please leave a message and I'll get back to you."

I hang up and dial again, this time I close my eyes and allow her sweet voice to wash over me and through me as I redial her number again and again until my eyelids grow weighty.

Times Square is full of people laughing and joking, and couples cuddling together on nearby benches. A car is flipped into the air and onto the sidewalk as everyone scatters, the sound of crunching metal and the smashed glass rings out through the streets. I rush over, desperate to help. My feet crunches through the smashed glass that litters the sidewalk. No one is around to assist as Rachael lies unconscious in the upturned vehicle. The streets that surround us are eerily silent, then she's lying on the sidewalk, blood pouring from her, turning the concrete red. I try to compress her bleeding, but nothing can stop it, the streets are deserted as I look around for help.

"Someone help!" I scream but no one comes.

I hold onto Rachael as blood trickles out of her nose and runs down her face.

"Rachael?" I whisper but she doesn't respond.

I place my hand on her face as she turns pale, her skin like ice. I shrug off my jacket and drape it round her.

"Rachael?" I attempt again, giving her a shake.

A shadow looms from behind. I turn, still holding onto her lifeless body. Tobias sneers down at me.

"She's gone, Mark," he crows.

I clench my fists.

"You twisted monster," I spit.

He continues to sneer and laugh, his bitter breath filling the air.

"You shouldn't have got involved with her. She would still be alive if it wasn't for you. Her blood is on your hands," he says.

I rest my head against her chest, knowing in myself that maybe he's right. He places his hand on my shoulder, but I shrug him off.

"Re-join me. End your suffering, that is all love has brought you," he says.

"No," I whisper.

"Mark, join me."

He pulls me from her and begins to drag me away. I thrash and struggle.

"No! I won't leave her."

"You already have."

I look helplessly back at her on the sidewalk, alone, cold, and dead.

I scream and sit bolt upright in bed. I'm soaked in sweat and still fully dressed. Trent dashes out of his bedroom, dressed in a tatty old beige bathrobe. He stares straight at me as I breathe deeply, my heart palpitating. He rushes over and sits on the bed beside me.

"You alright, bud?"

I wipe my face with my hand and stare at him.

"She's dead, isn't she?" I whisper.

His mouth falls open.

"What? No. She's fine. The doctor said she's stable, remember?"

I frown, trying to recall those words, they may offer me some solace, but they do nothing.

"Bad dream again?" he says, narrowing his eyes.

I nod and take another gulp of air.

"Can we go back to the hospital? I need to see her."

He checks the clock that hangs in the kitchen then turns back to me.

"In a few hours. Let her rest a little while longer."

I open my mouth to argue, but don't have the energy.

"Do you think you can get some rest?" he asks.

"I'm not going to that place again. I'm staying up. You can go back to bed, Trent."

He frowns, then stands up.

"You'll be okay?"

"I'll be fine."

His mouth twists but he turns on his heel and returns to his room. I swing my legs out of bed and rush to the bathroom to splash myself with cold water. *Snap out of it.*

\Dawn breaks over the horizon. I sit up in bed attempting to watch something on Netflix, but I keep zoning out, returning to my nightmare. My head is pounding, I place my fingers on my temples and rub firmly. *Get the hell outta there.* Trent's bedroom door opens, and he walks out dressed in a pair of striped pajamas. He glances at me. I nod at him which he returns as he pads into the kitchen and turns on the coffee machine.

"Coffee, Mark?" he calls.

"No thanks."

He looks back and narrows his eyes.

"You didn't eat last night. At least drink something."

I groan.

"Fine, but just a small mug."

He turns back to the machine. I switch off the TV, it's doing nothing to calm me as he walks over carrying two steaming mugs. He hands one to me, I take it, but my hands are trembling, my wedding band clinks against the china. He sits beside me and takes a sip. I do the same, but it tastes like ash in my mouth. I put it on the floor beside my feet and take my cell from my pocket; 8:45 a.m.

"Can we go back to the hospital now?" I ask.

He peeks at the clock, downs his coffee and heads back to his room, but pauses in the doorway and looks back at me.

"I'm just going to get changed," he says, then closes the door.

I look down at my own clothes, I slept in them last night and don't smell great due to me sweating but I don't have a change of clothes with me. He reemerges and grabs his keys.

"Can you cope on a bike?" he asks.

I think for a moment, unsure if I can deal with it then plaster the best smile I can manage and get to my feet.

"Sure. I could do with the air hitting me in the face."

He looks down at my clothes.

"Are you wearing those?"

I stare down at my scruffy apparel.

"I don't have anything else to wear."

He frowns then pockets his keys and heads back into his room. I check my watch. *What's he doing now? I'm desperate to see her.* I'm about to call for him to hurry up but he returns with a duffel bag. He throws it at me. I look down at it.

"What's this for?"

"We'll stop off at your place, collect some bits," he says.

I don't want to collect some bits and live here with Trent, I want to be in my own apartment, in my own bed with my wife. My mood dips some more, this isn't possible right now.

Trent pulls up outside my apartment, I look up at the red brick building and my heart drops. I climb off the bike and walk towards the underground garage, wanting to avoid Tom. Trent rushes after me and grabs my arm.

"The entrance is over there," he points.

"I know that. I want to go this way," I say, proceeding to the underground entrance.

He follows me as we walk down the ramp and into the cool garage. I stop when I see Rachael's white Mercedes and stare. Slowly, I approach and stroke the bodywork. We've only been back from Bear Mountain a couple of days and my life has already turned to shit. I shake my head as Trent stands behind me and watches.

"C'mon," I say, continuing to the elevator.

We stop outside my door. I fish the keys from my pocket and unlock it. Trent walks in first and I trail in after him, but something rustles underfoot, like paper. I glance down and sure enough, there's an envelope on the doormat. I pick it up, pocket it and walk inside, closing the door behind me. I stare round our apartment and head into the bathroom to collect my things. I grab my bodywash but then stop and grab Rachael's shampoo. I open the lid and inhale deeply; her sweet scent of roses fills my sinuses. I exit the bathroom to find Trent in my bedroom packing a few of my clothes.

"I doubt you'll want your suit for work?" he says, looking up.

I shake my head, unable to face going back at a time like this.

"I'll have to talk to Mr. Levitt," I say, sitting on Rachael's side of the bed and stroking her pillow gently.

"No need. I've already spoken to him."

"Thanks."

I grab her favorite book; maybe I'll read it to her in the hospital. I hand him the book which he stows in the duffel then I remember the envelope that I picked up on my way in. I fish it back out of my pocket and turn it over in hand. It doesn't have my address on it, it just reads 'Mark Flint' in curvy writing. He glances up.

"What's that?"

"I dunno. I found it on my way in."

I turn it over again and rip it open. Inside, there's a small, folded piece of card and a crushed carnation. My stomach drops as I fish everything out. I show Trent the flower and unfold the card. It reads: *'I'll see you soon. Kindest Regards'*. I slam my fists down on the bed and crush the petals in my hand. He jumps up and grabs my arms, holding me still.

"Easy, bud. Take it easy."

I shrug him away, get up from the bed and thump my fists against the wall.

"This has gone too far," I groan into the wall.

"What's going on?" he asks, looking back at the crushed flower which is now on the floor.

"I need to speak to Steph, urgently."

"What's going on?"

"He was at my apartment. How the fuck did he get past security?"

"Who?"

"Who do you think?"

He folds his arms and twists his mouth, then his eyes bulge and his mouth drops open.

"Tobias?"

"Yeah… Or one of his goons. I don't know and right now, I don't care. They were here, outside my damn door!" I shout, pointing towards the front door.

He grabs my arm and tugs slightly.

"We'll deal with it. Let's get outta here. Call Steph from the hospital," he says, grabbing the full duffel and throwing it over his shoulders.

I pick up the wilted flower and the card, and pocket them both. I'll show Steph with the hope that she can provide some sort of closure to this heinous crime and if I'm lucky, a suggestion to stop this monster once and for all. If she can't, I'll deal with him myself. I still have a few tricks left to play.

Chapter Eighteen

I sit at Rachael's bedside while Trent sits in the lone plastic chair in the corner. I stroke her hair and read from her book, Pride and Prejudice. He clears his throat, slaps his knees, and stands. He takes his cell from his pocket and waves it at me.

"Just going to give Stephanie a call," he says.

I nod at him and return to the book. I peek over at her intermittently and grasp her hand in mine, she doesn't respond to my touch or my reading, she remains still and mute, the only sound is the beeping of the heart monitor and the air hissing through the ventilator. I close the book and place it on the small table beside us. I sigh and look through the blinds at the window which looks out into the hospital corridor. Trent paces back and forth, one hand on his head and talking into his cell. He nods, says something else then hangs up and comes back into the room.

"Stephanie will be coming to my apartment a little later," he says.

"What did you tell her?"

"I just told her that you got something in the mail that you need to show her. Said it was urgent."

"That doesn't sound strange at all."

He chuckles.

"Thought I'd add to the mystery," he jokes before glancing down at his watch.

"Sorry, bud. I've got to get to work. I'll be back to collect you later."

I nod and glance back at Rachael.

"You going to be okay?" he asks.

"Sure."

He smiles, pats me on the shoulder, then strides out of the room. I climb onto the bed beside her and lie down, clinging onto her hand tightly and inhaling her scent. It's not how I remember it; no longer roses but now the strong smell of disinfectant.

"Rachael," I whisper close to her ear, hoping for a small bit of movement, but she doesn't budge.

A tear trickles down my face and splashes onto her hand as I plant a gentle kiss on it.

"Come back to me. I miss you so much."

I lie my head down beside hers.

"It's Mark, isn't it?" A gentle voice says.

I sit up. Nurse Crawford stands in the doorway, smiling. I climb off the bed.

"Yes, it is."

She steps further into the room and eyes the book on the table.

"Pride and Prejudice?"

I look at the book then back at her.

"It's Rachael's. I thought I'd read to her when I visit," I say.

"Good idea. Keep talking to her."

"Can she hear me?"

"Who knows? But I believe she can. I think it gives her comfort knowing that those she loves are close."

I smile and glance down at Rachael.

"I need to do my checks. It won't take a moment," she says.

"Would you like me to leave?"

She shakes her head.

"You're welcome to stay."

She stands beside Rachael and starts looking over the machinery and wires, opening one eye and shining a light, followed by the next, then she changes the IV bags.

"When will she wake?" I ask.

Nurse Crawford peeks up and frowns.

"It's hard to say. Whenever she's ready. However, it might comfort you to know that she had a comfortable night last night. We did another scan this morning, the bleed on the brain is starting to go down. The blood transfusion seemed to help too. She's recovering fast. If she continues like this, it will only be another day or two."

"That's reassuring. Thank you. Am I allowed to know the doner?"

Nurse Crawford twists her mouth and holds a finger up.

"I'll check. One moment."

She retreats from the room. I sit back in the padded chair beside her and continue reading from her book.

Nurse Crawford returns after an hour. She's carrying a clipboard and flips through the papers.

"We've spoken to the doner. They're happy for us to disclose their information to you," she says.

I lean forward, my hands clasped.

"Who is it?"

She glances down at the clipboard again.

"His name is Trenton Wilkinson."

My mouth falls open and I sit back in my seat. *Trent did this. Why didn't he tell me?*

"Do you know him?" she asks.

I look back at her and nod.

"My friend."

"The man that's normally with you. That's him?"

I nod.

"That's some friend you have."

"My best friend. He means everything to me."

She grins widely, places the clipboard down and proceeds with Rachael's checks. She pulls back the sheets and checks her blood pressure then tucks her back in.

"All signs are normal... Oh, one more thing, her uniform is in a bag behind the nurses' station, should you wish to take it home with you."

"Thank you."

"Collect it before you go."

She smiles then leaves the room. I look back at Rachael. Her hair is all out of place, mahogany waves splayed out in all directions across her pillow. I root around in the duffel bag hoping that I packed a comb. *Yes.* I sit on the edge of the bed, then slowly and gently comb out the tangles, so her hair falls round her shoulders in her usual silky wave that I love and miss so much.

I read more from her book, occasionally glancing up from the pages at her.

"It's time to go," Trent says.

I close the book, leap from my chair, and kiss him on the forehead. He pats me on the back and gently pushes me away.

"Wow. Dramatic much? What was that?" he asks, his eyes widening.

"Why didn't you tell me?"

"Tell you what?"

"About the blood transfusion."

"What about it?"

"It was your blood… You saved Rachael's life. I owe you everything."

"I didn't know until this morning when I got the call. They told me someone was asking for the information, I agreed… I didn't know it was you, though."

"Trent, I couldn't be more grateful."

He raises his hand.

"I've been donating blood for years. It was nothing really. Just a lucky coincidence."

"Well… Thank you anyway."

"Anytime. It's late. We need to go."

"Okay. One sec."

I walk back to her and gently press my lips to her forehead.

"I'll be back tomorrow," I whisper.

I leave the room, collect Rachael's uniform from the nurses' station and leave the hospital, with Trent by my side.

"Can I tempt you to eat today?" he asks, looking back at me from the kitchen.

I rest my back against the counter. My stomach rumbles angrily as the aroma of the hot dogs that sizzle on the stove hits me. Trent smiles, his eyes crinkling at the corners.

"Please. But let me take over," I say, taking the tongs.

He cocks his head to the side and watches as I rotate the sausages. For the first time since this happened, through the dark storm clouds, a ray of sunshine peeks through. All the same, what if my nightmare was trying to tell me something? Will Rachael pull through? And if she does, will she ever walk again? My mood nosedives again, but I shake away my morbid thoughts. I place the sausages onto a plate and cut up the buns, then walk into the lounge and place it all on the dining table.

"You're very helpful tonight," he says, nudging me.

"Just keeping myself busy. And I owe you a massive thank you."

He pulls a chair out.

"Mark, really it was nothing. Let's save the gratitude for when she's back, huh?"

I lean forward and surprise him with another hug.

"I'm sorry I lashed out last night."

"I understand. You're going through a really bad time right now. Now, please eat," he says, picking up the plate and offering it to me.

I pick up a hot dog and take a small bite from the bread. Once I have a taste for it, I can't stop. I'm famished.

We eat the last of our hot dogs and watch a couple of episodes of Breaking Bad, then there's a loud knock on the door. Trent quickly stuffs the last of his hot dog into his mouth and stands to open the door. I take the empty plate into the kitchen as I listen to whispered voices. He reemerges with Steph. She stares at me and removes her cap.

"Mark, good to see you again. How's Rachael?" she asks.

"She's improving, according to the nurse. The bleed is going down and hopefully she'll wake in a day or two."

She smiles, but her eyes are glazed.

"Well, that's good at least. She'll remain in my prayers."

I take a seat on the couch beside Trent as Steph perches on one of the blue dining chairs. Her radio crackles but she reaches up and turns it down.

"Trent said that you have something for me?" she says.

I peek at him. He strokes his nose and looks away. *Do I? Oh, right that, the flower and note I received this morning.*

I pull the crushed carnation from my pocket and hold out my hand. Steph stands and glances down at it.

"A carnation?" she asks.

I nod and root in my pocket some more for the small card that came with it. I hand them both to her. She takes the card and scans the words. She flinches and shoots her eyes back to mine.

"'Kindest regards'?" she says, her lips curling into a snarl.

"He was at our apartment, Steph."

"How do you know?"

"The envelope it came in had no address on it, only my name. I'm scared for me and Rachael's safety when we return home."

She pulls out a plastic evidence bag and places the card and carnation into it.

"We'll put measures into place. An officer will be stationed outside your apartment complex for protection."

She stands and places her cap back on.

"Thank you for this, Mark. I'll take it back and request analysis. Maybe there'll be prints. We'll catch this son of a bitch."

"I hope so."

She pats me on the shoulder and heads towards the door.

"Steph?" I call.

She turns and raises a brow.

"Did you get the security van that you were after?"

In the periphery of my vision, Trent slowly glances at me.

"It meant a lot to Rachael that it was caught. I was just… curious," I continue hastily.

She sighs.

"We did."

My heart pounds against my ribcage.

"And?" I ask, jumping to my feet.

"One of O'Malley's men was inside. He swore allegiance to him as he was arrested."

She exhales, removes her cap again and twists it in her hands. I frown. *What isn't she telling me?*

"So, you have the money back?"

She scrapes her shoes against the hard floor.

"Steph? What's going on?"

"The money wasn't there. It was a dud."

My mouth drops open. That means Rachael ended up in hospital for nothing. It was drawing attention away from the *real* van. *Or the money's already gone.* I slump my shoulders and hold onto the wall for balance. The room is spinning, and my legs feel weak. She steps closer.

"We may have the real van. Driven by this man."

I look up as she pulls a folded piece of paper from her duty belt and hands it to me. Trent stands quickly and rushes over to join us. I unfold the paper and look at the image. It's a black and white, grainy CCTV photo of another security van. Driven by a man that I think I recognize. I squint at the image.

"Rusty?" I whisper.

Steph blinks at me.

"You know him?"

"He's Tobias' muscle. One of his most loyal followers. He was with him the same time as me."

"Does he have a real name? Maybe we can put him through the database."

"Yeah, um… Leigh Rogers."

She takes the image from me.

"Does he have a brother?" she asks.

"No idea. Why?"

"The man we arrested yesterday, the same one driving the dump truck, he was identified as Gary Rogers. He had a tattoo of a carnation on his left wrist and a larger tattoo of a scorpion on his back."

"Of course," I say, stepping back.

"What?" she asks, following me.

"Most of us were given code names to hide our real identities and tattooed with a red carnation on the left wrist. Gary got the name 'Scorpion' for always sending vehicles into a tailspin. I didn't know they were brothers. I rarely saw him. He's one of Tobias' outside men."

"Well, we have him at least. Time to find his brother and put them both where they belong; behind bars," Steph says, placing her cap back on and pressing a button on her radio.

"All units. Be on the lookout for Leigh Rogers, A.K.A. 'Rusty'. He's a six-foot-two male with short red hair and a distinctive tattoo of a red carnation on his left wrist. Approach with caution, he is to be considered armed and dangerous."

"Copy that," the radio crackles back.

She looks back at me and opens the door.

"Rachael will be justified. You have my word."

I nod as she exits, the door clicks gently behind her.

Trent's gone to work, leaving me on my own. I pace the apartment, blinded by the sunlight that emanates from the window as my anger flares anew in my gut. Tobias has hurt me enough times. He has destroyed my life for the last time. When will it be enough for him? I need him out of my life. *How about 'dead'?* I shake my head and screw my eyes shut. *No way.* I distract myself by taking Rachael's police uniform out of the bag; the pants are ripped in several places; the shirt is stained with dried blood and her badge is covered in scratches. I fold it up neatly and place it all gently back into the bag. I pick up her duty belt and place it on top of the clothes. The handle of her pistol catches my eye. I bend down and pick up the gun, turning it over in hand. I open the chamber. It's loaded. With my anger continuing to spiral, I place the pistol into the waistband of my jeans and grab my leather jacket. Just as I make for the door, Trent walks in.

"Hey, man," he greets.

I swallow and pull my shirt down over the handle of the gun.

"Hey."

He furrows his brow and looks down at my trembling hands.

"Where you goin'?" he asks, eyeing me.

"For a walk."

His eyes widen, then he licks his lips and pulls up my shirt before I can stop him. He eyes the gun, then looks up at me, his mouth held open.

"What's that for?" he asks, pointing at it.

"What do you think?"

He goes to grab it from me, but I turn away quickly, avoiding him. He follows me.

"Mark, give that to me," he orders.

"I need to end this," I say, still avoiding him as he stalks me.

"You're no killer. You don't want to do this."

"Well maybe I do! I need to stop this from happening again."

He finally stops following me. We stand on opposite ends of the room. He sighs and puts his hands into his spiky hair.

"Mark, please don't do this. You'll wind up back in jail, not just for a little while, but for good. How do you expect me to tell Rachael?"

I blink at him and look down at the gun.

"This isn't you," he continues.

I lower my head. He's right. I don't have the nerve to kill anyone, not even a snake like Tobias. He steps closer and outstretches his hand.

"Give me the gun," he says quietly.

"It's all I have left of her," I say.

He shakes his head and continues to tread closer.

"She's still here. She'll come home to you soon. Give me the gun."

He outstretches his hand again. I look down at the gun then back up at him, his eyes bulging. I sigh then slowly place the gun in his hand and drop to my knees. He sits down on the hard floor opposite me and wraps a hand round my back.

"What's Rachael going to think of me?"

He smiles and pats me hard.

"I won't tell if you don't. It'll be our secret. Just think with your heart next time and not your head."

I crack a half smile. Trent leans back on his heels and blows out.

"Impulse is dangerous. Am I right?" he says.

I scoff.

"You don't know the half of it."

He pats me on the back and grips my shoulder just as my cell rings. I jump up and dash for it: unknown number. I frown and show Trent who still kneels on the floor. I answer.

"Yes?"

"Hello. Is this Mark Flint?" a female voice speaks softly.

"It is."

"This is Nurse Crawford. I'm just phoning to let you know that Rachael is now breathing unaided."

I sit on the couch.

"That's great news."

"Also, she has started to show some movement. We think that she may be starting to stir."

I widen my eyes as Trent places Rachael's gun back with her uniform.

"Thank you. I'll be right there," I say, then hang up quickly and leap to my feet.

"Rachael is starting to wake."

He grins.

"You see, what'd I tell you? Back home in no time."

I slip on my leather jacket and grab my bike helmet.

"Let's go," I say.

He grabs his keys and we run to the front door.

Trent drops me off at the entrance of the hospital as he goes to park. I remove my helmet, tuck it under my arm and rush towards Urgent Care. I push through the sterile double doors where Nurse Crawford is sat at the nurses' station. As I rush over, she glances up and smiles.

"How is she?" I ask, panting.

She stands from behind her desk and gestures towards Rachael's room.

"We took her off the ventilator last night. She's doing well on her own," she says as I rush alongside her.

"Is she awake?"

"Not yet. We did see movement last night, but it may still be a couple of days, we'll have to wait."

I frown.

"How's the bleed?" I press further as we arrive at Rachael's room.

"It's completely healed. We expect her to make a full recovery."

I look through the window at her. Her eyes are still closed, but less wires surround her. Without the ventilator, her face is fully visible; her straight nose, her full lips; the cuts and bruises that tarnished her beautiful face are slowly diminishing. I immediately go to sit beside her, lean down, and plant a delicate kiss on her lips. They're just as warm and sweet as I remember. She continues to lie still. I sigh and pick up her book just as Trent enters the room.

"Where were we last?" I say to Rachael, opening the book.

"Ah yes. Chapter Seven."

I sit back in my seat and read the first paragraph in my head and chuckle slightly.

"Wow, this is soppy, but I like it."

Trent sniggers. I glance over at him as he glares at me through one eye. I ignore his probing stare and look back at her, square my shoulders and start to read aloud.

Hours have passed and she remains asleep. Trent gets up from his chair and walks over to us. I stare up at him, feeling a little disheartened.

"We should get you home."

"But she could wake any minute."

He glances down at me.

"Well then, you'll need to look your best. When was the last time you had a shower?" he asks, crinkling his nose.

"A while."

"I'll tell you what. Get yourself cleaned up, then I'll bring you back. Deal?"

"Okay. Deal."

Trent makes for the couch as I close the bathroom door behind me. I look in the mirror and blow out. Wow, I am a mess. He wasn't lying. My hair is greasy and sticks to my face, my eyes are baggy and dark, my lips are dry and chapped, my white shirt is beginning to turn gray, and my muzzle is thick and bushy.

"I don't hear water running," he calls.

I roll my eyes.

"Okay, 'dad'," I call back, but then my heart sinks.

I strip out of my smelly old clothes and discard them on the floor, then I climb into the shower cubicle and turn the faucet. Warm water rains down on me and I begin to wash myself thrice over, washing away the dirt on my body and the doubts in my mind.

I step out of the bathroom, feeling refreshed and cleansed. Trent turns off the TV and stares at me down the corridor.

"Aren't you forgetting something?" he grins.

I roll my eyes and sag my shoulders.

"What?"

He rubs round his chin prompting me to do the same. My fingers are pricked by my long, spiky muzzle.

"Oh."

I walk back into the bathroom and shave. When I'm finished, I rush by Trent into my bedroom where I change into a striped, blue shirt and pair of black jeans then I enter the lounge and stand in the middle of the room. Trent looks up from his Stephen King novel.

"How do I look?"

He grins and gets to his feet.

"Less like a bum."

I titter.

"I've heard that one before. Can we go back now?"

He removes his keys from his pocket.

"Sure. Let's go," he says, heading for the front door.

I'm dropped off at the all too familiar hospital entrance. Trent waves, then revs his bike and drives away. I stride back towards Rachael's room. Nurse Crawford grins at me on my way through.

"Looking good, Mark," she calls, waving at me.

I grin and offer a quick wave on my way past. I bump into a doctor who's just leaving Rachael's room. He drops his notes on the floor at my feet.

"Oh geez, sorry," I say.

I bend down and scoop up the papers, then hand them to him and step back. Mitch smiles at me in his doctor's coat.

"Mitch?"

"Hello, Mark. Surprise."

"What are you doing here?"

"Trent called, told me about Rachael. I transferred myself here. Let me just start by saying how sorry I am about Rachael, but I'm now the lead physician of your wife's care. She's doing well. She surprised us all at the speed of her recovery."

I pull him into a one-armed hug.

"Thank you for this, Mitch. I owe you."

He shakes his head and holds up his hand.

"Nonsense. It's what I do. I'll leave you two alone for a moment. I'll be back later."

He walks past me, his footsteps echoing off the polished floor. I head inside hoping to see Rachael awake, but she's still asleep. I sigh and sit in the chair beside her bed where I retrieve the book and open it to where we left off.

"Sorry I left so suddenly... 'Miss Bennet,'" I chuckle.

"No problem, 'Mr. Darcy,'" she groans weakly.

I freeze, the book falls from my hands and slaps onto the floor. I leap out of my seat and bend over the bed. Rachael's eyes twitch ever so slightly, then the moment I've been dreaming of, her dazed hazel eyes open slowly and glance around the room before coming to rest on me. My mouth falls open and I drop to my knees beside her.

"Rachael?" I whisper.

She stares up at me and weakly lifts her hand to my face.

"Hi, Mark," she rasps.

Chapter Nineteen

I continue to stare down at Rachael, overjoyed that she's come back to me. Her hand falls away from my face and limply drops onto the bed. She slowly looks around again and attempts to sit up. I leap from the ground, place my hands gently on her shoulders and slowly lower her.

"You need to lie still," I say, pressing the call button above the bed.

Her eyes squint.

"What happened?" she rasps.

I purse my lips and perch on the side of the bed, then run my fingers deftly through her hair.

"You were in an accident. You've been in a coma for a couple of days."

She furrows her brow and looks down at her right arm. She fingers the wires protruding from it, then she widens her eyes, and sits up again.

"The van!" she shouts.

I gently push at her shoulders again, lowering her back onto the stacked pillows.

"Don't worry. I've spoken to Steph; they're dealing with it."

Mitch appears in the doorway, a clipboard tucked under his arm. He looks towards Rachael, his glasses catching the light from the nearby window. He smiles and steps into the room.

"Welcome back, Rachael," he says.

Her mouth forms a perfect 'o'.

"Mitch? What are you doing here?"

His face splits into a megawatt smile as he perches himself in the chair beside her.

"I transferred myself here after I heard about the accident."

"Well, thank you. You didn't need to go through so much trouble for me," she says.

He takes her hand in his and taps it.

"It's no trouble, it's what I do. Now, I must ask, do you know where you are?"

"Yes. Hospital."

"You were in a nasty accident. You've been in a coma for a couple of days."

"Mark told me."

"Do you remember the accident?"

Her eyes narrow, then she shakes her head.

"No, I don't. I remember chasing this van that was loaded with stolen cash, then... everything went black."

She closes her eyes and rubs her forehead firmly.

"Are you in pain?"

I peek at her.

"A little sore, and I have a headache."

"You'll be sore for a few days. Would you like some pain killers?"

She nods and lowers herself back down.

"I'll get Nurse Crawford to bring you some," he says.

He stands and leaves the room as I take her hand and stroke it with my thumb. She sighs, shuts her eyes, then reopens them and glances at me.

"Were you worried?" she asks.

I nod as I recall the ordeal; seeing the upturned cruiser, Rachael unconscious on the wet ground, thinking that I'd lost her, the dread when I was told she had a bleed on the brain, Louise and Sara bursting into tears before me. I was full of uncertainty and anger. *I still am.*

"I was there," I say.

She struggles up onto her elbows.

"You were?"

"Yeah. I saw you chasing the van, then I heard a bang and I rushed to the scene. Your car was upside down on the sidewalk."

"I don't remember that."

"Why should you? I ran over to you and held you… I cried. I thought you were gone."

She reaches her hand over and glides her fingers through my hair.

"I'm sorry."

"Please. Don't be. You're here."

She leans her torso against mine and wraps her arms tightly round me. I envelope her in my arms and bury my face into her shoulder. She caresses my back with her hands. Tears flow from my eyes as I plant my lips on her neck and feather her hair with my fingers.

"Please don't leave me again," I muffle.

"Not happening."

I sniff against her. We break away and I remove my phone from my pocket.

"I gotta make some calls," I say.

She smiles weakly.

"Don't let me stop ya."

I dial Sara's number; it rings several times.

"Mark?"

"Hi, Sara. Rachael's awake."

She's silent, then gentle sobs sound through the phone.

"She is?"

"Yes, she just woke up."

She bursts into tears.

"Colin?" she shouts, making me draw the phone away from my ear.

"What? What? Is it Rachael?" he asks.

"She's awake. Mark just told me."

"She is? Grab your coat."

"We'll be over soon. Thank you, Mark," Sara says.

"No problem."

Now to call Trent. He answers almost immediately.

"Mark?"

I repeat my news to him that she's woken. He laughs.

"That's great, buddy! See? I told you she was a strong one. I'll visit after work. Does she know about my donation?"

"No. Not yet."

"I'd like to tell her… if she's up to talking."

I remove the phone from my ear and look back at her. She's sitting up in bed, looking through the window at me with hooded eyes.

"Hold on," I say to Trent.

I head back into the room and offer her the phone.

"Trent wants to talk to you. Is that alright?"

She nods and takes the phone.

"Trent?"

I place my hand on her forearm and stroke back and forth.

"Sore, but I'm gonna be okay."

I glide my fingers down to her hand and grasp delicately. She gasps.

"What? Really? But how?"

Her lips part, and she strokes my hand.

"I- Thank you so much. I owe you a big wet kiss."

I snigger. She laughs but winces and clutches her ribs. My eyes dart to hers. She smiles and nods.

"Nice talking to you too, Trent. Thank you again. See you soon."

She hangs up and hands the phone back to me.

"You knew about that?" she asks.

"What?"

"What he did for me."

I nod.

"He told me yesterday. And like you, I gave him a big wet kiss."

She giggles and yawns just as Nurse Crawford steps into the room, holding a small paper cup.

"Doctor Baker said you needed pain relief."

She hands her the cup and pours her a small glass of water.

"Careful now, drink plenty of fluids."

Rachael downs both capsules with a large sip of water.

"Thank you," she says.

"Of course. Get some rest," Nurse Crawford smiles, before leaving the room and closing the door softly.

"I'm going to need some more sleep," she murmurs.

She releases my hand and lies back on the bed, her eyelids fluttering.

"Don't drift too far this time."

She smirks as her eyes shut. I tuck her in, kiss her on the lips and cling to her warm hand.

Rachael is in much better spirits after waking up a couple of days ago. She ate her first meal yesterday and sat up in bed, laughing with each of her visitors. I sit beside her and read more from her book as she leans in, but then she frowns, causing me to stop.

"You alright?" I ask.

"Did they catch the driver?"

I close the book, using my thumb as a bookmark.

"We don't need to discuss this now."

Her frown deepens.

"I want to know."

I sigh.

"They got him."

"And the money?"

I shake my head.

"It wasn't in there. It was a decoy. Sorry."

She exhales and slumps back against her pillows.

"How do you know?"

"Steph."

"Of course."

She folds her arms under her bosom and sniffs.

"So, where's the *real* van?" she asks.

"They don't know. They've been tracking it but…"

She sighs.

"I should've stopped him."

"It's not your fault. You had no idea what was going to happen."

She purses her lips.

"What about the bastard that put me here?"

His hideous smirk breaches into my mind. *I can't tell her what I was thinking.*

"He's behind bars too. I don't want to think about him. The important thing now, is for you to get better."

"Good to know two of those assholes are off the streets, I suppose."

I reopen the book.

"Shall I continue?"

She lifts her head up, grins, and crosses her hands on her lap.

"Proceed."

After several more tests from the doctor, Rachael is declared fit to go home in a few hours. I get out of my seat, quickly peck her on the cheek and make for the door.

"Where you going?" she calls.

I peek over my shoulder and smile.

"Just going to make our apartment presentable before you get home."

She laughs.

"Been throwing parties without me?"

I laugh loudly. *I've missed her wit.*

"I haven't been able to get my lazy ass to work. No way would I have been able to host a party."

She laughs as I return to kiss her again.

"I'll be back soon," I whisper.

I've made the bed and cleaned the dishes covered in congealing stains that were left over from our meal the night before the crash. The crunching metal and the smashed glass underfoot erupts in my ears again; I shake my head and try to divert my thoughts to happier things, She's been discharged from hospital and when I'm finished here, I'll go back and bring her home. I make for the door but as an afterthought, I plump the cushions on the couch and grab her car keys, it'll be better and faster to bring her home in her car and I'm sure she'll appreciate it more. I rush down to the underground garage where I press the key fob. I climb into the driver's seat then pause. I've never done this alone; my gut twists and I feel a little sick. I take a few breaths, then start the car and pull out of the garage.

After an arduous search for a parking space back at the hospital, I finally manage to park up and rush back to Rachael's room. She's sitting on the bed, already dressed. She smiles as I enter.

"Hi," she breathes.

I lean down and kiss her.

"Hi. Ready to go home?"

She nods then struggles to her feet. I quickly grab her arm to support her. She clings onto my shirt and finally manages to pull herself up. She winces and clutches her right side.

"You okay?" I ask.

"Yep. Just still sore. I'll be fine. Take me home."

She limps out of the room, still holding firmly onto my arm. We walk past the nurses' station. Mitch chats quickly to Nurse Crawford, who strokes her index finger across her lips and nods. They stop talking and stare at us both as we approach.

"Thank you, for everything. Both of you" I say.

Mitch smiles and comes out from behind the desk where he hugs first Rachael, then me.

"My pleasure. Take care of yourselves," he says as he releases me.

We make for the elevators, ride them down to the ground floor and out into the balmy afternoon heat. She stops and takes a deep breath, then looks around.

"Shall we hail a cab?" she asks.

"A cab? I have something better in mind."

She raises her eyebrows.

"You do?"

I lead her to the parking lot and towards her car. Her eyes widen and she whips her startled expression at me.

"You *drove* my car here?"

"I thought you'd like to ride in something more familiar."

I lead her to the passenger side door where I open it wide and help her in.

"M'lady," I bow.

She giggles and brushes her hand through my stubble, making my breath catch in my throat.

"Mr. Darcy," she says, slipping into the car.

I slam the door shut and walk round to the driver's side, twirling the keys round my finger. I'm so happy to have my Rachael back and I can't wait to get her home.

Chapter Twenty

W e're stopped at a red light just outside our apartment. Rachael peers out the window as I tap the steering wheel with my thumb.

"Why are there officers outside our building?" she asks.

A tight knot forms in my chest as I recall the note. Bile rises in my throat. I hastily swallow it back down and grip the wheel tighter causing my knuckles to pale. Thankfully, the light turns green, and I make a sharp left. In the periphery of my vision, she stares at me, her perfect brow furrowed, and her mouth forms a thin line.

"Mark?"

I'm not going to escape this. Gotta give her something.

"There was… a disturbance while you were away."

"A disturbance? What kind?"

I turn into the underground garage a bit too harshly, the tires shriek in protest.

"We don't have to discuss this now, honey. You need to rest."

Her frown deepens as I park up and cut the engine.

"I want to know. Please. Or I'll call Steph."

I fold my arms and turn in my seat to face her.

"There was a note outside our door. No address. It just had my name on it."

"Who from?"

"Tobias… or one of his goons. He was at our apartment. We're currently under protection."

Her mouth pops open, her cheeks slowly turn red, and she slumps back in her seat.

"What did it say?"

I run my hand through my hair. When I look back at her, she's still regarding me closely.

"*I'll see you soon*."

Her lips thin, then she wraps her soft hand round mine.

"I wouldn't worry. He must be doing this to scare us."

"You were only just put into the hospital when the letter came through. It's not a coincidence."

"I know, but it won't matter once we get him off the streets. For now, let's just go inside."

I squeeze her hand and smile.

"Yeah, let's."

I fish the keys out of my pocket and unlock the door. Rachael heads in first, I rush after her, closing the door behind us and locking it. She stands in the hallway and glances around the apartment before she limps into the lounge and sits on the couch. She throws her head back against the cushions and lets out a long drawn-out groan. I lean against the wall and watch her, my legs crossed at the ankle. She raises her head, smiles, and pats the cushion beside her. I join her, drape my arm over the backs of her shoulders and stroke her gently. She lies across me, her head resting on my lap.

"It's so good to be back," she says.

"I couldn't agree more."

I lean down to kiss her, my long floppy hair brushing her face as she combs it away with her fingers. I sit up and flick it back.

"Sorry," I chuckle.

She giggles and reaches up to stroke her fingers through it again.

"I've always loved it."

I kiss her again but this time she deepens it. I lie down with her, so our bodies are pressed together. I've missed her touch, her sweet scent and there's nothing I want more than to rekindle with her, to forget about the past week. There's a loud knock on the door. We break apart and look towards it. I groan and roll my eyes, but she bursts into laughter and shrugs.

"Sorry, Mark."

I get up from the couch and look through the spy hole. It's Steph, clutching a small bouquet of flowers. I unlock the door and open it.

"I heard Rachael was home," she says.

I look behind me. She's still sitting on the couch, staring down the hall.

"She is. Come in," I say, opening the door wider.

Steph steps inside and rushes towards her. I close the door and lean against it as Rachael and Steph hug.

"Hey, Steph. I'm alright," she whispers, stroking her hair.

I join them both and take the flowers.

"I'd better put these in some water," I say.

Rachael nods.

"Thanks."

I head into the kitchen and root in the cabinets for a vase. I find one under the sink, then place it under the faucet and fill it with water before putting the flowers into it. Rachael and Steph speak incoherently from the lounge. I pick up the vase, carry it into the lounge and place it on the windowsill, then I sit beside Rachael and drape my arm round her back. She peeks at me, strokes my face, and looks back at Steph.

"Mark tells me that you caught the driver and my attacker," Rachael says.

Steph's grin slips as she peeks at me. I look down at the ground.

"We did," she says.

Rachael looks from me to Steph.

"And that the van was a dud."

Steph swallows and sits back in her seat.

"Rachael, it's not important. I just need you to get better," Steph says.

"I'm fine. I need to be in the know."

Steph swallows again, glances at me and sighs, then looks back at Rachael.

"We may have another lead on the *real* one. It's still in the city," Steph says.

"Was there anything in the fake one?" Rachael asks.

"Just old newspapers."

Of course. I remember.

"Tobias' crew pulled off a few of those tricks while I was with them," I break in.

They both glance at me. *You idiot. Why did you say that?*

"I didn't play an active part, I just umm…"

I clear my throat.

"...I counted the money after the job was done... while Tobias would tell me about how they pulled the switch with the vans."

Rachael's brows knit together.

"You never mentioned that."

"Yeah. It only just came back to me. Sorry."

She sits back and clasps her hands together.

"I see," she says.

I clear my throat again and quickly stand up. *God. I feel like shit.*

"Anyone want a drink?" I ask.

They both continue to stare at me. I hold my breath before Rachael smiles as does Steph.

"Yes please," Rachael says.

I rush into the kitchen, away from her probing stare where I quickly examine what we have to offer. I eye the whiskey left over from Christmas; I could do with a stiff drink.

"Whiskey?" I call.

"Please," Rachael calls.

"Just water for me, I need to drive," Steph says.

I grab some glasses from the cabinet, pour out some water for Steph and whiskey for me and Rachael. I head back in with the drinks and hand them out, thankfully, the conversation has shifted to something lighter as they chat about when Rachael ran twenty-five minutes late for our wedding. I grin and laugh.

"I thought you were going to abandon me at the altar," I laugh.

Night has fallen over the city. Me, Rachael, and Steph have just finished pizza and are now watching Breaking Bad on Netflix. Rachael shushes anyone who dares speak. Steph checks her watch and stands from the couch.

"Sorry, guys, I'd better be going, I'm on shift soon."

Rachael switches off the program and gets to her feet shakily. I rush to help her, and we all walk to the front door together. Steph opens the door, then stops and turns. She hugs me, then Rachael.

"I'm so glad you're okay," she whispers close to her ear.

Rachael gently pushes her away and smiles.

"Thank you for coming and for the flowers."

Steph grins then walks down the corridor and disappears into a waiting elevator. We head back inside together, Rachael closes the door, leans against it, and eyes me.

"What now?" I ask.

She lunges for me, kisses me hard and pushes me against the wall. I run my fingers through her long silky hair and kiss her back with my own fervor. I run my hands down her body and pull her against the length of mine. She winces and gasps. I freeze and loosen my grip. She stops kissing me and runs her nose down mine.

"Why are you stopping?" she asks.

"I can't, Rachael. You're hurt."

She frowns and strokes my face.

"I don't care. I need this," she says, kissing me along my jawline.

"I know, me too. It's just…"

She breaks away and runs her nose down mine.

"What?" she whispers.

"I don't want to hurt you."

She smiles and kisses the corner of my mouth.

"It'll be fine. Please, Mark. I need this."

She continues to kiss me across my jaw. I melt against her and stare down into her hazel eyes.

"Are you sure?" I ask.

"Yes."

"Anytime you want me to stop…"

She nods and nips my earlobe.

"I'll tell you."

I smirk, kiss her again then scoop her up into my arms and carry her to the bedroom.

I twirl a lock of her hair round my fingers as we lie in our post coital bliss. Her body heat and sweet fragrance fills all my senses. She rests her head against my shoulder, her breath radiating me. Sweat beads on my chest and forehead as I delicately run my hand up and down her spine. I eye the bruises that cover her legs and arms. There's a small one still visible on her right cheek and under her left eye. A small cut is still clear on her bottom lip.

"I didn't hurt you, did I?" I ask.

She peeks up through her lashes and smiles.

"No."

I roll onto my side as does she.

"You know, I wanted to kill that asshole," I hiss.

There, it's finally out. She props herself up on her elbow and combs a stray lock of hair from my eyes.

"Which one?"

"The one who nearly took you from me. Trent and Steph stopped me."

"Well, I'm glad they did. It's okay to be angry, but not like that."

"I know. I just… really want them out of our lives."

She lies her head on my chest and sighs softly.

"We all do. We'll get them. Just give it a little time."

"I can live with that."

"Good."

I peek down at her. Her eyelids flutter slightly, and she yawns loudly.

"You okay?" I ask.

"Yeah. Just very tired."

I pull the duvet up, covering us both, wrap my arms round her and close my eyes. The sound of broken glass, crunching metal, shouting, and distorted sirens ring through my head unannounced. Tobias' voice from my earlier nightmare reflects in my mind's eye. *'Join me.'* My eyes snap open and I bolt out of bed, breathing rapidly and running both hands through my hair.

"Mark, what is it?"

She's by my side; her slender hands clasp my shoulders. I blink at her, the cuts and bruises that cover her flawless body are my undoing. I sit on the edge of the bed and rub my face frantically.

"I just wanted to protect you. It's what I promised on our wedding day. I can't help feeling responsible for the crash," I say through my fingers.

She gasps and the bed dips, then her hands are round me again.

"How can you say such a thing about yourself? This wasn't your fault."

What I would give to believe her words, but I can't accept them. She places her hands either side of my face and gently turns it until I face her.

"It wasn't your fault," she reiterates.

I place my hands on top of hers and get lost in the deep depths of her loving stare; my sanctuary; my shining light.

"You know, you've always been so good to me. So patient. So understanding," I say.

"I'm a good judge of character. Got that from Mom, I suppose. You're a good man. You need to stop doubting it. The crash was awful, sure, but that wasn't your doing. All this madness comes from a deluded psychopath. Not you."

"How do we stop him?"

She sits back on her heels.

"There's nothing you can do. This is for the police to do."

"I can't just sit here and do nothing. Watching the news, staring at my phone, just preparing for the worst. I've been left alone enough already. Don't you leave me."

My voice hitches and I pant. *Alone, sobbing incessantly on that sticky couch.*

"I'm going nowhere. It's been an awful week, I know, but try to relax. Everything will be fine. I'll make sure of it."

"Okay."

She exhales and rises smoothly.

"I don't know about you, but I'm exhausted. Let's just get back into bed and cuddle. Whaddya' you say?"

"Sounds nice."

She throws the duvet aside and pats the mattress.

"Shall we then?"

The morning traffic report rouses me and the sun beams through the gap in the curtains. I roll over, slam off the traffic report and stare down at Rachael. She groans and rolls over in bed so that her back is facing me, she remains asleep. I slip out of bed and retrieve my briefs that lie in a crumpled mess on the floor. I pull them on and sneak out of the bedroom and make for the kitchen, I want to make her breakfast in bed. I look in the fridge and try to decide on something hearty for breakfast. I spy the eggs. Scrambled eggs, maybe? I take a pan from the drawer, place it on the stove and heat a little butter, then I crack some eggs, pour in some milk, and whisk hard. I pop some bread into the toaster and stare out of the kitchen window at the street below while I wait for everything to cook, but the smell of burning gets my attention, I turn to investigate, it's not coming from the toaster so it must be the pan. I stir the mixture swiftly, but the bottom of the pan blackens. I turn off the heat and frown just as the toast pops up.

"Do I smell burning?"

I swing round. She leans against the door frame, dressed in just her silk robe. I rest my back against the marble counter.

"I thought I'd make you breakfast."

She walks further into the kitchen and looks over my shoulder at the burnt monstrosity that was supposed to be breakfast.

"I'll try it," she says.

I turn my heated face away from her smirk as I busy myself with buttering the toast and pouring what's left of the egg onto it. I hand it to her as she glances down at her plate.

"Looks nice."

I settle with just coffee. I walk into the lounge and sit on the couch as she tucks into her breakfast. She chews slowly and looks up.

"It's bad, isn't it?" I say.

She swallows and grins.

"You need to have a bit more confidence in yourself. It's lovely, thank you."

I sip my coffee and cock my head to the side. *I think she's just trying to be nice.*

"Want to try it?" she asks, holding a fork full of food up at me.

I get up and eat the fork of food she's offering. *She's right. It's delicious.*

"See?" she smiles as she continues to devour her eggs.

"What do you want to do today?" she asks, her mouth half full.

"Well, first thing, I need to call Mr. Levitt and apologize for my sudden absence, then…"

I twist my mouth.

"…Shall we stay home?"

She crinkles her nose.

"What? Boring. I want to go out, I need some air."

"Fine. How about rowing in Central Park again?"

She pushes her empty plate away and laughs.

"You're not going to throw me into the water again, are you?"

"I won't, I promise."

"Sounds fun. Let's do that… Unless they've banned us," she grins.

It's mid-morning and the sun beats down. We walk hand in hand towards the Loeb Boathouse as I quickly dial Mr. Levitt's number.

"I won't be a moment," I say, shaking my phone at her.

She nods and pulls me towards a nearby bench. It rings a couple of times before he answers.

"Good morning. Neapolitan."

"Hello, sir."

"Mark? Hello. Lovely to hear from you. Any updates?"

"I just wanted to apologize for my disappearance. My wife was in a car accident, and I rushed to hospital to be with her."

"Relax, son. Trent told me everything after it happened. I didn't call because I thought you wanted some privacy. It must have been very distressing for you. Believe me, I've been there."

His son. Of course.

"Thank you for your understanding, sir. I'll be back to work soon."

"There's no rush. Take your time. How is she now?"

I glance at her; she rubs her legs and blows out. I think she's still in pain.

"She's on the mend, thank you."

"Oh, that's wonderful. Thank you for calling and letting me know. See you soon, I hope."

"Of course. See you soon. Thanks again."

I hang up and pocket my phone.

"Sounds like that went well," she says.

"He's a very considerate man. I'm lucky to have a boss like him."

She smiles, stands, and offers her hand.

"Let's keep moving. I'm feeling a little stiff."

I take her hand and get to my feet.

"Would you like to head home?" I ask.

She shakes her head.

"I like being out."

We stroll past several street artists and performers, couples walking their dogs as they laugh carefree together, and children play around us with their parents watching on. We stop outside the Loeb Boathouse. The boats row slowly on the lake. She chuckles and gives me a sideways glance.

"What?" I grin.

"Don't throw me in this time."

"I promise."

She takes my hand and leads me towards the jetty where we spot the same man from last time, pushing a boat into the water with a family seated inside. We approach as the man glances up at us and frowns, I don't think he likes me very much. I stand tall beside Rachael and clear my throat.

"We'd like to hire a boat, please," I say.

He glances from me to Rachael and his frown deepens.

"Are you going to behave this time?" he grumbles.

She stifles a snigger beside me, I look down at her and back at the man.

"We will. Won't we, honey?"

She nods and grins at me. He sighs heavily and rubs his forehead.

"Alright."

He gestures with his hand towards one of the boats. I lead her towards it, help her in and pay the fee, then I climb into the boat myself as the man pushes us into the water. He continues to glance at me, his mouth sets into a flat line and he narrows his eyes. *Hey, while you're busy scowling at me, there's a queue behind you.* The boat glides smoothly away from the jetty, I grasp both oars and row us towards Bow Bridge. Rachael lies her head back and like she did last time, she places her hand in the water and splashes lightly. Other boats glide around us. Excited children squeal and point in all directions and happy couples laugh around us. Ducks bob up and down on the gentle ripples of the lake, and the nearby trees sway softly in the calming breeze. She glances up at the blue sky, her eyes are closed and her hair glows in the sun, burnishing hints of red and deep purple.

"Lovely day," I say.

She sits up and glances at me through one eye.

"Quite stunning."

"Hey, you stole my line."

She shrugs and looks back up at the sky.

"So, sue me."

I chuckle and pull harder at the oars. My legs start to ache with the effort, but I don't care. I ignore the niggling pain and keep rowing. The sun slowly fades behind the clouds and the sky turns an eerie gray, promising rain. She glances back up at the sky and frowns. All the other boats around us begin retreating to land.

"We should get back," she says quietly.

I nod and like everyone else, we make for the jetty. On our approach, the heavens open and the rain arrives, light at first but gradually, it gets heavier and lashes down on us. There are three men at the jetty, hurriedly getting the boats out of the water. A young man grabs our boat and pulls us ashore. I climb out and take her hand, pulling her up with me. The rain pats down harder and both of us are soaked. She hasn't got a coat or a jacket, she wraps her arms around herself and snuggles in close to me. I quickly shrug out of my jacket and drape it over our heads, then we run home as the rain and thunder worsen.

We barge through our front door; both soaked and cold. I hold my dripping jacket in my hand and shake it off as best I can. She heads into the bathroom and wrings the water out of her hair then bursts into hysterics. I stand in the doorway, my hair wet and stuck against my face as I watch her double over.

"Want to share the joke?" I smirk.

She recomposes herself and smiles at me.

"That was so much fun."

I step into the bathroom to join her until we're nose to nose. I raise my hand and comb her drenched hair from her face as beads of water form on our skin. She glances up into my eyes then she leans in slowly and plants a gentle kiss on my lips. I open my eyes and glance down at her.

"I love you… You know that, right?" I whisper.

She nods and rests her head against my damp shirt.

"I love you too."

I wrap my arms around her, and we stand in the middle of the bathroom, cocooned in each other's damp but loving embrace. Eventually, she pulls away and glances down at our damp clothes.

"We should dry off. Don't want to catch a cold."

"Agreed."

I walk towards the bedroom with Rachael following. We strip out of our wet clothes and place them in the laundry hamper.

"I'm going to take a shower," she says.

She retreats from the bedroom, leaving me standing only in my briefs as the thundering rain lashes against our bedroom window.

We're both showered and draped in our bathrobes. We're snuggled up on the couch with a bowl of popcorn, watching movies together. We've watched The Notebook for what feels like the hundredth time since we got together, and I yawn loudly. She jabs me in the side with her elbow.

"Boring?" she asks.

"No, but we've watched this film a lot. Can't we watch something else?"

"Well, we can relate to the boat scene don't you think?" she arches a brow and grins.

I chortle.

"Sure. It was fun. I just thought it would be nice to watch something… new."

"What would you suggest?"

I try to think of a suggestion, but I don't know much about movies. She continues to stare, but I shrug my shoulders, wrap my arm round her back and rest my head against hers.

"This is fine."

She looks back to the TV as I sit back and mouth along with the words.

The film credits roll as Rachael dabs her eyes with a tissue. I roll my eyes and blow out, then my cell rings. I leap off the couch and grab it from the kitchen. It's Trent. I answer quickly.

"Hey, man," I greet warmly.

"Hey, bud. How's Rachael?"

I glance out of the kitchen; her slender legs are tucked under her.

"She's on the mend."

"Oh, I'm so glad to hear it. When are you coming back to work?"

I breathe out and pinch my nose, not looking forward to my return. I'd prefer to stay home and nurse Rachael back to health.

"I dunno," I respond.

He falls silent for a moment.

"You can't stay away forever you know."

"I know, Trent… hold on."

I walk back into the lounge just as she switches off the movie. She stares at me and cocks her head to one side.

"When do you think I should go back to work?" I ask.

She shrugs.

"That's up to you."

"But I need to stay home and care for you."

"I'll be just fine."

I frown, then place the cell back to my ear.

"What would you suggest?"

"What if you have a half-day tomorrow?" he asks.

"I'd have to ask Mr. Levitt."

"I already have. He agreed, said he'd speak to you when he sees you next."

My throat constricts as I try to squeeze the words through.

"I'll come tomorrow," I say.

"I'll let him know. Looking forward to seeing you."

"Me too," I respond truthfully, then he hangs up.

I flop back onto the couch; she snuggles in close again and glances up.

"What's wrong?"

I peek down at her and sigh heavily.

"I don't want to leave you on your own."

She sits up straight and places a hand against my cheek.

"I'll be fine. Nothing's going to happen to me here. Besides, we've got protection outside."

I rub my face, but her soft hand caresses my arm, causing me to peek through my fingers.

"I promise you," she grins.

I remove my hands from my face and cup both her hands in mine.

"You will call if you need anything?"

"I promise."

I grin and lean in to kiss her softly which she reciprocates then we lie back on the couch and continue with our movie marathon.

Trent picked me up from home today and brought me to work kicking and screaming. I reluctantly left Rachael home alone and I'm hating every second. I manage to crack a small smile as I remember her helping me with my tie this morning and her constant encouragement that she'd be fine, but the crash refuses to leave my mind. I shake my head and try to continue with my shift. Mr. Levitt and I reached an agreement that I'll be on a half shift until Rachael has made a full recovery. Trent sits beside me, focusing hard on his computer screen as I attempt to do the same. We're in the middle of check out time, so it's all systems go. Thankfully, it's approaching lunchtime. I log out of the computer and head up to the staff room, keen to check on Rachael. I grab my cell from my locker and quickly dial her number, it rings several times and I fear that she's not going to answer but then, her sweet voice comes through the phone.

"How's work going?" she asks.

"It's tiresome. I can't wait to come home."

I feel her warm smile down the phone.

"Me too."

"Are you okay?" I ask.

"Yeah, of course I am. Why wouldn't I be?"

I rake my free hand through my hair and sit on one of the nearby armchairs.

"I just can't stop worrying about you."

"I'm fine, honestly."

I grin at her sincerity, but my mind refuses to stop replaying the events over and over.

"Mark?"

"Yeah, I'm still here."

"You need to try and calm down, okay? I know what happened was bad but I'm fine now."

I nod. She's right. I need to get a grip, then an appealing thought comes to mind.

"Would you like to go out for dinner?" I ask.

"That was a quick change of subject. I'd love to."

"Be ready by four. We're going on a date."

"I'll look forward to that. Thank you."

"See you at four."

I hang up and immediately go online to make reservations. *But where to go?* I browse the internet, trying to remember the name of the restaurant where we went together on our first date. I sit back and think about that night. God was I anxious. We talked about our feelings for each other, we learnt more about each other, then she took me by surprise when she invited me back to her place where we hugged for the first time. How far we've come since that day. I shake my head and try to think of the name of the restaurant; it was some sort of Italian name, Storo, Storiano, Stocco... Storico, that's it. I go onto their website and book a table for four-thirty tonight. I check my watch, 1:55 p.m. I'd better get back to work. I leave the staff room and head for the lobby in a much better mood as I think about our dinner date where we'll finally forget about the awful events from last week.

The last hour of my shift drags. I'm checking my watch more than I'd like. *The time is going backwards, not forwards!* But it's coming to an end now. Me and Trent leave the hotel together and walk in separate directions.

"Hey, want a ride home?" he calls after me.

I turn back to him.

"No thanks. I'll see you tomorrow."

He smiles and waves which I return.

"See you tomorrow morning," he shouts then turns and strides towards his bike. I carry on with my walk home. I'm looking forward to seeing her again and taking a trip down memory lane. We dine at Storico tonight.

Chapter Twenty-One

I unlock our front door, stride in and make a beeline for the lounge. Rachael isn't there, but her smartphone rests on a dock on the windowsill as music fills the room.

"Rachael?" I call.

"I'm in the bedroom. Just getting my shoes on," she calls back.

I sit on the couch and clasp my hands together. The music shuffles to the next song; a man croons softly and I think I recognize his voice, a distant memory of Grandma liking this sort of music comes back to me and I try to think of his name… Chris de Burgh, I think. I listen to the lyrics and recognize it as 'The Lady in Red'. The bedroom door clicks open, I jump to my feet, ready to greet her, but my mouth dries when she appears. She looks incredible, she's wearing the same red dress that she wore the first time we met up for dinner with glossy red heels, her hair hangs over her right shoulder and is tied into a messy ponytail. Her cheeks are flushed, and her lips are a sharp, eye-catching red. I lick my lips and step forward.

"You look… Wow."

She blushes a delicious pink as I take her hand and plant a delicate kiss onto it. She peeks away.

"Do you think so?" she asks.

With my index finger, I gently place it under her chin and lift her face to mine.

"I know so. You're… quite stunning."

She grins as the song comes to an end. I walk over to the phone dock and replay the song. She stands frozen to the spot, her eyes firmly on me. I stroll back towards her and outstretch my hand.

"May I?"

She produces an all-tooth smile and places her soft hand in mine. I press my body up against hers and slowly sway us to the music as she rests her head against my shoulder, following me step for step.

"You surprise me at every turn," she says softly.

"In what way?"

"I didn't know you could dance. It was a surprise at our wedding."

I chuckle and look down into her sparkling eyes.

"You'll have to thank Trent and Louise for that one."

I place my head against her shoulder and hum along with the words.

It was nearing 11 p.m. and I was exhausted.

"C'mon man. Can we stop this for now?" I moaned.

Trent stood back and shook his head.

"You get sleep when you stop treading on my feet. The bride and groom are expected to share their first dance together and you have a week to shape up," he chastised.

I collapsed onto the couch, groaning while Louise smirked beside me. Trent walked over and pulled me back to my feet as I grumbled my protest.

"We'll get it this time... Like before, put your hand on my waist," he instructed.

I turned my nose up and felt awkward as hell but slowly, I placed my hand against his waist and Louise replayed the song. Trent began to move slowly, making me feel sick.

"This is weird," I moaned.

"Shut up," he grumbled.

I tried to focus, but again, I trod on his feet, and he jumped away. I was utterly frustrated and again slumped back onto the couch as he sat on the floor rubbing his toes.

"I can't do this," I said, throwing my hands up in the air.

Louise huffed beside me and jumped up from the couch.

"You boys are rubbish. C'mon, Mark, I'll teach ya."

She outstretched her hand to me. I furrowed my brow.

"Please. For Rachael?" she said.

I sighed, took her hand and we danced.

"One, two, three. One, two three. See? Easy," she gushed.

I've finally nailed it. Trent stared openmouthed.

"You'll be ready for this in no time," she smiled, squeezing my shoulder.

I park Rachael's Mercedes round the corner from the restaurant, then we walk hand in hand through the bustling streets. We enter the New York Historical Society Museum, walk through the lobby and into Storico. A middle-aged blonde waitress rushes over when we enter.

"Good evening. Table for two?" she greets warmly.

"Please," I say.

The waitress collects a couple of menus then gestures with her hand.

"Right this way."

We follow her as I observe the familiar surroundings. It's just how I remember it; white and yellow furniture with old Italian art, mirrors and shelves stacked with fine china. The rich aroma of herbs and wine tantalize my senses. We arrive at a booth, Rachael slides in delicately, and I take a seat opposite her, unbuttoning my jacket as I do. The waitress places the menus on the table in front of us and rushes back to the door where another couple are waiting to be seated. She picks up her menu and scans quickly, I do the same. Every so often, we catch each other's eyes and quickly look away again.

"I know what I'm having. How about you?" she says, laying the menu flat in front of her.

"Me too."

The waitress walks back over with her notepad and looks from me to Rachael.

"Are you ready to order?"

"Yes. Can I have the vegetable linguine with a side of asparagus and a glass of Pinot Grigio please?"

The waitress writes down the order quickly then diverts her gaze at me.

"Same, please."

Again, she writes down the order then collects the menus from us.

"Thank you. We'll get on it."

The waitress turns and heads towards the kitchen.

"This place holds some fine memories. Do you remember, Mark?"

"How could I forget? This is where we came to talk through our feelings… not so long ago. That's why I booked it."

"And look at us now," she says as she twists her wedding and engagement rings round her finger.

I take her hand. She stares up at me.

"Are you happy?" I ask.

She flinches and blinks.

"Of course I am."

"Good. Me too."

She brushes her thumb across my knuckles. The waitress returns with our drinks, places them down and scurries away again. We both take a gentle sip and I become lost in my own thoughts. The crash refuses to leave my mind, it continues to whirl and nag. Tobias will know that his attempt was unsuccessful, that will just make him more determined. I press my fingers to my right temple.

"Hello?" Rachael whispers close to my ear, causing all the hairs on the back of my neck to stand.

I look at her through hooded eyes, she's smiling at me, her glass still in her hand.

"You were far away. Is something the matter?"

I take another sip of wine, not knowing how to tell her. I don't want to spoil our evening.

"It doesn't matter," I say.

"Tell me."

I put my wine back on the table as I glance at the bruise under her left eye.

"Are you in pain?" I ask.

She shakes her head.

"Not really. It's more annoying than anything."

"Right."

"Where's this coming from? Are you still thinking about that?"

"It's all I can think about. What if Tobias comes for you again?"

"You need to stop doing this to yourself. I'll be fine, I'm safe with you. Nothing is going to happen to me."

"Are you sure?"

She smiles and leans closer until our lips hover close. I can almost taste her.

"I promise," she whispers, her soft breath melting me internally.

I lean into her so that our lips finally meet, and we kiss each other deftly. We break away just as the food arrives. The waitress places it down in front of us, the aroma makes my mouth water. I hadn't realized just how famished I was.

"Enjoy," the waitress smiles, then departs.

We both look down at our food, then I reach for my fork and tuck in. *Delicious.*

"How was your first day back at work?" she asks after a mouthful.

"As to be expected. Busy, but tiresome."

She chortles.

"It's a living."

She shrugs as she picks up a spear of asparagus and clamps it between her teeth slowly. My blood runs hot and fast through my veins. My body responds further as she takes another slow bite. *Is she doing that on purpose? Is it hot in here?* I clear my throat, loosen my tie, take another mouthful and chew slowly as she continues with her torment. I'm drawn to her, and I want her now, in this crowded restaurant. Her eyes dart to mine and she giggles.

"See something you like, Mr. Flint?"

I swallow and lick my parched lips.

"With you, Mrs. Flint, every sight is a pleasure."

She wipes the corner of her mouth with her thumb. *That is not helping.* She carries on with her meal as I try to do the same, but my appetite vanishes fast as I squirm in my seat. Right now, I just want to go back home. She takes a few more bites from her linguine, then returns to the asparagus, takes the spear in her mouth, glances at me and slowly bites down. A slight moan escapes my lips, I place my hand up to my mouth and grip onto the tablecloth.

"Do you have to eat them like that?" I say, shifting in my seat.

"Like what? I'm just enjoying my food."

I take a breath in a feeble attempt to calm myself down but as expected, it doesn't work. I desperately try to distract my wayward thoughts by drumming my fingers against the table then I form a fist, trying to keep my hands busy; again, it doesn't work. I hastily return to my dinner and try to ignore the seductive game that she's playing, but it's no use. I'm drawn to her, like a moth to the flame. I can't wait a minute longer. I push my half-eaten food away just as she polishes off hers. She eyes my bowl and frowns.

"Didn't you like it?"

"No, I loved it, but... you know."

She glances down at my lap.

"Uncomfortable, Mr. Flint?"

"Extremely," I say through gritted teeth.

She quicky summons the waitress who hurries back to us.

"Check, please."

The waitress nods and heads over to a small desk and taps at the screen. Moments later, she's back. I take my card from my wallet and swipe it without checking the amount.

"Have a good evening," the waitress grins.

"We will," I smile, eyeing Rachael who blushes.

I take her elbow and steer her out of the restaurant, back outside into the balmy summer air. We walk down the street and back towards her car while dodging the crowds.

"That wasn't cool what you did in there," I whisper close to her ear, her hair tickling my face.

"What? What I do?"

I shake my head as she continues to plead the fifth. We reach the car; I walk round to the passenger side and open the door.

"M'lady."

"Darcy," she chuckles.

I close the door and rush round to the driver's side. My pants are becoming tighter by the second. I pull at them in a vain attempt to give myself some room. She looks at me through the glass and gestures with her head. I climb into the car and peek over at her, one side of her face is shrouded in darkness, the other is illuminated by the overhead streetlamps.

"What took so long?" she asks.

"Just a little tight."

She reaches over and squeezes my leg.

"I have ways to cure that."

Oh, good god. Time to get home. I turn the engine on, wait for an opening in the traffic then quickly glide in.

We're silent for most of the journey home. I shift in my seat in an attempt to get comfortable; my pants are *really* starting to chafe.

"I think my plan worked too well," she laughs.

I keep my eyes fixed firmly on the road ahead but the corner of my mouth lifts.

"Indeed."

I pull into the underground garage, park into our spot, then cut the engine. We stay rooted in our seats, neither of us speak or look at each other. My deep breathing and the beeping traffic from outside cuts through the silence.

"So, now what?" she says.

She smirks, and I can't stand the wait much more. My adrenaline fully takes over. I unbuckle my seatbelt and swiftly lean across to her side of the car. I push her up against the glass of the passenger side window and kiss her deeply, my mouth insistent. She lets out a small yelp before she leans into me and deepens the kiss. Our breaths mingle and our teeth clash as we continue our passion, she pulls my white linen shirt free of my pants and begins to unbutton it. The handbrake digs into my pelvis; I will myself to ignore it, but it's really beginning to hurt. I pull away.

"Let's take this upstairs," she whispers.

We leap out of the car and run to the elevators in haste. I repeatedly bash the call button and fidget uncomfortably. She quickly takes the car keys from me, presses the fob to lock the car, then places them in her purse. The elevator finally arrives. She pushes me inside, slamming my back up against the mirrored wall, then her lips find mine once more. She takes my bottom lip between her teeth and grips hard, sending a shock of electricity through my bloodstream. I savor every tantalizing touch from her tongue as she glides it through my stubble and invades my mouth. I pull away frantically, nip her earlobe and trail small kisses down her jawline as she runs her fingers through my hair. A loud ping sounds, and the doors open. We pull away from each other. A smartly dressed man in his mid-forties, wearing dark black specs is waiting to board. I freeze while she quickly straightens her hair as the man blinks at us.

"Cooper. Hi," she rasps.

He blinks once more at the two of us, then he diverts his gaze slowly to me.

"This is Mark, my husband. Mark, this is Cooper; he lives across the hall from us," she continues.

Really? Now!? I take her hand and leave the elevator.

"Hi, it's so nice to meet you," I say, outstretching my free hand.

Cooper takes it and we shake quickly before he looks back at Rachael who continues to neaten her hair and straighten her dress.

"I didn't know you were married, Rachael," Cooper says.

"Yeah, last month."

I shuffle from foot-to-foot, feeling awkward to have been caught but at the same time, pent up as hell.

"Well, it was nice meeting you, Mark," Cooper says.

"You too."

He enters the waiting elevator. She wraps her arm round my waist and proceeds to pull me towards our front door, she rummages around in her purse. I lean over and kiss the back of her neck. She rolls her head back against me, granting me more access. She pulls the keys out and unlocks the door. We tumble in together, then make out through the hallway until we emerge into the lounge where we collapse onto the couch. I run my hand up her thigh, hitching her dress up as I do, while she continues with the buttons on my shirt, but then she stops again, breaks away and gets to her feet. I lie sideways on the couch, staring up at her.

"What are you doing?" I grunt.

"I'm just going to freshen up. One minute."

"Are you kidding me?"

She leans down and kisses me swiftly on the forehead.

"One minute."

She runs into the bedroom, closing the door behind her.

I groan; I'm growing increasingly uncomfortable. I unbuckle my pants and slide them down my legs, but it does nothing to comfort me. I sit back on the couch and ruffle my hair back into place in a vain attempt to keep my hands busy. *What is she doing in there?* I contemplate bursting into the bedroom to check, but begrudgingly decide to leave her to it. I drum my fingers against the coffee table then stand back up and pace the room. The bedroom door opens, I whirl round as she slowly walks out. My mouth dries and my eyes widen as I look her up and down greedily. She's changed out of her dress and is now wearing black stockings held up with suspenders, her duty belt, police shirt with a few buttons undone to reveal the soft swell of her cleavage, and her police cap. My jaw hits the floor and I'm unable to move, she walks closer to me until she's so close, I could just reach out and touch her, but my body refuses to budge. She smirks and glances down at my naked legs.

"I see I've caught you with your pants down," she says in a sultry tone.

I lick my lips to talk, but just nod instead. She steps back slightly and like I did to her, she looks me up and down.

"I'm sure you can help me. I'm looking for Mr. Flint. Do you know him?" she asks.

I shrug my shoulders and smirk.

"Maybe."

She regards me; her widening hazel eyes are like melted chocolate; her brow forms a firm 'v'.

"Where is he?"

"Closer than you think."

Suddenly, she slaps me hard across the face. I cup my heated cheek but feel aroused as hell.

"I won't ask you again…"

I run my nose down the length of hers and place my lips close to hers, nearly touching.

"I am he."

She smirks and grabs my shoulders.

"That's all I wanted to know."

We kiss deeply again as she walks me backwards until I feel the couch at the back of my knees, then I hear a click. I look down; she's cuffed my right wrist. I glance up at her and she smirks.

"Other wrist. Now," she orders.

I slowly hold it up for her and she hastily cuffs that one too, then she breaks away and pushes me down onto the couch. She jumps on top of me, I get lost in her eyes as the tendrils of her hair tickle my cheeks, her nostrils flare, then her lips seek mine once more. I cradle her in my arms as best I can while the cuffs dig into my flesh.

"Could you remove these?" I ask, holding up my wrists.

Her pupils dilate.

"No."

I groan and pull against my restraints but as expected, they don't budge. The cold metal bites into my heated flesh, making me wince.

"But I had plans for you," I moan.

"Oh, well in that case..."

She takes a small key from her pocket and releases me from my bind. I rub my wrists, then stand quickly, scoop her over my shoulder and stride towards the bedroom. She shrieks and slaps my behind.

"Mr. Flint! Put me down!"

"As you wish."

I throw her onto the bed and stare down at her as she smirks up at me, then I crawl over her and possess her once again. Finally, the moment I've been waiting for, we make love with a fiery passion, utterly consumed in each other.

The warm summer sun heats the side of my face. I rub my eyes and peek down at Rachael, tucked tightly under the duvet. Her hair is a dark, messy haze spread over her pillow, her arm drapes over my bare chest and our legs are entwined like ivy. I carefully prize myself from her, climb out of bed and sit on the edge. I retrieve my briefs from the floor and smirk to myself as memories from last night flood back. I pull on my briefs just as she wraps her arms round my shoulders, her warm bare chest presses against my back as she kisses me on the cheek.

"Good morning," she whispers, nipping my earlobe.

I turn in her arms, folding my legs beneath me. I brush my hand down the side of her face and kiss her neck.

"Good morning. Sleep well?"

"I did. You?"

"The best."

She smiles, then her eyes dart to the floor. I look down with her to find the crumpled heap of clothes scattered on the floor.

"Fun night?" she asks.

"More than fun."

I climb off the bed to begin clearing up, but she grabs me and pulls me back down onto the bed. I lie on my back and stare up at her as she straddles me.

"I'm not finished," she whispers.

"You're trying to murder me, woman."

She laughs, then bends down and kisses the tip of my nose.

"There are worse ways to go."

I open my mouth, but she places her index finger over my lips, silencing me, then her mouth seeks mine. A loud knock rings from the front door. *Seriously!?* She sits up and scowls. I grumble under my breath and sit up.

"Leave it," I implore.

She peeks at me, smirks, and kisses me again, but then more rapping echoes down the hall. I groan loudly and climb off the bed. I grab my robe from the back of the door, slip it on and head for the door, muttering under my breath. I open the front door, Trent stands on our threshold in his biker leathers, grinning at me, but then his smile turns to a crooked smirk as he eyes my robe.

"You're in a bathrobe," he says.

"Am I not allowed?"

He checks his watch.

"We've got to be at work in thirty minutes."

I huff and gesture with my head, holding the door wide.

"Come in. Take a seat, I'll go and get changed."

He follows me into the lounge where he sits down as I retreat into the bedroom. She's already dressed in a light blue blouse and loose denim jeans. *Dammit. Thanks, Trent.* She glances up as I enter.

"Trent?" she whispers.

I nod and quickly collect my suit from the floor. I hurriedly get it on and make my tie presentable. She wraps her arms round my neck, and we stare at each other's reflections in the mirror.

"You owe me," she whispers.

I turn away from the mirror and kiss her swiftly.

"I'm on a half shift. I'll make it up to you when I get home."

"C'mon, Mark," he shouts.

I huff as she chuckles.

"Jeez, is he bossy," she jokes.

"You don't know the half of it."

We enter the lounge; he glances up and smirks widely, his head cocked to the side and his eyes hooded.

"What?" I ask.

"I take it you two had a good time last night."

She turns beet red.

"I don't know what you mean," I say.

His smirk broadens, then he clears his throat and holds up her cuffs.

"Then maybe you can tell me about these," he crows.

My mouth drops open as she covers her face with both hands. I stalk across the room and snatch the cuffs from his grip.

"I am married to a cop you know. These things are bound to happen."

I throw the cuffs back to her, then she quickly pockets them.

"Yeah, I'm sure they do... nice welts by the way," he continues, pointing down at my wrists.

I glance down at them, there are two large red welts on each wrist where the cuffs once were. I pull my sleeves down in a bid to hide them as he continues to grin crookedly at us both.

"Oh, and by the way, Rachael. Out of curiosity, does N.Y.P.D. stand for 'Nuzzle Your Penis Dear'?"

She sniggers and rubs her nose.

"What are you? Twelve?" she says.

He laughs and I slap him on the shoulder.

"Now, if you can grow up and stop teasing for a moment, shall we?" I say.

He clears his throat, stands from the couch, and walks to the front door, stifling a laugh on the way. I grab my leather jacket on the way out with her following and holding a brown paper bag. I take her into my arms tightly and press my lips to hers.

"Your lunch, Mr. Flint," she breathes, pressing the bag into my hand.

I lean into her ear.

"See you later. I owe you," I whisper.

She flushes beet red again and shoots a glance in Trent's direction. I look round. He scratches his nose and stares down the corridor.

"Get outta here," she shoos.

With one last wink, I walk down the corridor with him and towards the elevators.

We ride down in silence as I slip on my leather jacket. Trent clears his throat loudly and shakes his head.

"What?" I say.

"You can play stupid all you want. I know what you two were up to."

"Still not gonna speak a word."

He hoots with laughter and slaps me on the shoulder.

"You know, you need to be careful, bud. Don't want her getting pregnant."

I pale. *Me? A father? Ludicrous.*

"You do want kids, right?" he asks.

I lick my lower lip.

"I don't know, Trent. I haven't put a lot of thought into it."

"You know, the name 'Uncle Trent' has a ring to it. Do you know if Rachael's interested in having them?"

"We've never really discussed it. Listen, we only just got married. I'm sure the conversation will happen someday, but one big event at a time, huh?"

"Sure."

I regain my composure, just as we alight at the underground garage.

Chapter Twenty-Two

———∾∾———

The activity at the Neapolitan is hectic; the high season is in full swing, but my mood has been the lightest it's been in weeks. My Rachael is slowly returning to normal, her wit, her charm, her stamina. *Oh boy, her stamina.* I blow out and comb my fingers through my hair as my mind flits through the various scenes of last night, her police outfit, unbuttoned so her supple cleavage was on full display for my eyes only, our breaths and tongues mingled, and when she cuffed me. *That was new.* I shake my head and focus hard on the monitor just as a young family approaches the desk. I sit up straight in my seat and smile broadly.

"Good afternoon. Welcome to the Neapolitan, my name is Mark. How can I help you today?"

I log out, stand, and stretch. Another day done, now to get home and make it up to Rachael. *Oh my, I can't wait.* I rush up to the staff room, but bump into Trent.

"Whoa, what's your rush?" he says, grasping my shoulders.

"Just eager to get home."

He smirks and nudges my elbow.

"Yeah. I bet you are."

I roll my eyes and shove past him, but his footsteps pad against the soft carpet behind me. I look over my shoulder.

"Do you need a ride?" he asks.

"I'll walk. Thanks though."

I drag my rucksack from the locker and shrug it on.

"Are you sure you don't want that ride? It's a hell of a walk."

I shake my head and pat him on the shoulder as he stands in the doorway, his hands on his hips.

"You're worried about Tobias again, aren't you?"

He slowly lowers his hands down to his sides and brushes his shirt.

"We all are. We just want you safe."

"I know. But I'll be just fine."

He opens his mouth.

"Afternoon boys. Heading home?" Mr. Levitt calls.

Trent shuts his mouth and we both turn to face him in the doorway.

"Yes, sir," Trent and I answer in unison.

Mr. Levitt sniffs, then turns his gaze slowly to me. I stand rooted to the spot and stare back.

"Thank you for today, Trent. Mark, could I have a moment of your time?"

"Of course."

He turns and strides back down the corridor. I walk past Trent who clutches my shoulder and squeezes.

"Glad it's always you and never me," he whispers.

"Thanks."

He releases me and I follow Mr. Levitt back towards the all too familiar surroundings of his office.

He opens the door and gestures towards one of the seats. I sit in the same leather chair and wring my hands together. Bile rises in my throat. He closes the door and slowly makes his way over to his desk. He removes his jacket and drapes it over the back of his chair.

"It's a hot one today," he says, glancing towards the windows.

I look with him and nod.

"Yes, sir."

He sits down and glances at me before laughing.

"You're not in trouble."

I slump back into my seat as the nausea slowly fades into nothing.

"I just wanted to ask how your wife is getting on?"

"Oh. She's well, thank you, sir. She's back to her normal energetic self."

He smiles and places his clasped hands on the desk before him.

"That's wonderful, I'm glad to hear it. Would you consider coming back for your full hours tomorrow? As you're probably aware, the high season is starting up and it's only going to get busier. I need all the staff on board if I can."

I sit back in my seat and purse my lips. Rachael should be returning to work at some point next week. She's healed faster than all of us expected. I smile as her laughter during our boat ride rings through my ears, but then my smile fades. I fear her return to work.

"Mark?"

I shake my head and glance back at Mr. Levitt. He peers at me through his right eye.

"That shouldn't be a problem. Yes, I'm happy to return to full hours."

He smiles and sits back.

"Great, but know this, I'll always try to be flexible with my employees' personal lives. If you need to leave for any reason, all I ask of you is to let me know."

"Of course. I'm sorry again for just disappearing on you."

He raises his hand.

"Nonsense. I was more worried about you than anything, but then Trent barged in and told me… well, you know. I'm sorry about what happened to your wife, but I'm thrilled to hear she's on the mend."

"I couldn't agree more."

He nods and points his hand towards the door.

"You're free to go. See you in the morning. 9 a.m."

"Thank you, sir."

I stand from my seat and exit the office.

I step out into the blazing heat as it continues to beat down fiercely on the city. I fan my face and remove my jacket. *Still getting used to this.*

"Hey, man," Trent calls.

I turn round. He leans against the brick wall next to the hotel entrance, his jacket and tie draped are over his arm and a couple of buttons are undone.

"I thought you would have gone home by now," I say.

He stands up straight.

"I was worried about you. What did old man Levitt want?"

"He wants me to come back for my full shift. I start tomorrow."

He frowns.

"Are you ready for that? Is Rachael well enough?"

"She goes back to work soon. She'll be fine."

He pats me hard on the back, shunting me forward a little.

"Good to have you back. Last chance for that ride."

"Go home, T. See you tomorrow."

"You're impossible," he whispers.

I laugh and wave, then stride through Times Square.

I cross the street and head towards Columbus Circle as I open another sext message from Rachael.

Undress me...

I smirk and tap out a reply.

...Slowly.

I dodge and weave through other pedestrians who talk around the circle while others take photos. I look up from my phone and notice a man striding towards me. He looks familiar but I can't place him; he's in his late twenties with short dark hair and wearing dark rimmed glasses. I squint my eyes to get a better look, then it hits me; it's the man from the park a few weeks ago, the same one that was at the Neapolitan shortly after. What's he doing here? He walks towards me from the right, so I swiftly head left. I flick my sunglasses down and look at my phone. *Hopefully he hasn't noticed me.* He walks straight past without a backward glance, and I exhale. My phone beeps again. Another text from Rachael.

I can't wait to have you home. I'm waiting.

I peek back at the suspicious man. He looks over his shoulder, then pulls up his left sleeve and checks his watch, strapped backwards on his wrist. He has a tattoo, a red carnation. I flinch. *He's one of Tobias' men. I knew it. But what's he up to?* I look back down at my phone and reply.

Be home soon. I can't wait. Be ready.

I pocket my cell as Tobias' boy strides along the sidewalk by the south wall of the park. I cross over to the opposite side of the street while glimpsing at him every few seconds. He pulls a cell out of his pocket and speaks into it. Someone hits my shoulder; I spin round at a couple who scowl at me.

"Excuse me," I say.

They look away and I keep walking forward while scanning the other side of the street. *Where's he gone?* Groups of people walk in opposite directions, but the darkly dressed man emerges into view again, still mouthing into his cell. He pockets it and keeps walking through the crowds. Another buzz comes through on my cell. Rachael again.

Oh. I will be.

I smile, but my heart sinks. I should be going home to her right now but following this guy could help bring Tobias down for good. He looks behind, I dart my eyes away from him, then glance up slowly; he's looking ahead of him. He veers into the South entrance of Central Park. I pick up the pace until I stop at a crosswalk. *Not too much traffic.* I take my chance and dash over the crosswalk. He walks past the Jose Marti statue and down a flight of stairs. I stop at the top and wait for him to reach the bottom. He gets to the end and glances left and right before perching himself on the stone wall, looking out at The Pond. I turn away and lean against the brick wall with my back to him. I whip out my phone and keep my eyes down on the screen.

"You're late," the man says.

I peek over my shoulder; another man has joined him; he's tall and broad shouldered, wearing a black hooded jacket, dark jeans, and a Yankees baseball cap. I lean a little closer to get a better look, he looks up momentarily and I catch his face. I gasp and turn away sharply. *Craig? What's he doing here?*

"Sorry. The subway was murder," Craig says, sitting beside him.

The man scoffs and turns his lips up in a crooked smile.

"There'll be another murder if you don't live up to your side of the bargain."

He flinches and sucks in his lips. I raise my phone up and snap a picture of the two men.

"He's not as easy to catch as people make out. How am I supposed to do this? And another thing, you never told me that injuring Rachael was part of the arrangement."

The man laughs and claps him across the shoulder. *He knew about that!? I could kill him.*

"We were trying to soften him up for you. Then would have been a perfect time to strike, but you failed the boss… again. He's growing impatient."

"Look, just give me a couple more days."

"You don't have it. A day. I can buy you a day. If he isn't delivered, you'll be taken out of the equation, and

I'll collect that son of a bitch myself. Have I made myself clear?"

"Yes. You've got it. A day it is."

The man sniffs, then gets to his feet.

"Good. Don't disappoint us again."

"You got it."

The man nods once, then turns and strides off to the left. I get up off the wall and wait until he's disappeared through the crowds. I turn my head slowly and glower down the stairs at Craig. He sighs, removes his cap, and wipes his forehead with his arm. He slowly gets up and strides right. I pocket my cell and rush down the stairs. *This lying bastard nearly got my wife killed and I need answers.* I follow closely, he occasionally glimpses over his shoulder, but I keep my head down. The busy crowds begin to thin as he approaches Inscope Arch. He places his black hood over his head and strides through, his hands jammed into his pockets. I stride faster towards him, following him under the arch. He freezes and turns slowly. I grab him by his collar and push him up against the wall. His eyes widen and his mouth slacks.

"Hey! Hey! I told you! I was going to get him for-"

I remove my sunglasses and tuck them into my shirt. His eyes narrow.

"Mark?" Craig whispers.

"It's Mr. Flint to you. We are not friends," I hiss.

"What do you want?"

I scoff.

"I could ask you the same thing. You looking for me? You're responsible for nearly getting Rachael killed."

"I didn't know they would do that."

"*They?*"

He screws his eyes shut.

"Shit."

I throw him to the ground. He grunts and grips the back of his head. I pull my phone out as he coughs.

"Shall I call her or are we going to talk about it?"

He outstretches his hand.

"No no no! Please!"

He gets to his knees.

"Some guy called me a while back, like a few weeks ago, said he was an undercover cop or somethin'. He told me that he was investigating you, that you were planning to rob that hotel- whatever it is. Told me you married Rachael, but you had ulterior motives with her, so I went to ask her about you, but…"

"I was there?"

"Yeah. Obviously, you weren't too keen to chat back then."

"Well, I'm not one to get bored of my wife. You, on the other hand, lost her through your own stupidity and selfishness. Now you think you can win her back by getting rid of me?"

"I don't want to get rid of you."

"No. Tobias does."

"Who?"

I scoff.

"I'm fed up with these games."

"You gonna let me finish?"

"Fine."

"After I met you, I told the cop that you attacked me. He told me that you've had a history of violence, that you attacked him before, left a scar on his face."

"That's Tobias. Tobias O'Malley. He fooled you," I spit.

"Yeah. I know that now. *Thank you*. After you were framed and when I saw her crash on the news, I denied his calls, I knew who that guy really was. I tried to lie low, but that guy back there, he called me and said that they'd pay me a visit if I didn't cooperate with them."

"And that's why you met up with him just then?"

"Yeah."

"And what do you get out of all this?"

He shrugs.

"Safety from him? And money."

"Of course. Well, if it's me they want, it's your lucky day."

"What? But I don't want you dead. I just wanted Rachael back."

"By taking away her husband? I never broke her heart, I haven't and will never for a second consider it."

"And what about what you're about to do? Hmm? I take you to him, you're dead. You might as well kill her too."

I purse my lips. *I need to stop him, but I don't want Rachael in harm's way again.*

"I've dealt with him before. He and I are not strangers. Take me to him, or I'll call Rachael and the police."

"No. I'm not having any part in this."

I gaze at my phone and tap on contacts. I hover my finger over 'Rachael'.

"Okay, let's see what she has to say."

"Don't!"

I look at him and put my cell away.

"I'll take you to him, but you're going to regret it," he says, getting to his feet.

"My actions aren't your concern. You got a car?"

"Yeah, just round the corner."

"Move."

He staggers out the other side of the arch and I follow behind.

Craig has driven me into Staten Island and parks outside an old warehouse on Edgewater Street. The exterior of the warehouse is rusted and covered in graffiti; its windows are smashed and surrounded by a brick wall with overgrown leaves; and a high fence surrounds the compound.

"He's in there," Craig says, pointing with his chin.

I look at the car park entrance. Several armed bodyguards patrol the grounds.

"I'll be sure to let him know that you delivered me."

I open the door and lean out, then he grabs my arm.

"There's still time to reconsider," he says.

"It's a bit late for that. You don't get to lecture me after what you've done."

I shrug him off and close the door. He drives away and I look back at the compound. *What the hell am I doing?* I rake my hands through my hair and check my phone. A message from Rachael.

Mark, where are you?

I sigh deeply and reluctantly pocket it. I need her out of this. I'll explain everything to her when it's over. I begin to head to the opposite side of the street, then a hand wraps round my mouth. I muffle, struggle, and hit at the assailant.

"Ssh. Easy, buddy," a man's voice whispers.

Wait, I know that voice. He drags me away and pushes me up against a white wall of the neighboring warehouse. *Trent.* He uncovers my mouth, stares at me and puts his hands on my shoulders.

"Trent? What are you doing here?" I hiss.

"I could ask you the same thing. What are you playing at? Who was that guy who brought you here?"

"I can't believe this. Were you spying on me?"

"I was keeping an eye on you, to keep you safe, as per Rachael's request. Now, you answer my questions."

I push his hands from my shoulders.

"I need this over with, Trent. I'm fed up with the continued threats this guy throws at me. Don't you remember what he did? To me? To you? To my wife?"

"Mark, I don't know what you're planning, but this is reckless, foolish and above all, dangerous, even for you. Now, I implore you, please don't do this."

"I have to."

"No, you don't. Come back with me. We can go and get the police together. Do this right."

"No one else will die for me. I can't live with it."

I place my head in my hands and rub my face fiercely as Adam's face just before he died flashes through my mind.

"But you'll die," he whispers, stepping away.

"If it means keeping you and Rachael safe. It's a price I'm willing to pay."

His mouth drops open, he steps back further and his eyes rim.

"Please don't do this. You've only just returned to my life. We've missed out on so much together. And what about Rachael? You're a newlywed. Don't do this to us… please."

He sits on the sidewalk, his head in his hands. I sit beside him and wrap my arm round his shoulders. He peeks through his fingers at me.

"I won't let him kill me. This isn't the end. But I need you to go."

He sits back on his hands and shakes his head.

"I can't."

"Trent, please go. Call the police, get them here. I'll keep Tobias busy until they arrive. Just do this for me."

He gapes and wrings his hands on his lap.

"I can't lose you. Not again. I've already lost Dad."

I pat him on the back and give his shoulder a squeeze.

"I'll be fine. I promise. Now, go."

I get to my feet and walk back towards the fence. I look over my shoulder, Trent's gone. I exhale, and peek round the corner. There's a lone guard standing nearby, holding his weapon over his shoulder as he lights a cigarette. *Damn.* I press my back up against the fence and scan my surroundings. A couple of loose bricks lie in a heap at my feet. Slowly, I pick one up, feel the weight of it in my hand and, while staying low, approach the guard. He turns slowly as I reach him, without hesitation I hit him round the head with the brick, his eyes roll into the back of his head and he falls backwards, landing with a thud on the dusty ground.

"Hey. Did you hear that?" a voice says in the distance.

"Jeez, can I not take my break in peace?"

"C'mon. Let's go check it out."

Shit. Sweat runs down my forehead, I wipe it away hastily and scramble for a plan. I look down at my hands, at the brick. *Just like baseball.* I stand up straight, swing my arm and throw the brick into the distance; it lands loudly on a pile of twisted metal on the other side of the courtyard.

"Over there!" one shouts just as they emerge round the corner of the building, weapons drawn.

"We know you're there, asshole. Come on out."

I crouch down and sneak through the shipyard, avoiding the patrolling guards and towards a half-open door. I peek in. The warehouse is full of machinery. Laundered dollar bills are pegged across the ceiling; a table with disassembled firearms are being put together by several men; and in the far left corner, money is being unloaded from a van. I flinch back. *The stolen security van? It's here.* In an office cubicle in the opposite corner, there he sits, puffing on his cigar while polishing his much loved murder weapon. Tobias.

"Come on, boys. This merch needs to be ready by tonight. We've got three hours till the buyers arrive," Rusty shouts from the floor.

I get my phone out and snap photos of the machines, the men, the van, and Tobias, then pocket the phone and start sneaking towards the stairs. A hand grabs the scruff of my shirt and hauls me to my feet.

"I've caught our intruder. The boss has been dying to see you," the man says.

He drags me through the aisles of machinery. Several of the men stop and look at me, their decaying teeth are on display as their grins broaden. He opens the door of Tobias' office. He looks up from his lint cloth and sneers. I'm thrown onto the hard dusty ground; the dust particles rise into the air and up into my nostrils.

"Where did you find him?" Tobias asks.

"He was skulking around outside. Took out Tommy," the man says.

Tobias raises an eyebrow and stands from his seat.

"Dead?"

"Nah, boss. Just knocked out."

He holsters his revolver.

"Things never change. Do they, Mark?" he says, glancing down at me. "Leave us."

The man nods and backs out of the room, slamming the door shut. He looms over me, hoists me onto my feet and pats the dust off me.

"I apologize for my men. They can be quite heavy-handed."

"Yeah. Clearly."

"I assume you received my letter?"

I exhale through my nostrils.

"Yes," I snarl.

"Remind me. What did it say?"

"*'I'll see you soon'.*"

He wheezes and shakes his head.

"And here you are. It's nice to see you again."

"I'd be lying if I said the same."

He widens his eyes and his lips slowly form a smirk.

"Okay… Vibes aren't great in here. What say we get some sea air in your lungs?"

He grabs my arm and steers me towards the door. He twists it open, and we walk out.

"Keep up the good work, boys. Remember our deadline. I'm showing an old friend of mine around. We need to have a little chat."

Tobias releases my arm at the opening of a broken down wooden jetty. Boats bob up and down on the gently rippling water, moored either side. Water buoys ring in the wind and the sun starts to fade into the horizon, staining the clouds in a cocktail of blood orange and deep purple. Manhattan is just a small speck in the distance.

"So... how's the wife?" he asks.

My fists clench.

"Recovering. Should be here now, taking you down."

He chuckles.

"But yet, here you stand. Trying to be the hero as usual. What does that tell you about the police's abilities?"

"This has nothing to do with them."

He steps a little closer as he pulls a cigar from his pocket and lights it.

"Sure it does."

The end of his cigar glows red as he takes a puff and blows smoke in my face. I cough and fan it away.

"So, I need to ask. What do you want? Why come and find me?"

"The police will be here soon. They're after the merchandise you're planning to sell, the cash you stole from the banks and from the hotel I work at."

He looks around, then cups his right ear with his hand and widens his eyes. He chortles.

"No one's coming, Mark. You're alone here. You're a fool hunting me down."

"I didn't necessarily hunt you down. I found your guy. He talked. Brought me here. In fact, he was very forthcoming."

He smirks.

"Well, I'll let the boys know that he delivered. We'll leave him be. Don't need that dumb piece of shit anyway."

I snigger.

"Something we can agree on."

He takes another puff from his cigar.

"Stealing money from the hotel where I work; you must have known that the charges weren't going to stick," I continue.

"Of course."

"So why do it?"

"Simple. While the police apprehended the wrong man. We robbed a bank right under their nose. And here's where it gets funny; the bank we hit was right opposite the 17th precinct. Can you believe it?"

"This is all just fun and games for you, isn't it? But I must know, how did you get my prints?"

He laughs.

"It's amazing what you can achieve with just a piece of sticky tape. And hairs… well, that's much easier. Got them while you were in our-"

"-clutches?"

I instinctively rub my scalp.

"Well, I was going to say 'care', but whatever you want to believe. You've gotten very bright since you left me."

"You didn't give me a choice."

He takes another drag from his cigar, withdraws it from his mouth, then tosses it into the river.

"So… I'll ask you again. Why come here?" he asks.

"I'm going to make you an offer."

"This oughta be good for a laugh."

"Shut down your operation and surrender your goods to the police."

He sniggers.

"And… what do I get out of this?"

"You take your boys, leave town and never return."

He pats me firmly on the shoulder and leans in close, his stench of tobacco and cheap booze invades my nostrils. I grimace and step out of his reach.

"That sounds beautiful, Mark, but the thing is, me and my boys, we've made quite a nice home for ourselves here, much like you, only we hold faith in something that's real; controlling our destiny and ambitions, not relying on another group of people that manipulates it for us."

"Murdering? Stealing? That's what you call 'destiny and ambitions'?"

He squints and his lips form a thin line.

"I'll make a counteroffer. We have some buyers coming soon to collect. You help us load all the merch onto the ship and we won't hurt you, your Rachael, and those so-called friends you hang out with, ever again. Oh, and as an extra sweetener, a quarter of the profits we make will go to you. Think of all the things you could get for Rachael."

"You really think I'd believe that?"

"Well, it's no different from how she treats you."

"You don't know anything about her."

"I know more than you think, more than she lets on. Tell me. How did it feel when your wife arrested you? Knowing once and for all that they're not on your side."

"You didn't give her a choice. She had to go with what she and the police were provided with at the time."

"Of course, they did, but they like to leave things out, the *really* good stuff."

"I'm done with this. I'll leave you to your 'destiny.'"

I turn on my heel and walk towards the exit of the shipyard.

"The Chicago police told you that your parents went missing, didn't they?" he calls.

I freeze, then slowly look over my shoulder at him. *What the hell?*

"What?" I ask.

"Didn't they?"

"Yes. But Rachael told me they were gunned down. Found with gunshot wounds. What game are you playing now?"

He shakes his head and walks closer.

"Oh, Mark. I feel for you. Your beloved just feeds you half the truth."

Shit, the folder. She tried to give it to me last year. I never read it.

"What the hell do you know about my parents?"

"Oh, I know plenty. It was twenty-four years ago, on this very day in fact. Your father borrowed a considerable amount of money from me to fuel his drug and gambling addictions. But when it was time to give it back, he tried to avoid me. One day, one of my men tracked him down. He agreed on a meeting. He was foolish enough to bring his wife into danger with him, and they were even negligent enough to leave poor six-year-old Mark all alone on some hairbrained belief that their troubles will all be over."

I shake my head and step back, but he follows.

"They arrived. Your father told me bluntly that I won't be getting my money back. He was very much like you, y'know. He thought he could tell me what to do. Leave his family alone."

He pulls his revolver from his holster.

"During the argument, I pulled my gun from my pocket. We tussled and I pulled the trigger. Your mother tried to protect her pathetic husband. She took a bullet, right here," he continues.

He jabs at my chest, just above my heart with the barrel of his gun. I stand frozen to the spot. Tears prick the backs of my eyes and my mouth dries.

"You're lying."

"While your father groveled over his dying wife. I put my gun to the back of his head… and fired. The bullet went in so fast it came out the other side and landed in the opposite wall. Beautiful in its own way."

I drop to my knees as pain lances through my chest. Tears start streaming down my cheeks. *I'm back there. Crying incessantly on that mangy couch. I can't escape.* His shadow still looms over me.

"Yes. Your parents died at my hand."

Chapter Twenty-Three

"You're very much like your father; you act tough to hide that scared vulnerable little boy. I tried to take care of you, but you spat in my face," he says, leering over me.

He raises his foot and kicks me over. I land hard on my back as he cackles. I scramble to my feet and raise my fists.

"You're lying!" I shout.

"Look me in the eye and see if I'm lying. Then take a good long look at Rachael and tell me that she's telling you the truth."

I swing my right fist, pounding him across his scarred cheek. He quickly recoils, stretches his arm out and fires a bullet past my ear. He spits blood out.

"That's something else we have in common, Mark. We go for the weak spots."

"RACHAEL WAS GOING TO TELL ME, YOU ASSHOLE!"

I swing my foot up to his stomach, but he grabs me by the ankle and twists. I scream out as I spin round and land face first on the floor.

"But she didn't."

I swiftly roll over and get back to my feet. My ankle seethes with pain, I stumble, but quickly regain my composure. I charge again hitting him three times in the face. I'm grabbed by the arms and hauled back. I look at the two rat-faced men who grip me, their long yellow fingernails dig into my flesh through my shirt.

"And she never will. Take him back inside. Make it slow for him, slower than how his folks felt," he continues.

I struggle and writhe as a humming whir looms from above. I look up as a helicopter shoots overhead and hovers just above the jetty. Tobias looks back at it as it touches down.

"And that's my cue to leave. If you're tough enough to survive their wrath, I'll be seeing you soon," he says.

He turns around, then stops.

"Oh, and one more thing. My deepest condolences."

He rushes towards the helicopter, accompanied by Rusty and two other associates. They hop aboard as I'm dragged inside the warehouse and thrown to the floor.

One of the men cracks his knuckles while the other puts a knuckleduster over his fingers.

"The rest of you, keep working, we're going to keep this one busy," one of them shouts.

I raise an arm to defend myself, then the noise I've been dying to hear rings through the broken windows, police sirens. The men swing their heads round. *Now's my chance.* I roll over and swing my leg at the man's ankles, toppling him onto the ground.

"Shit!" the other man yells.

I hoist myself up and block the man's fist. I pull his arm down and twist it back. He screams and swings a punch, but I avoid it and kick him hard in the back. Another man jumps onto me and punches me hard in the small of my back. I yell and swing round, trying to shrug him off, but he holds firm. Several loud bangs can be heard from outside the metal door, then at last, armored police officers swarm the building, their rifles drawn.

"Lower your weapons and get down on the ground with your hands on your head."

Tobias' men crouch and comply. The officers begin to cuff them. Another officer gets hold of me and presses a button on his radio.

"Sarge, we got 'im," he says.

"Bring him to me," a female voice rings out. *Rachael? What's she doing here?*

We head outside into the slowly fading light.

"Bring it down!" Rachael yells.

Several officers fire up into the air at Tobias' helicopter. Several bullets ricochet off the bodywork, but it continues its course and flies into the horizon. All the officers holster their weapons.

"Get our bird in the air now. Find him," she orders.

I'm frog marched towards a casually dressed, but red-faced Rachael. Her eyes blister into mine, her mouth twists and her hair sways softly in the breeze. Her nostrils flare and her pupils dilate. She tears her gaze from mine and smiles at the officer who continues to hold me.

"Thank you, Forrester."

"Ma'am. The chief doesn't want you on duty."

She raises her hand.

"I'll deal with the chief."

He nods and releases my arm, then assists his colleagues as several of Tobias' men are loaded into vans.

"Thank you for coming," I say, stepping towards her.

She steps out of my reach and scowls deeply.

"What. The hell. Are you playing at!?" she seethes.

I lower my head.

"I dunno'. I was a fool. I'm sorry."

She grunts.

"The car's this way. We're going home."

She walks towards her Mercedes.

"I don't mind taking the subway."

She whips her head round.

"No. You're coming with me before you get into any more trouble. Now get in the goddamn car!" she shouts, pointing towards it.

I slink to the car, open the door, slide in, and slam it closed, reverberating the car. She climbs in, starts the engine and drives away.

We cross Brooklyn Bridge and head towards Midtown Manhattan. Darkness has descended on the city, the streetlamps are now lit, the traffic is heavy, and the streets are full of life. Rachael has been silent throughout the entire journey; her eyes have stayed rooted ahead. I slump into my seat and rest my head against the cool glass, my breath condensates on it. My stomach is knotted into a tight ball and I'm cold and shaky on the inside as my mind replays my encounter with Tobias. *Was he telling the truth? Did he really kill my parents?* We pull up at a red light, I sigh and glimpse at her. She peeks over at me, I offer a small smile, but she looks straight ahead again.

"Are you going to ignore me long?" I ask.

She looks back at me again just as the light turns green and the traffic slowly pulls forward.

"I honestly don't know what to say to you right now."

"Look, I'm sorry. I know what I did was foolish."

"*Foolish*? 'Foolish' is too kind a word for what you did. If you had just done what I asked and let the police do their jobs, this could have ended differently. We stood a good chance of catching him, but yet again, you had to be reckless and be the hero. Do you know what you put me and Trent through today? He was in bits when he phoned me."

"Tobias killed my parents."

She slams on her brakes and veers towards the sidewalk. I clutch onto the door panel as several cars beep at us and shoot round. She parks up next to the sidewalk, cuts the engine and turns her whole body towards me.

"How do you know that?" she asks, her eyes widening.

"He told me."

She sighs and rubs her face with both hands.

"He told me *you* knew about it. Do you?" I ask.

She slowly uncovers her face and sighs deeply.

"Yes… I knew."

My heart free falls through my chest. My mouth falls open and I sit back into my seat.

"You did? Why didn't you tell me? Don't you think I have a right to know what happened? They're my parents goddammit!"

She stares at me wide eyed, her mouth turned down. I shake my head then look away and open the car door.

"Where are you going?" she calls, but I slam the door shut and start walking, my hands jammed into my pockets. A car door opens and closes, then frantic footsteps click behind me. She grabs my shoulders and stands in front of me.

"Please let me explain. I tried to tell you... Remember when I told you they were found in 1993? I tried to give you that manilla folder? You didn't accept it. That has all the information you need. I tried to tell you, but you ran off like what you're doing now."

I exhale.

"I just don't know how to cope with this. I've spent all these years wanting to know what happened to them. Grandma would never tell me, but now that I know..."

I place my hands over my eyes and press my back up against the cold brick wall.

"Ah. I just don't know." I continue.

She gently prizes my hands away from my face and stares at me.

"I know this is hard, especially finding out the truth through... *him*. I'm sorry, I should have just told you outright, maybe I could have spared you all this pain."

The corner of my mouth twitches a little and I run my nose down hers.

"It's okay. I'm sorry for my outburst and for running off. It's just, after the crash, I swore revenge against the man who hurt you. All I ever want is to keep you safe and protect you."

"I know. But running off like that is dangerous. You know better than most what sort of man he is. What if he killed you on sight? What if I get a call that a body has been found? That's not protecting me, getting yourself killed. I don't want the next call to be from the morgue."

I never thought about it like that. My mind was clouded with wanting Tobias out of our lives as soon as possible, but at what cost? She's right, I should have just returned home.

"You're right. I'm so sorry. Do you forgive me?"

She smiles and wraps me in her arms.

"I'm just glad you're safe."

I press her against the length of my body and inhale her sweet familiar scent. It's a calming balm, slowly piecing my broken soul back together.

"Shall we go home?" she asks, as we break away.

"Let's. And I need to see that folder when we get back."

She stares into my eyes and runs her hand gently down my face.

"Of course."

Being back at the apartment does nothing to comfort me as my gut continues to gnaw and grind at my insides. My head is primed to burst as I desperately try to piece together what I've discovered. I just want to have a hot shower and wash off the feeling of grime that clings to every sinew, muscle, and bone, I want to crawl into bed and curl into a ball in the hope of a dreamless night sleep, but I can't. I have to face this. She hangs her keys on the hook beside the door and brushes past me.

"Would you like a drink? Coffee? Wine?" she says.

"Something stronger."

She blinks at me, but then heads into the kitchen and clinks around in the overhead cabinets.

"Take a seat," she calls.

I move slowly into the lounge and collapse onto the couch. I roll onto my back and throw my arm over my eyes. She taps at my legs with her foot, and I stare up at her. She frowns, her brow forming a small 'v' as she offers me a small cut glass, half full of amber liquid. I sit up, take it from her and throw back the liquid in one mouthful. It burns the back of my throat as it slowly slips down, but it goes little way in soothing me. She takes a sip from hers then places it on the table in front of us and opens a drawer in the cabinet beside the TV. She pulls out the manilla folder and holds it in both hands.

"You sure you want to look at it now? It *will* hurt," she says.

I purse my lips.

"I don't care. I need to see it."

She closes her eyes and exhales before coming to sit beside me. She rests her hand on my thigh and hands me the folder. I breathe in, take it from her and stare down at it. *Time to face the truth, Mark.* I open it and am confronted by a three-page crime report and a few photos. I turn my attention to the report. A picture of my parents is paperclipped to the top left corner followed by their information, the location of the incident, any suspects that have been identified and lastly, a summary of what the police discovered. I pick up the first page and read aloud.

"Chicago, Cook County, IL – 32-year-old Imogen Annie Flint and 34-year-old Jonathan Roger Flint were both found in a pool of their own blood in an alleyway just off West 15th Street on June 27th, 1993, at 3:58 a.m. Witnesses phoned with concerns after hearing several gunshots in the vicinity. Police responded and found their bodies. They were both removed and taken to hospital but were pronounced dead on arrival. The medical examiner determined that they both died instantly from their injuries. Imogen had a gunshot wound to her chest and Jonathan on the back of his head. Despite the pieces of evidence that we gathered from the scene including a shell casing and a red, blood-stained carnation, no suspects have been identified and no arrests have been made. Next of kin has been informed and their son, six-year-old Mark has now been placed into the care of relatives. Reports suggest that the child was left unaccompanied at their home at the time of their deaths. The reason for this is as of yet unclear. Investigations and questioning are ongoing."

My hands shake as I lower the folder.

"The carnation. They had no idea it was him back then," I say.

"They do now. Maybe he was unknown to the law enforcement at the time."

"Maybe."

I scoff.

"Y'know, I remember the look on Tobias' face when he first picked me up from that train station back in Chicago and I told him that my parents had disappeared; he just made a thin line with his lips and said that he'd 'take care' of me. It was completely unlike what he turned out to be. He wanted to keep the truth from me so that he could keep me all to himself, but why? Why did he want me so much?"

"I wouldn't know."

I focus on the file photos; one of Mom, wide-eyed, with long hair; and another of Dad, sporting the same floppy hair as mine, albeit longer; both of them stare at me, wondering how long it took me to find this out; another photo is blacked out, I presume the suspect. I go cold as I stare at a photo of Mom and Dad, lifeless on the wet hard floor, bloodened gunshot wounds to Mom's chest and Dad's head, and between them, the carnation, its delicate petals coated with blood. Several 'DO NOT CROSS' tapes surround the horrific scene. I squeeze my eyes shut, holding tears back and press the paper to my forehead. Rachael's smooth hand rests on my shoulder. The dam bursts and my tears start to flow. She gently takes the folder from my hand and places it down. I collapse onto her warm chest and let all the emotions from that traumatic night flood out. Her fingers glide slowly through my hair.

"It's okay," she whispers.

I weep harder into her like that young heartbroken boy again, but I'm not alone this time. I embrace that memory, no longer hiding from it. I lean up, rest my chin on her shoulder and wrap her in my arms. Her steady breaths calm the waters that flow from the emptying dam of my soul until it dries up and I bring myself back from the surface. I release her and breathe out.

"Thank you," I say.

She smiles weakly and wipes the tears from my cheeks with the backs of her knuckles.

"Now you know."

I sniff.

"Somehow, I had an inkling. But I need to know. How did you get your hands on this?"

She crinkles her nose.

"When you were first arrested, I did some research on you. There was nothing I could find until I found a news article detailing…"

"…my parents?"

She shuts her eyes and nods.

"I saw the carnation and I knew right then. I asked my superiors about it, and a few days after you were released, Dad said he'd ask some old friends over in Chicago for some insight, then after another week, this came back," she says, tapping the folder.

I look down at it again.

"Thank you for showing me this, but could you put it away now please?"

She jumps to her feet and places it back into the drawer.

"I hope that's put some of your questions to rest," she says, turning back to me.

I nod and smile weakly, my face still heated from my earlier emotion.

"Yeah, it has, but there has to be more to this."

"Possibly. And if there's more, we'll dig it up. But we need to do this together, we can't shut each other out this time."

"Okay."

She checks her watch.

"I'm going to have a shower. Hell knows I need one. Afterwards, we'll go and get a bite to eat. How does that sound?"

I get to my feet and hug her hard.

"Sounds good to me."

She pulls away, grabs a towel from the closet and disappears into the bathroom, the door clicks softly behind her. I head into the bedroom and pull my dirty work clothes off and discard them into the laundry. I stare at my reflection, topless. A bruise forms on my cheek and chest through Tobias' firm hand. I turn my nose up, sit on the edge of the bed and rest my head in my hands. I listen to the running water coming from the bathroom and lie flat on the bed. Nothing soothes me, I sit up, punch my pillow, and lie face down on it. My head starts to hurt, I climb off the bed and pad into the kitchen where I find some aspirin. I sink two tablets with a glass of water and stand in the middle of the room. The only sounds being my deep breathing, the wind whistling from outside the apartment complex and the running water. I look at the cabinet that houses the dreaded folder, I slowly open the drawer and pull it out. Placing it on the coffee table, I open it and remove the photo of my parents. Their casual faces stare back at me. I sit on the couch and do nothing but stare back. Tobias took them away from me, he has no remorse or regret for his actions. He nearly took Trent from me, he nearly took Rachael from me, well, no more. I don't know how I'll- no- how *we'll* do this, but we'll find a way. Tobias will be stopped. I don't care whether he lives or dies, but redemption is no longer possible for him, he doesn't deserve it. He's taken so many lives needlessly. It's time his reign of terror comes to an end. That is my mission, that is my goal, that is how I'll seek the redemption for what I've lost.

The stench of stale water and mold of the old warehouse invades the man's nostrils as he glares through the cracked discolored window as the sun sinks into the horizon, shrouding his hideout into darkness once more. He takes a cigar from his pocket and lights it, overpowering the smell of decay. *Much better.* His men hurry around downstairs to ignite barrels for light and warmth while others haul in machinery.

"Keep up the hard work boys. We have a lot of orders to fill," he called loud and clear without a backward glance.

His mind is firmly fixed on one man. *Mark Flint.* He takes a long draft from his cigar and blows out smoke rings. *The truth is out... Well, most of it at least. He doesn't need to know how deep my relationship went with his petty father. He was dead to me long before I put a bullet through him.* He smirks to himself as memories of the night he murdered them ring through him anew. *That was a good day. Now he knows. The pain of the truth will burn a hole right through him. Especially that, of all people, his wife, a police officer kept that from him. He will push her away, everyone closest to him will fade, he will tear his own life apart and return to me... defeated and ready for death.*

"Boss?" Rusty says.

He turns around and arches a brow as smoke wafts from the cigar.

"An update for you. The police got several of our men and… we've lost the money and the van."

"Anything else?"

"Yeah… Flint's still alive."

Of course he is. He thinks he has something to live for. The fool.

"Anything else?" he says, looking over his shoulder.

Rusty looks down and swallows.

"Umm… The police have also confiscated most of our merch. We're going to have to start from scratch. Where does this leave us with our plans?"

He discards his cigar, stamping it out under his polished shoe.

"Don't despair, Rusty. All wrongs can be righted. Tell the boys to work harder and prepare for the breakout. We already have everything we need. It's time I reunited with my brother, and it's time for us to expand our numbers."

"And what of Flint?"

"Leave him be… for now. He'll slip up, make foolish mistakes. We'll tighten our hold on this city, he'll keep running from his problems until he runs out of road."

"And then?"

He tittered and inclined his head to the side.

"Why spoil the surprise? Go."

Rusty nods once then turns on his heel and barrels down the stairs.

"C'mon, boys. Pick up the pace!" Rusty shouts.

He turns back to face the ever darkening sky. *Mark thinks he's safe from me, cowering behind that scum police wife of his. She can't stop me. The police can't stop me. I will give Mark salvation. He has to go, and it will be through my hand. Or maybe, there's still time to bring him round. Succeed me. Take my place. Either way, I'll free him from his life of lies. Liberated. Redeemed. Saved.*

www.ingramcontent.com/pod-product-compliance
Lightning Source LLC
Chambersburg PA
CBHW050844210726
48290CB00004B/1069